DINAFAR

pressed her hand against her mouth as she watched
the meie circle slowly about Sten. She must have
taken a saber from one of the bodies while
Dinafar distracted Sten because she held one now
—and looked like a child playing with its father's
arms, her short fingers barely able to circle the
hilt, the weight and size of it looking too great for
her thin arms to lift. Her face was intent as she
concentrated on the man in front of her, staying
just beyond his reach, watching, waiting. *Like that
first Kappra,* Dinafar thought. **Teasing him until
he made the mistake that killed him. She's going
to kill this one too; he outreaches her, outweighs
her, has to be three or four times as strong as she,
but she's going to kill him.**

JO CLAYTON

has also written:

DIADEM FROM THE STARS

LAMARCHOS

IRSUD

MAEVE

STAR HUNTERS

THE NOWHERE HUNT

MOONGATHER

Jo Clayton

DAW BOOKS, INC.
DONALD A. WOLLHEIM, PUBLISHER
1633 Broadway, New York, NY 10019

FIRST PRINTING, MAY 1982

3 4 5 6 7 8 9

 DAW TRADEMARK REGISTERED
U.S. PAT. OFF. MARCA
REGISTRADA, HECHO EN U.S.A.

PRINTED IN U.S.A.

AT THE CUSP THEY MEET

"I'm bored."

Raiki janja looked up from the cards she was shuffling, laying out on the leather in front of her knees, gathering in and reshuffling. In the cruel light of the early morning sun thousands of small wrinkles webbed her face, deeper wrinkles rayed out from eyes made larger and darker by the uneven lines of black painted around them. She sighed and her double dozen gold chains with their pendant coins lifted with the sigh, clanking fitfully. She sat on a huge hide nearly as ancient as she, her small feet tucked neatly under her heavy thighs, her robes billowing about her bulky body. She looked what she was, a minor tribal sorceress—except for her eyes. They were a shadowy, shifting, brownish green like water in a shady tarn, calm and wise and eternal, the only external sign of that which dwelt within her. "No," she said. "Not bored, just greedy."

Haloed by the rising sun, Ser Noris stood on the edge of a cliff, his hands clasped behind him, white hieroglyphs against the stiff black of his robe. He turned and walked toward her, his booted feet soundless on the gritty stone. A ruby like a teardrop with a fine gold ring through the tail hung from his left nostril—a relic from a youth so distant he couldn't remember when he first eased the gold ring through his flesh. He wore it still, since the weight of it against his lip was part of him now, though the blood-red gleam of it ill suited the cool austerity of his face. When he smiled at her, the ruby lifted and rolled, glowing at the touch of the rising sun. "No, janja, I need a challenge. I'm ossifying." He stamped a boot heel against the stone. "Much longer and I'm as responsive as this rock."

Raiki shuffled the cards, squared the pack. "The penalty of your success, Ser Noris."

"A very small success, janja."

"You want too much." Holding the cards low in her lap, she gazed past him at the valley glowing green and beautiful beyond the edge of the cliff. "That's not for you."

5

"Because I'm of the Nearga Nor? I won't be bound by them, janja. I hold the Norim here." He closed one shapely hand into a fist. "None of them can touch me, singly or in concert. I wield more power than most men dream of, but . . ." He waved his hand at the valley. "When I stand here, knowing what lies behind that, I know how small a triumph I can boast. I need more room, janja." He wheeled, bent with liquid ease and took the top card from the deck she held, straightened and stood tapping the card's frayed edge against his thumbnail. "Match me, janja."

Raiki frowned. "A game? Absurd."

"Play the game, janja." He smiled once more, a wide charming smile that warmed his cold face. "Why not?"

She slipped the next card from the deck, held it a moment face down. "I shouldn't warn you, my beautiful wrong-headed Noris, but I've got fond of you a little. Don't do this. The game will destroy you."

His smile turned wry. "I don't think so. Consider this, janja, even if you're right, what choice have I? I can rot alive or live while I live, however short that be. If you were I, what would you choose?"

"So be it. Play your card, Ser Death."

"Order, janja. Control, not death." He placed the card on the hide in front of her knees.

IMAGE: *head and torso of a girl child, green blotches spat-tered across her fair rosy face. A darker green oval in the center of her forehead just above her nose was half concealed by tumbling red-brown curls. The four-year-old gazed from the card with desper-ate defiance, her orange-amber eyes opened wide.*

Raiki smiled down at the image, affection and sorrow mixed on her face. "A misborn of the windrunners." She looked up. "Poor child. Must you?"

Ser Noris waited without speaking, his dark eyes fixed on the card in her hand.

"If you must." Sighing, Raiki laid her card beside his.

IMAGE: *The misborn grown older. The green blotches had spread and joined until her skin was a light olive green. The darker blotch on her forehead was more cleanly defined, an oval eye-shape between her brows. Her hair was shorter, a cap of soft russet curls. She wore a time-rubbed leather tunic that hugged the meager curves of her slim torso like a second skin. The tip of a bow rose over one shoulder.*

"Think that's clever, Raiki janja?" Ser Noris touched the card with the toe of his boot. "I'll teach the child. After that, try taking the woman."

Raiki gazed at him sadly. "You don't understand. By your nature, you can't understand. Take your next card."

IMAGE: *a man in a loose black robe, a silver flame embroidered on the breast. His arms were held out from his sides, elbows bent, palms turned up. A fire burned on the right hand, a scourge was draped over the left.*

Raiki shook her head. "Ah my friend, that's bad. The Sons of the Flame. Tschah! you're calling on the worst in man. I'm afraid I've got no place in that world you're shaping. My stomach couldn't take it. I'd be angry all the time and turn sour as an unripe quince." She laid her second card down.

IMAGE: *a short pudgy man, surplus flesh veiling the strong, elegant bone structure of his face and body. He looked lazy, sensual, intelligent and arrogant, a man who had everything he wanted without having to ask for it, who was saved from decay by an exuberant enjoyment of life, who yet was so indolent he didn't bother to probe deeply into the things that excited his wonder or prodded his curiosity. A man with much promise, little of it realized.*

"Hern of Oras. A flawed weapon, janja."

"Perhaps." She gathered in the cards. "Flaws can be useful." Struggling to her feet, she moved past him to the cliff's edge where she stood gazing down into the Biserica valley. "Ser Noris, my Noris, too many people are going to die from this game of yours."

He crossed to stand behind her. "They die every day in that chaos you call life, janja. What's the difference?" He squeezed her shoulder lightly, an affectionate gesture odd for one of his training—a training which should have killed the capacity for affection in him. That it had not, that he had

contrived to ignore the more restricting requirements of the
Neärgate and flourish in spite of this, was some slight
measure of how far behind he had left his colleagues and
how high his ambition could leap.

Raiki patted his hand. "Take care, my Noris. If you dis-
cover the answer to that question, I'll have won the game."

THE WOMAN: I

Lightning whited out the street. Slowing her stumbling run, Serroi clapped small square hands over her eyes. *That was close*. The eye-spot on her brow throbbed *danger, danger, danger,* giving her a headache, telling her what she didn't need to know. Behind her the shouts of the guards were growing louder; over the scraping of her own boots she could hear the thuds of their feet. She bumped against a wall, pulled her hands down, the corners of her wide mouth twitching into a momentary smile at the absurdity of trying to run self-blinded. As she rounded a bend in the twisting street, the lightning flashed again, showing her Tayyan stumbling heavily over the body of a drunk stretched limp against the wall.

The lanky meie got to her feet, wincing as she tried putting her foot down. Serroi stopped beside her. With a last worried glance behind her, she knelt beside the injured leg. "Bad?"

Tayyan shook her head, her short blonde hair shifting about her long face. "Don't think so." She brushed the pale shag out of her eyes. "How close do you think?"

"Couple turns behind us, but closing." Serroi felt the injured ankle, ignoring Tayyan's gasp of pain. "I don't think anything's broken. Can you walk?"

Tayyan lifted her head, squinted as lightning cracked the darkness again, grimaced as a hoarse yell sounded to be swallowed almost immediately by a thunder crash. "I'd better, hadn't I." Her short laugh was harsh, strained. She pushed away from the wall and limped a few steps, sweat beading her forehead, teeth clamped on her lower lip.

"Lean on me." Serroi slid her arm around her shieldmate's waist. "All right?"

Tayyan chuckled, an easier, more natural sound this time. "Fine, little one." She ruffled Serroi's tangled curls, then pressed her hand down on her shoulder, resting enough of her weight on the small woman to enable her to swing along at a fast walk.

Every glare that shattered the stifling blackness of the

9

stormy night showed storehouses sharing sidewalls on each side of the winding street, blank stone faces two stories high locking them into the way that was looking more and more like a trap. *A vinat run to the slaughter*, Serroi thought. *Maiden grant we find a sideway soon. Or we have to fight.*

The street twisted again, an abrupt, almost right-angled bend. The two women staggered around the bend and stopped, dismayed, as the lightning showed them a solid stone wall blocking the passage—a warehouse, its massive iron-bound doors the only break into two stories of rough-cut stone. Serroi looked up at Tayyan, touched the coil of rope on her weaponbelt. "You're the climber. What's the best way?"

Tayyan urged her forward, hobbling with her halfway to the end. Then she halted, gave Serroi's shoulder a little push. "The warehouse. You climb, I'll keep them off your neck." She limped to one side of the street, her eyes fixed on the corner they'd just turned.

"But . . . Tayyan!"

The taller woman glanced back, grimaced. "Get a move on, will you? You're going to have to haul me up as it is."

Serroi stared down at shaking hands until they steadied, then she ran over the cobbles until she stood before the double doors. She unclipped the line from her weaponbelt, snapped on the small folding grapnel, began swinging the weighted rope in widening circles. She let it go. The rope went streaming upward, butted playfully at an overhanging beam, then fell back to clatter on the cobbles. Serroi's breath whined in her throat as she pulled in the grapnel and swung it again, around and around until it hissed through the heavy air. When she let it go this time, she heard the grapnel clunk solidly home and saw the rope jerking like a thing alive in front of her. She drew her hand across her sweaty forehead, straightened her shoulders and turned.

Tayyan was standing in the middle of the street now, her hand on the hilt of her sword, her body balanced and alert in spite of her injured leg. Serroi breathed a prayer of thanks, then shouted, "Tayyan! Get your skinny self up this rope." She reached for the bow clipped to the wide leather strap that passed diagonally across her back. "I can hold them off better with this."

Tayyan snorted as she limped a few steps closer. "You first, love; you'll have a better angle of fire from the roof."

"Tayyan!"

"Don't you argue or I'll spank you black and blue when we get home, little windrunner." She grinned. "Get!"

"Bully."

"Scrap." Still chuckling, Tayyan turned to face the corner again. Lightning burned the images of four men out of the darkness. Her voice cutting through their shouts of triumph, she cried, "Go!"

Serroi ran at the rope and began hitching her way up it. A quarrel from a guard's crossbow thudded against the stone and skittered off. Curses and the clank of sword on sword sounding behind her drove her faster and faster up the rope, her arms burning with the intensity of her effort. Finally she swung herself over the parapet and collapsed onto the flat roof. A quarrel hummed past. She shifted position hastily and risked a glance over the edge.

Tayyan was down, a quarrel through the thigh of her injured leg. As Serroi watched, she struggled onto her knees, then onto her feet, using her sword as a brace until she was up. She lifted the sword and waited for the guards to attack.

They advanced cautiously; a Biserica trained meie, even one handicapped by a wound in the leg, was to be respected. Her back against the wall of the storehouse, she waited for them, calm, resolute and deadly.

Serroi unsnapped her bow and strung it. The man with the crossbow slapped a quarrel in place and clawed back the bowstring. She nocked an arrow and let it fly, taking him in the throat. Then she methodically dropped the other three as they scrambled for the bend in the street. Bow in hand she leaned over the parapet to call to Tayyan.

Tayyan took one step, slipped in her own blood and crashed onto the cobbles. The quarrel in her leg must have nicked an artery for the blood was pumping out of her, gushing whenever she tried to move. She managed to drag herself a few feet. Her hands slipped and she went down; she raised her head, called hoarsely, "Serroi, help me."

Serroi dropped her bow and started to swing back over the parapet. Three more guards plunged around the corner. She leaped back to the bow, pulled and loosed with the calm sureness trained into her by her years at the Biserica. As the last man toppled, the Norid stepped around the bend. His hands were raised. There was a sharp agony of light flashing between them, a small fireball. Serroi froze. He threw the fireball. It came at her, growing, growing.

Bow clutched forgotten in one hand, whimpering in terror,

forgetting everything but her need to get away, Serroi fled over the roofs, sliding, leaping, blind and deaf. Lightning and thunder cracked around her. The wind rose, battered at her. Great drops of rain spatted down. She fled over the rooftops, eyes blind, mind numb, body only animal competent, leaving her shieldmate lying in her own blood, forgetting the oath she swore on sword and bow, caught in an agony of terror touched off by the dark figure of the sorcerer.

She fled until the roofs ended at the city wall, scrambled desperately onto the broad walkway and into an arrow slit then threw herself toward the uneasy water far below, not caring whether she lived or died.

She hit the water feet down, body vertical, slicing into it, going deep then fighting up, mind blank, body struggling to live. With the storm breaking over her, lightning almost continuous, the wind snatching at the water, turning the harbor into treacherous cross-chop, she swam blindly until she slammed into the side of a moored boat. Without hesitation she swung herself over the rail and lay gasping on the deck. As soon as she'd caught her breath, she fought the sail free of its cover and got it raised, slashed the mooring lines, and sent the boat into the heart of the storm, her tears mixing with the sea spray and the rain.

The wind drove the boat far out to sea before the storm dissipated and left her bobbing like a cork between great swells of water with no land in sight and little idea of what direction she was moving in. She unclamped cramped fingers from the tiller, uncleated the sheet and let the sail crumple down, then dropped her head on her knees, trying to summon the remnants of her strength. After a time she sat up, touched her forefinger gently to the soft warm green spot that sat like a third eye in the center of her forehead. With the spot quivering under her touch she *desired* land, then closed her eyes and moved her head in a slow half circle trying to feel the pull that would tell her where she had to go.

Once the tugging had steadied, she raised sail again and sent the boat after the pull.

It was still dark when she neared a line of chalk cliffs. The clouds were breaking up overhead and the Dancers were visible, the last of the eleven moons to join the Gather, three small glows that always moved together, crescent or gibbous or full. They were close to full now and their light was sufficient to show her the brief interruption in the line of surf beating against the base of the cliffs. She sailed into the short tappata, the finger of water, dropped anchor in the middle of the channel—the tides around Moongather were extravagant. When she was as safe as she could make herself, she collapsed onto the wet deck, too tired to worry about soaked clothing and chill air.

And the nightmares came; over and over she replayed her flight. Over and over she saw Tayyan's face, her pleading, accusing eyes. Over and over she heard, "Help me, Serroi, help me." And saw herself running like an animal. And over and over she saw the Norid's smiling face, the solid line of brow running handsomely over dark warm eyes, the triangular white face with its finely drawn lips, its beaked nose, delicate nostrils, pendant ruby—not the Norid in the street, not the worthless brass imitation, but the other one, the first one, Ser Noris, her Noris.

Serroi woke panting, her heart choking her, terror possessing her—until she saw the sail slapping idly against the mast. The boat rocked under her, blown about by the wind, tugged at by the receding tide. She sat up, groaning and sore, still part lost in nightmare.

The early morning sun was a squashed orange, bit off at the bottom by the mountains called the Earth's Teeth. Last night's stormclouds were crowding around it, sucking up red, gold and purple light. The wind brushed at her hair, plucking loose coils from the sorrel mass and tickling her face with them. She touched the green oval, closed her eyes, stretched out the invisible feelers she always felt went out from her in this kind of search and swept as far as she could reach. No thinking being within her range. She stroked the spot delicately, shivering with pleasure, remembering the caress of other fingers. Tayyan. . . .

Help me, Tayyan called. Serroi looked down at her shield-mate sprawled in her own blood, then she looked past her at the Norid, the Black Man, the terror that ran in her blood. And she ran. Scurried like an animal over roof tiles and walls. Ran with Tayyan's accusing eyes always behind her.

Serroi shuddered and rubbed at her eyes, leaned her head back against the seat by the tiller and watched the sun drift upward, beginning to realize just how hungry she was. She laid her hand flat on her stomach, marveling at the desire her body had for life. Blinking away tormenting memory, she got to her feet and started rummaging through the lockers. She found a wineskin and shook it, squeezed a few drops of the sour wine into her parched mouth, shuddered at the taste. She broke a fingernail working open a tin of biscuits, sat sucking at the finger as she poked through the pale brown rounds inside. Fishing one of them out, she continued her exploration of the boat, chewing on the hard biscuit and sipping at the sour wine.

The boat was clean and well-kept, obviously the darling of some poor fisherman's heart. There was extra rope, pieces of canvas for patching the sail, cord for reweaving nets, neat coils of fish line, a small packet of needles and coarse thread—and much more. Halfway round, she kicked into her bow, lying where she'd dropped it, still strung. "Yael-mri would have my hide." She knelt, slipped the loop, ran her hand along the carefully tended stave, pleased that the wood seemed strong still in spite of its repeated inundations. She hung the bow over a mast cleat to continue drying, stretched, patted a yawn.

Higher up the cliffs hanguli-passare nested in hollows in the chalk and were flying about, their long leathery wings and small furred bodies coping easily with the thermals along the cliff face. Their cries blended with the steady roar of the surf and the creaking of the boat as wind and tide shoved it about. She moved slowly along the rail, running her hand over the neatly patched and oiled wood, shamed by her carelessness with her bow, shamed by the theft of this boat. Even if she sent gold back to pay for it, this kind of loving care had no price. She stopped her wandering and stood, eyes closed, listening to the harsh wild cries of the circling passare, drawing comfort from them as she had before and would again from similar sounds and smells and touches. Animal and earth and green growing things—they were always the same, always what they were with no pretense, never soul-hurting as humankind could be, as humankind had been to her over and over again.

Standing by the mast, she faced toward Oras, wondering what was happening there, if Tayyan was still alive. *I should go back. I have to go back. He'd take her to the Plaz, he'd want her alive so he could question her. Damn that fool Lybor, trying to use a brassy Norid in her plots. Question her!* She threw her head back, flung her arms out. "Ahhhhhaaaaiiiiy, Tayyyyaaaannnnn!" The cry was torn from her throat, an agonized recognition of the terror that ran in her blood. The Norid. She saw again the narrow black form, saw his stiff black hair, his gaunt red-brown face, Norid, Norid, cheap street Norid with his petty tricks. Then the image changed to the one that haunted her, the face she couldn't forget, couldn't ever forget—the elegant spare face, colorless as moonlight, with a black bar of eyebrow, a mouth thinned to a blue-pink line, with a fine gold ring and a pendant ruby dangling from one nostril, moving with his upper lip as he spoke. The ruby grew and grew, flooded her in bloodlight, pulsed until she danced with the pulsation, small wild girl child marked as misborn, thrust apart as misborn, small girl dancing, unseen fire searing her, swallowing her. . . .

When she was again aware of what she was doing, the boat was in open water, the cliffs a dark line on the horizon. She shuddered and swung the boat back to the shore. Her mouth was dry; she drank the sour wine, gulping it down until her head swam with the fumes. She slipped the tether over the tiller bar and curled up on the deck, dizzy with the boat's movement and the wine in her belly, cuddling the sagging skin against her breasts. She shifted position and drank again. And again. Then she fumbled the stopper home and cradled her head on her arm, drunk and exhausted, already half asleep. Her money sack hit the planking and the coins inside clanked dully.

Tayyan wrinkled her long thin nose. Hitching her weapon-belt up over her narrow hips, she eyed her shieldmate. "Dammit, Serroi, we're not on duty now. Who cares if a couple meie stray out of the harem? Who cares if Morescad put a curfew on us! Not me. What he doesn't know damn well won't hurt us. And he won't know a thing if we go out over the wall. Look, little one, Lucyr set up this race. Only man I ever met that knew more about macain than my father. Five macain, none of them ever beaten, one of them bred in my family's plexus." Her dark blue eyes laughed as she ruffled Serroi's mop of sorrel curls. "A mountain-bred macai from Frinnor's Hold, love, out of Curosh's stable. Cousin to my mother's sister's husband. You got any idea how long it's been since I saw a good race, a really good race?" Her fingers tangled in the fleecy curls; she tugged gently at them. "Come with me, love?"

Serroi sighed and gave in despite painful twitches of warn-

ing passing across the eye-spot on her forehead. She pulled
away from Tayyan's fingers, caught her hand and brought it
to her lips, kissed a finger lightly then bit down hard on a
knuckle, laughed and danced away when Tayyan grabbed for
her.

The race grounds: an hour's brisk walk outside the city. A
long rough oval scratched in the dull brown earth of the arid
ground south of Oras. Torches. Wine-sellers scooping wine
from purple-stained barrels into pressed clay bowls. Noise
and laughter and wine and excitement whirled around Serroi
until she felt as if she moved in an expanding bubble that refused to burst. In the center of the whirl, five macain plunged
and snorted—racing stock, big bones, long ugly limbs, claws
digging and tearing at the coarse earth, throwing up bursts of
small rock that spattered the crowd and pinged down
unheard among stamping boots. The roar rose to a shriek.
Powerful hind legs launched the macain into a series of long
jolting leaps.

Tayyan clutched Serroi's shoulder, beat up and down on it
as the animals swung around the far curve and headed back
to the finish. A lanky greenish-brown macai with a wiry hill-
man perched high on its back was gradually opening distance
between it and the other four.

"Curosh, Curosh!" Tayyan whooped with glee as the macai
came plunging toward them. "Come come come come!"

Serroi shrieked along with her shieldmate, her alto counter-
pointing Tayyan's squeal, her premonitions forgotten as she
surrendered to the noise and excitement around her. Yells.
Curses. Stamping boots. Arms whacking into her back and
sides. Wine bowls splashing over her. Flecks of gravel striking
her face. Smells of mansweat and animalsweat washing over
her. Bits of foam splattering her. Crowd roar. Surge of
bodies pushing the two of them forward. Jostling. Yelling.
Laughing. Crowd madness absorbing them as the watchers
surged around the snapping winner.

The bubble burst. Serroi came back to sanity, dizzy from
wine fumes, nauseated, her head throbbing. Tayyan was stuffing gold and silver coins into her money sack and talking en-
ergetically to a smallish man with hair like straw and a
brown, weathered face like a withered old root. Serroi
hauled her away and the two meien edged out of the scattering mob, crunching over the gritty earth toward the Highroad
and the city gate.

Tayyan was still excited, pouring the contents of her money sack into her hand, counting her winnings, crowing her triumph, ignoring Serroi's growing withdrawal. The eye-spot was throbbing, each small nip a warning shout. *Danger ahead. Watch out.* She said nothing—there was nothing to say, the warning was unlocalized in time or space and there was nothing around them but the moonlit plain and the plodding sportsmen returning to the city. Even these grew quieter as they approached the gates. More than one of them had passed wine and coin to the guards on duty there, bribing them to leave the gates open a crack. By good fortune none of the guards belonged to the Flame. Or perhaps fortune had nothing to do with that. Domnor Hern enjoyed a good race; only harsh and unyielding pressure from counselors, wives and the Sons of the Flame had brought him to banning races and condemning the wagering that went on at them.

The two women passed unnoticed through the gate, but once inside, Serroi walked faster, pulling Tayyan after her with some urgency. In the city there was a growing hostility to the meien, a hostility fostered by the Sons of the Flame. Domnor Hern still used them as harem guards but the other meien were gradually being dismissed by their employers. Outside Oras, in the small villages of the Mijloc, the priests of the Flame called them devil's whores and other names even less polite, led campaigns against those followers of the Maiden who still sent problem daughters to the Biserica valley for training as weaponwomen, healers or Servants of the Maiden. The custom—its origins lost in the mists of mythic time—of providing sanctuary at the Biserica for runaway girls and women had created a reservoir of resentment among the more conservative Mijlocim that was easy enough to stir into revulsion and fear.

Tayyan dumped half the coins back in her sack and stepped suddenly in front of Serroi, grinning broadly as she hugged her shieldmate, then caressed the eye-spot with the back of the fisted hand that held the rest of the money. "Little borrower of trouble," she said affectionately, still rather drunk with wine and excitement. "Here. This is yours." She stepped back, caught hold of Serroi's right hand and dropped a pile of coins into the palm. "I bet a couple of decsets on Curosh for you."

"Tayyan, you know I don't play those games." Serroi tried to give back the money.

"You'll spoil no sport tonight, love." Tayyan laughed and

danced away, lifting her hands to the gathering clouds, yawn-
ing and groaning with the pleasure of stretching her muscles.
She stopped, hands on hips, grinned at Serroi. "I'm for bath
and bed. Join me?"

Serroi nodded, unhappy because she couldn't match Tayyan's high spirits. She walked several minutes in silence, then
she sighed and tucked the coins into her own money sack.

The boat heaved as the wind shifted. Serroi stirred, her
tongue furry, her head throbbing. She pushed against the
deck and lifted her upper body until she was sitting with her
legs crossed before her, hands clutching at her temples. She
swallowed, swallowed again. *People*, she thought. *I need
people. And water. And food.* She focused her *desire* then
followed the tugging of the eye-spot southeast toward the
cliffs.

She beat her slow way against the wind to the distant shore
but she was still some way out when the sun touched zenith
and the wind dropped to an erratic series of puffs too weak
to lift a feather. The sail flapped against the mast, then
sagged, flapped, sagged. She shook the wineskin, unstoppered
it and lifted it high, let the thick sour liquid trickle into her
mouth. The sun steaming the moisture out of her until she
felt her skin frying, she sucked at the wineskin, her eyes on
the faint line of the horizon, the tantalizing dark line, so close
and so impossibly out of reach. She dozed a little but sleep
brought the nightmares back; finally she kept awake, trying to
drift without thinking.

Late in the afternoon a cooler breeze tugged at her hair
and teased the sail into slapping noisily at the mast. Sodden
with wine and sweat, she staggered to her feet, collapsed onto
her knees as the boat rocked under her. She shook her head,
groaned, then looked over her shoulder at the sun hanging
low in the west, almost touching the flat line of ocean, tipping
the waves with crimson. Crawling because she couldn't stand,
she got to the mast, pulled herself onto her feet, her head
slowly beginning to clear. People, she thought, *desired*, then
sent the boat where the eye-spot pulled her. The sail filled
and the small boat danced lightly across the swells. She
blessed the builder. A sweet ship, steady and responsive, built
with love and maintained with love, skimming over the
darkening water with a singing hiss.

As she drew near the white cliffs she saw another tappata
with a pier angling past the outlet, small store-sheds, and a

crude stone fort. Driven by wind and the incoming tide, the boat was a bird under her hands swooping down on the pier. The sheds and the fort were deserted, crumbling. She frowned with disappointment, but her eye-spot still tugged her strongly inland, so she settled back and let the wind blow her along the finger of water winding between perpendicular cliffs of chalk.

THE CHILD: 1

The small dirty child was playing with the chinin pups, tumbling recklessly about on the tundra, mashing down grass and flowers, ignoring the prodding of scattered fist-sized rocks. The chinin were play-growling, small sharp teeth worrying at her torn and mud-streaked clothes. Tugging at the ankles of her boots, stomping on her, rolling on her as they wrestled with each other. She was filthy and wet, bruised, scraped in a hundred places, and she loved it, she bathed in the trust and warmth the chinin gave her, felt herself one of them, a chini among chinin. And forgot completely, or refused to think about the scold she'd get later on from her weary mother, the strapping her father would give her, the tormenting she could expect from her normal brothers and sisters. In this play she lived utterly in the present and was supremely happy.

"Serroi!" She recognized the harsh voice of her grandfather and got reluctantly to her feet. She slid her eyes to his face, then stared down at the toe-peaks of her boots. He looked angry and embarrassed. She sneaked a second glance at the man beside him, puzzled by the stranger's presence. The green blotches on her skin and her smallness offended her grandfather's sense of self-worth; she was a symbol of his son's lack of control, conceived against custom at the radiant hot springs where the windrunners wintered, usually kept well out of sight when there were visitors to the camp. Yet now her grandfather was calling her to meet a tall man in a narrow black robe. She came scowling to her grandfather's side, furious with him for spoiling her joy and too familiar with his heavy hand to dare show her fury.

She stood away from her grandfather, knowing by instinct and experience that he didn't want her touching him, stood with her head bowed, her curls tumbling forward hiding her face, stood sneaking looks at the strange man because he was beautiful in her eyes and she was starved for beauty. He was tall. Grandfather who was a mighty man among the People came only to mid-chest on him. He was snow-pale with finely chiseled lips and a nose straight as a knife-slash. A small gold ring passed through the outside of his left nostril. A gleaming red stone hung from the ring and moved when he smiled at her. His hair was black smoke floating around his narrow high-cheeked face. His eyes were black too, the black of the polished jet ornaments her mother wore to the Iangi-vlan festival at summers-end. He seemed to her more a strange wild animal than a man and because she felt most at home with animals she dared smile back at him and lift her head, forgetting, for once, the green blotches that marked her as misborn.

"This is the child." Her grandfather's lips were stretched in a wide humorless smile; he was almost fawning on the stranger.

"Her parents agree? She must be a free-will gift." The man's face was low and musical. Shivering with pleasure at its beauty, Serroi paid little attention to what the two men were saying. Adults talked over her head all the time about things she found complicated and uninteresting. Instead, she concentrated on the singing joy his voice made of his words.

Grandfather shrugged. "Summers-end she goes to the priest anyway. My son consents."

"The child's mother?" The ruby flashed sparks of crimson as he spoke.

Serroi sneaked a look at Grandfather at the stranger's question. His red-brown eyes opened wide with surprise that anyone would bother about what a woman thought. "The out-daughter will do what my son says."

"Then put your mark on this." The beautiful stranger slipped fingers inside his sleeve and drew out a short roll of parchment which he handed to Grandfather. "It is a deed of gift." He proffered a tiny pot of black grease and showed Grandfather how to set the mark of his thumb on the deed. When that was done, he took the parchment, rolled it again and tucked it back in his sleeve. Once again he smiled down at Serroi, held out his hand. "Come, child."

Lost and bewildered, wanting to do what he said, afraid of what was happening, she looked from her scowling grandfather to the beautiful man, then walked hesitantly toward him. After a final glance at the chinin pups who stopped their playing and sat on their haunches watching her, she took the stranger's hand and trotted beside him, her short legs taking several steps to his one. After a few minutes she looked back. The pups still sat in a ragged half circle, their eyes mournful as they watched her leave. A chini pup howled suddenly and the others joined him. Disturbed by the sound, she bit down on her lip and walked faster beside the dark figure striding across the tundra toward one of the many outcroppings of rock rising like snaggle teeth from the rolling land.

Behind the rock a vinat was tethered to a heavy stone, grazing at the soft spring grass. He was hitched to a carved and painted cart like those the Iangi priests rode in when they traveled between the windrunner camps. Around the four sides, carved vinat with gilded horns leaped and ran on a yellow ground. Above and below them ran chains of red and yellow flowers, green leaves and twisting vines. Over the top of the car arched carved ribs with loops where a covering could be tied, though there was no cover on them now. Serroi watched as the stranger lowered the back gate of the cart and began untying thongs on a large leather bag.

With an odd quiver in her stomach, she moved away to the grazing vinat and stroked tentative fingers over the thick fleecy curls along the animal's front legs. The graceful narrow head lifted, the limber neck curved round and the vinat was nuzzling at her, its nostrils quivering, ears flicking with pleasure as she scratched along the jaw line just above the fibrous beard that could sting like fire when the vinat brushed it over an attacking predator. More stiff short fibers shone like gold wire on the palmate horns. With its throat protected, with its horns given an added sting, with its razor-sharp hooves, the vinat was a nasty fighter and hard to handle, even half-tame.

"Come here, child." The musical voice had a touch of warmth that surprised her. Her heart beating erratically, hoping for she knew not what, she left the vinat and circled the cart. The man took her hand, smiled down at her from his great height. He looked gentler now, less like a long-tooth sicamar prowling a herd. "Sit here." He pointed to a small rock sunk deep in sweetgrass and limul flowers. As she sat, he brought a basin filled with water and perfumed white foam. He knelt beside her, settling the basin in the grass by her boot toes. After turning back his sleeves, he dipped a rag in the water and gently cleaned her face. The cloth caressed her skin though the foam got in her eyes and stung them. The water was deliciously warm. She sat very still, vibrating with pleasure at the warmth, the gentleness which she took for tenderness, the first she'd experienced since her mother weaned her. When he finished with her face, he washed her hands thoroughly, even cleaning out the small arcs of dirt under her short bitten fingernails.

Finally he sat back on his heels, dropped the rag in the basin. "Clean the rest of your body, child, then put those on." He pointed at the back of the cart; her best trousers, tunic, belt and cloak were there. "Your mother sent them." He stood. "Don't dawdle. Join me when you finish." He walked away and pulled himself onto the driver's seat of the cart, his back to her.

When she climbed up beside him, he flicked a whip at the vinat's haunches and they started off across the tundra.

THE WOMAN: II

The precipitous walls of chalk confined the tappata to a worm of salt water poking into the side of the Earth's Teeth, the chain of mountains hugging the shore from Oras south to the Aranji gulf where the great round bulge of Sankoy thrust out into the Ocean. The water was rising in the channel, going faster as the tide came roaring in. Winds fell over the top of the cliffs and mixed with the strong air currents following the water from the sea, tangling in a confused knot that twisted and turned unpredictably.

Serroi fought to hold the boat in the center of the tappata, blessing fervently the builder since all that kept her from crashing a dozen times was the stability and responsiveness of the small craft. She sailed through the deepening shadow under the cliffs, beginning to smell green from the mountains as the side drafts picked up the scent of growing things and mingled this with the tang of the salt air.

A mellow brazen note sounded above the noise of wind and water, then was repeated several times. Serroi blinked and leaned forward, listening intently as the boat swept around the first section of an elongated double curve. *A bell. And close.* When the boat nosed into the second half of the curve, the bell no longer sounded but fragments of shouts drifted to her. The tappata widened suddenly, the cliffs beginning to move back and fall away. She dropped the sail, riding the slowing surge of the tide, her eye-spot throbbing with its danger-warning.

About a dozen boat-lengths ahead of her the right-hand cliff broke off. Beyond the white chalk a rolling grassy meadow rose gradually toward the mountains. As the boat crept forward, still drowned in shadow, the battle scene unreeled before her, a section of wall lengthening like a ribbon pulled from a slot—then the fisher village separated itself from the cliff.

Heads lined the top of the wall and thrust out from window slits in the gate towers. Three fisher bodies were sprawled outside, one bristling with a dozen crossbow bolts,

24

the other two slashed to bloodied rags. A little farther out, two smaller darker bodies lay in pools of drying blood, skewered by fish spears.

The setting sun gilded the shouting, milling groups of macai riders gathered on a rocky knob just out of bowshot from the village. They were small dark men, their bodies wrapped in leather straps, boiled leather shields on their backs, sabers brandished high or swinging along their thighs. *Kapperim.* Serroi sucked in a long breath, exploded it out. *A raid at Moongather? Here?* Something was wrong. They were too far north, too far from their burrows in the mountains behind Sankoy, something was stirring them up. She licked her lips, uneasily aware that this could fit in all too well with what had happened in Oras. That could mean the Nearga-Nor's reach was a good deal longer than she'd suspected, something she didn't want to think about. She searched the knob for the Shaman but saw only the Warleader, a bearded man whose leathers were set with thousands of tiny mirrors that caught the sun and clothed him in a web of golden light.

Five raiders broke away from the others and rode at top speed down the slope. When they reached the flat ground in front of the village wall, they reined the macain back on their haunches, swung slings over their heads and lobbed smoking globes into the village. Wheeling their mounts, they raced away, shouts and shrill curses following them.

The globes sailed back outside to burst on the ground, sputtering, fuming and finally subsiding. Out on the tappata, Serroi wrinkled her nose as wisps of the stinking smoke reached her.

A flight of arrows and a few fish spears streamed after the Kapperim. Though most of them glanced off the shields on their backs, two raiders fell from their saddles, one with an arrow through his leg, the other skewered just above the waist by one of the fish spears. The wounded Kappra dragged himself onto his knees and started crawling uphill, but another spear took him in almost the same place as the other, the lower back. He sprawled on the grass, twitched a few times, then was still.

Serroi's boat emerged from the cliff shadow, slowing even further as the tide-drive lessened. Several raiders yelled and pointed at her. The Warleader waved an arm glittering with light, sending three men plunging to the edge of the tappata. They waited for her to come within range, ignoring the fisher arrows that skittered around and off them. When she was close enough, they raised their bows and sent quarrels skimming at her.

Serroi slipped the tether over the tiller and sank behind the boat's side, watching the bolts hiss past. One clunked into the mast and bounced back onto the deck; one cut the air two feet behind the stern, hit the water, skipped twice, slowly sank as the heavy point pulled it down. The third hit the side of the boat close to the waterline, slid along it, sank. Serroi snorted with contempt and sat up.

The Kapperim saw her head and loosed another flight. She ducked again, scornful of their marksmanship but not ready to tempt their luck. Sitting crouched on the deck she strung her bow, worked the weaponbelt around until the long case rested in her lap. She flipped it open and counted the arrows. *Twelve shafts left. Not enough. Have to pick my targets.* She lifted her head above the rail and frowned at the men on the knob.

They were backing away, forming a ragged half-circle about a fire. Four Kapperim rode forward and one by one thrust torches into the fire. As soon as they were blazing, the men whirled them about their heads, howled their war challenge, jerked their macain around, raced down toward the walls. One rider fell when an arrow from the village caught his mount in an eye. As he tumbled from the saddle, another arrow socked into his chest. Two of the Kapperim reached the walls and flung their torches against the planks of the great double gate. The third stopped a little way out, whirled the torch over his head and flung it in a high wheeling arc over the wall. As it swung through the air, the flame raced the whole length of the handle. The moment it cleared the wall, a fisher sprang up, caught the torch, shrieked as the fire ate into his hands. Refusing to let go, screaming obscenities, he hurled it into the tappata where it rocked up and down on the water, burning furiously. The fisher stared at white bone coming through charred flesh, moaned and dropped from sight. The other torches flared up with unnatural swiftness, the wood of the gate already beginning to smoke and blacken.

A small man, naked except for a greasy leather apron, stood hunched over a replica of the village. A tiny fire licked slowly higher and higher at a miniature gate. Body strained, the Shaman was chanting sonorously, his voice in its lowest register. Eye-spot throbbing, Serroi knelt on the deck, nocked an arrow, then was on her feet, feeling for her target, feeling the flow of the wind, breathing slowly, deeply, centering herself. Ignoring the shouts from the bank, the quarrels flitting past her, she loosed the shaft. The arrow sang through the air, swung through a high arc, sliced into the greasy naked back of the Shaman. He fell over his model, extinguishing the tiny fire.

The fire eating at the gate snuffed out and the torch in the water sizzled to blackness and sank.

On the bank the Kapperim howled with rage and spurred their macain until they came up with the boat. This time two of their bolts flicked by less than an inch from her head and the third skinned her arm. She ignored them and loosed a second arrow at the Warleader. The light-gilded figure on the knob went rigid. His head dipped down as if he stared at the shaft protruding from his chest, then he toppled off his mount, his fall like the sun suddenly going out for the raiders. She heard screams and curses from the bank, then the quarrels were thick above her as if the shooters were too blind with fury and grief to notice that she was no longer standing, too blind to do more than shove the bolts in and shoot them out. Then the bombardment stopped.

She rose to her knees. On the knob the Kapperim milled about, wailing the death chant for their leaders. On the village wall fishers were cheering, a small boy had climbed the bell tower and was swinging on the broken rope, the successive peals of the huge bell a roll of triumph booming out over the meadow, nearly drowning out the sorrowing yips of the raiders. The charred gate split in the middle and the village men swarmed out, shooting a rain of arrows from their longbows, hurling spears at the wailing, disorganized raiders. Serroi dropped the anchor overside and sat watching the melee, her part in the raider's rout completed.

The confusion out on the grass increased. Demoralized by the death of their leaders, a death coming so suddenly it was like evil magic to them, under attack by the reheartened villagers, the Kapperim scooped up their dead Shaman and Warleader and fled into the band of trees hugging the mountains' feet. Left behind, dead and dying raiders lay on the grass and abandoned macain were snuffling around, tearing up tufts of grass, chewing placidly now that their riders no longer prodded them into irritated rebellion.

Serroi ran a bit of leather along the bowstave, smoothing a few roughened spots in the wax as she watched the fishers move among the downed Kapperim, cutting the throats of those who still lived. After a few minutes of this, she set the bow aside, worked the anchor loose and drew it back in the boat. When the boat had enough way on, she swung it around, raised the sail, and began tacking back toward the line of boats drawn up on the bank of the tappata in the shadow of the village wall's. It was near full dark, the shadows long on the grass, the western sky filled with rags of crimson and amber as clouds gathered for another storm. The tappata was quieter, the tidal surge leveling off. She angled the boat into a last tack, drove its nose up onto the mud slope.

When she bent to pick up her bow, her head swam and dark blotches danced before her tearing eyes. Sinking down on her heels, knees shaking, head throbbing from fatigue and the fumes of the wine, she clutched at the rail to steady herself until the dizziness receded. She could hear the voices of fishers as they gathered on the bank but she paid them little attention while she clipped the bow to its 'strap and shifted it around until the stave lay diagonally across her back. The heels of her hands pressed against tired eyes, she knelt a moment longer, gathering the remnants of her ebbing strength, then shoved herself to her feet and dropped overside into the mud.

A growing number of fisher's moved about on the patchy grass at the top of the bank, waiting for her, exchanging muttered comments, scowling at her, not looking particularly grateful for the help she'd given them. They were a surly lot toward outsiders, these inbred villagers. She smoothed her hair down and started up the incline, frowning as her feet slipped on the gelatinous mud that coated her soles and caked in a thick lump under her instep. When she reached firmer ground, she scrubbed her boots vigorously across a patch of wiry grass, inspected the soles, knelt and used a handful of the grass to rub the rest of the mud away, ignoring the men who were waiting for her until she was satisfied that her boots were as clean as she could make them. She wiped her hands on another bit of grass, then rose to her feet to confront the man standing a step ahead of the others.

The Intii—the fisher headman. That much she could read from the pattern of scars running across his forehead, thanks to her Biserica training. The Valley scholars had gathered fragmentary reports about the fishers and woven them into a sketchy picture of their lifeways, enough to give Serroi some confidence in her ability to deal with them in spite of their reluctance to accept outside contact. Obviously not going to speak first, he waited for her to explain herself, growing impatient as she scanned his face without saying the words he was silently demanding. He was a lanky long man, grey-streaked brown hair and beard twisted in elaborate plaits, thin lips pressed into near invisibility, eyebrows like hedges drawn down over hooded hazel eyes. Behind the hair his weathered face was a mask carved from nut-brown cantha wood, unreadable except for a general aura of shrewdness and strength.

She straightened her shoulders, fixed her eyes on his, said firmly, "As meie of the Biserica, under Compact I ask a night's shelter and help on my way. What is expended will be repaid without the need to ask."

His eyes traveled over her plain leather tunic, knee-length divided skirt, her battered dirty high boots, the weaponbelt slung around her hips, widened a little as he noted the absence of a sword. "Meien travel two by two," he said finally, the fisher lilt twisting the words until she had a hard time understanding him. He looked past her at the boat; from the set of his face she thought he recognized it, something he confirmed when he spoke again. "Ferenlang's boat, how come it here without him?"

"The boat was borrowed."

"Borrowed, woman?"

"Meie, Intii," she snapped, suddenly furious at his stubborn resistance. Fingers trembling from fatigue and anger, she jerked the thongs loose on her money sack, pulled out a handful of coins and threw them at his feet. "Pay for the usage of the boat and for the fisher who returns it. Forget the rest, I'll sleep under the trees where the dark lives that prowl the night show more courtesy than men."

The Intii contemplated the coins scattered in a ragged line in front of his toes, then fixed his eyes on her face, not about to be hurried into decision either by anger or insult. He rubbed a bony thumb along his lower lip, looked from the tip of her unstrung bow thrusting up past her shoulder to the boat, from the boat to the rocky knob where the Shaman and Warleader had fallen victim to her marksmanship. The silence lengthened, broken by the sounds of shuffling feet and more muttered comment from the men gathered behind the Intii. "A meie without a sword?" he said finally, another quibble, though this time his voice was more thoughtful than accusing.

Serroi swallowed a sigh; the prospect of hot food and a bath was the only thing keeping her from carrying out her threat and leaving the man to his tortuous reasonings. "You will have noted my size." She spoke with exaggerated patience, knowing this could annoy him, unable to swallow her resentment at the way she was being catechized. The way she was dressed, the skill with which she handled the bow, what the hell else could she be but a meie? "I haven't the reach for effective swordplay though I'm trained in sword use; must I prove this on one of you?"

To her surprise, the Intii's thin mouth curved in a tight smile. "If you're half as quick with sword as you be sharp with bow, I think I'd lose the man, meie." He wheeled and with a few brisk words ordered the shifting crowd to disperse and take care of work left unfinished at the onset of the raid. He stood silent beside Serroi until the last straggler had passed through the gate, then he chuckled and relaxed, a different man away from his followers. "You're a stingy fighter, little meie; two arrows and raid's a rout." He glanced over his shoulder at the line of boats, shook his head, tongue-clicks underlining his disgust. "Fishers and we never thought of using boats. Next raid, we clean their guts; those bows of theirs, they got no range."

Serroi frowned. "This is the Moongather year and only one more week before the Gather's complete. I've never heard of Kapperim raiding this close to the Gather—or this far north with winter on the way." Wearily she moved her shoulders, rubbed at the back of her neck. "Any idea why they're breaking custom?"

"The stink in Sankoy. Worse'n fish a week out of water. We don't fish south any more. What I hear, Kapperim're part of the stink." He smoothed the toe of one sandal across the gritty earth, his face thoughtful. "Could be they're opening a way for the Sankoy stink to spread." Pulling the mantle of the Intii back around his shoulders, speaking with grave formality, he said, "What do you require, meie of the Biserica?"

Once again Serroi straightened her back, squared her shoulders, answering with equal formality, "This I require, Intii of the fishers. A macai from among the abandoned." She nodded at the dark blotches wandering about the rolling meadow, their shapes lost to the descending night. "A hot meal, a bath, a bed and in the morning supplies for my journey."

THE CHILD: 2

Letting her short legs swing, Serroi watched the hairy haunches of the vinat ripple as the beast pulled them steadily over the pathless tundra. They were traveling west, cutting across the migration route of the vinat herds and the windrunner clans that followed them. Narrowing her eyes, she sneaked a glance at the tall silent figure sitting beside her, the reins resting loose in lax fingers. He'd been kind enough, but after her first glow faded, she was afraid to trust that kindness without trying it some more. Her five years had been enough to teach her how little she could depend on outside herself. Though she was beginning to understand that the world had patterns she could learn if she watched them long enough, each spring was still a revelation to her; she wasn't sure, even now, that the sun would keep coming back, but could remember enough times when it had to be reasonably certain spring would come again. In the same way, she'd come to expect pain and spite from humankind and see momentary kindness as a trap for her stumbling feet.

Still, she had fallen into hope, seduced by the beauty of the man and the music of his voice. It seemed to her as she continued to sneak looks at him that no one so beautiful could be cruel or indifferent, that the man's outward appearance must reflect his inner nature. She smoothed her hands over the supple leather of the cushions. Smiling timidly, she asked, "How may I call you?"

When he didn't answer, she shrank back into her own silence, afraid she'd offended him. Some moments later he looked around, black eyes coming back from vast distance, warming with visible effort. "Your pardon, child?" The soft deep voice wooed her back from her fear, cradling her in its music. She wanted to snuggle against him, be comforted by him, but she didn't quite dare. There was a barrier unseen and undefined between them; she sensed her affection would not be welcome, at least not now. Later, when she knew more of him, perhaps she could move closer. She needed to be touched, to be given the casual physical affection she'd received from her animals.

"My mind was elsewhere, child." He shifted the reins into one hand and brushed the wild fleece off her forehead. It should have been a light caress but was not, was too stiff and forced, as if he calculated even the speed and weight of touch required by such a gesture. Deeply disappointed, she forced a quivering smile to hide her confusion. "What did you ask?" he said, looking down at his fingers as if he too didn't know quite what to make of the failed gesture.

"How may I call you?"

"I have no name." He spoke slowly, thoughtfully; she saw him give his shoulders a small shake like the twitch she sometimes gave to her boots when her feet were swollen and the boots didn't want to slide on as they should. Like the boots, too, he grew easier with wear. When he spoke again, he had relaxed until she could feel the return of the warmth that had made her happy enough to come with him. "I am a Wordmaster of the Nearga-Nor. You may call me Ser Noris."

Serroi shook her hair back over her eyes. "Ser Noris, why did you take me from Grandfather?"

"Were you so happy living with him?"

"They're my family." She didn't want to think about them; after all they were all she had; they made up the greater portion of the only world she knew. She rubbed her hand back and forth over the leather, leaving behind small wet tracks from her sweaty palms, but stopped asking questions, sensing under his calm exterior a warning restiveness.

Ser Noris dropped back into his silence, his body beside her, his mind far away in some world he alone knew. The cart jolted steadily along, the vinat clicking off the hours with the strong rhythmic scissoring of his legs while the long sun rolled around the horizon, the passage of time measured more intimately for Serroi by the growling hunger in her belly. She sat in miserable silence, too shy to speak again.

Perhaps he sensed her need, perhaps it was only a part of his plan, but soon afterward Ser Noris stopped the cart. He fished in the back, gave Serroi a flask of water and some pieces of dried meat. While she ate, he poured water in a basin for the vinat, then stood with his arms crossed over his chest gazing steadily southward while the beast grazed. After a half hour's halt, he remounted the seat and flicked the vinat into a quick walk.

He drove westward until Serroi was dizzy with sleep,

clutching desperately at the seat arm beside her, jerking in
and out of a light doze, only half aware of it when the cart
stopped its bouncing and the seat creaked as he swung down.
She sat blinking hazily while he unharnessed and hobbled the
beast and came back for her. He lifted her down and carried
her around behind the cart, setting her on her feet and plac-
ing her hands on the dangling rear gate so she could hold
herself up while he lifted out a bulky bundle whose outside
wrapping was a finely tanned vinat hide with the long hair
still on it; the bundle was nearly as big as she was and
weighed heavily in her weary arms when he handed it to her.
"Spread these under the cart, child," he said. "They'll give
you some shade."

"Thank you, Ser Noris."

"Are you hungry, child?"

"No thank you, Ser Noris. Only sleepy."

"Then sleep." He left quietly then, walking off toward one
of the ever-present outcroppings of rock. Serroi blinked,
yawned, spread out the bed roll and was asleep almost before
she pulled the hide over her head.

By the next nooning they came to a river, the first Serroi
had ever seen. She stared at the rushing water, wider than a
dozen streams, fascinated by the swirls of bright blue and
green, the rooster tails of foam, the roar that seemed to
merge with something deep inside her.

For several more sleeps they followed the river west, eating
fish the water threw out at them when Ser Noris commanded
it. She watched the water as it widened, watched the land as
it changed its form, even its substance, watched the houses
they were beginning to pass, her eyes round with wonder.

They reached the sea on a brilliant day when sunlight
danced in shards among the waves and the blue of the water
was a promise of delight. Where the river poured into a wide
shallow bay there was a huddle of steep-roofed buildings,
four or five piers reaching out to deep water, a few ships
moored at the piers, visible as pointed dots against the bright
blue of the sky. Some men, not many, sat in small groups on
the piers, old men with yellow-stained beards and pale blue
eyes sunk deep in nests of wrinkles, long lean men very different from her windrunner kind. The pale blue eyes followed
them as Ser Noris drove the cart onto the first of the piers
and out to the end where a small sailing ship was moored. A
hunched grey man came limping from one of the buildings

and followed them onto the pier. He took the reins from Ser Noris, stood with dull grey patience as Ser Noris climbed down and moved around the end of the cart to hold out his hand for Serroi.

His flesh was cool and smooth, his life running strong under the skin. Serroi shivered as the hand closed over hers. Once again he'd changed; something about him, she didn't know what, frightened her. He was suddenly the savage animal again, his power visible as a predator's teeth, as if he'd put a part of himself aside when he traveled inland and was only now reclaiming it. She jumped down from the cart, careless in her distraction, wanting so to get free of that disturbing touch that she stumbled and fell against his legs. With a gasp of dismay, she scrambled away and stood with her back against the cart's wheel.

He smiled down at her after a moment, patted her gently on the head, took her hand again and led her toward a narrow gangplank. The grey man took the vinat and cart away; as she trudged onto the deck of the ship, Serroi looked over her shoulder at the animal, watching it trot off with a damp sadness about her heart. For the first time she realized she might never see her people again, that she was being cut off from everything she knew. She looked up at the silent Noris, then down again, closing her teeth hard over her lower lip to fight back the surge of loneliness that made her eyes burn with tears.

"Hold onto the mast—this—and don't be frightened, child." Ser Noris placed her hand on the smooth wood and waited until she was clutching at the softly humming mast, her cheek pressed against it, then he stepped aside and spoke a WORD.

Invisible hands raised the sails, cast off the mooring lines. Invisible hands held the wheel and turned the ship toward the open sea. Though the wind blew inshore elsewhere, the white sails filled and the ship skimmed over the water, driven by a mage wind that left the old men on the piers gaping.

The humming grew louder in Serroi's ears; the wind flirted past her, tugging at her curls, flattening her tunic against her narrow body. For the first few minutes she was excited enough and pleased enough at this new experience to forget her sorrows, then her stomach began to protest as the deck moved up and down under her feet and the railing beyond tilted up and down up and down. She looked up at Ser Noris, sweat beading her face, one hand pressed over her mouth.

He rushed her to the rail and held her as she voided her stomach. Even through her wretchedness she sensed his distaste; desolation and emptiness of another kind grew in her. Tears dripped from her eyes to mix with the sweat and sour liquid from her stomach as the convulsions diminished and finally stopped. She hung limply over the rail, so weak and distressed she was unable to move.

Ser Noris carried her back to the mast and settled her on the heaving deck. He squatted beside her, frowning. "I'd better leave you in the open air until you're over that." He touched her cheek with a ghost of his former gentleness. "You may think you're dying, little one, but it will pass. I promise you, it will pass." He stood briskly, brushed at his sleeves, spoke another WORD.

A rope end snaked from a coil hanging on the mast. Serroi watched it wobble through the air toward her and cringed away, but was prevented from moving far as the Noris squatted again and held her still, his hand on her shoulder. The rope slid around her waist and wove itself into a knot. She stared down at it, then at the other end which was looping itself about the mast. She reached down and touched the knot at her waist, jerked her hand away from the unnatural warmth of the rope fiber. She looked fearfully up at the Noris.

He touched her cheek again. "This for your safety, child. Otherwise you could be swept overboard. My servants will care for you." With smooth unobtrusive grace he was on his feet and moving away. About a body-length away from the mast, he stopped and faced the sea, spoke a WORD into the wind. When he'd paced out a square around her, speaking a WORD at each corner, the air touching her gentled and turned warm. He came back and stood looking down at her. "Remember, child, if there's anything you need, call for it and my servants will bring it."

When he'd disappeared below, invisible hands fetched a basin of warm soapy water and bathed her face. They brought her more water to drink and a savory broth to fill some of the emptiness inside her. They tended her neatly and impersonally, went away as soon as they were done. Serroi crouched against the humming mast, the only thing that seemed real and comforting, too sick to care.

Twice more she succumbed to the urgency of her stomach. The hands cleaned her up and left her alone. Finally she managed to sleep and found to her surprise that when she

woke, her body had adapted to the dip and fall of the ship.
She sat up, pushed aside her blankets, blinking at the sun
which shone directly in her eyes as it dipped to its lowest
point near the horizon. "Hands," she called. "I'm starved.
Bring me something to eat."

A moment later she had a platter of steaming rolls with
butter and jam, a pot of cha and a dainty small cup with no
handle and long thin slices of cream-colored posser flesh. She
sniffed, grinned, began eating hungrily. The wind was crisp
and fresh even filtered through her invisible walls, the sea
jewel blue, singing past the sides, rising and falling like a
breathing beast. Fish leaepd in schools from the water making tiny whistling sounds like damp, iridescent birds.

When she finished her meal, she submitted to the invisible
hands while they bathed her and brought her fresh clothing,
more things her mother had packed away for her. With their
usual wordless efficiency they polished her and the deck until
both were painfully clean, then they left. Serroi shook out her
tether, wrinkled her nose at it, then moved toward the railing,
testing how much range of movement she was going to have.
The rope proved long enough to let her lean on the rail and
stare down at the water hissing past.

A whale broached nearby. Breaking water first, its back
was a shining curve of dark grey with black mottles like
sooty hand prints. It spouted a rush of steam, then sounded
with a comic flirting of its tail flukes. Laughing her delight,
Serroi raced back along the rail, the rope whipping behind
her until it pulled her to a stop. She leaned out over the rail,
still laughing, her eye-spot tingling. She called the whale
back, clapped her hands in joy as it played with the ship,
loosing it finally when it began to chafe at the restraints she
put on it.

Birds flew by overhead, riding the wind that drove the ship.
Sometimes they settled around Serroi to preen russet, gold,
green, or blue fur with long narrow tongues, to search each
other for fur-mites, crunching them between tiny dagger teeth
lining the lips of their leathery beaks. Serroi scratched at
small heads, coaxed some of the birds into her lap where they
twittered with pleasure under the probing of her fingers.

The ship moved south without pause, the days growing
shorter and the stars shifted into new patterns. Serroi contented herself with the birds and the creatures of the sea, left utterly alone by Ser Noris. Yet she wasn't lonely; her happiest
times had always been when she ran and played with the an-

imals drawn to her by the siren-song of the eye-spot. These days were an endless playtime without the painful and often incomprehensible demands of adults. The rope confined her and at the same time freed her from the need of watching her feet so she ran heedlessly about, tagging the birds, racing the fish that sometimes leaped the rail and slid across the deck into the sea on the far side.

The ship danced southward until days and nights matched and the winds were warm as her own breath—always no land, only the blue water, the blue sky and the mage wind blowing them into summer. Her life in her father's wagon following the vinat faded into vague dreams. She had a child's perception of time, the hours stretching out and out until one day was swallowed by the next, until she might always have run about the deck of the ship surrounded by an endless sea.

The rising sun was red in her eyes when she woke on the last day of the voyage; she blinked and yawned, sat up rubbing her eyes. Kicking the blanket away, leaving it in a heap for the hands to carry off, she trotted to the railing to see what was happening, squinting against the glare of the morning light. Her eye-spot tingled, a sourceless itch crawled about beneath her skin, and she had an uncomfortable sense of waiting-about-to-end. The nose of the boat pointed toward a triangle of black cutting up to spoil the smooth line of the horizon. She shivered. What there was about that rising dark fang to make her so uneasy she couldn't tell, but when she looked at it, she felt a hollow coldness spreading inside her. She watched it grow for a while then went slowly back to the mast and her cooling breakfast.

The black form became a tall cone-shaped mountain breathing out a wavering plume of steam. Other small dots grew into dark islands, an archipelago of stone whose tallest peak was an active volcano.

Having begun to think the South was all water, Serroi went to the rail again to watch, fascinated, the nearing islands. The ship dipped neatly through a ring of foam and slid past a large island of brown-black stone, then past a blunt stone pier with a huge stone house high above it rising from a glass-smooth cliff, a house that seemed big enough to stable her family's vinat herd. She stared up at it as they went past, wondering about it, pounded small fists on the rail in frustration because the hands were mute and couldn't answer her questions and Ser Noris was out of touch and she wouldn't have dared question him anyway.

The ship nosed through the twisting passage between the islands, past more tall houses and silent piers. The air felt heavy and dead, except for the mage wind driving them. The islands were barren with no touch of green. Even the water had lost its brilliance and sighed heavily and darkly under them.

The mage wind died and the ship glided smoothly along one of the stone piers. As it nudged into place the sails came down with hasty snappings and sighing slaps and the mooring lines snaked out to snub it against the pier. Serroi felt the rope about her waist come alive and writhe loose. It wriggled away from her to coil itself back on the masthook. Rubbing at her waist, she tilted her head back, her eyes moving up along the dark shiny face of the cliff to the tower that continued its ascent into a heavy sky. A dead place, cold and unwelcoming. She turned to face north, yearning for the tundra where life was thick and warm even when it snowed.

Ser Noris came up onto the deck moving with a calm, slow dignity. He stood a moment, she heard the soft sounds of his feet stop and knew he was watching her; she refused to look around. "Come, child." The music of the words wooed her and surprised her almost as if she were hearing his voice for the first time, having forgotten the magic it made for her during the silent weeks on board the ship.

She turned slowly and walked across the deck to him, her feet dragging, her head down. She wanted to say to him that she needed to go home, that she didn't like this place, that it was dead and made her feel dead—but she didn't quite dare. She could feel an itch building in her that she couldn't describe or even fully understand, a growing resistance to being pushed along without understanding what was happening. When she forced herself to look up at him, his beautiful face was quiet, he was even smiling a little—but he was still a long, long way off and the smile was a grimace that didn't touch his eyes. She said nothing, simply took the hand he held out to her.

He lifted her onto the pier and led her down it to the cliff face which was glass-smooth and without a break she could see anywhere. She opened her eyes wide, wondering what the Noris was going to do, then gasped with surprise and fear as her feet left the stone of the pier.

They rose smoothly, soaring with the ease of the sea birds

lately her companions. After her fright passed away and she was certain she wasn't going to fall, she laughed with delight and kicked her feet through the flowing air. The Noris ignored her antics. At the top of the cliff he halted the flight and glided smoothly to a landing inside a deep alcove cut into the tower's outer wall. Facing the tall bronze doors at the back of the cut, he spoke a quiet WORD. The doors sprang apart, crashing against the stone not far from his impassive face. He strode between the age-greened slabs into the thick blackness beyond, pulling Serroi along with him, a draggled kite tail almost forgotten.

As soon as the Noris stepped over the threshhold, the door clashed shut again, almost nipping Serroi's cloak between its jaws. She gasped and stumbled, blind and frightened in the sudden darkness. Clinging to the Noris's cool fingers, she turned and twisted with him through darkness, having to trust him to lead her back to light. He walked as freely as if the dark were light to his eyes, but she felt her terror growing until her breath was near strangled in her throat. When she knew absolutely she couldn't take another step, he stopped, dropped her hand, spoke a WORD.

The wall split before them and a cool pearly light flooded into the blackness. The Noris stepped through into the room beyond. To Serroi's watery eyes, he was a tall black column with opaline fringes. She rubbed at her eyes with fisted hands, then went timidly through after him.

The room was a domed cylinder that looked as big as the inside of a mountain to her. The light came from all over as if it filled the room like air. There were tall chairs around the walls, some tapestries—images of plants and animals in bright splashes of color, three long narrow ink-paintings—again natural images suggested in splashes of black and white. On the far side, opposite the doorway, a dais jutted from the wall with a massive throne-chair centered on it, the dark wood carved into serpentine twists of vine with animal heads snarling through the leaves. On the floor the rug was a shimmer of brilliant leaf and flower forms. Serroi gave a soft exclamation of delight and stooped to caress the thick silky fibers, to trace one of the twisting vines and stroke a crimson flower the size of her hand. She glanced at the Noris, a question on her lips that died when she saw the look on his face. "All the things I'm denied," he said. She felt the pain and self-mockery in the soft voice and crouched trembling on that magnificent rug, more frightened than she'd ever been in her short lifetime. Then he was calm again, his face a sparely sculptured mask. He held out his hand. Slowly she straightened, got to her feet, crossed the rest of the rug to him and took the extended hand. He led her to the tapestry that hung behind the throne chair, pulled the edge aside to reveal a barrel-roofed corridor. "Through here, child. Walk ahead of me."

Serroi frowned down at her toes, resisting the urging of his hand. All the small rebellions of the long journey came together in her at the sight of that dimly lit wormhole. Knowing she would be punished, having rebelled and been punished for it countless times before, struggling against the torments her older brothers and sisters inflicted on her, rejecting their instinctive attempts to break her spirit and turn her to something less even than the animals they at least tended with some care, she snatched her hand from the Noris, scowled up at him. "My name is Serroi."

THE WOMAN: III

Serroi gasped out of her troubled sleep and sat up. "Maiden bless," she groaned, clutching at her throbbing head. When the pain steadied to a dull ache, she flung the quilt aside and drew her knees up, sitting in the cool darkness of the pre-dawn morning, struggling to come to terms with the forces contending within her.

No more running. She pressed her fingers against her eyes, feeling the familiar wall of resistance rising in front of her. *No more. Feet won't go no more.* She pulled her hands down and smiled at her toes, wriggled them, then sighed, her brief flash of humor subsiding. Staring at the crumpled quilts beyond her feet she saw in her mind the Valley of the Biserica, her Golden Valley, the place of peace she sought for and fought for and suffered for. *Fifteen years. After fifteen years he should be cleaned from my blood. I was surprised, that has to be it. I didn't have time to prepare for the fight.*

With a groan and a yawn she stretched her torso up as far as she could, then bent forward until her forehead touched knees still trying to shake. When she straightened, she stripped the case off the small hard pillow and rubbed it over her sweaty body, the coarse fabric scratching at her skin, stirring her blood. After she finished, she sat quietly, elbows on her knees, hands cupped over her eyes. *I have to go back. I have to find Tayyan if she's still alive. I have to warn Domnor Hern about his number two's plotting against him, the lovely Lybor. Wonder if he'll believe me. He has to know what she's like—but if he does, why the hell did he marry her? Or Floarin, for that matter. Tall and beautiful and gloriously blonde. Why do I bother asking? Both of them near a head taller than him. What's he trying to prove? Doesn't he know how ridiculous he looks beside either of them, little fat man prancing along beside golden goddesses?* She scowled. *Though I've seen a look in his eyes sometimes—he's laughing at himself or us or the whole damn world. I don't know.* She stopped a moment. *I should have known I couldn't just run off. All that wine and I still had nightmares. I suppose I'll*

41

have to face my Noris someday if I'm ever to win free of him. She grimaced; she wasn't ready to face the great nightmare in her life, perhaps she never would be—though she didn't care for that thought.

The darkness was greying with the dawn; she stretched out again and lay scratching at her stomach and staring up at massive rafter beams as their outlines slowly sharpened, wondering just how she was going to get back into Oras. The Plaz-guards would be on the watch for her and the Norid. . . . She grimaced again then forced herself to remember him. He wasn't much, only a Norid, a street-Nor, capable of a few cheap tricks, selling false gold and charming quartz to fool jewelers. *Not like . . . no, I won't think of him.* She winced away from the face that had haunted her for the past fifteen years. *Calling up demons. That's what he promised Morescad. Him? He wouldn't dare try it unless he had backing. Backing Morescad and Lybor couldn't know about or they wouldn't have gone near him.* She frowned as she recalled more details of the scene in the secret room. *Lybor's nurse. She had the circled flame embroidered on her sleeve. The Sons of the Flame. Are they involved in this? Connected with the Nearga-nor. Can't be. They rant against the Norim almost as virulently as they do against the Maiden.* She chewed on her lip. *This is all speculation. I need more information. Still, Yael-mri should know what we saw. Another reason for getting back into Oras. Coperic's birds. But how . . . how . . . how . . . if they're looking for me, if the Nearga-nor goes after me? Or Ser Noris.* She whispered his name into the grey morning. "Ser Noris. Why am I alive?" Tears flooded her eyes. "Why did you let me live?" This was a question she'd asked a hundred times before and as before she got no answer. Rubbing impatiently at her eyes, she rolled over and slid off the bed.

Her feet made soft slipping sounds over the pole floor as she walked back and forth, back and forth, hearing the noises of the stirring family on the sleeping platform on the other side of the flimsy wall. The wide low bed behind her was the Intii's own. He'd moved his woman and himself out to join the immediate family who slept on pallets rolled out on a wide platform jutting out over the single large room of the great hall. Other dependents slept below, anywhere they could find space to spread their bedding. Though she was grateful enough for the privacy she suspected it wasn't so much a matter of courtesy as it was a protecting of the people from the corrupting presence of an outsider. She stretched again, did a few quick bends and twists, then started dressing.

The sky was reddening in the east when she stepped into the street but the village was still dark and quiet, though most of the halls had lines of yellow light around doors and shutters. As she moved slowly along past the big square buildings built of white chalk and red sandstone, she caught glimpses of fisher vassals milking the varcam and feeding other stock, of the sheds and pens and corrals tucked in between the halls and the wall. She heard a grunt just behind her and wheeled to see a posser amble past her, cross the street and lean into a housewall, rasping its stiff bristles against the soft white stone. More of the squat shadows loomed up beside her and crunched past. Apparently the fishers turned their posserim loose to forage outside the walls where they rooted among the grasses for tubers and dug small rodents out of their nests.

She moved slowly toward the open gate; after last night's violence the peace and the simplicity of the dawn was almost disconcerting. Even the sky with its faded stars and the rags of last night's storm was tranquil. Then she saw the dark heads thrusting out the tower windows, turned toward the mountains. Life was going on as usual, but the Intii was taking no chances on a sneak attack.

Torches lit the dark forms of men working about the boats, turning them upright, sliding them into the water, stepping the masts. When they spoke, which they did seldom, their voices echoed hollowly over the water. Their shadows jerked and wavered over the grass and mud.

Serroi leaned against a massive gatepost sunk halfway into a groove in the chalk wall while more posserim trotted past her. She watched the busy men getting ready to ride the retreating tide out to sea and felt a restlessness that had little to do with her nervous apprehension about returning to Oras. She fidgeted a while longer then followed the posserim along the wall, walking out onto the grassland. The sun was showing layer on layer of transparent color as it came from behind the jagged peaks of the Earth's Teeth. The forests carpeting the lower hills began to emerge from the smoky shadow still clinging to the earth.

"You'll be crossing the mountains?"

The voice behind her startled her; she wheeled. The Intii

had left the laboring men and come up so quietly behind her she hadn't heard a whisper of sound. She looked into the wrinkled mask. "Yes." The word trailed out as she tried to read him and determine how much she should say. It seemed safer to lie; no matter how little contact the scattered fisher villages had with outsiders and each other, accidents still happened. A hundred eyes—a thousand—might be looking for her, searching every shadow for her traces. *In an odd way I'm safest going back to the city. That's the last place they'd look for me.* "I'll be taking the Highroad south to the Biserica," she said.

The Intii looked from the village walls to the dark smudges on the grass where the dead raiders lay still unburied. "The Kapperim will be waiting for you." He pointed at the trees. "You won't see them. One or two at a time, they'll be waiting for you. Never forget an injury, those animals." His mouth stretched into a slight smile as he reached out and touched the tip of the bowstave. "Do you ever miss with this, little meie?"

"Not often." She watched the boats moving into the middle of the tappata. The men left behind were walking silently back toward the waking village. On the bank she could see at least half the boats still perched high above the water. "You expect the Kapperim to come back?"

He jabbed a long bony thumb at the sprawled bodies. "That bunch, they won't be back but others're sure to come behind them. Already had half a dozen raids hit us." He tugged at a beard plait. "I tell you this, meie, I bear you no ill will, but better you go quick, you hear? My woman is fixing up the things you asked for. No need you going back in there." He nodded at the village. "Fetch your macai." He grinned suddenly and as suddenly sobered. "Lots of them to choose from." Without more words he turned and strode off toward the gate.

A macai honked mournfully, then strolled past her chewing at a succulent louffa, the long slim leaves dangling from the mouth jerking rhythmically and gradually shortening. Chuckling now and then, Serroi moved through the grazing macai, looking them over with an eye trained by Tayyan until she found one that pleased her.

She edged cautiously toward it, using her eye-spot to send out waves of reassurance. It watched her warily but didn't move off, only shied a little when she rested her hand on its skinny neck. She scratched at the slick warty hide, then rested her forehead against the macai's shoulder, the sharp dusty smell of the beast triggering memory. . . .

A long skinny blonde with scraped knees, a tear in her sleeve, a small bandage on her nose, Tayyan strolled into the stable, looking the macain over, her inspection accompanied by an assortment of sniffs, mostly scornful. Serroi was stroking the neck of a new hatched macai, pleased by skin striped a brilliant amber and umber and softer than new spring grass. Tayyan knelt beside her, hard blue eyes softening. She held out her scruffy hand for the colt to sniff, then settled herself beside Serroi. After a moment she edged her hand close enough to touch the quivering nose, stroked it gently until the little macai honked its treble pleasure. More moments passed in companionable silence, then Serroi and Tayyan began talking.

Tayyan's father was mad about macai racing and shared that obsession with his daughter. She rode almost before she could walk, refused to sit meekly with the women and learn the maidenly arts her aunts struggled to teach her, escaped to the stables at every opportunity where she was treated more like a son than a daughter. But all this ended on the day they brought her father home belly down over a macai's back, his neck broken.

Her oldest uncle moved in, a rigid man, dull and lumpish, jealous of his popular older brother, seeing slights in nearly every word. He shut her in the women's rooms, demanded that she learn a woman's tricks, had her beaten, beat her himself, when she defied him or sneaked away to the stables when life became too much for her. When she reached her twelfth year, her uncle betrothed her to a friend of his, thinking to rid himself of her. And so he did, though not the way he intended. She crept out one night, saddled a macai and took off for the Biserica.

Serroi sighed, rubbed the back of her hand across her nose. Humming a ragged tune, she stroked her fingers along the macai's neck, then scratched at the folds of skin under its jaw. The beast nudged her, then butted its head against her shoulder, honking plaintively, begging for more scratching. With a shaky laugh, she complied. Then she pushed away, sighing, and swung up into the saddle.

The macai hopped about a little, but calmed immediately

as she kept a firm hand on the reins and sent him toward the village. With every step she was more pleased than before with her choice. A smooth rolling gate. The saddle and halter well-crafted. Made to the measure of the small-hipped Kapperim, the saddle with its high front ledge and trapezoidal back fit her well enough. The stirrups were a little long, but that could be easily fixed. Saddlebags, lumpy now with the dead raider's possessions, big enough to hold her own supplies. *Ten days*, she thought. *Only ten days to Moongather. Ten days to get across the mountains and back to Oras.*

By the village wall, she slipped from the macai's back, stripped off the saddle and used the pad to scrub his skin clean of all sweat.

She was pulling at the saddle's belly band when she heard slow steps behind her. "Set the things down by me," she called, then grunted and jabbed her knee into the macai's side. The beast whooshed and honked, then sucked in its stomach. She pulled the strap taut and tucked it home. When she turned, she saw a girl crouching beside a heap of gear, a ragged girl with a sullen stubborn face, big hands spread out over the waterskin on the top of the heap, fierce determination in her scowl. Her skin was several shades darker than most fishers', though her eyes were a greenish-brown, much like the Intii's. Her hair was long and dirty, very dark, almost black. *Mixed blood*, Serroi thought with a touch of sympathy. She could remember all too well how closed societies treated those among them who were different. "What is it?" Serroi asked quietly, not wanting to frighten her more than she was already, a fear that was glazing those green eyes.

The girl's tongue traveled over dry lips. She rose slowly to her feet. About twelve, still flat-chested as a boy, she was nearly a head taller than Serroi. "The Intii sent these things and says it would be best to hurry." She stumbled over the words, her voice hoarse and uncertain.

"Yes. I know." Serroi took the saddlebags and shook out the Kappra's rubbish, not bothering to see what was there. She took the bundles of food and the utensils provided by the Intii's wife and stuffed them hastily into the bags, slapped the bags over the macai's back, then reached for the blanket roll that the girl was holding out to her, her hands shaking badly. "Take me with you, meie," she said rapidly. She let go of the bundle, pressed fisted hands against her chest. "I want to go to the Biserica, meie. Please?"

Serroi stared at her. Her first impulse was to refuse; she was in enough trouble without this added complication. *Maiden bless, can't I be excused this? I'd never get out of the village with her. And what do I do with her once we're over the mountains, send her south alone?* "I'm riding into a lot of trouble, child," she said. "I can't take you with me. You could be killed or worse."

"Killed?" The word was low and intense. "Worse?" She shook the coarse hair out of her eyes. "Nothing could be worse than staying here. You have to take me, you have to."

Serroi turned her back on her, started tying saddle thongs around the blanketroll. Over her shoulder she said, "You don't understand what you're asking."

"I don't care, meie." She bent and picked up the waterskin, moving a little awkwardly, her thin body coltish, uncertain as a young macai. "Listen. My mother was raped by a Kappra and left for dead. Kappra!" She stretched her mouth into a snarl, then shook her head impatiently. "Better if she'd died. Or me. I eat the scraps after the posser and the oadats. Each time the Kapperim raid, the fishers who are killed—their families take it out on me. Meie, I'm a woman almost and there's no one here to protect me, not even the Intii, though my mother was his own sister. I used my knee on a man this morning, I got away, but he'll be waiting for me tonight. I don't want to be the village whore, meie. Take me with you."

Serroi took the waterskin from her and tied it slowly in place. "They won't let you go."

"I know. But I'm supposed to watch the posser and keep them out of the trees, what I thought—I'll go away now and meet you out there, behind the knob where the Kapperin were."

"You've thought this out very carefully."

"Meie, I had to." She glanced nervously around. "Please, I should go now, I've been here too long."

"Wait a moment. There's something I must do first." She tapped the macai on the rump, sent it a few steps in a tight half-circle. "Start going through that junk." She pointed to the pile of Kappran leavings on the ground. "At least you'll look busy. There are some questions you must answer. It's ritual. Do you understand?"

"Yes, meie." The girl dropped on her knees and fumbled with the bits and pieces, touching them with a determined attempt to conquer her revulsion.

"You ask to be one of the company of the Biserica?"

"I ask it, meie." Her hands stilled, began moving again.

"The way is long." The required words came smoothly enough to Serroi though she felt little joy in speaking them. "We promise nothing."

"I have learned to endure, meie."

"What do you bring us?"

"Only my hands and my heart, meie. I'll do anything, I don't care what. To get away from here, to be someone, not an animal, I'll do anything."

Serroi took a deep breath. "If you join the company of meie, you must abandon the hope of children."

"Better than being raped by whoever takes the notion. I want to rule my own life, meie." Her body was taut as a bowstring with passion. "I want to be . . . I don't know . . . I want to mean something."

"Then let it be." As the girl gathered herself, Serroi added hastily, "Don't move yet, not for a minute. What's your name, girl?"

"Dinafar." Her tone turned bitter. "Outsider. That's what my mother named me before she threw me into the street."

"And I am Serroi. I'll wait by the knob, but I meant it about the danger. I can't explain, but think carefully before you come."

Dinafar's face flushed, then paled. She jumped to her feet, staggered, ducked her head in a awkward bow, then ran for the meadowland.

Serroi chuckled, shook her head as she turned to the macai and checked all the ties and straps, then she pulled herself in the saddle and started riding after Dinafar toward the rocky knob rising like a brown-grey pimple from the rolling green.

THE CHILD: 3

The Noris's head jerked, the red gem flickering in the pearly light coming from the room behind him, then flickered again as his mouth twitched into a ghost of a smile. "So it is. Serroi," he said. "Come, Serroi, I want to show you where you'll sleep."

Rebellion melting away for the moment, she walked carefully past the raised tapestry and into the corridor, glancing repeatedly up at him, surprised at having surprised him, trying to fit his reaction into what she knew of people. The Noris spoke a WORD and the stone to her right gapped suddenly. Stone seemed as malleable as water to him. Light crawled up stairs folding in a tight spiral as the Noris dropped the tapestry and urged her forward with a hand on her shoulder onto steps that seemed to be driving into the stone, forcing it open as they climbed. Serroi trudged reluctantly up those unreeling stairs, feeling very strange. The narrow space made her skin itch; she didn't like being so enclosed, was glad the Noris followed close behind.

She came around the last curve of the spiral and stepped into a short hallway with an arched roof, little more than an alcove shut off by a large panel of bronze. She turned and looked up at the Noris, puzzled.

"Open the door." His voice filled all the space, stroked her like a caressing hand.

"How?" She scowled at the metal.

"Examine it."

She marched up to the slab of bronze and looked it over. A little higher than her head a bronze hook stuck out of a slot. She pulled it down and pushed. Nothing happened but a metallic clunk. She rubbed at her nose, then pulled the hook down again and tugged the door toward her. It slid smoothly open. She pushed it against the wall and swung around with a wide grin. "I did it."

"So you did. Now, go inside." The Noris folded his arms over his chest, his eyes twinkling at her.

She stepped into the room, eyes wide with excitement.

49

There was a bed set up on legs like a cart without wheels. She had no trouble guessing what it was though she'd slept most of her five years on piled-up vinat skins only inches from the frozen earth. She crossed to it and touched the shimmer-soft coverlet, then stroked her hand over the bright, blue-green smoothness, oohing her delight. Still petting the cover she looked around at the other strange things in the room. With great zest she trotted from wall to wall, touching everything she could reach. There were two tapestries, simplified plant forms in strong rhythmic designs, worked in threads that gleamed richly in the brilliant light pouring in through the open window. A bronze chair and a table with a marble top and bronze legs stood next to the window, on the table a bottle of ink, several sheets of paper, two pen-holders with silver nibs. She lifted the holders, touched the points to the tip of her forefinger. "What are these?"

"For writing." At her blank look, he joined her at the table, took a pen from her, dipped it into the ink, pulled a sheet of paper close and wrote SERROI on it.

"What's that?" She touched the first letter with the tip of her finger, pulled the finger away and scowled at the small blue-brown stain on it.

"Your name, child."

"Show me how to do that." She fumbled with the pen, started to plunge the end into the ink bottle.

The Noris caught her hand and took the pen from her. "Later. Come here." He led her to a rack on the wall a little way from the table. "These are books." Slipping a roll of parchment from the top of the small pyramid, he unrolled it in front of her. She stared at the black marks on the smooth cream-colored surface, touched them tentatively, exclaimed with delight at a delicately painted design on the border. After returning the parchment to its place, he slid a section of the wall aside. Serroi gasped with surprise as she saw her own clothing hanging on hooks and a spare pair of boots pegged to the back wall. "The servants will keep these clean for you. You can dress yourself?"

"I'm not a baby," Serroi snorted with disgust.

He nodded, the twinkle back in his eyes. He opened a door and displayed a small neat bathroom, showed her how to use the toilet and bathtub. With a chuckle he led her away from the toilet, which fascinated her almost as much as the pens, taking her back into the bedroom. In their short absence the hands had been busy scattering potted green plants around the room. The Noris turned to Serroi. "Does this please you?"

Serroi nodded shyly. "It's beautiful," she murmured.

"Good. Come. There's another thing I want to show you."

She followed him out of the room and back down the spiraling stairs, still disliking intensely that wormhole in stone.

The Noris moved down the corridor, his booted feet making no sound at all. Serroi was startled by this; her own boots made scuffing and grating sounds that echoed dully in the dimly lit hall. As she followed him, she looked about curiously, saw a number of alcoves sealed off with bronze slabs like the door to her room. The corridor wound downward, widened abruptly into a high-walled, four-sided court open to the clean blue of the sky.

A hundred eyes watched as she stepped, blinking, into the brilliant sunlight. Cages lined two of the four walls of the court, walls made of the same shiny black-brown stone as the tower. Each cage was roomy enough to provide its inhabitant with pacing or climbing room. Since the shapes and sizes of the beasts varied considerably, so did the sizes and shapes of the cages. There were dead sections of trees in some, ledges of molded rock, paddings of straw or gravel on the solid floors; in some cases a total environment was provided for the beast, nothing living, though, no green in any cage. Each cage had its feeding tray and waterwell. She recognized several of the animals—chinin with pups about two passages old, an unhappy looking vinat, a prowling irritated sicamar, several carrion birds of the kind that followed the herds—but most of the creatures were strange. There was one sad-faced grey beast with long skinny arms and legs that looked like a parody of man. She watched it as it stared at her then began rooting about in its straw. It startled a giggle out of her when it came up with a piece of nutshell and threw it at her. She dodged the shell and started toward the chinin.

"Serroi, come here." The Noris sounded amused but she hastened to his side. She was still uncertain about him. He'd done nothing to hurt her, had, in fact, taken good care of her, but she still didn't know what he wanted from her and he changed sometimes into something she didn't know. She was gaining a certain amount of assurance, progressing step by tentative step, but she did sense there were things he wouldn't accept from her. He smiled down into her eager face—but changed again, an empty charming smile; he'd withdrawn himself, she felt he was tired to trying to keep tied to her needs against his own need to soar. "These animals will be your responsibility for the coming year," he said. "Keep them well and content, feed them, water them, give them exercise. Open any cages you feel safe about. Go up and down between your room and the court whenever you wish, day or night. Anything you need my servants will bring you."

Serroi plucked nervously at threads in the embroidery on her cloak. "Will I see you?"

He was silent a long time. She sneaked several glances at him, wondering. He was staring at the cages, not seeing them, an odd expression on his face as if she'd startled him again and he'd startled himself by his reaction to her question. She endured the long silence as best she could. He was thinking and when he'd finished, he'd give her an answer.

He looked down at her, his eyes warming again. "You can come talk to me. I'd like that." He swung a hand in a wide gesture, encompassing all the cages. "Start getting to know the beasts, Serroi. Get yourself settled in your room. My servants will give you your first lessons in writing later this afternoon." He looked away from her, gazing instead into the featureless blue above. "I'll send for you after the evening meal." His feet still making no sound on the stone flags, he walked quickly to the center of the court where a gleaming copper pipe rose from the paving stones. The top end made an abrupt right-angled turn with a bronze hook projecting from a vertical slot. "Come here, Serroi." When she stood beside him, he pointed at the hook. "Pull down on that."

Serroi wrapped her small fingers about the hook and tugged. Water gushed from the pipe's end. Laughing, she thrust her free hand into the cool rushing stream, bent and drank, then let the hook snap back and straightened to look up at the Noris.

He'd put aside, for the moment, his irritations and was smiling gravely down at her. "You can get water for the animals from this. The servants will bring the other things you need to care for them. Can you do this?"

Serroi nodded; hesitantly she stepped closer to him and dared to touch his hand, sliding her fingers along his strange disturbing flesh. She sneaked a look at his face and saw that he was uneasy at her touch, yet at the same time pleased by it. Without another word he walked away, disappearing through the doorway.

The silence in the court lasted several minutes after his de-

parture then died before the coughing roar of the sicamar, a
long-haired beast with a flat face, ripping teeth, yellow-green
eyes and small round ears. His long fur ranged in color
from the palest tan on his underbelly to a brindled chocolate
on his back. The tips of the longer fur on the top of his head
and around his neck were a yellowish green while the deeper
fur was a misty blue-green like the color of new spring grass
that rose above the last year's growth now dead and faded
brown. He paced restlessly up and down his cage, a powerful
beast, magnificently muscled, in the prime of his life—but
not well. Patches of his fur looked dull, ruffled; the yellow-
green eyes were filmy and his mouth hung open now and
then as if he lacked the will to keep his jaws together. Serroi
sucked in a deep breath, shivered. There was an almost im-
perceptible taint of sickness to the air in the court. Perhaps
nothing lived on these islands because nothing could live
there. Her head began to ache. There was so much she didn't
understand, so much she couldn't understand—but she knew
the sicamar was suffering; her eye-spot throbbed to his pain.
She began walking along the cages, peering solemnly at the
animals inside, tilting her head back to inspect those piled
high above her. Her eye-spot continued to throb as she
started feeling her way into them, but she redirected her efforts, not absorbing now but projecting, reassuring them,
caressing them with that deep love she had for all of them,
the love pent up inside her that had no other outlet. By the
time she finished her round even the air smelled cleaner. The
animals were settled in drowsy comfort, in silence or making
their various kinds of purring sounds. Content again, she
went to the cage with the chinin and opened the door, whistling her old call, laughing as the adults and pups leaped out
and pranced around her, sniffing at her, rearing up to lick at
her face.

Serroi hesitated in the doorway. The room was lit by a few
candles; a fire snapped and crackled in a dark-stone fireplace.
Bathed in rich golden light the Noris was stretched out on a
divan, propped up on velvet pillows watching the flames
dance. She wanted to go to him, he seemed as lonely as she
sometimes felt, but she knew instinctively that he was uneasy
with her no matter how relaxed he seemed.

"Come here, Serroi." His voice was soft and dreamy. He
hadn't looked at her but he knew she was there anyway. Serroi licked at her lips. "Sit beside me," he said. One pale hand

dropped onto a thick pillow on the floor beside the divan. The gesture was too deliberately graceful, another betrayal of his lack of ease. Serroi moved silently to the pillow and settled herself stiffly beside him, her head by his shoulder. Though she couldn't have put what she felt into words, her discomfort came from his. She stared into the flames, waiting for him to speak.

After a lengthy silence she looked up to meet his eyes. They were fixed on her and bright with curiosity as if he were tasting his reactions and hers, probing at himself with a curious objectivity that confused her. Among her own people emotions rode surfaces. No man paused to examine his anger but was simply and thoroughly angry.

"You've settled in comfortably?"

"Yes, Ser Noris." She brooded a minute. "The hands showed me how to draw a lot of funny marks."

"Pictures of sounds, child."

Because he sounded amused, she sniffed and complained, "Hands don't talk, Ser Noris. How'm I ever going to tell which mark means which sound?"

"Learn the marks." He yawned, drawing back from her mentally as well as physically.

She sensed she'd moved too fast; this was like taming a wild and wary beast. So he wouldn't send her away, she said hastily, "What is a Noris, Ser Noris?"

"Mmmm." He lay back on the pillows staring into the wavering shadows dancing across the distant ceiling. "A Noris is a shaper. Wind and water and stone answer his words. A Noris is a reacher into strange subworlds that would frighten you, child. A tamer of demons. A focus of forces great enough to rock the world. A Noris is a man of terrible power forever shut off from the greatest power of all." The bitterness in the last words made her regret that she'd asked the question, but the soft voice swept on, leaving the bitterness behind. "You should have asked what is a Nor, child." He reached out and stroked Serroi's curls, an absent-minded caress he was not even aware he was giving her. "Nor is the generic term for what I am. There are several kinds of Nor. Some are weak futile creatures who because they have mastered a few cheap tricks delude themselves into believing they belong among the mighty; often they serve as priests of the Flame among the Sons of the Flame, only group foolish enough to pander to their egos. These are the Norids, the street Nor. Some Nor are good competent jour-

neyman sorcerers, but they need elaborate paraphernalia or
their spells will go awry; they need the incense and the
candles of dead man's fat, cat's cradles, pentacles, sigils, tal-
ismen. They can be arrogant and foolish and they often reach
beyond their grasp and end up food or slaved to the demons
they seek to raise. You'll find them in the courts of those
kings who like to bask in a second-hand sort of power, preening themselves that they control men who control such wonders. These are the Norits." He sat up suddenly, staring into
the dimness over her head. "Finally there are the word-mas-
ters who by much study and inborn gifts move beyond the
need for apparatus, who need nothing but the actualizing
WORDS to command what we are permitted to command.
And there are those who try to push the limits of what we
control back until . . . it's not as easy as it looks." He
blinked, suddenly back with her from whatever dream he
kept secret in his heart. "No, child, it's not so easy. One
doesn't simply learn the words and bellow them into the wind.
Each of the great words rests on vast amounts of study and
discipline and denial, on a preparation invisible beneath the
surface. I walk, my little Serroi, in the middle of a web of
potencies woven over the many lifetimes I've known; I speak
the WORD and a part of the web is actualized. I speak another WORD and it sinks back into the web." The corner of
his mouth turned up as he gazed down at her blank face.
"But you don't understand a word of this, do you." His eyes
twinkling, he reached down and stroked the tips of his fingers
along the side of her head, then across her brow, something
no one else had ever done. His fingers caressed the eye-spot
and she felt a flush of warmth, a great rush of love for him.
She could have curled up beside him and let him go on petting her forever, content as a chinin pup after a long day's
play.

He dropped his hand onto his knee. "Go to bed, child.
We'll talk again tomorrow. You can tell me about your
special gifts."

Confused and dazed, Serroi wobbled onto her feet and
walked silently from the room, leaving the Noris staring into
the flames, brooding over something, perhaps turning in
again on himself, studying himself, toying with his unaccustomed emotions as a sicamar will toy with a small rodent it
has caught away from its burrow.

THE WOMAN: IV

The macai ambled around the base of the rocky knob, stopping as he saw Dinafar walking back and forth, taking a pace or two in each direction, careful to keep the knob between her and the village. The beast went down on his knees and rubbed his head over the grass; he tried to roll but the saddle prevented him. Honking mournfully, he lurched onto his feet and edged up to Dinafar. He pushed his head against her chest, sending her sprawling against the rocky slope. He whined and nudged at her again. She began to be frightened—then she heard a chuckle and jerked her head up to glare at the meie.

The small woman sat casually in the saddle, leaning on arms crossed over the saddle ledge, amusement vivid in her small green face. "He isn't trying to hurt you, poor beast." She leaned forward and whistled three warbling notes.

The macai's head twisted around. With a series of anxious hoots he trotted to the meie, stopped to rub his head against her leg. The meie slid off her mount with a supple grace that woke a sudden envy in Dinafar's breast. *I'll do that some day*, she thought. *I won't be afraid*. She scrambled to her feet, brushed her long straight hair out of her eyes, watched the meie strip the saddle from the macai and ease the halter off his bobbing head.

The meie looked back over her shoulder, her large orange-gold eyes sparking with anger. "Your fisher kin left these beasts out here all night with their gear on." She looked down at the gear, scowled. "Maiden bless, I haven't time. I haven't time. . . ." She knelt and tore up a double handful of grass, looked back at Dinafar. "Take the pad and shake it out." She jumped up and began scrubbing at the macai's back. "Look at these rubbed spots. Poor damn beast, he'll be sore for awhile." The macai moaned with pleasure as she worked.

Dinafar shook the pad vigorously, then beat it against the rock, smiling with satisfaction as the vermin tumbled out. "I suppose they'll do something about them today. We. . . ."

She dropped the pad, straightened her shoulders. "They don't know much about macai."

"Let me have that a minute." The meie took the pad after Dinafar had scooped it up again. She held it out at arm's length, narrowed her eyes. Dinafar saw the green spot on her forehead tremble a little, small waves passing across the oval of a green darker than the matte olive of her face. Black specks rained from the pad and vanished in the matted grass. Dinafar stood scratching absently at her stomach wondering just what she was getting herself into, the meie was stranger than she'd thought; still, she knew what she was leaving and that was enough. The little meie turned to her. "Stand still a moment, Dinafar. You've picked up some visitors."

Dinafar flushed uncomfortably. She knew some of the vermin were her own, parasites she'd picked up from the posser she'd herded, the stables she'd slept in. She looked down, hate like fire for the fishers who had shamed her from the moment she was born. Then she started as cool fingers touched the junction of neck and shoulder. A moment later, most of the itching was gone. "Maiden bless, meie," she mumbled. The meie said nothing, simply swung back into the saddle.

"Hand me that gear," she said.

Dinafar stared, then realized that she'd be riding the spare macai in a little while. The thought excited and frightened her.

The meie rested saddle, halter, pad on the front ledge of her saddle. "Walk beside me. The other macai will follow and help shield you from the village. As soon as we're under the trees, I'll rerig our ugly friend here so we can make better time."

Half an hour later, when they were moving through high brush and scattered trees, when even the white cliffs had passed from sight, the meie pulled the macai to a stop. Dinafar was tired and hungry. Clinging to the stirrup leather had helped but in all her life she could not remember having walked so far and so fast. The meie untied the waterskin and handed it down to her. "Don't be extravagant with this, Dina. We can't stop to fill it for a good long time." She glanced into the shadows under the trees and sighed. "Maiden knows what's waiting in there for us."

While Dinafar drank, then rested, trying over in her mind the shortened version of her name, deciding that she rather liked it, the meie saddled the stray macai and slipped the halter over his ugly head. Then she called Dinafar and boosted her into the saddle.

As they rode deeper into the forest, Dinafar clutched at the ledge of the saddle, trying to fit herself into the rolling rise and fall of the macai's gait. She was beginning to feel sick; her hastily eaten breakfast was sitting uneasy in her stomach. She looked enviously at the small woman ahead of her who was swaying gracefully to the gait of her beast, back firmly erect as if her spine had a sword thrust down it.

Dinafar thought of the village now far behind and smiled grimly. *Henser will have to find himself another girl to pester.* Her smile widened to a broad grin as she pictured an angry father taking the blunt end of a fish spear to his back. *I'm out of there. I'm really out of there.* She shivered, sickness churning in her stomach, exacerbated by the hatred roused in her by those thoughts. Clinging to the saddle she leaned out as far as she could, yielding to her need to vomit.

Then small strong hands caught her and pulled her down off the macai, held her as her body was wrung by spasms of nausea. Sour and exhausted, she let herself be moved away and laid out on a thick layer of rotting leaves that smelled like cool rich earth. She could feel the dampness creeping through her clothing as she lay with eyes shut, entirely miserable. Then the small hands were back. A damp cloth moved over her face, cleaning away the sweat and sour liquid. She stiffened, feeling awkward, confused by the surge of emotion the meie's gentle touch woke in her.

She pushed the hands away and sat up. Her stomach shifted uneasily but she swallowed repeatedly until the nausea went away. When she looked up, the meie was tying the waterskin back behind her saddle. The small woman turned and watched her quietly. To Dinafar's surprise there was a haunted look in the orange-gold eyes, an instant's revelation of pain instantly suppressed.

"Can you ride now?" The meie's voice was gentle, calm, remote. Her pointed face was a mask, all expression disciplined away. "If you feel more comfortable walking. . . ." The words came slowly. Behind the meie's outward tranquility, Dinafar sensed a nervous urgency that made her offer something torn from her by courtesy alone. Dinafar thought back to the helpless rages that had wracked her since she was old enough to feel, if not understand, the hate, disgust and cruelty she'd breathed in with every beat of her heart. This gentle courtesy accorded her by one who was a little more than a stranger brought her a sudden vision of life at the Biserica that gave her the strength to stagger to her feet and pull herself clumsily back into the saddle. She settled herself as best she could and looked down at the meie. "Tell me how to fit the macai's rhythms, meie. I can't seem to do it."

A half smile, little more than a rueful twitch of her lips, lit the small woman's face. "My fault, child. I should have realized that you knew nothing about riding; you even told me so." She moved her golden eyes critically over Dinafar, the green spot on her forehead twitching as she concentrated. The spot looked velvet soft; Dinafar was suddenly and intensely curious about the feel of it under her fingers, then she closed her hands into fists frightened by what she was thinking.

"That damn skirt." The meie wrinkled her nose while her eyes shone with amusement and disdain. "I cannot see why or how women endure this." She began fussing with Dinafar's bunched skirt, pulling out the wrinkles, pushing at Dinafar's thighs and knees until her legs were pressed more firmly against the wide leather aprons that protected her from the macai's knobbly skin. Dinafar swallowed a sigh at the pain as muscles complained against being stretched in unaccustomed ways. The meie patted her on the thigh, ignoring her uneasy blush, then swung into her own saddle. "It will take a day or two for your bones and muscles to accustom themselves to this." She laughed. "I remember my own aches. You'll be wishing the Maiden had called you home, but the soreness will go away, I promise you." She clucked at her mount. As it took a step forward, she leaned over and caught hold of the halter on Dinafar's mount, forcing him to walk beside her.

"Center your weight around your navel." The meie's orange-gold eyes slid critically over her. "Hold your back straight but not stiff. That's better. No, don't stiffen. Think of your spine as a plumb bob. Know what that is? Never mind. Think of a string with a weight at the end. No matter how you move the top of the string, the weight keeps it hanging straight. Your spine is the string, your buttocks the weight."

Her voice was tranquil and remote; it fell on Dinafar's ears like cool water as the two macai paced slowly along, side by side. Buoyed by it, she was able to relax and let herself become part of the flow, not even noting when the voice merged with the flutter of the leaves overhead and finally stopped altogether.

Dinafar rode with the meie in and out of cool green shadow, gold splotches of sunlight slipping over them where the leaves thinned. The wind whispered in a continuous murmur, a drowsy, comfortable sound with a resonant quality that such sounds lacked out on the grasslands. She let her macai fall behind and rode through the green world, filled with a joy as warm and bright as the patches of sun that danced over her.

Sometime later, the meie twisted around in the saddle and looked back at her, then pulled her macai to a slower walk until they were once more side by side. The little woman smiled, both surprised and pleased. "You learn fast."

"Mongrels are clever creatures or so the story goes." Dinafar smiled to take the sting out of her words. Old hates were slipping further and further behind as she left the village behind.

The meie grimaced. "How many times have you heard that?"

"All my life." She shrugged. "That's past now."

The meie nodded; her quick smile flashed out again. "Forget it—or, if you have to remember, be glad you're a clever mongrel. Stupidity's no blessing." She frowned as Dinafar clutched at the saddle ledge and shifted a little to ease some of the strain on her legs. "Tired?"

"A little."

The meie tilted her head back, eyes narrowed, measuring the height of the sun. After a minute she looked down, rubbed at the back of her neck. "A little longer, then we'll stop."

They rode on, the meie in front again, Dinafar trusting that the odd little woman knew where she was going. It was pleasant to relax that way, to let someone else take responsibility for her actions; Dinafar couldn't remember when she hadn't had to fight simply to stay alive. As time passed, though, and the macai rolled on and on, she began shifting about more and more, the burning in her groin and thighs mounting slowly until it was nearly unbearable.

The trees opened out; they rode into a wide irregular space that was a burned-over section of the wooded slopes where lightning had set a fire and cleared off the larger trees. Several charred corpses of the squat brellim trees and the jagged pomacin lay like black exclamation points in the brushy second growth. As they followed a twisting track through the tangle, Dinafar began wondering when the meie planned to stop. She examined the straight narrow back ahead of her, the turning head, its tight curls bobbing with the movement. The meie seemed uneasy. Deeper in the brushy growth Dinafar could hear rustles and snaps as if predators were following them. She caught the itch from the meie and nearly forgot the pain in her legs.

Bursting out of a clump of brush behind them, yelling his war challenge, a Kappra charged at Dinafar, his saber raised for a killing slash. The bronze blade hummed over Dinafar's head as her war-trained mount squatted, then reared and threw her. She landed against a stand of springy saplings that broke her fall but sent her rolling under the claws of the Kappra's macai. More by luck than any management on her part, she evaded them and scrambled into the brush on the far side of the track just in time to miss a second swing of the saber. Eyes ringed with white, mouth open in a damp snarl, the Kappra forgot her and rode at the meie.

The meie dropped to the ground, smacking her macai on the rump to send it out of the way. As the Kappra drove toward her, she leaped back before the swing of the saber, glanced rapidly about, then darted to her left, plunging into a small stand of second-growth pomacim; their multi trunks were hard and sharp as spears and grew so close she could barely fit her small body between them. The whippy branches bent before her and snapped into the macai's face when the Kappra tried to force his mount after her. Howling with rage and frustration, he swung down and bounded after her.

Dinafar crawled out of the brush, using some of the curses she'd collected in the fisher village at the broken branches jabbing into her and tearing her already ragged clothing. She crouched by the track, pulling leaves from her hair, watching with horror and fascination as the fight continued. The Kappra was quick and adept with his saber. Most of his cuts missed by a hair and a half and the meie was bleeding from a dozen small cuts and scrapes. But he was a rider and clumsy on the ground. She was quicker. She used the young trees to block many of his cuts. Again and again he swung at her and slashed off the tops of saplings. Dinafar began to breathe a little easier. The meie's face had gone utterly tranquil; she wove like a dancer through the second growth, like a were-light enticing the Kappra on to doom, she led him round and round. Dinafar dragged herself to her feet, casting about for a weapon, anything. She found a lopped-off branch and began absently stripping it of leaves and twigs as she watched the intricate duel in front of her.

The Kappra's breath was coming hard; his mouth gaped, dripped foam. He'd passed into a berserker rage that gave him a terrible strength and speed; he drove the meie back and back, his saber cutting through the saplings as if they didn't exist, a squealing whiffling passage like nothing she'd heard before. Dinafar gasped again.

The meie faltered. She stumbled over an exposed root and barely managed to escape the swing of the saber. Trembling with fear, Dinafar ran toward them, those death-dancers so intent on each other no one and nothing else existed for them. *His wrist*, Dinafar thought. *If I can hit his wrist. . . .*

The meie stumbled again, slammed into one of the larger trees. The Kappra howled, triumph in the ululating sound; driven with all the power in his arm, the saber cut at her, moving so swiftly it was only a blur singing its own lethal sound through the air. The meie seemed to hesitate, stare helplessly at the descending death, then dropped and rolled away, this time to the right, moving so quickly that Dinafar could only gape. The saber cut through the emptiness where the meie had been and sliced deep into the tree—the trunk was just a bit too thick for the blade to cut completely through. As the Kappra tugged futilely at the hilt, stupid and blind in his rage, the meie lunged up at him, buried her knife in his side, yanked it out, the blade drawing with it a great gout of blood.

The Kappra gasped and crumpled, the saber hilt bobbing over him. The meie knelt beside him, mouth twisted with a pain of her own. He groaned. With his last strength he spat in her face. No anger in her eyes, only sadness, she wiped the spittle away. "Maiden give you quiet rest," she murmured. When he was dead, she brushed her hand across his face, closing his eyes, pushing his mouth shut. She knelt another minute in silence, then she retrieved her knife, wiped the blade on the Kappra's loincloth and replaced it in its sheath. She picked up fallen leaves and rubbed them vigorously between her palms and over the bloodstains on her legs.

Dinafar looked down at the dead Kappra, back at the rubbing, shaking hands. "Meie?"

The meie sighed and got heavily to her feet. "What is it?"

"You killed two yesterday and you didn't . . . all this." She swooped her hand from the dead man to the standing woman.

"Yes." The meie started trudging back along the track to the macain who stood rubbing sides, gingerly snatching bites of the brush. She reached up and touched the arch of wood and horn. "When the arrow strikes, you don't feel them die." She sighed. "You don't feel them die." She shook herself, seemed to throw off her depression and spoke in ordinary tones. "Get mounted. We can't stop here."

When they were back in the green shadow under the trees, Dinafar saw the meie's head turning again, using her eyes, ears and whatever other senses she had to probe the trees ahead and on each side. Before they'd gone far into the forest, the meie unclipped and strung her bow. *No more surprises,* Dinafar thought. She smiled, then shifted in the saddle, her mouth twisting as she sought vainly for a more comfortable position.

The meie nocked an arrow, slowed her macai. A Kappra rode at them from the shadow, his challenge deadened by the close-huddling trees until it was cut off completely by the arrow in his throat. The meie slid down, cut her arrow free, murmured her quiet blessing while Dinafar pulled saddle and halter off the Kappra's macai and dumped them on the ground.

Twice more Kapperim attacked; twice more they died; twice more the macain were stripped and freed.

At midday Dinafar was following the meie through a twisting ravine deep in the shadows of the mountain peaks. The trees had been left behind. Her legs were numb; she kept herself in the saddle with the grip of both hands on its ledge, too exhausted even to complain.

When the meie stopped at last, Dinafar's mount stopped also. The halt caught her by surprise and she nearly fell off. After she regained her balance she leaned forward until her face rested on the spongy fringe curving along his neck. Then she lifted her head and watched the meie through a haze of weariness; she saw her turning her head again, side to side as if she were feeling out their direction. With a quick habitual gesture, she brushed back her sorrel curls, then kneed the macai into a slow walk. Groaning silently, Dinafar clumsily kicked the macai into motion.

After an eternity of climbing over rock slope, up and up, always up until Dinafar's legs were no longer numb but burning, as if the macai's barrel had turned to live coals, the meie rode into a narrow crack in an outthrust of rock that seemed to Dinafar the bones of earth itself thrust through its flesh. They plunged first into darkness then into light again as they emerged; the torment eased as the macai rocked to a stop. Small hands touched her thigh. "Slide down." The warm husky voice cut through watery waves of tiredness swamping Dinafar. "Lean toward me and let yourself go. I won't let you fall."

Dinafar sat swaying, unable to move farther, then she leaned out and let herself fall.

The hands caught her. For a moment she was pressed against the meie's strong little body, then she was stretched out on cool deep grass, savoring the pleasure of being utterly still. Hands straightened her legs and pulled her skirt down. A damp cloth passed across her face, then down her arms. She opened her eyes.

The meie was kneeling beside her, the haunted look back in her eyes. It vanished as soon as she saw that Dinafar was watching her. She smiled. "Good. You'll feel better in a little." She moved on her knees along Dinafar's body until she was kneeling at her feet.

Dinafar had never worn shoes; she knew her feet were scarred and ugly and dirty. She tried to pull them away, but the meie took them in her hands, her surprisingly strong hands; she ignored the dirt, the broken nails, the cuts and scrapes, the thick horn on the soles, and began manipulating first the ankle then the toes. Dinafar gasped with pain, then sighed with pleasure as some of the grinding soreness passed from her legs. After a moment she started to become acutely uncomfortable as the meie continued to massage her calves.

The meie looked up. "Don't worry, child." She sounded amused. The orange-gold eyes were twinkling at Dinafar. "No matter what you've heard about us, I'm not trying to seduce you."

Dinafar knew from the heat and tightness in her face that she was blushing scarlet. She stammered, "I'm not . . . I'm. . . ."

The meie smiled. "Relax, Dina." She continued to work on Dinafar's knotted calf muscles until she'd worked out most of the soreness and stiffness, then she stood and stretched, finally looked down. "That better?"

Dinafar sat up. "Yes." She pulled her legs up, wrapped her arms around them and examined the place with considerable curiosity.

She was sitting in the center of a tiny lush valley almost

like a deep hole in the rock. The turf under her was cool and green, thick-set blades of short springy grass. By one wall a spring bubbled clear, cold water into a pool that never seemed to fill. Above the spring, carved with some delicacy into the living stone, was a great-eyed figure, generously female but obviously not human. "Who is she?"

The meie glanced at the carving. "The Maiden," she said quietly. "As the creasta shurin see her. This is a shrine-place."

"Creasta shurin?" Dinafar frowned. "I thought they were just children's tales."

The meie laughed. "No, that they most certainly aren't." She unbuckled her weaponbelt and let it fall beside Dinafar. "Just shy and content to be unnoticed." She unclipped her bow and set it down more carefully, laying it on the belt to keep it off the grass. "For very good reasons they keep away from men, too many of them have been killed for their pelts, but they are allied to the Biserica so a shuri should answer my call. We need a guide to show us the quickest and easiest way through the mountains; Maiden bless, the Kapperim don't usually come above the treeline." She shook her head then, looking troubled. "Can't count on that, I'm afraid. Nothing holds the way it should this year." She glanced at the carved figure. "I don't understand what's happening." She shook her head. "No matter. In a little while I'll call a shuri and see what problems the mountains will present us with."

"Already?" Dinafar was dismayed; she'd thought they were settled for a while, this mountain cup felt safe and her body rebelled at the thought of climbing back on the macai.

The meie got to her feet and started toward the beasts who were grazing placidly not far from them. "I'm sorry, Dina, but I warned you. I'm pushed for time, I. . . ." She sighed, shrugged. "You'll have to keep up as best you can." But when Dinafar started to get up to help her with the gear, the meie stopped her. "Rest now, you've got a hard night ahead of you."

When the macain were stripped, the meie brought her saddlebags to the edge of the pool, knelt on the grass and started digging in one of them. She pulled a round loaf from the bag, glanced at Dina who lay sprawled comfortably on the grass watching her. "Catch." The loaf landed with a little bounce on Dinafar's stomach. She giggled and sat up. The meie dug farther and tossed over a parcel of fish paste. "Make us a sandwich; careful of this one." She lobbed a

long-bladed knife to Dinafar. It landed with its handle toward
her, a ıoot from her hand. "This too." The meie threw a tin
cup to Dinafar and jumped to her feet, a flat pan in her
hand. She nodded at the pool. "Good water." For a moment
she stood frowning, her fingernails clicking against the bottom of the pan. "I'll get us some brambleberries. There's a
vine over there." She nodded her head at the bramble web
climbing the rock in a mist of green and purple.

Dinafar caught the cup, gazed at it, then at the meie as she
searched through the leaves for the berries, dropping them
like purple rain into the pan. Her fingers trembled. The fishers wouldn't let her touch anything they ate from. She'd
drunk from an old cracked mug that she washed herself and
hid from children's malice. Some of the boys broke her things
whenever they could find them. She'd eaten from a wooden
dish flung at her head, using a warped horn spoon she'd scav-
enged from the midden behind the Intii's Hall. She'd been
beaten for that, for having dared to touch it without begging
permission—*begging*. They let her keep it, since it was already defiled by her touch. She looked down at the meie's
drinking cup, shared so casually, down at the loaf of bread
and the fish paste and the knife. She set the cup gently aside
and picked up the knife.

The meie came back, the pan heaped with berries. She
took the sandwich from Dinafar, cut it in half, took half and
raised her eyebrows at the empty cup. Her eyes searched
Dinafar's face, then she took the cup, filled it at the pool and
brought it back. "Drink," she said. There was pain in her
face; Dinafar lowered her eyes, uneasy; the meie read her too
deeply. "Drink," the meie repeated softly.

Dinafar took the cup in shaking hands and sipped at the
water. She handed it back to the meie who deliberately
turned it and touched her lips to the spot on the rim where
Dinafar's mouth had been. She drank, then dropped onto her
knees. Saying nothing—no words were needed—she placed
the cup halfway between them and wriggled from her knees
to a cross-legged comfort on the grass. She picked up her half
of the sandwich and began eating.

Dinafar hesitated. She tried to trust what she saw, but the
years of conditioning made it hard. Her body was stiff as she
reached for a handful of berries, then began eating the sandwich. She reached awkwardly for the cup to wash down a
mouthful of bread suddenly too dry. She drank, her hands
shaking, water spilling from her lips, embarrassing her. She

carefully wiped the rim of the cup against her sleeve, then drew her arm across her mouth. When she looked up, the meie was smiling gravely at her.

"Go gently, child," the meie said. The quiet understanding in her face should have soothed Dinafar's unease, but instead stirred her anger. It was an intrusion into places where the meie had not been invited. The meie shook her head. "Relax and accept what you can. You have to learn. There are no castes at the Biserica." She watched Dinafar a moment longer then settled into a physical tranquility that was curiously infecting.

Dinafar caught that infection and gradually managed to relax into a drifting dreaming state beyond irritation and anger. She ate slowly and when she was finished she brushed bread crumbs from her mouth and lap, then sat quietly across from the meie, her hands folded in her lap, letting the stillness of the shurini shrine-place and the serenity of the meie bring her a peace unlike anything she'd felt before.

The tiny valley was filled with sound—the macain cropping at the short succulent grass, the wind whispering through spindly trees growing in a thin line along one cliff, the water gurgling in its basin, an occasional bird singing a soaring song, a lazy insect drone. The sun was hot as it slid off zenith, but it was not uncomfortable. In a little while she stretched out on the grass and slipped into a deep sleep.

THE CHILD: 4

She was beginning to know him. After three years in the tower she knew his moods, when he could be coaxed into talking about himself, when he was unwilling to be touched in any way. That he had some affection for her she knew. That it was shallow rooted she also knew. She was never too secure with him, aware always that his feelings for her would stand little strain. She knew these things without working them out; in her eighth year she still had no words for much of what she knew from instinct, not logic. She watched him, tried to please him, gave him the love that filled her and tormented her, the love that no one had ever been willing to accept from her—no one but her animals. She struggled to be what he wanted her to be although often she couldn't be sure just what that was.

He was cool and precise with a passion for detail and a demand for perfection that sometimes drove her into angry rebellion. During the past two years he'd tested her again and again to find the limits of her special talents, what the organ behind the eye-spot was capable of, how far its influence reached and the number of things it could do. She worked herself to utter weariness to please him but he was insatiable. She survived and thrived because she shared with him his thirst for knowledge. She learned small spells to handle wind and water. She learned to deflect lightning and lift small stones. She watched the Noris dip into the sub-worlds and call forth demons, even talked with them when he let her. He continually touched the eye-spot, stroking his fingers over it, resting them on it as if he tried to absorb its substance through them. Sometimes he hurt her; sometimes he frightened her; sometimes it seemed to her that he was trying to slip into her skin he probed so deep into how she felt and what she knew when she woke the spot.

Everything he learned about that organ she learned also. She already knew that she could call animals; the Noris told her how she did it—enticing them through their pleasure cen-

68

ters, giving them a pleasure reward when they did what she wanted. The longer she knew a particular animal, the stronger her control grew until it went far beyond the original crudity of the pain-pleasure response—almost as if she and it grew together into one complex being. She learned also that the organ could *find* anything she *desired*, the finding and desiring being reaction and trigger. Anything she could picture in her mind, she could locate, establishing a direction line and following it until she came as close as she could to the thing. This need to have the image in her mind limited her to things she knew, but her limits were rapidly broadening as she learned to read.

Her days passed quickly, were packed with activity. She studied her books, tended the plants that always died no matter how much care she lavished on them and were always replaced, played with her animals, fed them, talked to them, kept them healthy. She knew them all now, even the sicamar. In the evenings she'd let him out of his cage. He'd run wildly around the court, leaping and teasing invisible prey like a great savage kitten, he'd lick her with his rough tongue until he nearly rasped her skin off, he'd butt his head against her, he'd stretch out on his back, four huge feet waving in the air, and beg her to scratch his belly. Sometimes in the roughness of his play he'd knock her sprawling, sometimes he sat with his front end in her lap, purring frantically as she scratched behind his ears, her hands buried in his thick green ruff. Of all the animals, though, her favorites were the chinin. They had free run except when the sicamar was out of his cage, she took them up the stairs into her room while she studied, the three pups slept on her bed, curled up at her feet.

To her astonishment, she found that there were more languages than there were kinds of speakers. She could puzzle out five of them now, though she couldn't speak them. She spent long happy hours bent over the scrolls stored in her room, drinking in knowledge of strange things and strange places.

Evenings she joined the Noris to talk a little, get his answer to things that puzzled her, or simply sit in quiet companionship. He was her father, her family, her teacher. She trusted him, finally, as much as she ever would trust anyone. And she loved him in spite of the unexpected chill he could wake in her when he *went away*, retreated into that mind space where she couldn't follow.

She was rolling on the floor of her room, playing with the new batch of pups when the Noris opened the door and looked in. Serroi sat up, startled, then jumped to her feet. "Ser Noris?"

He looked around the littered room, lifted his brows, then beckoned to her, eyes twinkling. "I've brought you something else to play with, Serroi. Come see."

The rock opened for them again, melting into a narrow spiraling staircase that circled high into the tower until they came to a bronze slab blocking off further rise. Serroi ran up the last stairs, then jerked to a stop. There was no hook. She looked over her shoulder at the Noris.

"You'll have to have my servants open this for you when you come here." He leaned over her and touched the bronze. The door swung slowly open.

The room inside was much barer than hers. There were a bed and a chair, some pegs on the wall with small tunics hanging on them. The window was high on the wall and barred. There was nothing else visible until a small blond boy came around the end of the bed and stood staring at them, sucking on his thumb, his eyes wide and frightened.

Serroi hated him immediately. Pressing against the Noris's leg, she said, "I don't want him. Send him away."

The Noris patted her curls and pushed her forward. "No, Serroi. We're done with animals for a time. I want you to learn to command him as you do your chinin." He stood in the doorway watching her.

She glared at the boy. He was three or four, almost as tall as she; his eyes were a deep blue like distant seawater; his tunic was as blue as his eyes; his feet were bare; his skin shone a golden glowing brown like amber in sunlight. He was frightened of the Noris, even frightened of her. She socked her fists onto his hips and scowled at him. "Boy, come here."

"Nescu-va?" The shrill voice trembled, tears filled his eyes.

"Ha!" She pounced on him, pinched his arm, then pulled him out into the middle of the room. "What's your name, boy?" She poked his finger at the middle of his chest. "Name."

He stared silently at her; his thumb came up and he put it in his mouth; the tears crept down his dirty face, cutting runnels in the dust.

"Serroi."

At the sound of her name she turned. The Noris was watching her, a lazy amusement in his eyes. "Use this." A shiny black pebble was suddenly in the palm of his hand. She took the thing and scowled up at him.

"I don't like that boy," she said.

"No matter. Learn to control him." The Noris bent and brushed his fingers gently across her eye-spot. "When you want to leave, call the servants."

Commanding humans was harder for her. They were slippery, with stubborn, strong egos. The boy resisted her. The more she slapped and pinched and yelled at him, the more he slipped away from her. Even with the black pebble to translate for her, she never got close to him. Her intense jealousy was one reason, the boy's own implacable hostility was another. She was jealous of him because he was male, able to be a Nor if her Noris so desired; she could never be.

She stood in her own small pentacle as he summoned a firedrake and used him to spin a strange and beautiful thing of gold and moonstones and crysoberyl. Part of it curved from view as if it dipped right out of this world; in the center of the tangle was an oval emptiness. Though she ached with curiosity, she knew enough to keep still until the Noris was finished and the firedrake returned to his subworld.

"What's that for?" She hugged her thin arms across her flat chest and stared with fascination at the construct in his hands.

"Be still!"

Serroi shrank back; his anger hurt her. She needed to please him. Her hand pressed against her mouth, she nodded, watched as he completed the thing he was making.

The anger faded from his eyes as he turned away. He held the construct in one hand, used the other to draw lines of blue fire in the oval vacancy, complex lines that might have been the symbolic representations of the great WORDS he used to command. The designs wove tighter, blurred into a shimmer then smoothed out into a blue-silver surface that filled the vacancy completely. A mirror. Serroi bit down hard on her lip to hold in an exclamation of delight. She watched as the Noris touched the immaterial shimmer, stroked it solid as if he froze light into metal fit to take the image of a face.

The hands carried the mirror away. Serroi watched it go, wistfully thinking that she'd never know now what it was for. She looked up to see the Noris smiling down at her. She started to go to him, stopped at his upthrust hand.

"Don't cross the lines of the pentacle, Serroi. Not yet."

He spoke a WORD and the lines drawn on the floor melted into mist. "Come now."

In her room the mirror was sitting on a small table under the rack of scrolls. Serroi danced over to it, then looked back at the Noris. He smiled and waved her around. She knelt in front of the mirror and looked down at the image of her greening face.

"What would you like to see?"

Serroi frowned. "See? The vinat herd?"

"Touch the mirror."

Serroi looked up at him, then touched the shining surface. It was cold and hard under her fingers. She trembled, bent closer. The blue-silver shimmer rippled, then cleared. She saw a vinat herd pouring across the tundra under the long sun. The grass was green and lush, the limul flowers thick, brilliant patches of red and yellow dotting the green, the sky clear, blue, cloudless. She could almost feel the whip of the brisk wind across her face as she watched small high-wheeled carts moving along beside the herd. She soared over them as if she were a hunting bird sailing through that crystalline blueness. Wondering if the people were her own or from another clan of windrunners, she bent over the mirror and peered at the miniature figures, trying to make out features. The mirror answered to her desire and the focus altered until she was hovering just above the carts. She saw her grandfather sitting on the lead cart, singing as he was wont to do. He looked content, well-satisfied with his life. Her brothers rode vinat beside the cart. Inside, her mothers and sisters were sitting as she'd sat so many times. She blinked. Seeing them made her feel uncomfortable.

The Noris dropped a scroll beside her. She picked it up and began unrolling it. Then she smiled. The scroll was a geography of the western continent. She looked at the paragraph by her thumb. *Sankoy. The rug weavers.* She touched the mirror again. When it cleared, she saw a long narrow room with a loom stretching from floor to ceiling. A dozen girls worked small fingers over the vertical threads, tying and tying and tying knots, never stopping, their fingers like machines, eyes large, glazed, in pinched and unhealthy faces. Serroi shuddered and touched the image away.

"Use the mirror to learn, Serroi." The Nori sounded pleased.

She turned; he was in the doorway watching her. She rose

from where she was kneeling and confronted him. "I want to be a Noris."

After a startled second, he brooded over what she'd said, obviously troubled because he didn't know what to say to her. Slowly, he shook his head. "That is not possible."

"Why? I'm not stupid. I can learn. You've already taught me some spells. I can learn more. I can."

"You're female." He said it with a quiet finality as if that were the only explanation necessary.

She refused to accept it. "I can learn as fast as any stupid old boy. I've been here three years now. I've learned lots of things. I can learn to be a Noris."

He moved a hand impatiently. "It has nothing to do with your intelligence, child. Or skill. Or any of your many talents. It is simply this, I fear. Nor are necessarily male. If a female took the Nor-route to power, she'd have to fight herself as much as she fought to learn and would burn herself out before she got to where she wanted to be." When she opened her mouth to protest further, neither understanding nor accepting his slow, halting explanation, he gave a small exclamation of disgust and left.

Serroi glared at the blond boy. He scowled back at her. His fear seemed to leave with the Noris. She tightened her mouth, her jealousy like a fire in her stomach. The boy could take her place with her Noris if she didn't obey him. She fought against the pain in her heart and closed her fingers tight about the pebble. "What's your name, boy?"

He blinked solemnly at her. Slowly his hand came up to his mouth and he began sucking at his thumb. He said nothing.

Serroi pinched his arm. "Name!"

He pulled away from her, his thumb popping from his mouth. "Bad," he shouted at her. "Ugly girl. Ugly frog-face. Ugly. Ugly. Ugly." When she jerked her hand back to slap him, he stuck out his tongue at her and ran away to hide behind the bed.

All that spring she struggled to fight her antipathy to the boy, for that blocked her efforts to learn him, then control him. He hated her back with all the passion in his small body. He was a handsome child with a clear, soft skin and shining dark-gold hair. He'd been someone's darling, spoiled badly; he cried often, was malicious and sneaky, running to the Noris, showing the bruises on his arms where Serroi had pinched him. If there were no bruises, he'd pinch himself; she'd caught him at that. Though the Noris said nothing to her, simply watched the two of them with an enigmatic cool amusement that continued to keep her on edge. She grew thinner, tense and exhausted with her struggle. Her long, painful, fruitless struggle. For it was fruitless. That worried her most of all. She couldn't control him. Even after three months of intense effort, he fought her every step. She finally managed to impose her will on him for brief intervals, no more than two or three minutes in duration. Sweating, her face twisted into a straining mask, she could force him to walk about under her direction, could make him pick up or set down small articles, nothing more.

She came to dread those sessions. She couldn't bear to fail at anything the Noris asked of her. As the hot dusty summer settled over the tower, she fought to master the boy until she was close to destroying herself. Then the Noris brought the experiment to an abrupt, and to her eyes arbitrary, end. One morning she came wearily from her room to find the stairs leading up to the boy's room no longer there. The stone was solid. She hoped the boy was gone, but didn't dare ask for several days. She neglected her studies and spent the next days playing with her animals, trying to console herself for her failure. She'd tried her hardest, but she'd failed. Her blood kin had always punished her when she made mistakes, no matter how hard she'd tried. She waited and waited for the blow to fall, then nerved herself to speak to the Noris. *This evening*, she thought. *When I go to him.*

He turned his head as she walked in, turned it back to gaze dreamily into the leaping flames. She settled on her pillow. He was in one of his unapproachable moods, not unfriendly, just unwilling to talk. She fidgeted on her pillow, straightening her legs out in front of her, then curling them under her.

The Noris stirred, frowned.

Serroi closed her hands into fists. "I tried. I couldn't," she whispered. "I'm sorry."

"What?" His head swung around. "What are you talking about?"

"The boy." She pulled her body into a small ball on the pillow, head down, knees tight against her chest.

"Oh that." He flicked long white fingers, dismissing the boy into nothing.

"I tried."

"Forget it, child." The Noris spoke shortly, making the brushing-away gesture again, annoyed at her persistence. "It was only an experiment. It's over. I sent him away."

She loosed her hands and lifted her head, brushed the curls out of her eyes. "Sent him away?"

The Noris's hand moved gently over her curls. "When you want to understand something, Serroi, you test it to its limits." He pulled a curl between thumb and forefinger. "Do you miss him?"

She sighed and relaxed, leaning against the divan, her cheek on its velvet, watching the flames dance and the shadows play, the Noris's hand resting lightly on her head. "No," she breathed. "I'm glad he's gone."

THE WOMAN: V

Serroi sat beside the sleeping girl, drifting in a mindless ease until she found herself on the verge of falling asleep. Disturbed nights had left her with a weariness that was like an ocean pressing down on her. She sighed, got to her feet, walked with quick nervous steps to the rock pool. She stripped and plunged into the clear snowmelt, gasping with shock as her warm flesh dipped under the surface. She paddled about until the last wisps of sleep and nightmare dissolved and her blood was thrumming through her veins.

Turning onto her back, she floated, gazing up at a sun that was low in the west, bisected by the top of the cliff. The cup was filling with shadow; night was close enough to call the shuri. She flipped over and paddled to the cliff wall with the carving of the Maiden. With water sluicing from her body, she climbed the crude ladder of foot and hand holds hollowed into the rock, though the holds were small and made for hands and feet differently shaped. She placed her hand over the Maiden's stone fingers where the stone was worn smooth by many other touches, smiled as warmth tingled into her fingers and flowed along her arms to fill her shivering body.

"Creasta-shuri." She sang the words in her husky contralto, paused to listen to the echoes playing with the sound. "Meie of the Biserica I am." She sang slowly, twisting her tongue around the gutturals painstakingly learned many years before. "Guidance through the mountains I ask. By the pact between us I ask." She waited again until the echoes died and the warmth faded from the stone fingers, then dropped back into the pool.

She paddled across it and pulled herself out, shivering and muttering as the cooling air touched her. Hastily she snapped her blanket roll open and dropped to the grass, rubbing briskly at herself with one of the blankets until her body glowed. When she was dry, she pulled on her tunic and skirt, then sat down beside the gently snoring Dinafar to wait for the shuri.

Though the vale swam in dark blue shadow, the top third of the eastern cliff shone gold long after the sun disappeared. One star, then another appeared, pin-pricks of silver in the darkening blue. As the gold finally melted away, the sky grew thick with furry silver points. She began to wonder if the shuri would come at all. *Nothing is holding.* She shook her head. *I can't waste another day here.* When she closed her eyes she could see Tayyan sprawled in her blood. She wrenched her mind away from that and began thinking about Domnor Hern. She remembered him as she saw him one day walking toward the women's quarters, laughing up at the much taller Morescad arrogant and stone-faced beside him. The Domnor was a pudgy man with constant laughter in his grey-green eyes as if he found the world more than slightly absurd. He ate too much, played with his women too much, enjoyed himself too much in too many ways. Lybor called him a pleasure-sated fool. Serroi shook her head. *I don't know. The Mijloc goes along well enough under his hand. Better him than Lybor and Morescad. Will he believe me when I tell him what Tayyan and I heard? It's crazy, the fools, thinking they can use a Nor, even a cheap street Norid. Calling up a demon to take over Hern's body. Do they think no one will notice? Maiden bless, Floarin will tie the pair of them in knots if they try to get rid of her. And Tayyan's hurt, maybe dead because of that numb-brained nonsense.* With considerable effort she subdued her anger and bent over Dinafar.

The girl was scowling in her sleep, her snores little more than soft whistles, her hands closed into fists. *Dinafar,* Serroi thought. *Outsider.* She looked down at her own hands, at the matte olive of her skin, sighed. *Outsider.* When she touched one of the fisted hands, Dinafar moaned in her sleep and pulled the hand away. Serroi rubbed at her eyes. *At least my mother loved me and saw I had food and clean clothes. To teach a child she's lower than dirt!* She thought of Dinafar crouching over the pile of supplies, at once defiant and hopeless, struggling to find a way out of the trap she was in. *I didn't want you with me,* she thought. *I still don't. What am I going to do with you? Take you with me to Oras and get you killed too? Maiden bless, I'll find a way to send you south. You'll find friends there, loyal friends, not oath-breakers. Oh damn damn damn.* She felt a pricking behind her eyes, forced the tears back. *I'll weep for you later, Tayyan. If I have to.*

The blue shadows deepened to indigo as clouds gathered

overhead, rolling across the star field until only a few sparks
were left. A shadow in shadows came whispering across the
grass and stopped in front of her, the whites of its eyes glistening unsteadily as they shifted from her to the girl sleeping
beside her.

"Haes angeleh, Shuri," she murmured, then sat without
moving, waiting for the shuri to speak.

"Hasna angelta, Meie." The voice from the shadow was
low and burred, the tone questioning. "Why you shurin call?"

She considered the quality of the voice, decided to use the
male affix. "Shurid, out of my need I call." She spoke slowly,
gravely. It was important to take care. Shurin were a proud
and touchy people—and formidable enemies when they chose
to be. Nervously she passed her hand back over her hair,
pushing wind-tousled strands off her face. "We two—this
child and I—the Kapperim seek." She dropped her hand onto
Dinafar's shoulder, felt it move away from her touch. "A
double hand of deaths do I owe them. This of shurid I ask, a
safe and quick journey through Earth's Teeth."

The shuri was silent. He stood very still, his only movement the shifting of those large round eyes, Serroi to Dinafar
and back, until Serroi began to worry about her assump-
tions—was the shuri in female phase after all? She let herself
relax when the shuri bowed its furry head. "The pact between
shurin and meien sworn is, Meie. Value for value, in the pact
it is."

Puzzled and wary, Serroi echoed the shuri. "Value for
value. Has Biserica ever denied its debts?"

"Moongather a nyok'chui has called from Earth. A den
has it made at Kabeel water. The glishnacht without water
wither. The season-mother among the first he took. The
kitunahan no water to the glishnacht bring. Wam'toten, our
children of this year, in fear and hunger, in thirst to me do
cry. Season-father I be. The season-mother he knife take; he
trap set; he eaten is." The husky voice trailed off, grown even
thicker with the intense grief that shook his small form. Ur-
gent as her own need was, she could not deny the shuri's
need. In the pact it was. She looked down at the girl stirring
in her sleep, smiled ruefully. *Another problem, another snag.*
She shook Dinafar awake.

When they rode out of the cup, winding through the
treacherous slit with its tumbled rocks and precarious walls,
the storm clouds were massing overhead, coming between

moongather and earth. The wind pressed her clothes into her skin, tried to lift her off the saddle. She glanced back, wondering how Dinafar was making out. The girl was bent low over the macai's neck, sensibly presenting little surface for the wind to catch hold of. Serroi laughed to herself. *She does learn fast, little mongrel.*

She felt an easing of the sorrow that oppressed her. The simple fact that she was moving forward, on her way back to the city, was sufficient to quiet her pain for a while. As always, the storm outside stirred her blood and helped to ease the storm inside. She moved easily in the saddle, settling into the macai's dip and lurch, feeling as if she rode the dipping and swaying wind, not touching the earth at all. Lightning flickered, turning the world into patterns of black and white. Flat blacks, flat whites, hard and bold, like the designs her mother used to weave into belts and deocrative strips.

As she followed the dark shadow scrambling along a crude trail, she laughed aloud, seeing again the plains where she was born, plains far to the north of here where some nights were passages long in summer-deep. She could feel in her bones the creaking rocking cart that was her cradle and her home for the first years of her life. She remembered running like this with her chinin, running through wild thunderstorms beside the slow flood of the herd and, remembering, felt a sudden rapture, wanted to lift her head and howl like a chini at the wind and the rolling clouds.

The shuri leaped onto a boulder higher than his head, perched there while Serroi hauled the macai to a stop beside him, euphoria blown out of her like weeds before the wind. Coldly alert, she waited for Dinafar to come up beside her. The girl was beginning to manage the macai with some skill, but Serroi saw her shifting cautiously in her saddle. It would take more time before she was completely at ease on macaiback.

"Meie." Answering to the shuri's call, she turned back. He raised a hand, pointing ahead toward the swelling breast of a mountain. "Nyok'chui down and around me, Meie. Best the macai left here be. Or he come and eat."

"Shurid, I hear." She slid off her mount and beckoned to the girl. Switching back to the mijloc tongue, shouting to be heard over the wind, she cried, "Dinafar, stay here with the macai. Please?"

Dinafar nodded. She slid stiffly from the saddle, almost

falling as her knees buckled under her. Serroi caught her and steadied her until she could stand. "You all right, Dina?"

"Oh yes, just stiff." She stumbled to a rock and sat down. "Wait here?" She pushed her dark hair back. The next flash of lightning showed her as an old woman with heavy, weary lines in her face. "Alone?"

Behind her Serroi heard the rasp of the shuri's claws as he fidgeted on the rock. She pushed her hair out of her eyes. "Not long. And I won't be far. You'll be safer here."

Grains of grit danced over the rock and pinged into them; the wind was heavy and damp, driving unsteadily against them. Serroi touched the girl's cheek, then followed the shuri.

Around the curve of the mountain the wind was softer. She knelt on the mountainside, leaning forward tensely, searching the flickering darkness below. In the narrow flat where one downslope ended and an upslope began a small round pool caught the last glimmers of light from the sky on its dancing surface and scattered it in sparkles of silver that raced across the stone and lit a round patch of blackness in the hillside. The Den.

The shuri touched her arm and pointed. "Nyok'chui."

Serroi sucked in a breath and let it trickle out. "I see." She straightened, pulling three arrows from her case as she came erect. Eyes closed, she slid her fingers along the shafts, remembering with her body the characteristics of each, weight and balance and soul.

When she opened her eyes again, the air was thick and black around her and the pool below had lost its glimmers. The wind tugged at her hair, plucked at her body in erratic gusts. She sat and pulled off her boots, stood again, working her feet into the coarse soil until she felt the earth below a part of her blood and bone. She stripped off her tunic.

His fur fluffed about by the wind, the shuri watched her with grave curiosity but he said nothing more, simply waited for her to do what she'd been trained to do.

Serroi dropped the tunic and raised her arms over her head, twisting and turning, letting the wind coil around her, taking the rhythm of its rise and fall into her body. When she knew it like her own breath, she smiled down at the shuri. "Air and earth," she murmured. "Earth my body lifts and air my shafts." She looked past him at the faint splotch of darkness on the far slope. "Come soon?" She touched—very lightly—her eye-spot, felt the tremble in it, then focused mind and body downhill, sensing a stirring in the blackness of the hole.

"He out come when he hunger feel. He shurin at water take or at homeplace." The shuri was a small sad lump of fur. "Soon come. Three days he not eat. Hungry." A shrill chittering sound was his version of ironic laughter. "Want a shuri snack," he said.

Serroi chuckled, surprised by the black humor of his words. Still chuckling, she strung her bow and tested the pull, lifting it, then letting it fall. She nocked one of the three arrows and thrust the other two delicately into the soil beside her right leg. As the Nyok'chui began dragging its bulk from the hole in the slope, she straightened again to stand, knees slightly flexed, her bared skin drinking in the wind, tasting its patterns. She held the bow loosely, watching the great Worm ooze slowly from the earth.

The Nyok'chui's head was a snarling mask with a coarse mane standing out around his hairless face, each hair like a wire, sparks leaping from one to another like small bolts of lightning until his head was ringed with blue-white light, pulsing and eerily hypnotic. The first section of its body was a broad barrel-shaped torso, supported by six double-jointed legs that ended in massive talons like those of some great bird of prey. As the Worm inched farther and farther out of the hole, the segments became more and more rudimentary until, near the end of the scaled body, the legs were little more than stiff stubs. When completely out, the Nyok coiled the tail in wide, sloopy loops and raised up his foreparts. The front pair of talons, flexible as human fingers, batted the air in slow curves; the lightning halo about its head lit up the adamantine claws at the tips of each of these powerful pseudo-fingers until they were a glittering jeweled threat with even a kind of beauty to them. Between talons and tail, it was as if the beast held several natures at reluctant truce under its various skins. Eyes glowing red, it swiveled to stare up the hill at her. Once again it pawed the air, opened its cavernous mouth, roared a challenge at her.

Serroi strained to see. Conditions for shooting could hardly be poorer with the uncertain light and the erratic wind. She shut her eyes, willed the unfamiliar change and opened them again in the uneasy night-vision she seldom used; she saw them in stark outlines, greenish black and green-tinted whites with little fine detail but a massive sense of solidity.

The Nyok'chui began flowing up the hillside toward her. Over the snapping of the small lightnings about its head she heard the burring hum it used to pacify its usual victims; she fought off the hum-induced lethargy, centered herself once more, lifted the bow, drew the string back, waited.

Sensing her resistance, the Nyok reared, roared at her.

She loosed the arrow, brought up the second, nocked it, pulled, released. Brought up the third, nocked, pulled, released.

The first arrow drove into the inside of the Worm's mouth. The second pierced the right eye, driving through the bulging sac of jelly into the brain beyond. The third socked home into the left eye.

The Nyok'chui roared its agony, writhing, biting at the arrow its curved teeth couldn't even reach, swallowing and swallowing the gouts of blood that poured from a pierced artery. It would not die. With two arrows driven into its brain, with a third in its throat bleeding it to death, it would not die.

Serroi cupped her hand a moment over her eye-spot, closed her eyes and switched off the draining night-sight. Ignoring the noises from the struggling Worm, she unstrung her bow and laid it aside, then settled onto the cold, gritty soil, the storm winds tearing at her. She pulled on her boots and her tunic, then sat still, waiting as the Nyok's struggles lessened and finally ceased.

A few large raindrops splatted down on her head and shoulders. The night was velvet black now, the wind more erratic than ever. Lightning flared, struck below her. The circling winds brought her the sweet strong odor of burning flesh. *The dead beast*, she thought. *The worm.* She rubbed at her nose. *I've heard . . . what have I heard . . . something . . . something.* The shuri fidgeted beside her then started moving downhill. Absently she noted his departure while she continued to dig for the elusive memory. *The Worm of the Earth. The many-souled Worm that crawls through the living rock. Worm. Eye.* She touched her throbbing eye-spot. *Yes. That's it. The inner eye, dead and alive.* "Tajicho," she breathed. *Maiden be blessed for this gift.* In a frenzy of excitement she scrambled to her feet and raced downhill to the coiling pile of dead worm. In the intermittent flashes of lightning she could see the shuri dancing in triumph on the Nyok's head.

She stumbled and slid the last few feet to rebound from the cold rubbery flesh, shuddered, then began climbing the coils until she reached the collapsed mane. The coarse hair was long and thick, more like copper wire than hair. Even

with the Worm thoroughly dead, the mane had sufficient
charge left to send tingles through her body as she pulled herself up onto the domed skull. The shuri stopped its dance and
jumped to a lower coil where it crouched, watching her with
bright-eyed curiosity.

Nerving herself, she knelt on the broad snout and drove
her grace blade into the web of sinew and nerve between the
bulging eyes, trying to avoid looking at the translucent orbs
bleeding a greenish ooze that bubbled around the fletching
of the arrows. While she worked the shaft ends tilted and
dropped away, the wood burned completely through. Serroi
shivered and kept more carefully away from the fumes beginning to boil up from the eyes.

In a complex of nerves, nesting in a special hollow in the
skull, she found an egg-shaped object small enough to fit
comfortably in the palm of her hand. The unripe focus of the
Nyok's power. She cut carefully around it and worked it
loose, then scraped at it, freeing it as carefully as she could
from the fragments of flesh and sinew.

She wiped the knife on the coarse hair then slipped it back
in its sheath. Fingers closed tight about the eye, she raised
herself slowly onto her feet and stood balancing carefully on
the Worm's head, feet half-buried in the mane, the draining
charge still strong enough to nip at her.

"Meie?"

She glanced down and saw the shuri. "Shurid, dangerous it
be what I next do, but it I must do." She pointed. "Up the
hill. Go. Wait."

When the lightning showed him halfway up the hill, she
looked down at the dull bloody thing in her hands, trying
over the chant she hadn't used for fifteen years, letting the
words and rhythm focus her mind and will.

Remembered pain was a sudden sharpness distracting her
from needed concentration. The chant brought back too viv-
idly the sweetness of the early days in the tower, days like a
paradise gone forever. She looked up at the clouds, sighed,
then tightened her mind about the chant. Singing the words
into the storm wind howling about her, whipping her hair
into a wet tangle, shuddering against her body, she held the
eye above her head and called the lightning down to her. A
bolt flashed beside her, struck at the Worm's head. The reek
of burning hair and charred flesh wheeled around her. She
sucked in a breath, spat it out, called again.

A great jagged streak struck at the eye; her body quivered

with shock and pain. She fell to her knees, started sliding down, bumping helplessly from coil to coil of already rotting flesh until her head slammed against stone and she knew nothing more.

She woke on the earth beside the Nyok'chui, her body sore as if her bones had been wrenched apart then allowed to snap back into place. She was bleeding from abrasions on arms and knees, a burn on one cheek. But the eye was still clutched in her hand. The shuri crouched anxiously beside her. She smiled at him as soon as she noticed him, but winced as the muscle pull hurt her seared cheek.

The eye was warm in her hands. When she opened her fingers it nestled in the curve of her palm, a new-made crystal with a soft orange-amber glow at its heart. She touched it with her other forefinger, smiled as it resisted being separated from her palm. "Tajicho," she whispered. "Ser Noris, my Noris, you taught me this." Tears blurred her eyes. "Do you like what you made, my Noris?" She wiped her eyes, sat back on her heels, exhausted by her ordeal.

Tajicho. Twister. Talisman of immense power, it was keyed to the person who made it, useless to anyone else. It twisted spells, turned them back on the spinners unless they were unusually agile; more than this, it wiped its master from the world as far as the Norim were concerned, even the most powerful of them—except perhaps her Noris. No magic mirror, no beast-eye, no demon could see her even if she stood in front of it. This Ser Noris had taught her and in so doing had given her a weapon against him, how potent she couldn't tell. For a moment she wondered about the coincidence of the Nyok-chui turning up just now, wondered if this were some part of his torturous schemes, then she shook herself out of her dismals, irritated at herself for falling into futile speculation. She tucked the crystal into her money sack where it clinked musically against the small store of gold coins, moved fingertips over the small lump, lifted a corner of her mouth in a one-sided smile. "Finished this be," she told the shuri.

The rain began coming down hard. Lightning still flashed, though less often. Serroi's hair was plastered against her head. Her leather tunic and divided skirt were treated with the juice of the nu-frasha herb that grew high on the slopes of the Biserica valley; they shed water a long time, staying supple and comfortable after many a soaking. The rain beaded up

off the surface of the leather and funneled into her boot tops
until she sloshed as she moved her feet. She was cold and
desperately tired as she collected her bow, clipped it to its
strap, and followed the shuri around the mountain to the flat
where Dinafar waited.

The girl was huddled against the crouching macai, soaked
through. Her head lifted as she heard them coming. Eyes
wide in her drawn face, Dinafar said, "That roar?"

"The Nyok'chui is dead." Serroi bent and took hold of the
girl's cold hands. "Come, it's time to move on." She tugged
gently, helping Dinafar struggle up. She stood silent, pulling
her waterlogged skirt away from her legs while Serroi urged
the reluctant macain back onto their feet.

After shoving Dinafar into the saddle and slapping the
bulky skirt into a modicum of order, Serroi swung up into
her own saddle, wincing at the contact with the cold wet
leather. "Shurid!" She shouted to be heard above the storm
noise. "Ride with me so I don't lose you." A tardy flash of
lightning showed her the water streaming off the shuri. The
upper layer of his fur had changed under the rain to a sleek,
water-shedding surface that glistened like brown glass. Water
sluiced off the coarse skin of his face and divided around the
blunt muzzle with its wide-set nostrils and perpetual smile.
She felt his small three-fingered hands close about her ankles,
then he walked up her body until he was perched on the
saddle ledge in front of her.

With the shuri guiding her, with Dinafar silent behind her,
Serroi rode up and up, winding, twisting, sometimes having to
dismount, and struggled up impossible slopes and over un-
stable scree. She coaxed the macain on, whistling and cooing
to them, stroking them into moaning content with her eye-
spot after they'd managed some difficult task. The rain fell,
endless and cold. The wind tugged and battered at them,
drove gusts of icy water into faces or backs as it shifted continually in sinuous currents funneling through the mountains.

The hours passed in noise and weariness. Overhead, the
clouds began to tear apart, letting a glimmer of moonlight
through. Once the breakup began, it spread quickly until the
slopes were darkly visible. In a moment of comparative calm
Serroi heard Dinafar gasp; she glanced back and saw the girl
looking down at the perilous track, eyes wide with horror.

The track they followed was littered with loose rock; it
hugged the side of the mountain, falling off on the right into
an abyss so deep its bottom was lost in shadow. The girl was

swaying in the saddle, close to the end of her endurance.
"Dina!"

Dinafar's head came up slowly, her face a mask of weariness, her eyes gleaming liquidly in the strengthening light.

"Hang on a little longer," Serroi shouted. "A little longer."
The wind caught the words and shredded them but she saw
Dinafar nod and try to straighten her back. Satisfied, Serroi
turned and rode on.

The hours passed, cold endless hours. They left the abyss
behind and slid steeply down into a narrow crack, the walls
on either side rising higher and higher as they twisted deeper
into mountain-heart. Seated in cracks that branched off on either side, groups of shurin watched them move past, large
round eyes greenly phosphorescent. Equally silent, perched
like a furry lump in front of her, the curve of his back fitting
against the curve of her front below her breasts, the shuri began humming, his song transmitted through bone and flesh to
her. He had led them through the worst of the peaks and
across the divide, through the secret paths of his people. Once
this crack was negotiated they'd be well on their way to the
gentler slopes of the landward side of the Earth's Teeth.

They wound on and on. The straggling Dancers hung low
behind them, gifting the stone with triple shadows, lighting
the way with their deceptive cold glow. Serroi glanced up and
saw dark silhouettes cutting across the starfield. Five black
not-birds with long narrow wings and oversized heads circled
high over her.

She began shaking, then remembered the tajicho and grew
calmer. They were traxim, demon-servants of the Nearga-nor.
Flying eyes. She touched the lump in her money sack and felt
its warmth through the thin leather. She smiled. It was working as it should, sheltering her from dangerous eyes. The
traxim went away without seeming to notice her.

The wind dropped abruptly, freeing the crack for a few
moments from its whine, freeing the riders from its continual
battering. Serroi shifted wearily in the saddle; a little apprehensively she looked over her shoulder. Dinafar was lying
against the macai's neck, her arms circling its thin neck, her
hands locked together. She shook her head. *Hang on, Dina,*
she thought. *We can't stop yet.*

They rode out of the crack into a steep descent and into a
predawn wind that helped pull the wetness from their bodies.
By the time the eastern sky showed a pallor near the horizon

and the peaks behind them had caps of crimson, Serroi was dry and only a little cold.

The shuri held up a hand. When Serroi pulled the macai to a halt, he climbed down her leg and crossed a few paces of bare earth to a pile of rock. He perched on top of the pile and looked about. In the dawn light she could see that the reddish fur around his blunt muzzle was stippled with white. He was growing old, not many seasons left for him as season-mother or season-father.

As if he read her thoughts the shuri nodded sadly. "Next year season-mother I be, Meie. For me the last of seasons."

"My sorrow, shurid. I intrude."

"The right you have. With three arrows the season for me you have won." He stretched out a thin arm and pointed to the glow in the east. "A Stenda hold there. Half-day riding. The Stendam to Oras have gone for Gather, though two be left for watching hold and stock. The hold they leave each morning and each night they come back to sleep within walls. No closer than this go I."

"By the pact then, peace between us be, shurid."

"By the pact peace be, Meie." The shuri sketched a gesture of respect, then scurried past the macain and vanished among the rocks behind them.

Serroi looked up at the thin scatter of paling stars. The traxim were gone. Touching the bulge in her money sack, she smiled then sighed as she rode back to Dinafar.

Still damp, the heavy skirt was plastered against the girl's legs; as she lay along the macai's neck, her face in the spongy frill, violent shivers coursed along her thin body. Serroi lifted a hand, dropped it. Dinafar didn't need encouragement. A fire, some hot cha, those wet clothes off, sleep, those she needed. Serroi sighed and swung the macai back around so she could scan the ground in front of her.

Though a thick band of trees obscured much of the slope, she glimpsed a shimmer of water winding in a narrow line. Without looking back again she kicked the tired macai into a slow shuffle toward the stream, the other beast following close behind.

She followed the water to a grassy clearing, stopped the macai and looked about. Because the soil was shallow and stony only grasses spread their matted roots here, holding the small space free of trees and brush. She slid off her macai, stretched, yawned, bent and twisted her aching body to work some of the stiffness and soreness out.

Dinafar groaned and pushed herself precariously erect, face flushed, eyes glazed.

"Dina?" The girl swayed; her swollen lips trembled but she couldn't speak. "Dina, lean over like you did before." Serroi sang the words past the barrier of Dinafar's exhaustion. "Loose your hands, little one, let go, let go, I'll catch you, let go." She kept up the quiet chant as she watched the girl's fingers begin to uncramp from their hold. The drooping body swayed, then dropped like a stone into Serroi's waiting arms. Serroi felt the cold clammy skirt slap against her, felt the fever heat in the girl's body, the shivering cold in her hands. She lowered her gently onto the grass then stripped off the sodden clothing, ignoring Dinafar's weak scandalized protests. She tossed the clothing aside and ripped the blanket roll from behind her saddle, snapped the blankets open, tossed one blanket aside and wrapped Dinafar in the other.

That'll do you for a little, she thought. She glanced at the weary beasts who were already grazing. *You later.* She trotted into the shadow under the trees, searching for down wood.

Half an hour later Dinafar sat blanket-wrapped, sipping at cha laced with pyrnroot from Serroi's weaponbelt. The fever glaze was gone from her eyes, the flush from her cheeks. She cradled the cup in her hands, her eyes on the macain busily cropping at the grass close by. "Hadn't you better tie them up, Meie?"

Serroi prodded at the skirt she was holding up to the fire. "They won't go far. Anyway, I can call them back easily enough." She flicked a finger across her forehead, smiled as the girl's eyes widened, tossed her the skirt and followed with the ragged blouse. "Warm enough?"

"Umm . . ." Dinafar yawned suddenly. "You put something in the cha?"

"A healing root. Do you mind?"

"No." Dina yawned again and fumbled at the blouse and skirt, her eyes drooping lower and lower as she pulled the clothing over her thin body, blushing repeatedly at having to bare herself. Serroi carefully looked away, made uncomfortable by the girl's embarrassment. She thought about the crowding of the Intii's hall, remembered the prudery of her parents. *Intimacy and prudery. Perhaps the second is born of the first.* When she turned back, Dinafar was slumped on the ground, snoring a little. Serroi moved around the fire and stood looking down at her. *She never complained. I wouldn't want to make that ride myself if it was my first.* She knelt beside Dina, straightened her crumpled limbs and shifted her onto the second blanket. She smoothed the long straight hair back off the girl's face then tucked the other blanket around her. "Sleep as long as you need."

She stood and stretched, the morning light brightening around her. In the east, above the treetops, a few last shreds of dawn lingered, but they were fading rapidly. She yawned, sat watching the fire as it died to a few coals, then snuggled down on the grass, dropping into a deep sleep.

She was startled out of sleep by a hoarse yell and rough, strong hands that clamped her wrists together. She stared up into a grinning face, then was dangling in midair as he held her out at arm's length.

THE CHILD: 5

Serroi bent over the scroll, puzzling out the words; they were written in a script she'd just begun to learn and described the travels of a trader and rogue whose humor was resisting her at the moment, but whose descriptions were vivid enough to keep her interest, especially as just such a caravan was moving slowly across dun-colored sands before her in the magic mirror.

She was nine years old, several inches taller, content with her life in the tower. She wore tunic and trousers, new ones, fetched from somewhere by the Noris's invisible servants. The patterns in black and white woven into the belt were strange to her; she'd used the mirror to search the tundra for the wind-runner clan with those patterns but had never managed to find it, had grown bored with the search and finally just accepted the clothing when it was provided. There were so many other interesting places to explore by the mirror.

Suddenly aware of eyes watching her, she lifted her head and looked around. The Noris was standing silent in the doorway. She touched the mirror to blankness, rolled the parchment into a neat tight roll and replaced it in its rack. Though the rest of the room bore the imprint of her careless passage, the roll books were in meticulous order. The pens and penpoints on the table were shining clean, the sheets of paper squared in orderly piles, edges exactly parallel to the edges of the table.

The Noris smiled at this touch of order. "Come, Serroi. I need you to help me with something."

Happiness warmed her. Almost dancing, she crossed the room to him and took his hand.

The rock flowed before them, collapsing into stairs. The tower seemed to be solid except for those cells of emptiness located through the stone like bubbles in a brick of cheese. He took her higher than she'd been before and touched open a door leading into a room she'd never seen before.

As she walked inside, a chini yearling trotted to her, sniffed at her, laid back his ears and crouched whining in front of the Noris. She'd noted that before. Wild or tame, creatures winced away from the Noris pantomiming their fear in postures of submission. Even the great sicamar crawled on his belly and yowled with fear. The Noris stepped past her and crossed to a chair. As he settled himself, she continued to stroke the chini's head and looked around.

The room was small and circular, a cylinder in stone rising high overhead, ending in a crisp blue circle of sky too far away to lessen the sense of oppression that weighed on her. Little by little her happiness slipped away. The air was too heavy in that roofless room. Her eye-spot throbbed. She turned to the Noris, a dozen unspoken questions in her eyes.

He sat in a black stone chair raised on a dais with a permanent pentacle incised in the stone around it, the lines filled with silver that shimmered in the brilliant light pouring through the roof opening.

The yearling pressed hard against her leg; she could feel him trembling. He was a tall gangling animal, his back about groin-high on her, not quite at home yet in an adult-sized body. She scratched behind his ears and smoothed her hand along his spine. Touching this strong life, she was aware again of the deadness of the tower. She was never sure that the Noris truly lived; he seemed a man like others, but sometimes she doubted it.

"Serroi."

She stared at him, startled. There was a heavy solemnity to his voice unlike his usual cool detachment. She wondered what was coming, certainly something different. She moved to stand before him, straightening her back and shoulders.

"You've been here four years." His eyes moved from her face to gaze blankly over her shoulder at the glass-smooth stone of the wall. "You've proved to have an unusual aptitude for learning. I am pleased to find it so."

Serroi sucked in a breath, feeling more uneasy than ever. The things he was saying should have come from the warm, pleasant side, but they didn't, they were like the false smile he wore sometimes, said without feeling, a sop to her feelings. She knew that he had a very limited understanding of those feelings. In the past four years, she'd learned to accommodate herself to these limitations, shutting down when she could some of her stronger reactions to his actions. A year ago jealousy had scorched her. He was startled at first, then amused. She'd been in agony and it had amused him.

"You asked me once why I took you from your kin. Do you remember?"

She nodded, her eyes fixed on his face.

He held his hands out before him, palms up first, then the backs; after a minute he dropped them on the dark stone chair arms, draped them gracefully. "Hands," he said. "My hands. They hold power; you know that." He tapped fingers against the stone. "But there are limits. We can manipulate, transform the non-living; we're sealed away from manipulating the living. I needed a gate in that wall. You." He settled back in his chair, smiling a little, more remote than ever, an ivory and jet image of a man. "You are my gate, Serroi."

Apprehension and excitement swirled in Serroi until she was dizzy with them. She understood little of what the Noris was saying, but she grasped her importance in his eyes and glowed at the thought. Still, she was afraid, she didn't know why.

"Look at me, Serroi."

She stroked the chini again, then raised her eyes to meet his. The shining black rounds grew larger and larger until she saw nothing but that blackness. She was weeping, could feel the tears dripping from her eyes and trickling down her cheeks while a terrible coldness flowed into her from the Noris, stifling all that she'd been feeling, anger and joy, love and despair, chilling her until there was nothing warm left in her, until the tears dried, until her body was unfeeling stone.

A thing crept into her body. She felt her fingers twitch, her arms move. Felt the eye-spot wake and send out its invisible fingers under pressure from the invader. Her body stirred. Sitting trapped in walls of ice, the seed of warmth that contained her essence saw and grieved as her body went awkwardly onto its knees beside the whining yearling. Her body leaned forward until her face was pressed against the chini, her brow touching the soft grey fur on the side of his head.

The chini stiffened. She felt the thing in her creep out through the eye-spot and move inside him.

The yearling moved jerkily away. She heard him whine, then growl, saw him leap high, crouch, crawl across the stone, scraping at the floor with spastic paws. He began to howl. She felt his agony. The frozen part of her watched critically while the tiny soft spot where she really lived could do nothing but mourn endlessly in darkness. Her body crouched in the middle of the room while the Noris working through her tore the chini to bits, driving him until he foamed at the mouth, dashed against the walls at full speed, bit at himself, tearing out gobbets of flesh and hair. Finally the chini yearling died under the torment, driven until his heart gave out from pain and exhaustion.

The part of the Noris working through her withdrew. She felt the cold flow out of her and couldn't move; her trust broken utterly, she felt like she was bleeding inside where no one could see it. Hardly aware of what she was doing, she lifted her arms, crossed them tight across her chest, her eyes fixed on his ivory face, begging him to reassure her, to let her love him again, to say something she could believe. He sat brooding, apparently unaware that she was in the room.

She rose shakily to her feet and moved to the body of the chini. Kneeling beside him, she touched the mutilated flesh, ran trembling fingers over the pointed ears, looked down at the mouth that hung open, the lacerated tongue lapping out over the yellow teeth, touched threads of blood congealing in long lines from the jaw.

She felt the Noris's eyes on her and got heavily to her feet. He was frowning, puzzled by the strength of her emotion. When she came over to him, he leaned forward and pushed her down until she was kneeling at his feet inside the lines of the pentacle. A WORD made the silver in the lines glow palely. Another WORD, one more complex than she'd heard before, crashed against her, struck pain from her. She moaned and huddled closer against the Noris, sick and terrified.

A grey fog gathered over the chini's battered body. It hovered a moment then began shaping itself into a likeness of the beast. Red eyes like hot blood, red tongue lolling over yellow teeth, pricking ears, a great grey body, the demon was a travesty of the living breathing beast yet she sensed that it shared some of the chini's nature, chini and demon melded into a horrible amalgam that made her stomach churn. It slunk from the diminished body and came to sniff at the silver lines of the pentagram.

Serroi cringed away from it, cowered against the chair, pushing harder into the Noris's legs while the thing paced back and forth in front of her, its stinking breath blowing into her face.

The Noris stood. A chain of shimmering silver leaped into being in midair and slapped about the demon's neck. It whined with pain and crouched submissively. With a WORD the Noris paled the pentacle's silver then turned to scowl down at Serroi. "Go to your room, Serroi. Put yourself in order." He seemed angry as if she had somehow hurt him by her pain. He stalked from the room, one end of the silver chain in his hand, the demon trotting beside him.

Serroi looked sadly after him, then at the body of the pup. She couldn't even bury it. There was no honest living soil on this barren crag. Catching hold of the chair's arm, she pulled herself onto her feet. With a last glance at the dead beast she stumbled out of the room and trudged slowly down the stairs to her room, pulled the door shut behind her, wincing at the dull clang of metal against stone.

She stood a moment in the center of the small space looking vaguely about. Several plants were beginning to droop. She moved blindly to them, touched the wilting leaves and the splotches of brown. Abruptly she was crying. She threw herself onto her rumpled bed, her body shuddering with sobs wrenched from her.

After the evening meal, a meal she couldn't eat, she paced restlessly about the room, picking things up, setting them down again, trying desperately to forget what happened. She needed to believe that he was at least fond of her. Finally she sighed and went to see him.

He looked up and smiled at her, then turned back to the fire. She settled silently beside him. After a minute she caught his hand and rested her cheek on his cool flesh. She had to believe that he valued her, that he had some affection for her even if he didn't truly understand her. Several minutes passed like this then she looked up to find his eyes fixed on her, examining her with curiosity and some puzzlement. She held her breath, but he said nothing. She sighed and tried to forget the chini. It wouldn't happen again. It couldn't. Things would go on between them as before. She would forget and be happy again.

A week later he called her back to the cylindrical room. She saw the small grey figure with its round wrinkled face like an ugly old man and great round nocturnal eyes; she cried out and took a step back. The Noris brought her in, almost shoving her as she begged him not to do it, her hands clinging to him, tears streaming from her eyes. He used her to drive the little beast to its death, coldly testing it beyond its strength. Once again the demon blended with the animal.

After that he let her rest a week, then called her back to the chamber with another chini, using it to strengthen the first demon, welding the two natures more completely. Week after week the animals died and demons were born or made stronger. Slowly the cages in the court emptied and slowly her anguish grew. She begged the Noris to stop; he couldn't understand, it was only a successful series of experiments, what did a few lives matter, there were always more animals, they were born and died every day.

Serroi knelt beside the great chair, struggling to hold back her grief so she could speak calmly, persuasively. "Please, Ser Noris." She sucked in a breath, fighting for that elusive calm. "Haven't you got enough things to work with? Can't you leave the rest of them, let them go, let me stop. Let me stop. Please. They're my friends, Ser Noris. Let me stop." She sucked in another breath, waited tensely for his answer.

"Look at me." His voice was crisp and hard. When she looked up, she saw that he was coldly angry, so angry his hands were trembling. "You are the gate." He leaned forward suddenly and caught her head between his hands. He held her gently enough but she couldn't move. "They're only animals, Serroi. I'm doing what I told you, pushing back limits, learning things I never knew before. You have to understand that, child." To her surprise he was almost pleading with her. "Remember the mirror, the books, the tests we did together? You like to learn, Serroi. We share the same need to learn. They're just animals, most of them would be dead already by predator or disease. We give meaning to that death."

Her head locked in place by those steel and silk fingers, she was forced to look up at him. "They're my friends," she said. "And you're making me hurt them."

He held her a moment longer, then pulled his hands away and leaned back in the chair, his eyes closed. After a moment he waved her away from him with a quick impatient gesture of a slim white hand. "Leave," he said harshly. When she was at the door, he spoke again. "Be here tomorrow after the noon meal."

She began to fight him, trying to keep from looking into his eyes. She failed. She tried to wall him out of her body. She failed. She tried to push him out once he was in. She failed. She exhausted herself struggling against him and lost every time, but she never quit. She could no longer endure sharing in the destruction of the beasts and birds she loved.

As she struggled, she felt herself growing stronger; he had to exert more of his power each time he called her to that room. Still she lost. One by one the cages were emptied.

The courtyard grew silent. She couldn't go near the animals anymore, those few that were left. They wouldn't let her. She kept away from the court. She couldn't bear to look at the empty cages—or at the occupied ones, knowing their dwellers would soon be tormented to death.

She suffered. Having given the Noris her love fully and freely, she hurt when she had to defy him, hurt more when she sensed his own hurt, when she had to face his anger, his accusations of betrayal.

Spring faded into summer. She ate and slept when she could, lay awake more hours trying to find a way out of her dilemma. One day she tried climbing the cages, but the highest were too far below the top of the court walls and set too solidly in place. She tried loosening one cage, but only bruised and tore her fingers. Without tools she could do nothing. She went through her books and searched the mirror to find out everything she could about the island chain of the Nearga-nor, but she found little that comforted her. The islands were miles out to sea. She knew nothing about boats, nothing about swimming either, and she could remember all too well the power the Noris had over wind and water. There was no way she could run from him.

The sessions continued. She settled into a numb grief and let him use her as he wished. She withdrew from him, no longer sat with him in the evenings. Most of the time she lay in heavy nightmare-ridden sleep, retreating into sleep to avoid the pain her waking hours brought her—then the walls began closing in on her.

She went finally from apathy to a shrieking rage, plunged from the room and refused to go back, prowled about the court like a tiny predator, ready to claw at anything that moved. The Noris found her there early in the morning, sitting huddled by the water pipe.

"You spent the night there."

"Yes." Shivering, miserable, she glared up at him.

"Come inside, Serroi. Wash yourself. Eat something."

"No."

He bent to touch her head. She jerked back. "Serroi. . . ."

"No."

His face a mask in ivory and ebony except for the glitter of the pendant ruby, he straightened quickly, almost as if she'd slapped him. For a moment he said nothing. When he spoke, his voice was harsh and cold. "That is your choice." He turned away, turned back as abruptly, flung out an arm to point at a rough wooden door in the towerside. "Live there if you must." Walking heavily, deliberately, without sign of hurry, he crossed the flags and disappeared inside.

Summer passed and the rains began. Day after day the rain dripped down. When the rain stopped, the fog moved in and more moisture dripped endlessly from the cage roofs and the walls and settled on everything. The cages were all empty, their straw and other contents rattling forlornly in the winds that sometimes crept in to blow the veils of fog about. Serroi stayed in the cell-like room in the tower wall and the stone radiated a gentle warmth that kept her alive. The invisible hands brought her food and fresh clothing. Sometimes days went by before she saw the sun and even when it came out, she couldn't endure going into the silent court to see the empty cages. She stayed in the small dark hole and brooded.

THE WOMAN: VI

Hands were pulling at her. Dinafar muttered and pushed at them, unwilling to wake. She was still tired, her body ached, even moving her hands quickened the soreness in her muscles. The pulling continued. She opened her eyes, blinked, then cried out as she looked up into a man's grinning face. He twisted his hand in the front of her ragged blouse and ripped it away, baring her chest and the slight swell of her new breasts. She kicked at him, but her legs were trapped in the folds of her skirt. She tried to wriggle away, biting and scratching as his hands fumbled over her nipples. She rolled away from him, scrambled onto her knees. Cursing good-naturedly, he grabbed her wrist and jerked her back. A man she hadn't seen before caught her other wrist. "Wild one," he said. "Hurry up, Lere." He wrapped his hand in her hair and jerked her head back.

The pain brought tears to her eyes. She bucked her body about but the two men were far too strong. The first man, Lere, the other had called him, sat on her feet and began working the tumbled folds of her skirt up past her knees.

A roar from behind her head brought a muffled curse from Lere. He sat back, his face blank. "Ay, Tercel," he said with a forced respect.

"Sten, Lere, off that tita. Tie her wrists. Got no time for that now."

"Ay, Tercel." Lere glanced at the other two and muttered, "Ay, ay, ay, not a bit o' stinkin' fun. Hunh! Hang onto her, Sten. I'll get a bit o' stinkin' rope."

Hands tied in front of her, Dinafar sat up in time to see the Tercel clamp one thick-fingered hand tight around the meie's wrists, holding her out from him like a strangled bereg he'd taken from a poacher's snare. Her face masklike, she hung limply as if his strength had drained all fight from her. Dinafar was puzzled. The meie had never just given up. Not like that. The Tercel was a giant of a man, dressed in a leather tunic and black wool trousers, his barrel chest covered by a black and green tabard with the sigil of Oras appliquéed on the center panel. All the clothing was worn and dusty. He had several days' stubble on his face, a greasy shine to his skin, a gaunted look from days of hard riding and little sleep. When the erratic breeze blew her way, she could smell his stale sweat. Beyond him, she saw the meie's mount and hers, saddled and ready, standing with three others. The Tercel started moving toward the beasts, the meie still dangling at arm's length. His strength was phenomenal. *His vanity too,* Dinafar thought. *He's showing off for his men.*

Without warning the meie twisted her body up and around. Before the Tercel could move, she slammed her small boot into his groin.

Bellowing with pain and rage, he dropped into a crouch, clutching at himself with his free hand. His other arm dropped until the meie was crouched beside him, her wrists still prisoned. She fought desperately to free herself, twisting and kicking, but she wasn't strong enough. He held her. His meaty face still a grey-purple and shiny with sweat, his eyes glassy, he straightened a little and flung her away from him. She landed close to Dinafar, hitting hard enough for Dinafar to wince in sympathy. She hit and rolled to her feet in a single fluid movement—and stopped quite still, a saber-point in her face.

"Sten, slit the bitch's throat if she move." The Tercel lowered himself to the grass and sat hunched over, glaring at the meie. He passed the back of his hand over his face. "Lere, tie her hands good. She get away, I have your skin."

Sweating, eyes narrowed, he watched closely as Sten made the meie sit while Lere tied her. When her hands were secured, he grunted onto his feet, stood swaying a minute, then waddled over to her.

The meie lifted her head and stared at him out of a blank face. "How'd you find me?"

He jerked a thumb up. Dinafar followed the movement and saw six black birds circling over the clearing. "Traxim saw the fire, bought us. Funny, though." He scowled, nudged her leg with the toe of his boot. "Speaker-trax said there was just one here." He ran his eyes over her, his tongue sliding over his fleshy lips. "Lybor and her Nor want you bad, bitch. You gonna be sorry your ma whelp you. I'm gonna watch that Nor make you talk. I'm gonna hear you scream, bitch. I'm gonna hear you beg him kill you and let be."

The meie smiled.

The Tercel shook his head. "No, you get no chance to kill

yourself. We take good care of you, not like you crazy friend." The meie's gasp brought a grunting laugh out of him. "Didn't know? After you run off, t'other, she see the Nor coming at her, she pull out. . . ." His thumb jabbed at the grace blade still sheathed on the meie's weaponbelt. "And . . ." He slapped his hand against the side of his neck. "Good-bye, meie. The Nor he kick her a couple times, mad as hell. Told us haul her outside the city and dump her." He bent down, grunting an oath at the pain, jerked back on her hair, forcing her to look up. "See them? You gonna end up in them bellies like t'other one." He straightened, wiped his hand on his dusty trousers, watching her intently, savoring her distress. Dinafar ached for her, angry at the guards because she was helpless, disgusted with herself because of her avid curiosity about the meie, but when the Tercel went on with his punish-tale, she cursed the meagerness of the information in his words. "We hauled that skinny tita out and left her by the place where they run the macai. Before we get back to the gates, the traxim are crawling over her, getting themselves a fine fresh meal." He laughed at the anguish on the meie's face, the moan these words tore from her. "When ol' Nor's done with you, bitch, I'm gonna stake you out there. Same spot. I'm gonna sit and watch them. . . ." He stabbed a forefinger at the sky. "Watch them chew on you, eat you alive."

The meie dropped her head onto her arms, her small body shuddering under the impact of emotions Dinafar could only guess at. The Tercel watched her with satisfaction, then beckoned to Sten and Lere. "Get titam in the saddle. Time we was going."

The meie was quiet as Sten threw her onto her macai. She caught hold of the saddle ledge with her bound hands and fumbled her feet into the stirrups. Dinafar could see that her eyes were closed and tears were slipping down her face. Then Lere's hands moved over Dinafar's body, tweaking her nipples, thrusting between her thighs. She stood quite still, wondering what he'd do if she vomited over him. At a roar from the Tercel, he hoisted her into the saddle, then pulled her skirt down. She refused to look at him. He left her after a final pat on the thigh and mounted the animal standing behind her.

They moved out of the clearing, riding in single file, the Tercel first, hunched over in the saddle, cursing in a low steady monotone, then the meie, then Dinafar, then Lere, with Sten coming last. The ride rapidly turned to torment for

Dinafar; she felt every overworked muscle from last night's
terrible effort. She hurt. All over. She hurt. It wasn't like a
wound that concentrated the pain at a single spot. She was
bone-deep sore everywhere. Riding downhill all the time
didn't help, though the slope was moderate. She glared at the
Tercel's broad back and hoped his pain was worse than hers.

Awhile later, though, she'd warmed up and exercise had
loosened much of her stiffness. Feeling better, her curiosity
roused, she looked around. They were passing through a
small clearing in the trees. Overhead the great black birds
sailed in lazy circles. As they rode on, she kept looking up.
Whenever she could see a bit of the sky, the birds were there,
following them. Dinafar shivered. *Traxim. They ate the other
meie. She warned me she was going into danger. What's this
all about? I wish I knew what's going on.* She scanned the
little meie's back, wondering how she was taking the presence
of the birds. *They mightn't be the same ones; I hope they
aren't.* She clamped her teeth into her lower lip, swallowed,
swallowed again, until the urge to vomit went away.

There was a slight breeze winding through the trees. Dinafar felt it lifting a few straying hairs, letting them fall, passing over her skin, cooling her. The meie's sorrel curls flipped
about under its tugging. Her head was up, turning a little
from side to side. She looked back. Dinafar could see a faint
pulsing in the green spot on the meie's brow as she stared
over her shoulder at the two guards behind Dinafar. Then she
was looking ahead again. Dinafar swallowed. *She's getting
ready to do something.* Apprehensive and upset, she clutched
at the saddle ledge waiting for the world to fall in on the
guards. Nothing happened. They rode on and on and nothing
happened.

They wound through thick-standing brellim, the two-fin-
gered leaves of the squat trees whispering in the wind over
their heads, so many leaves that they shut out most of the
sunlight until the procession was winding in heavy silence and
humid twilight along a beast-run beaten deep in the spongy
soil by years of trampling hooves. *Here,* Dinafar thought. *Do
something, meie. They can't get at us here, those birds. Do
something.* Still nothing happened. She began to wonder if
the meie had given up trying.

After an hour in deep shadow the way ahead began to
lighten. Gleams of the nooning sun broke through, a few
beams dancing with dust motes reaching down to gild the
ground. The Tercel broke into the sunlight, his massive form

black against the dusty gold. When Dinafar rode into the clearing blinking and half-blinded by the light after so long in shadow, she saw the meie jerk erect and pull her macai to a stop.

Behind Dinafar a macai shrieked, a high hoarse scream that merged with two others as the mounts of the three men reared, twisted in convulsive heaves, shaking their riders loose, throwing them to the ground. Screaming, prodded to a mindless fury, the beasts turned on their masters and tried to trample them. One caught the Tercel in the throat with a hind claw and ripped his head off, sending it bounding across the glade into the shadows on the far side. A second landed on Lere's chest, stomping in his ribs, scraping loose long strips of cloth and flesh. Sten was agile enough to roll clear and scramble back onto his feet. He ran at Dinafar who sat gaping at the sudden carnage, too startled to move.

Off to one side the meie was fumbling at her weaponbelt with her bound hands, trying to unsheathe the knife and cut herself free. She looked up, saw what was happening. "Dina, get out of there."

Waking to her danger, Dinafar kicked her heels into the macai's side, but she was too late. Sten caught her skirt and wrenched her from the saddle. The breath knocked out of her when she hit the ground, she tried to claw his hands loose, but he was too quick for her blind fumbling attempt at self-defense. He held her down with his hand wrapped in her hair. She stopped struggling when she felt cold metal along her neck.

"Come off that, meie." Sten's voice was hoarse; he was afraid and furious, so furious his voice shook. "Knife. Belt. Drop them."

The meie slid off her mount. Her hands were free, the wisps of severed rope dropping away. She gazed down at the knife in her hand, then dropped it by her feet. Face empty, fingers shaking, she unbuckled the weaponbelt and stood in the broken circle, a haunted look in her eyes.

"Come here. No more tricks. I see one of those beasts move. . . ." The saber slid across Dinafar's shoulder, then down her arm to rest on her wrist. "I see anything funny and this girl got no more hand."

"I hear you," the meie said dully.

Sensing the little woman's pain, guessing it had something to do with the dead meie her friend, tired of being a passenger and a burden—tired of this to the point of folly—Dinafar cried, "No!" Using the long muscles of her thighs, she forced her body up, jerking her hand from under the saber's blade at the same time. Ignoring the pain in her head, she twisted around and drove her fingers at Sten's eyes, clawing bloody tracks in his face. He loosened his grip on her hair and leaned back, cursing, his hand coming away with bloody strands of black hair clinging to it. As Dinafar scrambled away and stumbled to her feet, Sten rose from his crouch to stand lightly balanced, his saber ready. He smiled. "Come on, bitch; I'm waiting."

Dinafar pressed her hand against her mouth as she watched the meie circle slowly about Sten. She must have taken a saber from one of the bodies while Dinafar distracted Sten; she held one now—and looked like a child playing with its father's arms, her short fingers barely able to circle the hilt, the weight and size of it looking too great for her thin arms to lift. Her face was intent as she concentrated on the man in front of her, staying just beyond his reach, watching, waiting. *Like that first Kappra,* Dinafar thought. *Teasing him until he made the mistake that killed him. She's going to kill this one too; he outreaches her, outweighs her, has to be three or four times as strong as she, but she's going to kill him.* Smoothing her hair back from her face with nervous hands, wincing at the pain of her torn scalp, she watched the death dance work out its slow wary patterns.

Sten lunged, beating the meie's saber aside with careless ease, the point of his blade cutting a small wound over her breast as she leaped back, a trickle of blood coming through the worn leather tunic. Her face didn't change. Sten attacked again, using his strength to beat her down; she drifted back, not trying to fight him, only watching and retreating. He chased her about the glade, trying to close with her, but she was too fast, dancing away from him with taunting ease, avoiding the bodies of the dead guards and other obstacles as if she had eyes in her feet.

Sten began favoring his right leg. *He injured it,* Dinafar thought, *when he fell off the macai.* She sank onto her knees staring at the circling duelers, absently brushing away the web of long hair blowing across her face. Sten faltered briefly; the meie twisted past his saber and cut at his arm, a small victory that cost her some blood as she flashed away. He began limping. Several times the meie managed to draw blood and get away unscathed, laughing each time, her mockery bringing the blood to his face, disrupting what rhythm he had left to his attacks, teasing him into attacking without thought. The last time, she stopped close to the headless body of the Tercel, her back to it. "One little woman," she taunted Sten. "Pretty mimkin, dance for me."

He lunged at her, forgetting the weakness of his leg, forgetting everything but the need to beat her down. She started to leap back, caught her heel on the Tercel's knee, fell back over the body. Horrified, Dinafar held her breath, her fists clenched on her thighs.

When she fell, Sten yelled his triumph, hopped another step, landing on his weakened leg. His right leg buckled as he put weight on it and he went down on one knee. Before he could move, the meie was back on her feet in a neatly executed roll. She leaped the Tercel, slashed at Sten as she flew past, her blow partly deflected by the saber he managed to bring up almost by instinct; then she was behind him, slashing again, the saber catching him in the neck, nearly cutting his head from his body. As he crumpled slowly over the Tercel's legs, she flung the saber away and knelt beside him, chanting softly the blessing of the dead.

Dinafar began to breathe again. The glade filled with peace. The macai were grazing placidly at the grass, the three men were flattened bodies bloodying the earth, the little meie murmuring over each the blessing of the dead. Dinafar wiped the sweat from her face, then looked up as she heard a soft hissing behind and above her. One of the traxim had dipped low and was gliding over her head. A moment later the black-furred wings were beating strongly as it circled up to rejoin the others. As she watched, a second trax folded its wings and dived toward the kneeling meie. "Above you," Dinafar screamed. "The trax!"

The meie looked up, rolled away just in time. The trax missed its strike, but the next one was coming, with another behind it. And another. She snatched up the discarded saber and flipped onto her feet with that beautiful controlled flexing of her body that Dinafar found hard to believe.

When the second bird struck at her, the meie slashed at it with the saber, battering it aside, drawing blood from one of the stubby legs. With a wild shriek, the bird flapped wildly and rose out of reach. A third attacked.

Dinafar looked about, saw the saber that Sten had used. She snatched it up and swung it awkwardly, trying to use point and edge as she saw the meie doing. The saber's weight surprised her; she was so clumsy with it she came near weep-

ing with frustration. Lowering the point till it rested on the
grass, she wiped at her sweaty face. The birds were swooping
down on the meie, battering at her, clawing for her face,
snapping at her, screaming their harsh ugly challenges. Dinafar hefted the saber, gritted her teeth and ran toward the
melee, intent on doing something, she didn't know quite
what.

Somehow the meie saw her and knew her intent. Gasping
out the words in bursts between saber slashes, she called,
"Dina . . . behind me . . . don't try . . . to cut . . . hold saber . . . point . . . up . . . Uh! Keep . . . em off . . . my back!"

Three of the birds were down, flapping about, attacking
legs with their needle-toothed beaks. Dinafar first tried to ignore them, then kicked at them as they chittered about her.
She did what the meie had said, held the saber up, steadying
it, trying to concentrate on this as she'd seen the meie concentrating, drawing out of herself strength she hadn't known
she had. Teeth began gnawing at her ankle once more. She
cried out, kicked, couldn't dislodge the bird. The meie cut off
the leg of an attacker, glanced around, exclaimed with disgust, cut through the bird's neck with a single vicious slash of
the bloody blade, then was back fighting off the others. Dinafar kicked away the severed head and lifted her saber higher,
trying to fight down her nausea as the black body at her feet
boiled and shivered, dissolving into goo and stinking black
vapors.

After a weary interval of noisy, smelly struggle, the last
two traxim broke off the attack and flew up to circle overhead. The meie watched them, her face grim. She kicked
away a grounded bird, dispatched it with a weary jerk of her
arm, jabbed the saber point into the earth and leaned on it,
breathing hard, blinking sweat from her eyes, frowning at the
pools of goo where the birds had been. With an exclamation
of disgust, she straightened and limped to her weaponbelt.
When it was buckled around her again, she closed the fingers
of one hand about the small sack dangling at one side, her
head tilted back as she watched the circling birds.

Dinafar kicked at a wounded trax snapping viciously at her
ankles. Clumsily, she brought the saber down on the stringy
naked neck. The trax squawked and hopped away, head wob-
bling, neck bleeding. "Can't kill the blessed things," she
groaned, lifted the saber again and chased the fluttering
squawking bird across the clearing, hacking ineptly at that
tough neck. She finally managed to bring the saber down

straight enough to slice through the rubbery flesh. Looking at
the bloody blade with disgust, she dropped it and limped
back to the middle of the clearing.

The meie was still gazing at the sky. Overhead the remaining traxim were chittering and floundering, obviously disturbed about something. As Dinafar gaped at them, they
circled the clearing a final time, then arrowed off toward the
north. "Why'd they do that?"

The meie relaxed, wiped the film of sweat off her face.
"They can't see me anymore."

"Oh." Dinafar frowned. "Huh?"

"Later." She stretched and groaned, rubbed at the back of
her neck. "Want one of those tabards to cover you?"

Dinafar looked down at her naked front and blushed.
Hastily she stripped Sten's tabard off, disgusted by the flaccid,
flopping body, pulled it over her head, shuddering at the
patches of blood on it. The meie smiled wearily. "We'll have
some clean things for you by tonight." She yawned. "Maiden
bless, I'm tired. Still, we can't stay here. Help me strip these
macai."

They left the bodies sprawled on the grass and rode back
into the shelter of the trees. Talking quietly at times about
little things, unimportant things, nothing personal, at times
silent and withdrawn, the meie led Dinafar along the winding
beast-runs in the growing heat and humidity of the advancing
day. By midafternoon they'd left the trees and crossed into
brush-covered hill country. An hour later they came on a
wide stream of clear cold water. They stopped to drink and
wash away layers of dust—the macain stirred up clouds of
red dust that settled into every crevice. The meie sank into a
heavy silence; Dinafar concentrated on hoarding her strength.
Both women rode on only because there was no place to halt.

Near sundown the meie pulled her mount to a stop and
leaned forward, listening intently. After a moment Dinafar
could hear a muted roar ahead; the stream beside her was
rushing over a cliff somewhere not far in front of them.

They stopped again at the rim of a shallow cliff, the stream
leaping out over it in a short fall, dissolving into mist at the
base then winding through a boulder-strewn bed toward the
Stenda forthouse and outbuildings tucked into one point of
the green and lovely valley spread in a broad triangle below
them. Most of the corrals attached to the barns were empty
except for dust-devils and blowing straw; in one a macai was
standing at a water-trough, one foot held protectively off the

ground, a foal nudging against her. The house itself was shuttered and still. The meie glanced anxiously at the sun, then began riding along the cliff, looking for a way down into the valley. Dinafar followed, hoping that the house meant rest and food.

THE CHILD: 6

Serroi gloomed in a nest of blankets. The cell was littered with dirty clothes and fragments of rotting food. The hands brought her two meals a day and once a week they hauled her to the tap in the center of the court, stripped off her filthy clothes and scrubbed her down. Cool and impersonal, they kept her reasonably healthy and preserved her for the Noris who seemed unready to discard her. For the rest, she was free to do as much or as little as she chose.

A papery rustle broke the heavy silence. She watched a large roach using its front legs to pull its long flat body from one of the many cracks webbing the side wall of the cell. As soon as it was free from the crack, it shook itself, rattled its wing cases, then sat a moment preening its feelers, ignoring her with splendid self-absorption. Its absurd airs surprised Serroi into a fit of giggles.

The roach scuttled back into the crack. When she sat very still, making no further sounds, it poked its head out, looked warily around, then came out of its refuge in a series of quick, angular movements and rested flat against the stone, feelers twitching, bright black eyes swiveling about with a clownish imitation of intelligence. A small fizzing escaped her in spite of her efforts to suppress her laughter. The creature arched its thready neck and seemed to stare at her with indignation. She settled back into her blankets, her laughter trickling into a comfortable series of chuckles.

The roach lifted briefly into the air on whirring, straining wings, circled clumsily, then landed beside a fragment of food on the floor. It twitched its wings back under the cases, waddled briskly about the inch-high crumb, finally walked its front legs onto the bread and perched that way, feelers twitching, head turning and turning until it was satisfied that no other creature lay in wait to snatch its food. Assured of this, it crouched beside the crumb and began eating. Serroi stretched out on her stomach, head propped on her hands, watching it nibble at the bread.

When the insect finished its meal and flew up onto one of

108

the bedposts where it sat like a conqueror general surveying
his new kingdom, Serroi eased out of bed and pulled on her
clothes, careful to make no sudden moves that might startle
her new companion. For the first time in days she felt impatient with herself and her surroundings.

Some months before the hands had brought her, unasked,
some cleaning materials, a broom, a scrub brush, an old
bucket, a jar of greasy soap—they were shoved in a corner,
untouched. She snapped off the jar's lid and dumped a fat
dollop of soap into the bottom of the bucket, wrinkling her
nose at its acrid smell. She glanced at the roach, giggled and
went out leaving the door open behind her.

All that morning she scrubbed at her dirty clothing, sloshing each piece in the soapy water, then slapping it hard on
the stone pavement as she'd seen her mother beat clothing
clean in northern streams. She even stripped off the things she
wore and washed them. Then she rinsed everything at the tap
and hung the clothing on the cages to dry.

When she went inside, the roach was crawling about on the
wall. It whirred to the bedpost, its tiny head moving back and
forth as she moved, watching her with bulging eyes as she
scrubbed the cell clean. It watched as she finished with the
floor and walls. Watched as she made up the bed with the
clean sheets and blankets piled forgotten on a shelf. Watched
as she struggled with her hair, washing it awkwardly, knocking over the bucket several times before she finished, leaving
the room awash with soapy water. Sat magisterially on the
bedpost as she used the brush to scrape the water out the
door.

While she waited for her clothing to dry, it moved about
on the wall, scuttling in and out of cracks like a small silly
roach-Nor moving within the fluid rock of its residence.
Much of the time, though, it sat on the bedpost, triangular
head cocked alertly, feelers twitching with fussy importance.

As the days passed, she began talking to the roach, telling
it stories, some she remembered from the long winter nights
in the vinat-hide tents on the tundra, others she'd read in the
Noris's scrolls. The slow movement of its head created the illusion of intelligent listening, allowing her a shadow sense
that she was doing something more than talking to herself.
Sometimes the hard memories crowded in on her and she
went back to huddling on the bed. On these days the roach
would come out of a crack and sit watching her with a look
of ancient dark wisdom; she knew it was illusion like the rest,

but as the moments passed she felt a deep calm flowing over her.

Growing tired of repeating her stories, she began making up new ones about the heroic adventures of a girl like herself and a giant roach. A girl she'd like to be, not the small trapped animal she was. They had magnificent adventures in a world spun out of dreams and the images she'd seen in the magic mirror.

As the long but no longer lonely winter crept toward its end, she felt a great change in herself. She began going outside, climbing over the cages, raiding them for their bits of wood and stone. Somewhere in the long days of dreaming, her wounds had skinned over. She no longer shied away from the empty cages. Her spirit had awakened, reborn, as the flowers and grass were reborn on the tundra after each killing winter. She piled her bits and pieces on the cage roof, but the best construction she managed left her hands a body length below the top of the courtyard wall. After her last try, she sat on the roof, dangling her feet over the edge, kicking them back and forth, wondering what to do next, ignoring the gathering and dripping of the fog that smothered her in greyness.

A darkness bloomed in the fog, rising like a black finger toward the sky. She watched idly, wondering what was happening. Towering above the north wall, the dark smoke swirled and billowed, softly solidifying into the form of the giant Nor with a black robe, pale face and hands. The misty figure lifted a hand and flung lightning at the tower. Serroi gasped. Hastily she slid over the edge of the roof and swung down the cage bars to the ground. When she looked up again, she saw a second smoke-Nor to the south. This figure hurled another bolt at the tower. It struck high on the side and split in half, traveling in a ring of light around the stone. Frightened, Serroi dived into the cell, slamming the heavy door on the attack.

All winter the walls of her cell had radiated a gentle warmth, keeping her alive and comfortable. As the days passed and the attack continued, the keep walls began to glow with heat, the fog condensing on them turning to steam in a constant sizzle-hiss and her hole in the wall became unbearable. Huddling in a sweaty heap on her bed, she looked around. The roach had disappeared somewhere, maybe the streams of moisture rolling down the walls had driven it off. *I can't stay here,* she thought. She mopped at her forehead, scraped straggling sodden hair off her face. *I can't stay here.*

Unhappy and afraid, she tossed the bucket out into the court, stood a moment watching it roll toward the tap. *Fog still. The sun's up out there somewhere.* She winced as the shadow figures stirred outside the walls, watched them glide about, meeting and parting, looming over the tower like thunderheads. Inside again, she rooted out all the blankets and sheets she could find, dumped them on the bed, and started searching for the roach. She searched for it a long time before she finally bundled blankets and sheets together and took them across the court to the large cage where the sicamar had prowled so restlessly last spring. Inside the cage there were tree forms and broad shelves molded from a fibrous stone that would insulate her from the burning and make living possible in that oven.

She spread one blanket out on the ledge where the sicamar used to sleep, tossed the rest of the things in a corner of the cage, hesitated in the open gate, flicking glances at the prowling figures, wondering as she did so why her Noris did nothing, walked quickly to the tap across paving stones that seared through the soles of her boots. She filled the bucket and ran back with it, clamping her jaws together to stand the sudden sharp pain in each step.

The day passed.

During the long night the walls glowed red-hot and the air in the court was near unbreathable. She was hungry. There was no food. The hands hadn't come all day, didn't come all night.

Throwing blankets and sheets ahead of her like stepping stones she crossed to the tap sometime after midnight—without the moons and the stars it was hard for her to tell. She danced up and down as the heat struck up through the blankets while she waited for the trickle of near boiling water to fill the bucket. To the north and the south she could still see the great figures of the Norim as solid columns of black. *Tomorrow is going to be bad,* she thought, and frowned at the tower, wondering once again why the Noris did nothing. *He's not afraid. He can't be afraid.* She glowered at the northern giant. *He'll come out when he's ready.*

Dawn. She kept shifting about as the padding heated beyond bearing. Twice she went for water. The day went on and on, interminably on and on.

And finally ended. The sun went down. The moons

bloomed for the first time in days, a long scatter of opaline discs and arcs over tower and court walls glowing a sullen red. Serroi drooped on her pile of charring blankets and tried to sleep. She wasn't hungry anymore; hunger pains had gone away, leaving behind dizziness and an extraordinary clarity of mind. She looked out through the bars at the northern giant standing still and formidable. *This is a challenge, a test of his power.* She moved a little, nearly toppled off the unsteady pile of blankets and sheets, sucked in her breath in a gasp of pain as one arm hit against the stone. Cuddling her arm in her lap she peered out at the shadow-giant. *He's afraid. They're both afraid. My Noris is letting them stand out there and stew. He's sitting in that horrible room with his beast-demons waiting until they begin to crack.*

After a while it seemed to her that the air was cooler. The stone behind her was decidedly cooler. Eventually she worried the blankets and sheets out over the ledge and stretched out to sleep.

At dawn she sat up, her head aching, her mouth dry, her lips cracking. She took the bucket and trudged across the cooling flags to the tap. When she pressed down on the hook the water gushed out more strongly than before—and drops splashed on her legs, cool drops. Laughing with delight, she put her hand in the flood; she splashed water over her face, shivered with pleasure in the easing of her own heat. She laughed again and lifted the bucket over her head, danced about as the cool clear water splashed down over her. She filled the bucket a last time and started back to the cage.

A booming laughter echoed across the sky. She set the bucket by her feet and gaped as the shadow giants glided around the tower, circling until they stood together in the east, glaring at something behind her. She swung around.

A third giant rose behind the tower. Her Noris.

Lightning crackled, sliced like crooked spears at him. He lifted a vast translucent hand and deflected the bolt casually into the sea as a greenish mist swirled up out of the tower, coiling round him until he was half-hidden in a pale shimmer the color of scum on a summer pond. He didn't bother moving when the shadow giant flung a second bolt at him. It struck the green and vanished—without a crackle or hiss or any sign of travail, it simply vanished.

Serroi watched fascinated, her soaked hair straggling into her eyes, her eye-spot throbbing painfully at the power that hummed in the air.

Lightning crackled and flew and was as damaging as a gentle spring rain. Things howled about her Noris, demons and firedrakes, gouts of water, other things she couldn't name, could scarcely admit to herself she saw. The Noris watched all this with a vast amusement and contempt. Nothing touched him. The attacks spattered against the green smoke and screamed into nonexistence.

The two images went transparent a moment, then they merged into one, thick and solid and dangerous, a terrible figure roaring out a triumphant howl that bounded across the sky and faded in multiple echoes. The giant raised its arms high. Between its hands a black cloud formed—a cloud that rippled and coiled, rose high, drew back, rose again.

Ser Noris moved back one step then another as the cloud flew at him. Watching with distress, forgetting her hatred in the excitement of the conflict, remembering only that she loved him, that he was father and mother and teacher, she pounded on her thighs, screamed her rage at the giant. Then she stared open-mouthed as a great translucent beast leaped into the sky to stand beside her Noris, snarling its challenge at the blackness—the chini-demon, glowing with a green far stronger than the aura surrounding the Noris. He bent, touched the demon's head, pointed at the billowing darkness.

The beast went leaping for the cloud, tearing it into harmless shreds, leaping through it again and again, worrying it, pawing at it, whirling round and round until the cloud was reduced to small fragments that melted into nothing. Growling, the hairs on its insubstantial spine standing up like tarnished copper wire, it stalked around the Nor-meld, caught the lightning flung at it in cruel yellow teeth, breaking it into sparkles of light that dropped in a glittering rain over the isle to melt into stone like bits of mist.

The meld hastily separated into its two components. They would have run but could not. Wherever they turned, the beast was there. They struggled, shrieking with pain, shooting out gouts of blackness like blood as the beast's teeth tore into their smoke bodies. Their struggles grew weaker and weaker, they were only trying to escape, but escape was not permitted. The image of her Noris grew stronger and blacker as the attackers faded, as if he was drinking in their strength. When they melted into nothing, he smiled. The beast-demon lifted its head and howled, then trotted back to its master. The Noris tugged at the demon's ears, scratched at the distorted skull, then both figures melted and the display was over.

Serroi breathed normally again. Kneeling beside the bucket, she scooped up handfuls of water and splashed it over her face and shoulders, over and over again until her shaking stopped. She drank, sniffed, drank again, then sat back on her heels. The red glow was gone from the tower; she looked at the charred wood of the cell door, rose slowly to her feet and walked to the tower. Biting her lip she jerked on the latch-hook and pulled the door open.

All that was left of the roach was its shiny wing-case and a few leg fragments. She picked up the case and stood holding it in her cupped palm. With a quick violent motion of her arm, she flung it out the door.

THE WOMAN: VII

Dinafar followed the meie along the gravel walk beside the shieldwall of sharpened logs, wincing as the small stones dug into her bare feet. They turned a corner and she saw double gates slightly ajar, a space between the two sides a man could just manage to squeeze through. "Why . . ." she began.

The meie flattened her hand on Dinafar's shoulder and urged her through the gap. "So the caretakers can sleep in their own beds." She pointed at a line of small houses backed up against the logs. They shared sidewalls and their common roof formed a platform about three quarters of a man-length below the top of the walls. Dinafar walked backward, staring wide-eyed at the courtyard with its patterned paving and neat little areas of kitchen greens outside each small house.

"Watch out for the well." The meie caught her arm and steered her around a low circle of stone in the center of the court. "The Stenda take down the sweep when they leave. The men still here must lower a bucket on a rope when they need water."

The house was built of logs as thick as those in the wall. The only windows on the facade were twenty feet over her head and stoutly shuttered. Beneath those windows hung a ten-foot shield carved and painted with the arms of the Stenda lordling who ruled this hold. Beneath this, deeply shadowed by the outthrust of the upper floors, was the main entrance, a place of ceremony and subtle boasting, three posts on each side, carved with the sigils of ancestry, male to the right, female to the left.

Dinafar climbed the three broad steps and stopped beside the meie who was examining that formidable door with weary interest. She glanced up, stared. The upper floors jutted out above her, an overhang about two feet wide with a marching row of plugged peepholes just visible in the thick wood flooring the overhang. She took another step and stood beside the meie frowning at the door. Three iron bars crossed in front of it, forming a black metal star whose ends disappeared into deep slots. A heavy chain was twisted about the point where the three bars crossed, fastened into place by a padlock that looked strong enough to resist a war-ax. She lifted it, exclaimed at the weight, let it clank dully back into place. "You'd have to burn the place down to get in."

"Think so?" Tired eyes twinkling, the meie bent and fished for a moment in the top of her boot. Twisting her head up, she went on. "You can't see any way inside?"

Dinafar tugged at the chain, grimaced, stepped back and scanned the front of the house. "Maybe around back."

The meie straightened. "First lesson. Enter a house through the door."

"Meie!"

"Seriously, little one." She opened her hand and showed Dinafar the thin steel probes crossing her palm. "The strongest point of a fortress can also be its weakest if you look at it in the right way." She knelt before the lock. "And use your head properly. Doesn't just apply to locks either." She slipped a probe in and began waggling it gently about. "This looks hard. Isn't. All you need is a key." Humming softly, she slipped a second probe in beside the first and moved it delicately about. "Or a substitute for that key. Ah." With a heavy clunk, the padlock dropped open. She slipped the probes back into their pockets inside her boot. With a hand from Dinafar, she got off her knees, worked the chain from the bars and collapsed them into their slots. "As you see. Nothing difficult about this." She pulled the door open and went inside.

Shaking her head, Dinafar followed. The air inside had a stale smell as if the Stenda had been gone a year, not a few days, and with the door closed there was very little light entering to lessen the murky darkness. "Meie?"

"Up here, Dina." The meie was looking down at her from a hole in the ceiling. She leaned out a little farther and slapped her hand against the wall. "Ladder. Climb it. I need you up here."

Dinafar pulled herself up a series of carved slats and emerged into a dusty twilight space between the inner and outer walls, a space wide enough for two men to walk along, side by side. "What's this?"

"Part of the defense system." The meie knelt beside a smaller trap half a pace out from the one they'd come through. She knocked back the heavy iron latch and hauled the plug up, exposing a narrow hole, somewhat broader than her shoulders and about half as wide. Dinafar nodded to herself as she recognized one of the peepholes she'd seen in the overhang. Their purpose became clear when the meie beckoned Dinafar over and pointed. "Look." The front door was just below. Defenders could take out anyone trying to fool with it.

The meie unbuckled her weaponbelt and set it aside, unclipped her bow and laid it beside the belt. "I'm going to put things back the way they were. You'll have to help me up afterwards. Think you can?"

Dinafar nodded. She looked down at her big hands and nodded again.

"Good." The meie dropped lightly in front of the door. She pulled the bars out and wound the chain back through and around them, snapped the padlock home, stepped back a little and looked up. "Stretch out flat up there, then drop me the bow strap, it's strong enough to hold my weight. Don't try lifting me; I think I can wiggle up on my own."

When Dinafar lowered the strap the little woman leaped, caught hold of it, climbed it hand over hand until she could catch hold of the opening. With a quick flexing of her agile body she was through the opening, sprawled beside Dinafar. Then she was on her feet slapping at her clothing, brushing the grit from her palms. She kicked the plug back in the hole, stepped back as Dinafar slid the latch home.

Dinafar sat back on her heels. "What now, meie?"

The meie leaned against the wall, her eyes closed. In the dim light Dinafar couldn't see her too clearly, but the dark shadows around her eyes and the lines of strain in her face were marked too strongly for Dina to miss. The meie sighed and pushed away from the wall. "I'd like to say sleep, but that's not a good idea. Bath first, have to be cold water, but that's all right." She drew the back of her hand across her eyes. "Clean clothes. You'll want to get out of that." Her fingers flicked at the bloodstained tabard. "Hot food washed down with pots and pots of cha." She yawned, smiled. "Come on, I know a bit about how these holds are laid out. Friend of mine was a Stenda." The last words were spoken in such a deliberately matter-of-fact way that Dinafar needed no telling who that Stenda was—the other meie, dead and eaten by traxim.

Bathed and fed and dressed in clean clothes, they sat at a kitchen work-table sharing a comfortable silence in a long pleasant room with a huge fireplace, dark red tiles on the floor, cast-iron and copper pans hanging from pegs on the walls. A steaming cha-pot at her elbow, the meie was repairing a torn rucksack while Dinafar sorted dried fruit and jerked meat into two piles beside small wax-covered cheeses and tins of cha leaves.

When she was finished she sat back and watched the meie drive the needle through the leather, pulling the stitches tight with quick twists of her hand. "Why do you call that a weaponbelt?" Leaning forward she rubbed her fingers over the series of small pockets. "Salve and soap, needles and thread, anything you happen to need. But no weapons."

The meie looked up, smiled. "It carries the sheath for my grace blade."

"That's nothing."

"I know." The little half-smile was back. "Patience a minute." She examined the rucksack, then tied off her thread and cut away the trailing end with the grace blade. "Finished." She patted a yawn, smiled drowsily at Dinafar. "Most meien carry swords." Another yawn. "Maiden bless. Unh. My teachers laughed me out of it, taught me the bow. And to use my head instead of the muscles I haven't got. Like this morning."

"You fell on purpose?" Dinafar opened her eyes wide. "You could have been killed."

"That's the point. You know it; he knew it in his bones and he let that knowledge color his actions, let his anger overwhelm his skill. I had a bit of luck when his leg gave, but I'd have gotten behind him without it and once behind him. . . ." She spread out her hands. "You see?"

Dinafar nodded.

"The head, Dina, will. . . ."

A noisy hammering on the front door accompanied by muffled shouts interrupted her. Lifting from her chair with a swift smooth surge, all the tiredness wiped out of her face, she buckled on her weaponbelt. Then she was out of the kitchen, running through the house to the front hall. Dinafar hurried after her, was just in time to see her vanish through the trap. Dinafar pulled herself up into the walkway. The meie looked up, touched a finger to her lips. She was stretched out on the floor, her head close to the peephole. Moving as quietly as she could, Dinafar stretched herself out on the other side of the hole.

The hammering stopped. She heard men moving about the court, kicking open the doors to the small houses. Two men came stomping up the steps and rattled the bars. Her heart in her mouth, Dinafar blessed the meie's cool head. If that door had been open—well she didn't like to think about that. She heard them moving about, then they stopped close beneath the peephole.

"What the hell, she ain' here. Ol' horny tooth up there say so."

"Damn fool. Want to tell the Son you didn't bother checking out the Hold?"

"Cai-shit, Cap'n. You know it. I know it. T'lads know it. Meie drownt herself in that hoor-storm t'other night. Ol' horny he got hisself a bellyache and had hisself a bad dream. What's Son want with her anyway? Scrawny thing they say; not worth wearin' down."

The other man just grunted.

Dinafar heard several macai hoots and the scratching of claws on the courtyard paving. The riders stopped by the stairs. "No signa anyone, Cap'n. Couple herders out with t'stock. Saw their tracks. T'other Stendam, they musta gone down to Oras."

"What about you, Winuk?"

"Same. Want we should go get the herders?"

"Trax up there, he say you're right. Gegger's Hold the next over, five mile south." The men's groans were heartfelt. "Ever think the Son's looking down at you now through them eyes?" Dinafar heard a soft slipping sound, a creak of leather, and pictured him waving a hand at the circling bird. The sudden silence brought snorting laughter out of him. "Move it, Seyderim. We got half a day yet."

When the noise of their passage faded, the meie pushed herself up until she was kneeling and staring into the dimness beyond Dinafar's shoulders. "Sankoy," she whispered. "The Intii hinted at it. Sankoy."

"Meie?" Dinafar scanned the drawn face, worried by the hopelessness in it. Maybe she was just tired, but the meie sounded like she was ready to give up. "They didn't find us."

The meie pressed her hands against her eyes, sighed, dropped them onto her thighs. "Those men were the High Teyn's Berseyders from Sankoy, Dina. Berseyders being run by a Son of the Flame doing the work of a Nor from Oras. Maiden bless, Dina, I didn't know how big this is, Lybor and her feeble plots, she hasn't a glimmer . . ." She rubbed at her eyes, yawned. "Ay-ii, I'm tired."

"It's getting late. Why don't we spend the night here?"

The meie sat without answering, one hand draped across her eyes, then she got wearily to her feet. "No. There's no time. I want to make the Highroad early tomorrow; we need to keep moving as long as there's light to see by." She turned and started for the ladder.

Dinafar chewed on her lip. There was too much she didn't understand but she knew enough about exhaustion to see that the meie was traveling on will alone. *My, I'm not going so good either.* She stretched her legs out in front of her, rubbed at her aching knees. *It doesn't make sense, leaving here. She's let her need blind her understanding as bad as the Kappra and those guards. I have to make her see. . . .* She climbed down the ladder and hurried after the meie, catching her near the kitchen; she touched her arm and the meie swung around a frown on her small face. Dinafar licked her lips. "It's only an hour or two lost, meie. How much difference can an hour or two make?"

The meie's eyes flashed gold fire as she jerked her arm free, wheeled and stalked away. In the doorway she turned again. "We leave in half an hour. Be ready."

Dressed in the clothes the meie had found for her, Dinafar walked slowly into the kitchen, uncertain of the mood she'd find the meie in. The little woman's back was to the door. She'd taken off the weaponbelt—it lay in a broken circle on the table beside the two stuffed rucksacks. She wore black wool trousers stuffed into her boot tops, a loose white shirt whose sleeves were too long; she was fumbling with the wrist knots, finding this more awkward and difficult than she liked. When she spat out an impatient oath, Dinafar grinned and went to tie the strings for her. The meie smiled wearily. "Thank you, Dina. Sorry I snapped at you."

Dinafar grimaced. "You know what I think, meie."

"I know." The meie slipped her arms into a boy's vest, settled the heavy russet cloth down over her body. "If the stakes weren't quite so high, you'd be right." With a grimace of distaste she fitted a boy's leather cap over her head, tucking in her sorrel curls.

Dinafar looked at her, started to speak, then pressed her lips together.

Orange laughter danced momentarily in the meie's eyes. "Green skin," she said. "Makes a joke of any disguise, doesn't it?"

"Well. . . ." Dinafar looked down at the red tiles. "Anyone seeing you, meie, has to know you."

"Don't worry about it, Dina. Before we reach the Highroad I take care of that detail too." She touched the bow that lay beside the sacks, sighed and shook her head. "This too. I'll have to leave it somewhere." She stroked her hand along the smooth curve of the upper limb. "Perhaps I can come back for it sometime." She took the bow and arrow case and dropped them onto the pile of blankets and groundsheets. "Everything's ready. We'd better get out before the caretakers come in."

"What about that?" Dinafar pointed to a waxy button in the center of the table.

The meie grimaced. "Tarr." She went slowly to the table and picked up the grey-green bud. "You're right, Dina." Dropping into a chair, she leaned her head back and closed her eyes. "I'd fall off if I tried riding." Her voice slurred with her fatigue. "My teachers wanted me to study herbs and be a heal-woman, they said I had a talent for it. I didn't want to, it was too close to . . . never mind. Have you heard of the Biserica heal-women, Dina?"

Dinafar sat on the front edge of a chair, wondering if she was expected to answer; if she kept very still the meie might talk herself to sleep. She looked up, met the drowsy orange-gold gaze. "No, meie. But we didn't get much outside news in the village."

The meie's eyelids dropped again; her short slim fingers played idly with the grey-green bud. "South of the mijloc there's an island chain; barren rocks most of them, but the largest has a spring and lots and lots of little scraggly bushes." Dinafar could barely make out the words they were so blurred and slow. She smiled to herself, suppressed the smile when she saw the meie looking at her.

"Think you're smart, don't you. Won't work, my girl." The meie yawned, then fumbled the bud into her mouth. She chewed a moment, swallowed, shut her eyes. "Every spring those bushes produce these tasty little buds." Her mouth twisted into a wry half-smile. "Addictive and dangerous. But. . . ." She straightened, her eyes brightening, color returning to her pale face. "But, my tricky young friend, for the next five hours, I'll have my strength back." She stood. "Let's go. Get yourself an armful and follow me."

THE CHILD: 7

Seven days passed, slow and painful days for Serroi. She sat in the center of her bed staring at the walls until she could stand looking at them no longer, went out of her cell into the court, wandered aimlessly about, touching the bars of the empty cages, staring into the sky, going round and round, looking for something, she didn't know what, empty and aching. She touched the door to the court, stroked her fingers over the cold metal surface. She wanted . . . she wanted . . . she wanted the magic mirror and her book scrolls. She wanted to sit with the Noris and feel his hands caressing her hair. Yet—if he touched her, she would knock his hand away and run from him, she knew that. She wanted things to be the way they were—and they could never again be the way they were.

The hands came back on the morning after the battle, bringing hot food to her cell. She felt no hunger, sat staring at the steaming food. After a while she forced the first mouthful down. Hunger returned; she ate everything they brought.

Except for bringing her food, they left her alone those seven days. On the eighth day, they came back, hustled her to the cell, cleaned her hair—not with the bucket, cold water, harsh soap, but with a scented cream they worked into her hair then rubbed gently out with soft white towels, working with infinite patience until her hair was falling about her shoulders, bright and clean, coiling into masses of fleecy curls with red sparks in the brown. They brushed her hair until it gleamed and coiled in soft curls about her scowling face. She let them work because there was no way to stop them, though she sat staring at the floor unhappy and angry. There was only one reason they would bother so with her. "I won't go to him," she whispered. "I won't." Tears in her eyes, she tried to pull away from the hands, but they wouldn't let her go.

When the hands were gone, she ran out into the court. She would have bathed in mud but the battle fire had burned the courtyard clean. Yelling in anger, she ran about the court, found handfuls of ash where straw had been laid down in the cages. She rubbed the ash into her shining hair, feeling a flare of triumph, a flare that quickly faded into her former restless unhappiness.

On the ninth day her boots were gone when she woke. In their place were dainty silk slippers. She caught them up and threw them across the room. They bounced unharmed from the wall and fell to the floor with soft plops. She banged the door open, kicked the slippers out into the court, ran out after them and stood glaring up at the tower. "I won't," she screamed. After trying to pull a slipper apart with her hands, she hung it on the door's latch. Hanging onto the slipper, she lifted her feet and swung about until the silk ripped. She fell, bruising herself, fell again until the shoes were tattered fragments. She gathered them up and threw them into the center of the court. "I won't," she shouted. Later, the hands came, collected the fragments and cleaned her hair again.

On the tenth day her clothing was gone, even though she'd bundled trousers, tunic and belt under her and slept on them. On the hook where she usually hung her clothing was a white robe made of a soft clinging wool finer than anything she'd seen before. She crawled out of bed, touched it, hated it, reluctantly loved it. A cold emptiness inside her, she used the latchhook to shred the soft fabric. When she was finished she sat naked and defiant on the bed, her hands closed into fists on her skinny thighs. "I won't go to him. I don't want to go to him. I don't. Maiden help me, I don't."

The hands came, took the tatters away, brought food, then began working on her body. They rubbed creams into the rough spots and bruises, washed her, cleaned her, polished her as they would a badly used piece of fine furniture. They brushed her hair, brought another robe, more slippers from her feet, forced her to let herself be dressed. As soon as they were gone, she tore the clothing off, carried it into the center of the court, brought handfuls of ash and turned the water on full force. She rubbed the ash into the wet soft material and left the sopping mess by the tap and went back to sit naked and filthy on her bed.

On the eleventh day the hands washed her and creamed her skin, dressed her again. When she tried to rip off the robe, they slapped her hands away, held her wrists when she struggled. All morning she sat in the middle of her neatly made bed, glowering at nothing. When the hands brought her midday meal, she managed to upset the cha pot over herself. The hot liquid scalded her but she ignored the pain.

There was a pause in the activity of the hands as if they sighed impatiently. Then they cleared up the debris, brushed her rather roughly and left. She kicked off the dainty slippers so violently that they bounced off the wall. Ignoring the cling of the soggy robe, she ran out into the court, made a face at the keep, then climbed up the cages, swung over the protruding roof, scrambling frantically for a moment on the splintery shingles, then sat in the middle of the gentle slope to catch her breath. The Nor-battle had damaged the shingles and the supporting beams so the roof creaked under her slight weight whenever she moved.

She looked at the scattered pieces of dead wood she'd hauled up here almost a year ago. When the roof shifted slightly with a shift of her weight, she realized she could not build her pyramids again. She frowned over her shoulder at the wall, the brown-black stone glistening in the sunlight, shivered, turned to glare at the tower. *If I give in even a little, he'll swallow me. I won't let him . . . won't . . .* She tugged her robe over her knees. *Something to hook over the wall . . . rope? Wall cap is too smooth? What?*

Underneath her attempts to think out an escape, the refrain went on and on. I can't. I can't. I dare not. I can't. Like a blood-drum the beat went on. I can't. I can't.

A rope . . . something to catch . . . that bit of branch. She crawled about the pile of debris. A branch like a fishhook as big as she was shoved up against the wall; she tugged at it, trying to break it. To her satisfaction she found the seasoned wood almost as tough as the stone in the walls. She glanced back at the tower. "I'll beat you yet, Ser Noris. You wait."

For three days after that, the hands didn't come; Serroi wondered if she was being left to starve or simply being punished. She didn't allow herself to think about him, just concentrated on her preparations for escape. She tore sheets into strips and braided them into a rope, working new strips in until she had twenty feet of line. When she tied off the end, she pulled and twisted the rope, testing the length for weak spots. As soon as she was satisfied with it, she coiled it over her shoulder and stepped out into the court, rubbing at aching eyes. The shadow was deep in the courtyard, the sun floating just above the western wall. She drank from the tap, stretched and groaned, then walked to the cages.

Once on the roof she dragged the branch along the creaking shingles to the corner where the roof seemed to be in the best condition. She knotted the rope about her waist then to the long section of the branch. Bracing herself, feet wide apart, she swung the limb back and forth then heaved it as high as she could.

The branch bumped against the stone then fell back, almost knocking her from the roof. She dropped carefully to her knees, her heart bumping painfully. Three days without food had weakened her more than she'd realized. Head swimming, trembling all over, she tried again, a desperate expenditure of all the effort she could gather. This time the branch went over the wall, though with less than an inch to spare. She heard the dull clunk of the wood as it banged against the outside of the wall, felt the tug of the cord at her waist, saw the taut white line running from her middle to the wall and over. She tried to feel triumphant but inside there was only grief. Hands shaking, she began pulling at the line, hauling her improvised grapnel back up. *It has to catch, has to. . . .* The end came up over the wall, hesitated, then flattened out as the side branch that formed the hook caught and held.

She edged up to the wall and tugged at the rope. It held. She threw her weight on it. It held. After she untied the end from her waist, she reached up as high as she could and began climbing. About two feet off the shingles she felt a sickening lurch and stopped climbing. When she looked up, she saw that the branch had slipped a little. She hung a moment, teeth clamped on her lower lip, then she snorted in a deep breath and pulled herself higher. The branch held. She drew her feet up, reached again.

The branch came flying away from the wall, dropping her heavily onto the roof. The shingles cracked under the sudden weight and she went through to her hips. Slowly, painfully, she pulled herself from the hole, splinters forced into her flesh by her efforts. She lay out flat, close to the edge. Below, on the flags she could see the broken branch and the white coils of braided rope. She couldn't cry; she was too exhausted, hungry and discouraged to cry. She started at the stone paving twenty feet below, wondering dimly if she should simply let herself fall, but even at the depths she didn't seriously consider this, it would be the admission of defeat more profound than she was willing to admit. As long as the Noris lived, she'd fight him. She had to.

As the sky darkened, she sat up. She ripped off the stained

robe, got recklessly to her feet, not caring much what happened, balled the robe into a damp compact bundle and threw it at the top of the wall with all the strength in her small arms. Caught by a rising thermal it sailed over the top and disappeared. She stood with her hands on her hips and laughed until the breath caught in her throat, then she swung over the edge of the roof, kicked about until her legs wrapped around a cage bar. She climbed down and wandered about the court, drank at the tap, the cold water making her empty belly ache, splashed water over her face and body, mounted the stairs and beat on the door, took a last kick using the heel of her foot to make the door boom. Finally she went to lie down in the slowly evaporating pool of water by the tap, staring at the night sky with its dusting of stars and string of many-sized moons, willing a bird to fly past, anything alive. Anything at all to break her solitude.

On the fifteenth day, the hands came back. They fed her, washed her, dressed her, manicured hands and feet, brushed her hair to a high gloss, then stayed near her, watching—if invisible hands could be said to watch—to make sure that this time she found no way to spoil their work.

About midmorning they took hold of her arms and urged her out of the cell. She resisted, refusing to walk, lifting her feet from the ground, struggling against the grip on her arms, flinging her body about. "I won't go to him," she screamed.

They lifted her clear of the floor and carried her through the door and across the court. The slab of bronze in the tower wall opened smoothly ahead of them and they carried her inside, all the way into the great bright room she'd seen on her first day in the tower. A table had been placed against one wall with several chairs tucked under it. The hands pulled out a chair and dumped her in it, forcing her back when she tried to scramble out. She kept them busy trying to restrain her until the Noris entered the room.

He came quietly around the table and stood beside her. "Be quiet, Serroi."

Frightened and confused by the music of his voice, something she'd forced herself to forget, she clung to her determination to resist without let-up. Tears in her eyes, she spat up at his face.

He jerked his head back then stretched out a hand. One of the invisible servants floated a handkerchief to him. He wiped his face and dropped the kerchief to the floor. The servant picked it up and whisked it out of sight. The Noris caught her face in one long-fingered hand, forcing her to meet his eyes. Black and shiny, they grew and grew until she could see nothing else. Her arms fell limp into her lap. Her legs hung down without moving. She slumped in the chair, passive as a rag doll. He turned a chair around and sat facing her, frowning a little.

She stared hate at him and nearly wept when he looked troubled. "I don't understand you," he said. "Why do you keep fighting me, Serroi?" He rose with the controlled grace that pleased her without her willing it. "I thought we shared a common goal. It's not logical, the way you're acting. You can't hope to win." His face went hard. He glared at her, but at that same moment his hand reached out and pulled gently at one of her curls.

She tried to slide away but her body was taken from her control. She was helpless. Tears gathered in her eyes. "No," she breathed. "I won't give in. Never. Not ever." She sat, glowering at him.

The Noris stood over her, a black column against the pearly light. Five pale fingers swam in front of her blurring eyes. His voice came from a vast distance, whispered music. "Your hand, child."

For a moment the words echoed in her head making no sense to her; when they did, she refused to move, then cried out with frustration as her hand moved on its own, reaching up to meet his. He knew her too well, had learned too much from her—and she was fighting her own needs as furiously as she fought him. His hand closed over hers. She wanted that touch so much and feared it so deeply that her stomach convulsed, flooding her mouth with sour yellow fluid which burst from her lips and spilled onto her robe.

The Noris jerked away with an exclamation of disgust. He stepped back and stood brooding down at her while the hands brought fresh clothing and cleaned her up. When he took her hand again, he spoke a WORD that crackled through the pearly light and shivered it into darkness. Abruptly they hung side by side in a blue-green glow.

Water. They were deep under the surface. She panicked, but her body was clamped in place. After a moment she calmed as she found herself breathing without pain, floating like a fish in the water. The Noris's hand left hers and she was drifting about as his WORD shook the water about her. She dived and flew through the water like a strange fish, the

Noris forgotten behind her. She curved her body and
swooped in a grand spiral, silent laughter bubbling out of her,
filling the blue water with silver bubbles that tickled her when
she swam through them. A long blue-grey fish with a white
belly swam out of the blue and arched with her in her joyous
flight. The large dark eyes sitting forward in its head were
warm and friendly. As it swam under her, she caught hold of
the fin in the middle of its back and rode astride as the fish
danced with her, taking her down and down, then up to the
surface, bursting through the barrier film for a golden moment that piercing agony in her lungs; then they were back
again in cool blueness.

The summons came, twisting through the water, pulling
them back and back to something she'd forgotten but remembered as terror. A dark figure drew them, fishes on a single
hook. She tried to uncramp her fingers from the fin and kick
the fish away from her. She couldn't. She was bait to trap this
fish. Bait. She saw and remembered the Noris then, and knew
she was bait tossed in the water to catch this particular fish.
She lay along its strong muscular back, felt the knobs of the
spine moving under her, whispered soundlessly, I'm sorry,
sorry, sorry.

The fish hung in the water in front of the Noris, its body
moving slowly as it adjusted automatically to the slight tug of
a sluggish current. Serroi tried to move, but could not, lay
stretched out along the fish, struggling to lift her head, keeping it turned so that the eye-spot did not touch the fish anywhere. The Noris drifted closer. His hands curved with
terrible gentleness about her head and eased it down until her
face was flat against the slippery skin, her eye-spot pressed to
the fish's spine. The Noris's hand continued to rest gently on
her head as he used her to reach into things he would have
no access to otherwise, into the life-affirming forces. The cool
water that bathed her and sustained her began to stink and
thicken as she tried to fight him away. Things came swimming around, circling around her as she lay on the fish's
slowly rotting body, beautiful translucent things that thickened and rotted with the water, that came slowly to the Noris
and submitted to him. When he touched them, they black-
ened, were whole again, but whole in another way, solid
black, shiny, filled with a terrible energy and slaved to the
Noris. The water grew stiffer, blacker until everything was
dull black. . . .

When Serroi woke, she was in her old room, lying in a dainty bed, a new bed. There was a Sankoy rug like a woven sunrise on the floor. Chairs, familiar bookscrolls, a line of robes pegged on the wall, paper and pens on a familiar table, an alabaster lamp. The magic mirror. She lay in silken sheets, wore a brief silken shift. Dazed for a moment, she lay blinking at the splendor, then memory came rushing back and she scrambled out of the bed. With a scream of rage, she pulled the lamp off the table and slammed it to the floor, laughing wildly at the resounding crash and the skitter of alabaster fragments over the brilliant rug. Hoarse with anger, she tugged hangings down, tracked bloody footprints into the priceless rug, stripped sheets and quilts off the bed, more blood on the rug as she ran heedlessly over the alabaster fragments. When everything she could lift or tug down was piled in a tattered heap on the rug, she ran to the window.

The tower fell away beneath her, straight down to the sea far below as the cliff continued the line of the wall. For a long time she watched the water curling around the rocks, the white-tipped waves a painful reminder of what had happened. Finally she went back to the mess on the floor, rolled up the rug, stuffed the awkward bundle through the window. She leaned out and watched it turn over in the air, spewing fragments of glass and fabric, splatting finally in the surf to bob up and down or paste itself in sections against the jagged rocks. After a moment more she turned away, padded to the bed, leaving more bloody footprints on the naked floor. She crawled up onto the mattress and sat with her legs crossed, glowering at the door, waiting for the hands to come.

THE WOMAN: VIII

The double line of small fires went north and south as far as Serroi could see. "I didn't quite expect this," she said quietly. She tugged at the strap of the boy's cap as the bright dots blurred then steadied. The Tarr was beginning to wear off. She straightened her back and looked around.

"What are those fires?" Dinafar sounded awed.

"Pilgrim campfires. Along the Highroad. On their way to Oras, walking, I imagine."

Clouds were gathering overhead. The first half of the Gather was up over the horizon and still free of cloudcover, touching the hillsides with silver light. The moon-knot was pulling tighter. For a moment Serroi was tempted to renew her energy with another Tarr button and keep riding. There was certainly enough light. *No time, no time,* she thought. She looked to the North. *A day and a half riding, longer if I walk. And there's Dinafar to deal with.* She looked at the girl beside her. "Dina."

"Yes, meie?"

"The Highroad goes south almost the whole way to the Biserica valley. You could be there in half a passage, twenty days of steady riding. There and safe." She waited for questions, but Dinafar was silent, watching her. "The other way, that goes to Oras. You've seen the danger I'm in. Go south, little one. Knock at the Biserica gates, they'll take you in. You don't need me anymore—if you ever did."

"I'm going with you." In the moonlight Serroi could see Dinafar's face take on its sullen, stubborn scowl. "If you won't take me with you," she went on, "I'll follow you."

Serroi shivered. "We'd better camp." She scanned the hillside below. There was a small grove of brellim about a quarter of a mile ahead. "There," she said, pointing.

They tied one groundsheet on a slant against the wind and spread out their blankets on the other after Serroi weighted it down with a few rocks, some of the many dredged up by the brellim's mobile roots. As Dinafar gathered wood for the fire, Serroi unsaddled the macain and turned them loose to graze.

They worked in silence, putting aside the quarrel that lay between them until they'd eaten.

The fire had burned down to coals. Serroi shook the cha pot, poured the last of the liquid into her cup. Then she crossed to her blankets and settled down under the slant of the groundsheet. She sipped at the cha and looked down at Dinafar lying beside her.

"Five days ago. . . . Maiden bless, only five days . . . five days ago my shieldmate and I were part of the Doamna's guard in Oras." She rubbed at her eyes and drank some cha. "The Doamna, Domnor Hern's head wife, Floarin, a royal bitch. Tayyan . . . Tayyan was a mountain lord's niece. A Stenda. Her father taught her a boy's skills and a love for racing macain." She smiled. "A racing macai would make our pair look pale. She loved those savage, near intractable beasts with a passion no one could beat out of her and sneaked away to races whenever she could, even after our training was done and we were sent out on ward."

Dinafar wriggled around until she was lying on her back, her legs drawn up, her hands laced behind her head. "I don't see . . ." she began, then pressed her lips together, blushing because she dared to interrupt.

Serroi lifted a hand. "I know. I ramble. It's the drug, I think. I hope. Never mind, I'll get on with the story. Five days ago, just about this time. . . ." She flicked her fingers at the fragments of sky visible through the leaves. "When we were going off duty, Tayyan pulled me aside. She'd heard about a macain race, an illegal one, held outside the city walls. The Sons of the Flame had managed to shut down all the races at the arena, called them incitement to sin. For some reason, I didn't know what at the time, Morescad had ordered all the meien warding at the Plaz confined to their quarters for the night. Tayyan wanted me to go with her, said Morescad was a stiff idiot with bone for a brain and no reason to order the meien curfewed except he didn't like us. She said she didn't see any reason to obey him. She'd met one of her father's old riding mates. A distant relative. And he'd told her of the race. As I said, she loved the racing macain and she hadn't seen a good race for a long time. She was determined to go. I let her persuade me. We went out of the Plaz through the Doamna's private garden and over the wall into the stables on the far side." Serroi sighed and turned away, watching red run across black on the dying coals. "At least she had that. It was a good time. We came back into the city drunk with much wine and more excitement."

They clattered over the cobbles, Tayyan excited and counting her winnings, Serroi quiet and increasingly disturbed. Her eye-spot throbbed uneasily and she had a sense of impending disaster.

"Here." Tayyan caught Serroi's hand. "This is yours." She dropped coins into the small palm and closed short fingers over them. "I put down a couple of decsets for you."

Serroi shook her head. "You know I don't play those games."

"You'll spoil no sport tonight, little worrier." Tayyan lifted her hands to the gathering clouds, yawned and groaned with the pleasure of stretching stiff muscles.

Serroi walked several minutes in silence, then she sighed and put the coins in her money sack. "Thanks," she said.

They continued in silence until they came to the bulk of stone that was the Domnor's Plaz. The Plaz stable backed against the outer wall, close to a small, seldom-used door. Serroi and Tayyan stopped across the street. While Tayyan waited, Serroi probed for guards. "Nothing," she whispered. "Come on."

They climbed the pole gate, both of them having some difficulty with balance, Serroi grimly concentrating, Tayyan full of giggles and nonsense until they both nearly tumbled in the thick macai muck in the corral. They slogged through the muck, weaving unsteadily around the sleeping macain, then started fumbling through the dusty vines tumbling down the wall. "Hey, where's the rope?" Tayyan's hoarse whisper sounded loud even over the increasing wind. "Maiden's breasts, windrunner, what the hell'd you do with the rope?"

"Shh," Serroi hissed. "Wake the macai. Wake ol' Morescad." She jerked at the vines, sneezing as the leaves dropped dust and pollen around her. "Must be here. Who'd wade through that slop but a pair of idiots like us?"

Tayyan looked briefly offended, then she giggled and lifted a filthy boot. "Wash it off in Floarin's pool. Wonder what the royal cow'll think when she gets a whiff of its new perfume."

"Unh." Serroi shook the rope free of the vines. "You first or me?" Taking Tayyan's snort for an answer, she started climbing, making hard work of it as the wine fumes wheeled in her head.

They got up the rope with whispered curses and slipping

boots then slid down into the garden. Serroi started to shake
loose the grapnel and pull the rope in. Tayyan tried to drag
her away, but she jerked loose, stumbling back into a
pleshtree, bringing overripe fruit down around her. While
Tayyan watched, swaying and grinning, Serroi scraped a dollop of plesh off her front. "My rope, it's my damn rope, you
grinning beanpole," she hissed. "Be damned if I leave it hanging there."

"Scrap." Grinning still, Tayyan forgot her impatience,
stalked regally over to the shallow bathing pool and splashed
into it, sloshing about while Serroi reeled in the rope and tied
it back on her weaponbelt. Serroi watched the lanky form
dancing about, kicking up noisy gouts of water, then she ran
unsteadily to join her shieldmate, gloom forgotten for the moment. They splashed about in the pool, clutching at each
other, giggling at the thought of the dignified Floarin's rage if
she ever discovered what they'd done.

When the clouds began to obscure the moons Serroi
shivered and climbed back onto the grass. Tayyan was quieter also, the wine beginning to wear off. The two meie looked
at each other, sighed, climbed out of the pool, and walked
silently toward the guarddoor. Abruptly Serroi clutched at
Tayyan's arm, halting her. "Someone coming," she hissed. "I
feel. . . ." Her eye-spot was throbbing crazily and the stink of
danger was thick in her nostrils. "Bad," she murmured. Tayyan grew quiet and alert, the years of training clicking on.
The meien faded into the dense shadow of the shrubbery,
watching as two dark figures came through the small door in
the outer wall and strode across the patch of grass toward the
Plaz.

Serroi touched the hilt of Tayyan's sword. Tayyan shook
her head. They were in no position to challenge anyone.

The two men stood a moment in front of a section of wall
then seemed to melt into the stone. The meien waited a
dozen heartbeats then raced across the grass to that portion
of the wall where the men had stood. Serroi touched her eye-
spot, raised her brows. Tayyan nodded, a sharp assenting jerk
of her head. "Catch them inside," she breathed, then she
giggled softly. "Hanky-panky in the harem."

"Hush." Serroi felt along the wall until her eye-spot
throbbed. She pressed hard and felt a slice of stone tilt under
her fingers. Behind it there was a hollow with a T-bar protruding from the back. She twisted the end of the T.

With a whispery scrape, a section of the wall swung inward. Tayyan pushed past Serroi as she hesitated, unable to summon any of her shieldmate's glee to lighten the foreboding that was a cold hard knot in her stomach. Shaking her head, she followed Tayyan into the darkness.

For an eternity they twisted through the dusty passage lit at long intervals by guttering candles, their flames flickering in a sourceless draft. Serroi concentrated on moving soundlessly, cold with fear and with the certainty of disaster ahead; she had no thought of arguing Tayyan out of this; she knew too well her shieldmate's stubbornness when her curiosity was aroused.

In spite of her caution she almost bumped into Tayyan as she turned a sharp corner. Her shieldmate crouched by a break in the wall, peering through peepholes in a heavy door. She tapped Tayyan on the shoulder, braced herself on one hand and pushed her head against Tayyan's and peered through one of the holes.

Four people inside. She saw three of them as fluttering shadows, her eyes fixing on one. A Nor. She pulled away and leaned her forehead against the cold stone, colder than the stone. A Nor. She pressed her hand to her mouth, swallowed, tried to steady her breathing. She looked at Tayyan; her shieldmate's body was a taut arc, she was breathing quickly through her mouth. Serroi closed her eyes a moment, then forced herself to look again.

The room was square and small, walls covered by heavy tapestries woven into erotic scenes that brought a blush to her face. Her eyes slipped hastily over the Nor, then came back to him. Even as she shivered with fear she knew he was one of the lesser Nor, a street Norid or a fifth-rank Norit. That didn't matter, he still dominated the room, making the others look like paper cutouts. He was a thin man with red-brown skin and stiff black hair, his narrow body clad in a seamless black robe that hung from his bony shoulders and reached his ankles without touching flesh. Her stomach churned and she shook until she couldn't trust herself so she turned from him and examined the others in the room.

Lybor. Domnor Hern's second wife. A tall Stenda woman, richly blonde with the pale petal skin of the highborn and the soul of an adder, as Serroi know only too well, having suffered her tongue for the length of her ward. Lybor had a gift for finding her weakest spot and twisting a knife in it. She sat in the throne chair at the foot of a curtained bed. Her shadow and confidant, Picior the poisonous, stood beside her,

her deepset blue eyes dull and unreadable, her twisted wrinkled face uglier than ever. She was wearing a different robe, a black tube much like the Nor's robe, a silver flame in a circle appliquéed on the front, riding a slant as her high pot belly pushed against the black cloth. *A Follower of the Flame, Maiden bless, I didn't know.*

Morescad stood on Lybor's other side. Morescad the General. Serroi caught her breath, understanding now the reason for the curfew; he wouldn't want meien or anyone else wandering around loose. Advisor to the Domnor. Lord general of the Army. Head of the Domnor's Plaz. Head of the Noses, the men who threaded the land sniffing out trouble. Serroi wrinkled her nose. There was a sensual arrogance that oozed out of his voice, eyes, stance, whenever he spoke to her or any of the other meien technically in his charge. Something about her seemed to fascinate him. More than once he'd stroked his fingers over her forehead like a man casually caressing a pet animal.

Lybor touched her upper lip with the back of her forefinger, then ran the finger along the curve of her eyebrow. "You came to us offering your services, Ser Nor. This frail one wonders why." Without waiting for the Norid's answer, she lowered her blue eyes, then raised them suddenly to his. She smiled. Small hollows flirted in her cheeks. "Welcome, Ser Nor." Her voice was dark music. Serroi felt herself responding to its caress in spite of what she knew; she could see the Norid softening, although he controlled himself immediately. Lybor smiled again and held out her hand. "You honor us."

The Norid touched her fingers briefly. Bowing his head, he said, "Doamna, one who has services to sell seeks the highest market that suits his wares." He straightened. "You are displeased with the Domnor."

Lybor turned to Picior and stared into the dull blue eyes for a long moment, nodded and swung back to face the Norid. "Hern's a fool." She drew the tips of her fingers slowly along the smooth stone of the chair arm. "A fat little fool who lets scum walk over him. He laughs at me when I try to demand respect from the mud working in the woman's quarters. He doesn't care about anything but his food and some new little bitch he's hot for." She smiled at the Norid. "You know what we want, Ser Nor; you knew before you came to us, I'm sure of that. Strings to pull to make Hern look like a man. Strings to make him do what we want."

Again she touched her upper lip, let her finger slide along the lovely line of her jaw. "For the good of the mijloc, Ser Nor."

Morescad stirred beside her. "For the good of the mijloc," he repeated, contempt in his dark eyes. He smiled and dropped his hand on Lybor's shoulder.

The Norid's slitted eyes moved from the woman to the big man. "Your rationalizations are your business, Domani." He rubbed his thumb across his fingers. "Mine is the gold you pay for my services."

Serroi felt bile rising in her throat. *The fools, the stupid damn fools, don't they realize what they're getting into?* She pulled away, pressed her hands against her eyes, then touched Tayyan on the cheek; when her shieldmate looked around, she jerked her thumb along the passage. Tayyan shook her head impatiently and put her eye back to the hole. Serroi hesitated then looked for herself.

The Norid dropped his hands. "What you ask can be done. But not until the Moongather. The Demon Road is widest then. See that the Domnor is alone in his bedroom on the night of the Gather. Be sure the guards outside his door are ones you can trust to keep themselves and any snoopers out of the room, no matter what they hear within. The business will take several hours. Your part is to arrange this. Mine is to prepare myself to call the demon forth. I will have half my fee now, the rest when the work is done."

Lybor turned to Picior. A silent communion passed between them then Picior went out. Lybor turned to the Norid. "You will have it, Ser Nor. First, though, some wine to seal our bargain."

Picior came back with a tray and three glasses. A crusty, cobwebbed bottle rested between them. The old woman filled the glasses and offered them to each.

Morescad grinned and lifted his glass. "To the Domnor, dancing to the strings we'll be pulling."

Tayyan hissed with rage, forgetting where she was. Her scabbard scraped against the stone as she came to her feet.

Morescad heard both small sounds. He leaped for the passage, his sword snatched out and questing.

Shaking with fear and sick to her stomach, with a strength that came out of nowhere, Serroi dragged Tayyan away, breaking through the Stenda blindrage, persuading her to run.

Run—through the rat hole in the walls—run—feet pounding in pursuit—run—leap up the tree, fall over the wall, breaking the fall with handfuls of vine—splatting into the macai muck—guards pounding after them—another coming after them—shouts behind—darkness and fear behind—clatter through the streets, running blindly toward the city wall—run and run and run—Tayyan sitting in a pool of blood, clutching at a leg transfixed by a crossbow quarrel—crouch on the roof—shiver with fear—the Norid comes—run—scramble frantically over slippery roofs with stormwinds snatching at her, accusing eyes pursuing her—the Norid behind her—after her.

"So I abandoned her, broke my shieldmate oath and left her to die. I got over the wall, stole a boat. You know the rest, Dina. Know how the land itself seems to be searching for me. Plaz guards and Teyn's Berseyd. Traxim and Maiden knows who else sniffing for me. The Nearga-Nor and the Sons of the Flame moving against me and anyone who might dare help me. And I have to go back." She rubbed wearily at her forehead.

Dinafar closed her fingers around Serroi's ankle. "No. You heard what the Tercel said. You can't think she's still alive."

"No." Serroi jumped to her feet, emptied the last of the water over the coals and kicked dirt over them. She came back and pulled her boots off, then stretched out on the blankets. Overhead the lightning was beginning to flicker. The wind sang over and around the slanted groundsheet, bowing it in like a sail. The first raindrops splatted down around them. "I don't know," she said slowly. "He could have lied to frighten me or punish me for what I did to him. I've got to know, Dina. And that's not all, not the most important thing, I have to warn the Domnor." She dropped her head on crossed forearms; Dinafar's large hands patted her shoulder clumsily. She turned her head and met the girl's anxious green-brown eyes.

"You'll just get killed," Dinafar whispered.

Serroi turned onto her back and lay staring up at the wind-whipped leaves. "If that were all." She caught the girl's hand and snugged it against her cheek. "Fifteen years ago I escaped one Nor. Though escaped isn't exactly the right word; he left me to die, but I refused to oblige him. I lived, but I'm still not free of him." She chuckled drowsily. "Never mind, I'm talking mostly to scare away nightmares. Those fools haven't the least idea who'll be pulling those strings they boasted about. Not them, that's sure. The Nearga-Nor will make fools of them through that Norid. He'll be running the

Mijloc, though why he wants that, why they want that, I don't know. They don't understand feeling, life, like color to the blind. They put people in boxes and are surprised when they don't fit, lumpy feelings, lumpy people, don't fit in boxes. They've got Sankoy, must have Sankoy, the Berseyd only work on the Teyn's command. After the Mijloc now. And the Biserica." She drifted into silence, listening to the sounds of the breaking storm.

"Shouldn't you let the Biserica know what's happening?" Dinafar's soft voice arrested her slow drop into sleep. "Let's both go south in the morning."

Serroi blinked, rubbed her hands over her face. "Too long, twenty days to the Biserica, hard riding." She yawned. "Besides, there's still Hern."

The girl sat very still, her torso a dark silhouette edged with light from the flashing in the sky. The rain was coming down more steadily, drumming on the hard earth, on the taut skin of the groundsheet. "To live with myself, Dina, I have to go back." She yawned again, circled her fingers around the girl's wrist. "You don't have to come. Better go south, the traxim saw you with me but you should be safe enough alone. You can tell Yael-mri what I told you. Yael-mri, our Prieti-meien. You'll like her. Be a favor to me. I'll feel better with her knowing in case I fail."

"You won't fail." The girl's voice was very soft but totally certain. "You can't so you won't. And you needn't expect me to leave you. What would I do if one of those stinking birds came at me? You're dressed like a boy. They'll be looking for one person or for two females, not a brother and a sister—if you can fix your skin."

"I haven't got the energy to argue, girl." Serroi chuckled as she wrapped herself in her blankets. "Go to sleep. We'll be walking tomorrow, turn the macain loose, they'll have to forage for themselves. I think you're a fool, but I'll be glad of your company." With a last yawn, she closed her eyes and was soon asleep.

THE CHILD: 8

The year passed slowly. Through Serroi the Noris touched the vegetative world, the animal world, the wild red life of the predators, the cold, sly life of reptiles, the hurry-scurry of rodents and the touch-flight, placid, jittery life of the prey animals. He touched these, corrupted them, enslaved them, then withdrew from them to press on with his quest to extend his power over the whole of existence. She fought him at every step and lost every time.

A strange thing was happening. Although he was unaware of it, he was changing himself, becoming more accessible to her—as if the life he touched struck back through his shields and brought the dead parts of his body-mind back toward the living. Serroi was changing also. She grew stronger with each contact she had with the life forces he was seeking to understand and control. The moments when he forced her to be his gate fed the stubborn core of her being. As the year passed, she began to see a distant possibility that she could someday break free and strike back at him.

At the end of the year, when winter yielded to spring, he took her far south, into the coast mountains turning the bottom of the Mijloc. He stood with her on a broad cliff high over a green and lovely valley, a garden place with a golden glow shimmering over it that radiated health and vigor. She knew as soon as she saw it that she had to reach this place somehow; it called her with an urgency she couldn't deny. And she couldn't bear the thought of the Noris destroying that peace and that goodness. She glanced up at him and was surprised to see his calm face distorted by anger and desire.

She said nothing, but quietly turned her eyes back on the valley. There was something out there—she probed at the valley with her eye-spot and felt something similar to a force that had been resisting the Noris for the past month, fighting his invasion, repairing the damage he was doing. He'd left her alone the past week, spending his time refining his accumulated knowledge; the tower had quivered under the forces he invoked. Confident of his control over her, he let her wander outside the tower whenever she wished. She went down to the shore and kicked through the surf, sat on one of the rocks and watched the dead fish floating in. There was a tense feel to the air. The world was gathering itself against him. She felt stronger than ever as she breathed in the rebellion of the earth. Standing on the mountainside above the valley, she felt the same kind of strength reaching to her from the place below. *This is the heart of the resistance,* she thought.

The Noris dropped a hand on her shoulder. She felt him preparing to flow into her and set herself to resist, the glow from behind entering her also, fighting with her against his intrusion. She cried out as his hand slapped hard across her face, slapped again and again, distracting her, but she ground her teeth together and fought him off. He cuffed the side of her head; she screamed with pain, screamed repeatedly as blows kept coming, hard slaps on her eye-spot, but refused to yield. The valley fed her strength. She was a rock. There was no place he could penetrate.

Shaking with fury and hurt, the Noris dug his fingers into her shoulder and carried her back to the tower. He flung her on her bed and stood staring down at her as if he tried to understand why she would betray him. He bent down, his hands gentle on her head, the hurt in his eyes teairng at her, confusing her. For a long time he didn't move, then he straightened. "You have to be taught," he muttered. Stretching out a hand, fingers splayed into a pale star, he spoke a WORD. Without looking at her, he ran from the room.

Serroi blinked tears away, wondering what the Noris had done. She moved a hand, accidentally brushing it against her thigh. She gasped as pain seared through her. The pain got worse, burning all over her body. Her clothing became a torment. She tore off the soft silken robe that was like a nettle shirt. Her body was bathed in sweat. Her legs trembled. She pushed off the bed. The soles of her feet burned. She sat on the bed again and felt fire searing her buttocks. She stood. The air pressed against her skin and burned. Unable to stand or sit without pain, her nerve ends sensitized so that the slightest pressure was agony, she wept. She wept knowing that he'd done this to her out of the knowledge he'd gained through her, wept while the tears rolled like drops of acid down her face. When she could stand no longer, she sat on the edge of the bed until she could endure that no longer. She stood again. She trembled, collapsed on her knees, screaming with the agony she could not escape. She struggled back onto her feet. Weeping with pain, she staggered to the door, forced her fingers closed over the latchhook, intending to make her way to the Noris and beg him to remove his curse. Her fingers slipped off the latch. Sweat rolled down her face. She tried again. The door was locked.

The torment went on and on. Outside her window the sky darkened. Stars sprinkled across the dark blue rectangle. Her tongue swelled. She tried to drink, almost could not force water down in spite of her thirst. The hands brought food. The fragrant scents flooded her mouth with saliva but she couldn't chew. Even swallowing was an agony.

The night passed slowly. She burned. Time crept along so lethargically it ceased to have meaning. She couldn't think. Couldn't move. Couldn't weep.

The window paled, was streaked by red and gold. The gloom lightened in the room. Serroi crouched in the center of the Sankoy rug the hands had retrieved and cleaned and replaced. Where flesh touched flesh she burned, but she was too tired to stand.

The door opened and the Noris stepped quietly inside. She looked up. "Please," she moaned.

He spoke a WORD. As the fire died out of her skin, he lifted her, carried her to the bed, sat on the edge of it and held her until her shaking stopped. After stroking gentle fingers over her hair for a few moments, he laid her down on the bed, straightened out her cramped limbs, looked gravely down at her, then left.

Serroi stretched and sat up, smoothed her hands down her body. Her skin felt sticky with old sweat but the burning was gone, blessedly the burning was gone. Eyes heavy with her need for sleep, she moved to the ewer and began sponging off her body, enjoying the smooth slide of the cool water over her skin. She bent over the basin and poured water through her sweaty hair, shivering with pleasure at the coolness. By the time the hands came, she was dressed and ravenous.

After her breakfast, she slept. She woke an hour before noon, feeling intensely alive. When she pulled on the latchhook the door opened before her; she circled down the spiraling stairs through tower and stone to the beach, walked along the surf, letting cold salt water coil about her feet. The brush-brush of the water and the warmth of the sun made her drowsy. She curled up on the sand and went to sleep.

Several hours later she woke to find her lunch set on the sand beside her. She ate hungrily, then went paddling with

quiet contentment among the shallows, refusing to think
about her punishment. As the afternoon wore on, the shadow
of the pain moved closer and closer until she could ignore it
no longer. She sat on the sand, her knees drawn up, her
forearms resting lightly on them, looking out across the
water, wondering what the Noris was going to do to her. She
shuddered as she remembered yesterday's pain and knew she
couldn't endure that again, she'd do anything he wanted
rather than endure that again. When she closed her eyes, she
saw again the golden valley, knew she couldn't let the Noris
corrupt it, knew at the same time that she no longer had the
strength to stop him. How the two pulls were going to balance, she couldn't tell. She opened her eyes, stared out across
the endless flat blue of the sea, wondering where the garden
was with the great rambling structure that seemed to grow
out of the mountainside and the life of all kinds that seemed
so lush and contented. *I'm going there. I'll get away from
here somehow. That's where I belong.* She twisted her head
up and back, examining the black-brown stone of the cliff
that extended into the stone blocks of the tower. The contrast
between the life in the valley and the deadness in the stone
made her stomach cramp with desire to be there not here;
dimly she began to understand the Noris's desire to possess
that wonder, though by possessing it he would end it.

Rubbing at her neck, she watched the creamy surf creep
toward her toes. There were a few islands in sight, barren
snags of rock. Beyond them she could see nothing but endless
rolling sea. *I don't even know where land is,* she thought. *Or
where that valley is.* As she felt that intense desire for the
valley, her eye-spot throbbed, tugged her head around until
she looked to the southeast. "The valley?" she whispered.
"Yes, yes." She jumped to her feet, danced around and
around on the sand. "I can find you, I can, I will, oh yes, I
will."

The Noris left her alone all that day. She managed a good
night's sleep and spent the next day down on the sands trying
to work out a way to cross the water, the blue barrier that
mocked her efforts.

Dawn was red in her window when the Noris shook her
out of sleep on the next morning. He was standing over her,
his face sad. He put his hand on her shoulder when she
started to sit up, shook his head when she started to speak.

After several moments of silence he spoke a WORD and left her. The pain was back.

Morning again. She crawled to his feet, weeping and begging. He took the pain away. Again he held her while she shuddered and sobbed, again he left her, left her alone for three days. Each night she crawled back to her room, expecting more pain, but by the third day she began to hope her ordeal was over. He'd never punished her so long or hard before. She began to wonder if she really was betraying him. She loved him in spite of everything and wanted badly to please him. The valley—she didn't know anything about it, perhaps it was a trap, only a trap. She shivered each time she thought of the pain, shivered again when she remembered the sadness in the dark luminous eyes of her father, friend and teacher.

He stood by her bed the next morning. She tried to tell him that she surrendered, but he wouldn't listen. He was measuring her strength by his and wouldn't believe her. He spoke the WORD and left, almost running, pursued by her screams.

This time the pain lasted two days. When he came back, she crawled to him, out of her mind with the torment, no will left in her. He spoke the WORD and the pain was gone, but she lay without moving, still sobbing, still pleading, not even aware that the fire was gone. When he lifted her and carried her to the bed, she cringed away from him, lost in terror, unable to think, unable to control her body. He blurred and cleared, blurred again as she tried to see his face. There was a sadness there but she was unable to relate to that. The terror was etched into her blood and bones. He sat on the bed beside her and tried to untangle her curls, not noticing how stiffly she lay, not noticing her lack of response. "Serroi, my little Serroi," he murmured. "Don't fight me, little one. Don't make me do this to you, my little gate, my daughter." His voice softened on the last word. "Daughter." He stroked fingertips along her cheek. "The only daughter I can have in my condition. Be my shadow, Serroi, my other self. You told me once you wanted to be a Noris. That's not possible, but you can learn more than most. We can be happy, Serroi. Together we can control all that exists." He smoothed the curls off her forehead, but didn't see how she trembled at his touch. Calm and content with what he had done, he left her.

That evening he called her to the fireside and sat contentedly with her while she held herself stiff, shivering whenever he smiled at her or touched her. She hurt inside from remembered pain and from loss; tears gathered in her eyes and she blinked them back. She looked at the Noris's quiet beautiful face and mourned because of the fear she couldn't help, mourned joy gone without possibility of return.

The next day he came for her. She was sitting in the middle of the bed, her legs crossed, her hands limp on her knees, staring blindly at nothing. When she saw him, she gasped and edged away, her head turning, searching blindly for a place to hide. There was no place to hide. The Noris smiled. "Come with me, Serroi."

For a moment she couldn't move, then she placed her hand in his and slid off the bed. He spoke and they were transported to the mountainside above the golden valley. She looked sadly down at it then waited passively for him to use her.

He turned her to face him and stood looking down into her eyes, one hand closed over her shoulder. His eyes grew and grew, great soft black circles. She stood frozen, blank with terror, waiting to feel him entering her—but her terror blocked him far more effectively than her earlier defiance. Though she was helpless to deny him, unable to protest any longer, she was equally unable to surrender to him; the terror was beyond her control. He raged and slapped her until she was sobbing. She tried to open for him, but he thought she was defying him again.

He snapped them back to the tower and flung her on the bed.

She scrambled on her knees to him, pleading. "I tried, Ser Noris. I tried. I'm not fighting you, please, please."

His fingers shaking with rage, he struck her hands away and set the pain on her again. Blinded by his own limitations, he could not see the difference in her and made his final and worst mistake, rendering her useless to him. He left her in pain for three days, then took it away, let her wander as she pleased along the shore. Though he stayed away, she could feel his fury and his disappointment around her wherever she went. Miserable and uncertain, she sat on the sand and watched the water come in.

As the days passed, she relaxed tentatively, but still had little appetite for the food the hands brought her. She slept little and what sleep she got was broken by nightmares. The Noris continued to leave her to herself, perhaps because he hoped that time would heal her as it had done before.

On the tenth day he came suddenly to her room and stood

looking down at her as she lay frozen under the covers. It was very early, the sun still behind the horizon, sending up layers of red and gold. His face was a pale blur in the hazy light. She couldn't breathe, her vision blurred, her heart pounded in her throat, drummed in her ears. She felt him trying to enter her and struggled to batter back the terror but could not. With a buzzing in her ears, she fainted.

When she recovered he was gone. She waited, sick and faint, for his retaliation. Nothing happened. The day passed.

More days passed. She ate little and slept less. Flesh melted from her bones. There were great dark circles under her eyes. Sometimes she thought she saw her mother standing in front of her, scolding her for something, though she couldn't quite make out the words. Other times her brothers and sisters came and tormented her as cruelly as they had back on the tundra. At times the beach sand or the Sankoy rug turned to chill earth with its soft easily bruised grasses and thick scatter of spring blooms; the chinin would come and play with her, circling about her, barking with ecstatic joy, wrestling with each other, knocking her over, licking her face—then turning vicious, snarling and nipping at her, driving her into sobbing, screaming flight. At times, she knew these were hallucinations; other times she was lost in them. Sleeplessness and slow starvation weakened her until she seldom left her bed, but still she could not make herself sleep and could only force a little food down without bringing it up again.

The Noris came and stood at the foot of her bed, his face troubled. "Serroi, why?" She stared at him terrified. "What can I do?" His voice was soft and unsure. She blinked and tears flooded her eyes. She reached toward him, her hand shaking. He took it, stood holding it a moment then moved close to her and pulled gently at one of her curls. Sobbing and shaking, she threw herself against him. He dropped onto the bed, holding her against him until the worst of the storm was past, sat stroking her fleecy curls, saying nothing only holding her. Finally he dried her eyes on the sheet, then laid her back. He touched her cheek, smiled and left her.

Half an hour later he brought her a chini pup.

Serroi shrank away, horrified eyes fixed on the pup.

The Noris looked puzzled, then his dark eyes twinkled. "I don't need any more chinin, Serroi. I brought this pup for you, to keep you company." He scooped up the cowering chini and dumped him into Serroi's lap.

She let the pup sniff her fingers, then carefully scratched

him behind the ears. When she looked up, the Noris was gone.

A month slid past. Spring eased into summer. The days were long and hot but she spent hours on the sand playing with the chini pup. She slept better, ate with a good appetite; though she didn't tan, her skin toughened and thickened as she splashed naked in the salt water or lay on the sand. Her tough resilient body rebounded into health and her strength returned.

One morning she woke early with the chini pup whining in her ear. Blinking, apprehensive, she sat up wondering what was wrong.

The Noris was standing at the foot of her bed, his face somber. He waited in silence while she rubbed the sleep from her eyes, then said, "Get dressed, Serroi."

She closed her eyes, stiff with fear. "The valley?" she whispered.

"No. Do as I said, Serroi."

She scrambled into one of the white silk robes and pulled the soft slippers onto her feet. Hesitantly, her eyes on his still face, she took his hand.

The room blinked out, changed into rolling hills of sand with scattered clumps of scraggly brush. The Noris spoke. A dark robe dropped onto the sand and rock beside him. He spoke again, a small WORD, and a banquet was spread out beside the robe, steaming savory food on delicate porcelain, wine in a single crystal glass, a crystal pitcher full of water.

She glanced at the sun, frowned. It was a lot higher than it should be. When they left the room it was barely dawn. Here the morning was advanced enough for the sun to be the width of her hand above the horizon. And it was getting uncomfortably hot. She and the Noris were standing on a slight rise in the middle of the most barren and inhospitable land she'd ever seen. Her eye-spot vibrated but she could find no touch of life as far as she could reach—at least no larger forms, she wasn't probing for lizards or rats. There were only ripples of rock and sand, cut across by straggling black lines where rainy season run-offs had eaten into the earth. She looked up at the Noris, wondering what she was doing here.

He laid a hand a moment on her head, then stepped back. "Good-bye, Serroi." And she was alone in the middle of a desert.

THE WOMAN: IX

Serroi stretched and yawned, then rolled out of her blankets. Dinafar was crouched over the fire, cutting the borrowed tabard into small pieces and dropping them onto the flames, making quite sure they burned to ash. When she saw Serroi sitting up, the girl smiled and put the cha pot onto the fire. "Good morning, meie. Sleep well?"

"Mmmm." Serroi smoothed her tunic down then began rolling her blankets into a compact cylinder. Humming a burring tune, she dealt with Dinafar's blankets, then crawled from under the groundsheet, glanced up at the sky and gasped with dismay—half the morning was spent. "Dina, why'd you let me sleep so long? You know. . . ."

Dinafar sniffed. "I know you were making yourself sick. You needed that sleep." She tossed the last of the tabard into the fire. "I don't see any virtue in rushing to get killed."

"Dammit, Dina. . . ." Scowling, Serroi ran her weaponbelt through her fingers, opened the pocket she was searching for and took out a small enamel case. "Quit trying to run my life." She dipped fingertips into pale cream and started stroking it on her face. "You want to help, make sure I cover all of my face with this goo."

The water started bubbling in the cha pot. Its small lid bounced rapidly, letting out puffs of steam. Dinafar snatched the lid back, dumped in a handful of cha leaves; her hand protected by a fold of her skirt, she pulled the pot off the fire and set it on a flat stone beside her. "The macain have gone off somewhere."

"Just as well. As long as you're coming with me, we can't use them any more. Too conspicuous." She sighed, began working the cream into the skin of her forehead, cursing softly as she tried to keep her tumbling tangled curls out of it. Holding her hair up, she scowled at Dinafar. "You really shouldn't have let me sleep so long. Have I got it on smooth?"

Dinafar's green-brown eyes twinkled.

"Stop grinning, girl, this is serious."

147

"Yes, meie, of course, meie." Dinafar's lips twitched again. She swallowed, smoothed her fingers along her throat. "You forgot your nose, meie."

"Hunh!" She dabbed hastily at her nose.

All the spare gear cached high in one of the brellim, blankets and groundsheets tied onto rucksacks, rucksacks settled as comfortably as possible on their backs, Serroi and Dinafar stepped from the grove and started downhill to the Highroad. Serroi grimaced. "Crowded already."

Dinafar stumbled, caught herself. "I've never seen anything like that. How did they ever build it?"

The Highroad ran straight as a knife slash from the Biserica in the south to Oras in the north. It was a twenty-foot-high embankment with the top smoothed flat and covered with a thick rubbery surface, a dull black tarlike substance. The top was perfectly level and wide enough for two farm carts to pass without crowding.

Serroi tugged at the chin strap of the cap. She was rested and relaxed for the first time since she'd left Oras; no nightmares, not even any dreams she could remember to disturb a deep, deep sleep. The cap fit close to her head and was a minor irritation. She'd never liked wearing anything that covered her ears, but it was necessary as part of her disguise. She glanced at Dinafar. The girl was walking easily, looking down at the grass under her feet, a small satisfied smile quivering on her lips. "Cream-licker," she murmured.

Dinafar grinned, then she nodded at the Highroad. "How *did* that get built?"

"The Domnor's grandfather got tired of bad weather and muddy roads delaying his tax gatherers. He hired a second-rank Norit to build him a road that wouldn't fall apart under the first storm. The sorcerer did it in a day and a night and old Kleorn paid him well. And squeezed the land to replace the money he'd laid out." She waved a small gloved hand at the slope. "One used to pay tolls to use the road. Domnor Hern stopped that about ten years ago when his father died. Said the road's paid for a dozen times over. No use forcing a lot of folk to spend coin for what they already owned. Irritated the hell out of Floarin and Lybor."

Dinafar smiled shyly at her, reminding Serroi how young she was. She felt a surge of affection for the girl, a gladness that she was out of that village trap.

They climbed up the steep side of the embankment and

eased unnoticed into the stream of humanity ambling along the black ribbon, most of the travelers heading north to Oras and the Moongather. The families traveling on foot moved steadily along, enjoying the day and the walk. At times macai riders came clawing through the mass, ignoring the protests of the walkers. Some of them were Plaz guards, their faces gaunt and weary, their green and black tabards thick with dust and stained with sweat. Others were Stenda, blond and arrogant, the men on high-bred macain of uncertain temper, women and girls in curtained wagons with huge iron-tired wheels. The Stenda pushed all walkers off the sides, paying no attention to curses and complaints, ignoring the men and women on foot as if they didn't exist. Some were wealthy merchants on placid malekanim whose gold-plated horns stretched three feet on either side, winning their riders room without need for asking; their veiled wives sitting in open carts followed with less fuss but just as much arrogance. Now and then Sleykyn assassins rode by, swishing their velater hide whips on armored thighs. No one cursed or complained when they passed, only moved quickly out of the way.

Serroi stared at the road when the guards rode past, knowing that the changed color of her skin was her best disguise, that they weren't interested in a dusty boy. She began to relax, trusting to her misleading appearance. Then a Nor rode slowly past on a jittery macai.

Dinafar caught her hand and held it tight when Serroi flinched away from the dark rider. Her warm fingers gave Serroi the steadying she needed. She kept the girl between her and the Nor, watched him with a fear and an old hunger she thought she'd forgotten. This Nor was an ascetic minarka with the olive-tinged gold skin of his race; his russet hair, straight as corn floss, rippled in the wind of his passage; he wore the tight-laced black cloak, the narrow black tunic and loincloth, the Nor's riding garb. She squeezed her fingers tight around Dinafar's, watched the Norit ride unheeding past her. As the black figure melted into the crowd ahead, she drew a long breath and exploded it out. She was on foot and invisible. She grinned at Dinafar. "He didn't even see us."

Dinafar pulled her hand loose, giggling. She danced in front of Serroi, began walking backward. "We fooled him. We'll fool them all." A man ahead of her growled as the girl bumped into him. Subsiding, she dropped back to walk beside Serroi. "Meie, no, what am I going to call you? We haven't talked about that." Her green-brown eyes were suddenly wide and serious.

Serroi rubbed at her nose. "Right. A name. Jern. My next oldest brother, a good enough name. Jern." She examined Dinafar as they walked along. "Neither of us looks much like mountain stock." She sighed. "I'm not much good at this kind of thing." She shook her head. "Trained in all kinds of weapons, trained until I can't even move naturally any more. I know how to sew a wound and kill a fever, how to tame anything on four legs, and dammit, nothing much about putting together a good believable lie." She chuckled. "When I get back to the Biserica I'll have to suggest some courses in underhandedness to Yael-mri." She fell silent, frowning down at the black springy surface moving past under her boots, Dinafar humming and skipping beside her.

Pilgrims moved around them, peasants and landless farm-workers by the hundreds, cobblers, mountebanks, minstrels, acrobats, tinkers, beggars, children, some scowling Sons of the Flame with clustering Followers—a selection of all the trades and types from all corners of the Mijloc moving noisily along the Highroad. Only the sick or those too old or too weak to stand the journey, or those forced to stay behind as caretakers were left out of the great flood of humanity traveling north. Tiny motes in that flood, Serroi and Dinafar walked safe and unnoticed, Serroi more relaxed, even content, now that she accepted her practical invisibility. She watched Dinafar, relishing the change in her.

The once sullen, angry girl was blooming. Her eyes shone more green than brown, shone with interest and delight—though sometimes she edged closer to Serroi, brushing against her with tiny touches. Serroi felt these and was gently amused, a little sad, seeing her own need for reassurance reflected in Dinafar. *She's really attractive when she's happy,* Serroi thought.

Dinafar's skin was olive, browning to a deep fawn, unprotected in the sun. Her black-brown hair was straight and long; she wore it unconfined with a kind of defiant pleasure. It blew about on the breeze, fine and silky and very thick. Her mouth was wide and mobile, alternating this morning between quivering smiles and broad grins. She wasn't pretty but had a charm of spirit that gave her an illusion of beauty when she was happy, when her eyes shone, her skin gleamed bright gold, her cheeks turned a delicate pink. She was broad-shouldered and would be heavy bosomed like her mother's people, but her bones were fine, her wrists and ankles as narrow as Serroi's though both hands and feet were generously made. Young as she was, she was already a head taller than Serroi and apt to keep growing a while longer. Serroi quieted her uneasiness about where she was taking Dinafar by contemplating these changes, telling herself anything was better for the girl than her soul-destroying existence in the fisher village.

More Norim and Sleykyn assassins rode past. Though she shivered and felt a tremble in her stomach with each of them, she no longer succumbed to that mindless panic that had driven her into equally mindless flight. The memory of her betrayal darkened the day for her. She brooded until Dinafar slipped a hand into hers. She looked up into anxious green-brown eyes. "Maybe she *is* still alive, J-Jern." Dinafar bit her lip when she stumbled over the name.

"That doesn't change what I did." Serroi smiled at Dinafar, lifted her hand and lightly kissed the back of it. Dinafar blushed and trembled. When Serroi felt her withdrawal, she dropped the girl's hand. "I don't want to talk of that."

The ambling horde thinned around noon. Many of the travelers climbed down from the Highroad to eat and rest on the grassy slopes before continuing their pilgrimage. Serroi and Dinafar kept walking with the rest, the more impatient ones. Chewing on handfuls of dried fruit, sipping from canteens, they kept moving. Far ahead there was a darkening on the horizon like smoke against the sky. Serroi felt excitement begin to build in her. Oras. Another day and she was there, back in the trap. She turned to the girl beside her. "Dina, tired yet?" She scratched at her palms; they were sticky from the fruit. She wiped them down the sides of her vest, forgetting it was red thick cloth not the treated leather of her meian tunic. She looked down at herself and wrinkled her nose with disgust.

Dinafar giggled, then shook her head. "I'm all right."

Serroi heard the splat-scrape of macai feet coming up behind them and moved hastily to the edge of the road. She risked a glance over her shoulder, stumbled and stopped walking as her eyes met the casual glance of a Nor, a tall thin man with blue-black hair braided into fantastic coils, skin the color of syrup over coal, and eyes a brilliant indigo with flecks of azure that caught the light like small sapphires. The eyes grew and grew as she stood frozen, unable to turn away. Then two Sleykynin rode past, the claws of their mounts throwing up bits of the black surface against her, tiny stings that she brushed at absently as she watched the Norit ride past no longer interested in her.

Her breathing labored, her heart thudding in her throat, Serroi looked back along the Highroad. As far as she could see, until the road was lost in the blue mists of the southern horizon, there were no walkers left on the road, only clumps of riders. Stenda and merchants, Sleykynin and Norim. She looked up. Traxim in groups of five were circling idly over the plain, moving toward the city lost in dark smoke ahead of them. She began walking again, lost in thought.

Dinafar touched her arm. "Should we stop?" She gestured at the groups of walkers resting on the grass, laughing, sleeping, eating, or simply sitting and talking as they waited for the noon heat to pass. "We're the only ones still walking."

Serroi shook her head. "I'd like to get on as far as we can before nightfall. Unless you're tired."

"No, not really."

They moved steadily along the side of the road, keeping on the verge to avoid the trampling feet of the various beasts and the clumsy wheels of the carts. Several more Norim rode past, ignoring them, to Serroi's vast satisfaction. The road began to fill again as the walkers climbed back up the embankment.

A boy who couldn't have been more than four years old raced ahead of his family, scrambling up the grassy slope, agile as a mimkin. At the edge of the blacktop, he teetered a minute, looking back at his people, laughing and waving. Without bothering to check behind him, he skipped onto the roadway.

Dinafar giggled as he caught his heel and went down on his buttocks, then gasped with horror as a Sleykyn rode past her, eyes half shut, within half a step of trampling the small form frozen on the blacktop.

Without stopping to think, Serroi dived under the clawed pads of the macai, making him shy wildly. She snatched up the terrified boy and rolled away with him, feeling a slash of blinding pain, then she was tumbling over and over down the steep embankment, her body cushioned by the grass, unable to stop until she jarred against the bottom of the slope.

Stifling a cry of pain, she sat up and set the wailing boy on his feet. She touched her arm. The tips of her fingers came away covered with blood. She twisted her head around. A long straight line cut across the material of her sleeve and a ragged cut bit into her muscle. Blood was oozing from the wound and dripping down her arm. *The whip*, she thought. *That bastard used his whip on me.*

"J-Jern." Dinafar was stumbling down the embankment. Serroi looked past her to see the boy's family pouring toward her also. Dinafar fell to her knees beside her. "He used his whip!" The girl's voice shook with indignation. "His whip!"

Serroi rubbed her thumb across the blood on her fingertips then wiped her hand on the grass beside her. "Sleykyn. They're like that." Dinafar scowled and parted her lips to speak. "Hush, Dina. Later."

As the older women fluttered about the whimpering boy, his father stumbled to a stop in front of Serroi, stood gasping and passing a blue and white kerchief repeatedly over his round red face. Serroi ran her eyes quickly over him. A farmer probably, not rich, but prosperous enough to keep his family well-fed and healthy and support besides several hands and maids. Two of his children stood silent behind him, a boy and a girl, obviously in harmony with each other, twins perhaps, both watching Serroi and Dinafar with a cool, assessing intelligence. Serroi pushed her torn sleeve up to cover the bits of skin showing through the cut. "Thanks, lad." The big man waved a broad hand at the noisy group around the boy. "My youngest. I owe you."

Serroi shrugged, touched her hand to his, let it be swallowed up in the huge paw, pulled it away again. "A man has to live with himself, tarom." She deepened her voice; her disguise was good but this man couldn't be a fool, not with the smell of prosperity that hovered about him.

He tucked the kerchief away and grinned amiably at her. "I nomen Tesc Gradin, Tartineh from the west of Cimpia plain. My wife Annic." He waved a hand at the older woman. "Daughters Nilis and Sanani. Those brats. . . ." He grinned at the two standing with arms linked. ". . . Teras and Tuli, twins. The lad you scooped up is Dris. Spoiled brat." He looked fondly at the boy who was reveling in the attention of his mother and sisters, then turned back to Serroi, examining her with kind, shrewd eyes. "You and your sister are over-young to be on your own. You run away?" Disapproval was strong in his voice. "Leaving your folks to worry?"

Serroi moved her hand gingerly. The whip-cut was drying, beginning to sting badly. "I nomen Jern, tarom. This my sister Dina." She looked down at her hands, knowing that she was very bad at lying. Tayyan used to tease her about her compulsive honesty. If she'd thought, she'd have prepared a story. So many things she should have done. She reached up to touch her eye-spot, jerked her hand down again. Dinafar stirred beside her. Serroi reached out and caught her hand, hoping that the girl wouldn't yield to impulse. "No, tarom," she said slowly. "Well, not exactly." She flicked a glance at his frowning face, then looked down again. "Our father died, you see, when we were babies." She licked her lips, hating this, wanting to say as little as she could. "Our mother married again two years ago." She looked up again, feeling the strain in her stiff face muscles.

Tesc nodded his understanding. "And now there's a new family started with you much in the way." The big man's eyes gleamed with satisfaction as he put his own interpretation on her words. "So the two of you ran away."

"Yes." Serroi stared down at the grass, letting the silence grow, startled and amused to see how real this was becoming to the landsman as he built a story for her out of his own imaginings, a story all the more convincing to him since it was his own. *I've learned a new thing,* she thought and was a little sad because she hated having to lie, especially to this kindly man. It eased her conscience, though, when she saw how much he was enjoying his fiction.

"Stout lad," Tesc said. "Have you got a place to go? If not, you and your sister are welcome to stay with us and come back with me to my tar." He looked sternly at Serroi. "You'll earn your keep, that be sure. But a little hard work never hurt a lad or a lass." He frowned at his children who had come up behind him and knelt with the twins watching Serroi and Dinafar with avid interest.

Serroi glanced at Dina who was returning the stares with equal interest. She poked her back to alertness, then answered the tarom. "We thank you, tarom, but our uncle, our mother's brother, he lives in Oras. A fisherman with a tidy boat and no children."

"Well, lad, I wish you luck. You'll share our supper with us and travel with us next day? I'll feel better about you that way. Good hot meals and safe sleeping will make the walking easier." He nodded at the small shunca cropping patiently at nearby grass. The packbeast carried a load that looked bigger than he was. "We have tents and plenty of food."

Serroi nodded, hiding her reluctance. "My turn to thank

you, tarom." Dinafar's hand closed hard on hers; she smiled at the girl, but shook her head, enjoining her to silence.

Annic clucked her disapproval when Serroi wouldn't let anyone but Dinafar touch her. Dina washed the wound, tied a clean rag Annic provided around it, then sewed up the bloody sleeve, working with sufficient skill to pacify the woman. When she was finished and Serroi had tried out still shaky legs, the party climbed back to the road and walked companionably along, separating into small groups as they did so. Tesc kept Serroi beside him, his words flowing in a gentle ceaseless stream as he talked about his land and his family. Shy at first, Dinafar began chattering with the twins; to Serroi's relief, from what she heard of that conversation, Dina was getting them to talk about their part of the Cimpia plain, asking questions and giving them little time to ask questions of her.

By the time night fell, Serroi was weary and sore, grunting responses almost at random to the tarom's monologue. Her arm felt tight and hot. She had no appetite but was terribly thirsty. Dinafar left off her chatting and came quietly to her side, helping her unobtrusively down the embankment as the family left the road to camp for the night.

Serroi forced herself to eat and drink, then stumbled apart with Dinafar. The girl touched her forehead with a rough cool hand. "You're burning up." She jumped up, ran to the family fire and brought back a cup of cha. Kneeling beside Serroi, she said, "Drink some of this, then you have to tell me what to do."

Serroi took a few sips then pushed the cup away.

"Meie," Dinafar whispered, "you said you had medicine."

Serroi blinked, then fumbled the tail of her shirt out of her trousers and began running her fingers along the weaponbelt she wore buckled under the loose shirt. After a moment she let her hand fall. Dinafar shook her. She gasped, but the pain did break through the fever haze. She fumbled at the belt and dragged out her small stock of herbs. "Pyrnroot," she murmured. In the uncertain light from the fire and the first glow of the Gather, she looked through the herbs and took out a twist of parchment. She dropped two pinches of greyish powder into the lukewarm cha, then sat holding the cup a minute while the powder dissolved and released a pungent, sickly odor. She took a breath, let it out, then emptied the cup in several gulps. "Hah, that tastes bad."

Dinafar glanced over her shoulder at the family. They

were talking and laughing together around the fire. Once, when Dris started over to them, Tesc caught his shirt tail, spanked him lightly, and sat him by his mother, ignoring his outraged protest. "They're giving us privacy, Jern. If you keep your back to them, you can take off the shirt so I can fix the cut better."

Serroi rubbed at her temple, using the hand on her uninjured side. She was beginning to feel a little better as the drug took hold, but her eyes drooped from her need to sleep. She moved around so her back was to the fire and let Dinafar pull off the bloody shirt. When it was finally off, she was sweating profusely, her arm was bleeding again, her lower lip bleeding too where she'd bitten into it as Dinafar eased the sleeve off her wounded arm. Dinafar bullied her into finding her store of antiseptic salve which she spread over the wound before she bandaged it again. She dug a clean shirt from Serroi's pack and handed it to her, then bustled around, spreading the ground sheets and the blankets while Serroi sat regaining her strength, still shaken and sick from her ordeal. After a while, she moved slowly, carefully, to tuck her medicines back into the belt.

Overhead the wind was rising and lightning beginning to flicker among the rolling clouds. No trees here and that meant no shelter from the storm. Tesc had invited them under his tent but she'd refused as politely as she could and he hadn't pressed her. She looked enviously at the dark bulk as the first drops came splattering down. Then she worked her feet under her and stumbled across to Dinafar.

Both ground sheets were spread out with the blankets folded between them, the packs resting at the head where they could be used to keep the top sheet clear of the sleeper's face. Serroi lowered herself to the grass and began tugging at her boot, but found her hands gently set aside. Dinafar pulled off her boots and helped her get herself tucked in the blankets. Serroi touched her hand. "I'm glad you were stubborn and insisted on coming, Dina."

Dinafar smiled and pulled the groundsheet over the pack, tucking it in carefully. Then Serroi heard her footsteps moving around to the other side of the sheet. The girl sat down, pulled off her own boots, then crept under the groundsheet, wriggled about until she had her skirt straight and her body wrapped in her blankets. "Goodnight, meie," she whispered, then lay still.

"Maiden bless, Dina." Serroi listened for a moment to the

rain pattering down on the treated material of the ground-sheet. The pyrnroot was killing the pain in her arm and making her sleepy. *Tomorrow,* she thought. *Tomorrow around sundown, we'll reach Oras.*

THE CHILD: 9

"Why?" Serroi whispered. She stared at the empty space where the Noris had been. "Why?" She ran past the feast spread out at her feet, turned helplessly around and around, arms out, pleading. "Noris, Ser Noris, don't leave me here." Her voice trailed off as she realized that she was talking into air, that nothing listened. Her shoulders slumped. She wiped the sweat off her face. It was oppressively hot though the morning was young. She looked down at the food, then out at the desert stretching away on all sides. No other water or food anywhere. She flung her head up. "I don't know what you want, Ser Noris," she cried. "Whatever it is I won't do it." Pressing her lips together she glared around, then stared toward the west. "And I won't die out here either."

Settling herself by the fine white cloth spread over the sand, she began eating, choosing only the most perishable of the dishes, a delicate custard, slivers of raw fish marinated in wine and herbs, a salad, the wine. She set aside the roast vinat, the raw fruit and cheese, the small pile of rolls. When she was finished, she threw away everything she couldn't use and tied the rest into a compact bundle. She wrinkled her nose at the crystal pitcher nested in a hollow in the sand. "If I had anything else I could put that water in . . . you're going to be hell to carry."

She stood and slipped the brown overrobe the Nori had left her over her head, then held up the skirt and looked down at the soft slippers. "Won't last long." She sighed. "No matter. Now. Find water." She closed her eyes and began turning slowly, feeling the eye-spot begin to throb as she *desired* water. When the tug developed, she oscillated until she was certain of her direction, opened her eyes and found that she was facing southwest. Using her toe, she drew a direction line in the sand.

One arm thrust through the knotted corners of the cloth, carrying the crystal pitcher in the other hand, she set out.

The sun crept higher. Sweat was rolling down her face and body. She trembled under the hammerblows of the heat. The

earth burned her. The air burned her when she breathed it in.
After about an hour she began to feel dizzy; her face was
flushed and hot but she'd stopped sweating. Her feet were
blistered and the blisters were beginning to crack. She dipped
her sleeve into the pitcher and rubbed the wet cloth across
her face. It helped a little. Squinting, she peered ahead and
saw a ragged line, like a sooty scar jagging across the pale
sand. A promise of shade, if nothing else.

When she stood on the rim of the wash, she looked down
and sighed. Dry wash. Like everything else here, dry. Where
she was the wall had broken off, slanting steeply to the bottom of the crack, ending in a pile of rubble. A little farther
down, though, she could see places where the wall had
scooped out sections that held pools of shadow delicious to
her aching eyes. She began working her way down the crumbling side of the wash, her fingers sprouting blisters to match
those on her feet. She reached the bottom exhausted, shaking,
her knees folding under her. Leaning against her arm she
rested a moment with closed eyes, rested despite the heat of
the earth through the sleeve, then she trudged down the stony
bottom of the wash to the nearest pool of shade and collapsed in the welcome darkness; the air was no cooler but the
shadow gave her an illusion of coolness and her eyes relief
from the sun's assault.

Once again she dipped the end of her sleeve into the
pitcher and bathed her face, pressing the damp cloth finally
against her cracking lips until all the moisture was evaporated
from it, then she settled back as far as she could into the hollow, intending to wait for nightfall. Travel under the beating
of the sun depleted her too much. As she waited she fell into
a heavy sleep, a sleep filled with nightmare and pain.

When she woke the moons were up, a scatter of slender
crescents. Nijilic Thedom was rising, marking the beginning
of a new passage. *A new passage into a new life. If I live.*
Her head ached when she sat up and she was desperately
thirsty. She held the pitcher up and frowned at the disappearing water in it, wishing she could think of a way to cover it.
She drank deeply, drank until she could hold no more. The
water seemed less likely to be lost if she had it in her body
rather than in the open-mouthed pitcher. Wiggling her fingers
into the bundle, she pulled out one of the fruits, ate it slowly,
letting the juices trickle down her throat, flicking the seeds
out into the moonlit stones on the wash's rugged bottom.
Heavy with the water she'd taken into herself, she lay back in

the hollow and dozed until Thedom was directly overhead,
then she drank the last of the water and left the pitcher sitting on the sandy bottom of the hollow in the wash wall.
With the bundle settled as comfortably as she could manage
on her back, she started climbing.

After half an hour's struggle she stood on the rim of the
wash. Thedom seemed to hover close over head, the three
Companions creeping toward her; Serroi collapsed onto the
stone, breathing hard, heart pounding. Leaning back on her
arms she watched the moons drift past the star-flowers, more
stars than she could remember seeing since the tundra. *I
never learned the star-patterns*, she thought. *But I don't need
that knowledge.* She stroked fingertips across her eye-spot,
smiled, then sighed as she looked down at her slippers,
wiggled toes through the tears in them. "Rags." Sighing
again, she struggled to her feet and stood frowning at the
moon-silvered desert. "Why?"

There was no answer in the wind as it sent sand crystals
singing across the dunes, no answer in the crescents rocking
across the sky. And there was no answer in her head, only
that he had to have a reason for abandoning her; he always
had a reason for what he did. *I'll find out. When his time
comes, I'll find out; he'll see to that.* Wincing as her stiffened
body protested and her heat-wounded feet sent flashes of pain
up through her legs, she began walking toward the southwest,
following the pull in her eye-spot.

THE WOMAN: X

The dark blotch on the horizon grew slowly and by mid-day had resolved into a turreted wall with an irregular line of roofs behind it, rising like a terraced mountain to the slender domed watchtowers of the Plaz. The pilgrims were thick on the Highroad, spreading over the rocky plain on either side. The green abundance farther down the road had given way to sparse patches of dried grass poking up in the lee of rocks on the rock-littered plain that was swept by continual salty breezes from the sea, cool enough at this time of year to make sitting about uncomfortable. With Oras in sight many of the walkers scrambled down from the Highroad, leaving it to the increasing numbers of riders.

Tesc and his family were among the ones who climbed down to the plain, their fat little packbeast stepping daintily over the scattered rocks. The tarom brought out his blue and white kerchief and wiped vigorously at his face. Tucking the kerchief into his sleeve, he looked over the plain. "Not so good going," he said cheerfully. "But more of it." His wife and elder daughters shook their skirts in disgust as the fine brown dust settled on feet and hems and crept upward into every wrinkle.

The city rose higher and higher above the horizon while the sun slid into its final quarter. Serroi withdrew into herself, Tayyan's face swimming before her now, so close, so terribly close, she was to the clandestine race-course and the place where the traxim had eaten her friend, her lover, her shield-mate and second self. She tried to shake off her gloom but each step toward the city was harder to take than the one before.

They reached the wall as the sun was throwing up a fan of crimson and gold in the west.

Tesc wiped at his face with the sodden filthy kerchief. "We got some friends waiting for us at the Tiyrj." He waved a hand to the east where a large part of the foot traffic was heading, circling around the city wall and disappearing behind it. "You're welcome to join us. Plenty of room in the

161

tent, you know that." He looked gravely at her, his round
face troubled, his shrewd eyes narrowed with concern for her
and Dinafar. "The city's a bad place for young ones these
days."

Serroi shook her head. "We'd best find our uncle."

He stared down at the kerchief he was twisting in his big
hands. "You're a good lad, Jern. If your uncle can't keep
you, hunt me up. You'll do that?"

"The Maiden bless you, kind tarom." She held out a small
gloved hand. "I won't forget and am most grateful for the
thought." She looked around. Dinafar was just behind her,
green-brown eyes wide and glowing. She dipped an awkward
curtsey, then gave her hand to Tesc. "Maiden bless," she
murmured.

Serroi and Dinafar watched the family move off, the young
ones turning to wave again and again. Serroi smiled. "You've
made friends." She eyed the girl thoughtfully. "Dina. . . ."

"No." Dinafar's voice was firm. She turned and headed for
the embankment. "I know what you mean to say. You keep
trying to shunt me off where you think I'll be safe." She
shook her head. "I don't want to be safe, Meie." She stopped
and bit her lip. "Jern. I want more than just being safe. I
don't know what it is. Something. Help me learn."

"If I don't get you killed."

Covered with brown dust, anonymous small figures, they
climbed onto the Highroad and moved slowly toward the
main gates of Oras, lost among a throng of other brown-
dusted figures trudging into the city. Only one of the thick
gates was open; the crowd was narrowed to a thread as it
trickled through the gate under the gaze of half a dozen
cold-eyed guards. Ahead of Serroi and Dinafar a small
woman was hauled roughly to one side. The kerchief she
wore was jerked off her head and the guards used it to scrub
hard at her face, ignoring her protests and the vehement ob-
jections of those with her. While this was going on, Serroi
moved through the gate and stepped hastily into a side street,
Dinafar close behind her, her eyes sparkling with glee at
fooling the guards. Serroi leaned against a wall, her heart
thudding in her throat, unshed tears burning in her eyes She
pressed her hands against her eyes, struggling to control the
tides of emotion pouring through her.

Dinafar fidgeted about for a moment then went to the end
of the narrow alley and started talking to a pair of urchins
squatting on the stones, pretending to sell battered plums, ac-

tually begging. Hearing the noise, Serroi pulled her hands down and stood watching the girl's animated figure, hands flying in wide expansive gestures. She smiled at the assurance Dinafar had acquired. *She's trying to take care of me now. Sweet strong flower growing from a midden. The Biserica will be good for her—if she ever makes it there.*

Dinafar crouched beside the boys, listening intently to their interrupted bursts of speech, echoing their peculiar piping cries as they called out to the passersby. Serroi looked around. The alley was small and dark, a cul-de-sac between high walls. At the far end she could see a pile of refuse and discarded lumber. *Where the boys sleep, I suppose.* She walked slowly back toward the main street, waited a second, then touched Dinafar's shoulder. "We better be going."

The girl looked up, nodded, jumped to her feet. She walked without words beside Serroi as the two of them threaded through the noisy gaping crowd filling the street. Overhead the sky was rapidly darkening and clouds were beginning to gather. Serroi looked repeatedly at the girl, wondering what was bothering her; she was unusually silent and as somber as she had been back in the fisher village. "What's wrong, Dina?"

"Where are we going? Do you know a place were we can stay?"

Serroi rubbed at her nose. "When you're ready, I suppose I'll find out. We're going to our long lost uncle, little sister."

"But . . . huh?" Dinafar stared down at her. She stumbled against a man; he grinned and slid his arm around her, but moved on good naturedly when she pushed him away. "I thought . . . you've really got an uncle here?"

Serroi shook her head. "No, little one; no blood relative but a man who serves the Maiden by serving us." She glanced up at the clouding sky. "There's not much time. Let me do the talking when we get to his place. Hurry now." She walked as rapidly as she could, wriggling through the crowd, pulling Dinafar along with her, ignoring both curses and the indulgent cries of happy people. She led Dinafar rapidly across the city, leaving the main street and working back through narrower and narrower streets until she reached the portside section where the wall was lined with warehouses and grimy taverns.

Close up under the wall there was a battered building, a slowly rotting structure that was standing in pools of high-smelling ooze. The drains were badly plugged around here by refuse and dead men so the nightly rains could not escape and the falling water stayed on the worn pavement, turning a milky white with threads of ocher and yellow-green as if the water itself rotted. Lines of foam edged the pools and drifted in sluggish clumps around lumps of other unidentifiable substances. A few drops of rain splattered into the sluggish fluid, raising a stench that was thick and sour-sweet and strangling. Dinafar gathered her skirt close to her and walked on the tips of her toes with a taut wariness that amused Serroi. "When we go in, keep still," she said.

"You already said that." Dinafar pinched her nostrils shut. "Do we have to?" she croaked.

"Yes." Serroi moved ahead of her and pushed through the swinging door.

Inside, in the small dark foyer, the smells made a massive raid on their senses. What light there was shone red and obscured more than it revealed. Serroi crossed the foyer, Dinafar close behind, and stepped into the taproom. In the light of two lanterns they saw a number of men sitting in small groups at scattered tables, two leaning on the long bar; the smell was more wholesome or at least was overpowered by the varied liquors served here. The small wiry man behind the bar paused in the middle of drawing a mug of ale and stared at them while the hum of voices filling the room fell to silence.

The barman finished with the ale, set the mug before a one-eyed man and came to the end of the bar, scowling at them, his hands fisted against his hipbones. "Git, boy. This ain't no flowershop."

Serroi smiled up at him, letting her lips tremble. "Yael-mri speaks in me," she whispered. More loudly, she said, "Uncle Coperic." The men at the nearest tables lifted their heads and stared.

The barman set his hands flat on the stained wood, his scowl softening. "Jinnit's kids?"

"Yes, uncle."

"What'a doin' here? Where y' ma?"

"Home. She got married again two years since and is with child."

"Stepfather kick you out?"

"Sorta."

He turned away and yelled into the gloom. "Haqtar! Get over here." A dull-faced man came shambling to the bar. "Hold bar a while." He tugged irritably at the ties of his apron, jerked it over his head and thrust it at the man. "This's no place f'r kids," he muttered, scowling at the ugly, vicious man. "No credit," he snapped. "Get goin before you draw drink."

"Yah, berom." The words stumbled out of the thick-lipped mouth, the labored voice matched the dull face. His little eyes brightened as he looked past Coperic at Serroi and Dinafar.

"Get way, fool." Coperic caught hold of a doughy arm and twisted until the man backed off, whining with pain. "These ain't meat f'r you." He turned to Serroi and Dinafar. "Maiden's tits, I give Jinnit hell on this. No place f'r kids. Come on." He hustled them through a door behind the bar, then squeezed past and led them up a narrow wooden stair that creaked protest at every step, even under Serroi's light weight. Climbing behind him, Serroi smiled to herself.

Coperic was one of the network of newsgatherers and silent suppliers that the Biserica maintained about the land— and he had other things he did; not even Yael-mri knew them all. A clever man. The staircase was proof enough of that, an efficient and invisible alarm. No man could climb it without giving ample warning of his approach and few would suspect that this was precisely why the steps squealed.

At the top of the staircase a long dim hall stretched back into shadow with floorboards that sank and groaned under their feet. Serroi began to feel that Coperic was a bit too thorough in his precautions. The whole building seemed to be swaying and unsteady under her feet.

Coperic pushed open an unlocked door at the far end of the hall and waved them inside.

Dust covered every surface. Greasy plates sat on an equally greasy table. The dust itself looked as if it would smear over anything it touched. The sheets on the unmade bed were grey with long use and the quilts leaked batting through old tears and were dark with ancient sweat and greasy mottles. The stagnant air held many odors, the strongest being stale sweat and urine. She wrinkled her nose at Coperic. "Don't you think this is carrying things too far?"

When he didn't answer, she crossed to the window and peered out through a knothole in one of the rotting shutters. As far as she could tell, the tavern backed onto the citywall; its mossy stones were close by the window. A dead end? Frowning, she turned and scanned his bland wrinkled face.

The man who'd arranged those stairs and this squalid room had to have a back door even though that seemed impossible.

"Who the hell are you?" His voice was cold. He stood with his arms folded, his deepset eyes drilling into her.

"Not what I seem." She pulled the cap off and ran her fingers through her hair until the squashed curls stood out in a wild tangle, then stripped off the gloves and showed him her olive-green hands.

Coperic relaxed. "Maiden's tits, meie. The whole damn army's poking about for you." He jerked a thumb at Dinafar. "Who's she?"

"My business." She shook her head. "There's no danger in her, only to her."

"It's done." He shrugged. "What do you want here?"

"Shelter. A bird." She rubbed at her eyes. "Nearga-nor is moving on the mijloc; Sons of the Flame involved in it somehow; and there's a plot against the Domnor, a crazy stupid ... never mind, the Biserica has to know."

"No bird." He scowled at Dinafar. "Girl, you wait outside a minute."

Dinafar crossed quickly to Serroi, took hold of her sleeve.

Serroi patted her hand. "We'll both go. Call us when you're ready." She took Dinafar's arm and hurried her out of the room. In the hallway, the girl started to protest but Serroi silenced her with a headshake. "Wait," she murmured. "He has a right to his secrets." She looked off down the hall, remembering that she'd left the cap behind, hoping no one would come and find them.

"Come." Coperic stood in the doorway, his face unreadable.

As she stepped back into the room with Dinafar behind her, she heard the rain dripping steadily outside. Inside, the gloom had deepened but there was enough light left for her to see the black hole in the wall. She slipped out of her backpack and held it dangling by the straps. Behind her she could hear Dinafar doing the same. She reached out her free hand and the girl took it.

"Through here." Coperic stood back and waited until they crawled into the dusty hole. After a foot of stone the hole widened suddenly. Serroi had just time to curl her body and roll, then catch Dinafar as she fell through.

Coperic came through and clicked the panel shut. He brushed past them. There was a sliding clash in the darkness, a shower of sparks and a quick lift of flame. Using the tinder, he lit a lamp then pinched the first flame out.

They were in a small comfortable room carved out of the wall's stone, a room almost painfully neat. There was a padded armchair, a bed neatly made up, a rack of scrolls against one wall, a table with a straight-backed chair pushed under. Opposite the entrance there was another door, a narrow hole closed by heavy planks. Coperic sat on the bed and waved at the stuffed chair. Serroi dropped her pack and sat, Dinafar sinking onto the floor beside her knee. "No bird?"

"Right." He was more relaxed now, a tired cleverness in his face, shrewdness bright in his eyes, eyes that abruptly narrowed to creases as he yawned, then yawned again, belatedly masking the gape behind a narrow hand. "Sorry, meie, I've been on my feet since I don't know when. About the bird. I tried sending one out a couple of days ago. With Norim and Sons flooding into the city and all the fuss you and your shieldmate kicked up, I got nervous, thought the Biserica ought to know." He scratched at the crease running from his long nose to the corner of his mouth. "Lots of traxim around, damn stinkin' demons aping bird-shape, ought to. . . . I sent out a bird without a message capsule to see what would happen. It got maybe a quarter of a mile. Then the traxim swarmed it, carried it off midtown somewhere, couldn't track it all the way down, too many demons skitterin' around. I thought about sending a courier. Changed my mind. With everyone pouring into Oras, anyone heading out would have a lot of unfriendly eyes on him." He managed a smile. "Maiden's blood, meie, what the hell did you do?"

"Saw something we shouldn't." She leaned back in the chair, one hand over her eyes. "Coperic, did you hear what happened to Tayyan . . . what is it, Dina?"

Dinafar rose on her knees, wrapped warm hands about Serroi's. "I wish . . ." she began. She raised Serroi's hand and held it against her cheek. "What those guards said was true, meie. You remember I was talking to those boys?"

"Yes."

"Well, after we'd talked a bit, I asked them why all the fuss at the gate. They . . . they said that two meie . . . had . . . had tried to . . kill the Domnor. Guards chased them. One got away. The other . . . the other put a knife in her throat before they could stop her."

Serroi pulled her hand free, stood, looked blindly around, went to the far wall by the crude exit, folded her arms against the wall and leaned her forehead on them. She shuddered with anguish but she had no tears, no tears for her shieldmate or herself. All the time she'd known—known! But still she'd hoped, irrationally hoped, that she could retrieve her foul betrayal, make all right again. But Tayyan was dead. There was no changing that. No way to say to her I'm sorry. No way to say to her I'll do anything, anything, anything to make this up to you. A hand touched her shoulder. A quivering voice said, "Meie?"

She swung around, angry, wanting to hurt, but Dinafar's face was too open, too vulnerable. Serroi opened her mouth to tell the girl to get away from her, to leave her alone, that she couldn't take Tayyan's place and was a fool to try. She opened her mouth, then looked past Dinafar at the worn, weary face of Coperic. The resentment washing out of her, leaving behind only a weariness to match his; she sighed, pressed her back against the wall, and let herself slide down until she was sitting on the floor. She looked up. "I'm all right, Dina. Don't fuss."

Dinafar dropped to sit on her heels beside her, silent and unhappy.

Serroi swallowed. She was tired, so tired it was hard to think. She lifted a shaking hand, stared at it a moment, let it drop back into her lap. "Coperic, I'd better tell you what really happened. Get this to the Biserica however you can, soon as you can." Once again she went through the story, her voice dull and even, hiding nothing, excusing nothing. The race, their sneaking out, coming back more than a little drunk. The secret meeting. What she and Tayyan had seen and heard. What happened after, the flight, the boat, the village and what she learned there, the eventful return to Oras. Coperic listened intently, the fingers of one hand tapping restlessly at his knee. When she finally fell silent, he leaned forward, his thin body a taut curve.

"You got loose, meie, why come back here? You should have gone fast as you could to the Biserica."

"What I said," Dinafar burst out.

Serroi dropped her head back until the coolness of the stone came through the matting of her hair. "Listen, both of you. Right now I'm hanging on by my fingernails. Don't try stopping me from doing what I have to do." She closed her eyes. "Have to do!" she repeated fiercely, then sighed again. "Dina, I know you mean well, but please don't. I'm fond of you, but you're . . . I . . . I'm sorry, but you're interfering in something that's none of your business. I lived twenty-seven years before we met; there's no part of me you own, child, and a great deal you'll never understand. I'm sorry." She opened her eyes, stared blindly at the flickering lamp. "Sorry. People hurt you if you get close enough to them, you hurt them. Sometimes it's more than you can bear, but you do bear it, you bear it because you have to." She sat up, paused. "I'm rambling. Coperic, in the morning I'm going to the Temple. The Daughter can get me in to see the Domnor without fuss if she chooses to do so. If nothing goes wrong, I'll be back by noon. If I'm not . . . does she know about you, the Daughter?"

"No." He scanned her face, shook his head slightly. "Why?"

She dipped her fingers into her money sack, eased the tajicho out and held it in the curve of her palm. She stared at it a moment, seeing glimmers from the lamp dancing in the clear crystal; abruptly, she ran her thumb over the hard, bright surface, then tucked the egg-shaped crystal into her boot, squeezing it into a small pocket near the top. "I'm protected well enough from demon eyes and Norim spells. If I'm not back by noon, forget me. What now?"

He frowned. "Hard to say. I've been up here long enough; don't want Haqtar getting snoopy, got to go back down, grumble about having to look after a pair of brats, swear I'll send you packing come the Scatter." He stood. "I'd better get the two of you settled. There're several rooms up here. Not very clean, I'm afraid. Not as bad as that." He flipped a hand toward the hole in the wall. "I'll get some sheets, clean ones. Hungry?"

"Too tired to be hungry. Dina?"

"Yes." The girl stirred. "I'm half starved."

"That's settled, then. I'll bring you something to eat." He took a step toward the wall, stopped. "Morescad has slapped a curfew on the city despite the Gather crowd. This place closes in an hour. Come." He gave his hand to Serroi and pulled her onto her feet. "You'll be all right?"

She nodded. "I'm just tired."

He looked at her a moment. "Right," he said dryly. Taking the lamp, he preceded them out of the hidden room; when Serroi crawled from the hole, he handed her the boy's cap she'd dropped in the middle of the floor. "Better keep this around." Without waiting for an answer, he strode away, the floorboards creaking under his sandals.

Outside, he stopped at a hall closet to fish out fresh sheets. After handing them a pair each, he went on down the shivering hall to a door close by the head of the stairs. Like everything else here, the door creaked when he pushed it open. He lit the lamp inside from the one he carried, then opened the window a crack. "You'll be safe enough in here, girl. The door's stronger than it looks. Soon as we're out, you drop the bar. Hear? I'll be up in a little with your food."

Dinafar nodded, turned slowly, looking unhappily at the small, bare room. "Meie, can't I stay with you?"

Blinking wearily, Serroi murmured, "You'll be fine here, Dina." Followed by Coperic, she left the room, hearing the bar clunk home with unnecessary vigor behind them.

"Touch of temper there." Coperic brushed past her and shoved open the door directly across the hall.

Serroi stepped inside and looked around. This room was a twin to the other. "She'll make a good meie, if that's the path she chooses."

"A lot of passion in her."

Serroi chuckled softly. "We don't vow chastity, you know that well enough, my friend. Only childlessness."

He touched her cheek lightly, then moved past her and lit the lamp sitting in the middle of a dusty table. He looked down at the chair, frowned, crossed to the bed and pulled off the old tattered sheets. He flicked the ends over the chair and table, then came back to her to stand looking down into her face. He dropped the sheets, kicked them to one side as he lifted a hand and brushed its back very gently along the side of her face. "Now that the girl's not here, how are you really, little meie?"

"Hanging on." She dropped cap and rucksack to the floor, smiled tentatively then leaned forward, her head resting in the hollow beneath his collarbone. "I've got a job to do," she murmured. "That helps."

His fingers played in the small tight curls at the base of her skull. "What about tonight?"

She pushed back, looked up at him. A smallish man, he didn't tower over her; without the wariness he seemed a gentle, affectionate man entirely different from the cynical manipulator of the bar. She tried to smile. "You offer?"

"Comfort for both of us. A shared solitude. More, if you're willing."

"Comfort, ahhh. . . ." Her knees sagged and she began to

cry, hard painful sobs that wracked her body. Sobs she couldn't stop. Tears finally for the lost shieldmate.

Muttering under his breath, he steered her to the chair and got her seated. Then he slapped new sheets onto the bed, tucked the ragged quilt back in. Finished, he marched back to Serrli. "Stand up."

Hiccupping and gasping, she stood swaying in front of him. He stripped off her vest and tunic, folded them over the back of the chair. The weaponbelt landed in a broken circle on the table; he pushed her to the bed and sat her down, pulled off her boots, untied the lacings of her trousers, then eased them off and tossed them aside. He sat beside her on the bed, bending over her, smoothing a hand along her shoulders, working on the tight hard muscles there for several moments until she began to relax. He touched her nipple lightly, smiled as he heard her breathing quicken. "More than comfort?" he murmured.

"More, oh yes," she whispered huskily, pressing her hand over the hand cupping her breast.

He swung his legs up onto the bed, then jerked upright. "Shit," he muttered. "Forgot, little meie. Not yet, not yet." He swung back off the bed and tugged her onto her feet, taking her stumbling and unwilling to the door. "Bar it after me, then get back into bed. I've got to close up downstairs and get food for the girl. Bar the door. You hear?"

She yawned, then suddenly twisted around and pressed herself against him, locking her hands behind his neck. "I need you," she whispered. She pulled his head down and kissed him with a kind of desperation.

"Maiden's tits," he breathed, then pulled her hands loose. "Bar the door, meie."

Twisting restlessly about on the bed, she heard sounds in the hall, then a knocking. She sat up, then realized that the knocking was on the door across the hall. Coperic bringing food to Dinafar. She got out of bed and padded to the door, leaned against it, waiting. When a knock sounded by her ear, she deepened her voice. "Who is it?"

"Uncle." Coperic's voice.

As he stepped inside, she went back to the bed and sat on its edge, wiping the soles of her feet with the end of the quilt.

He pulled the door shut and barred it. "Far as I know, Haqtar's the only Plaz spy downstairs; the rest are thieves, a pimp or two, one smuggler. . . ." He dropped into the rickety chair and unlaced his sandals.

"A friend of yours?" She inspected her feet, then slipped into bed.

"Now, little one, is that a friendly thing to say?" He pulled off his tunic and draped it over hers. "Haqtar's a fool, no danger to you or anyone. Still it's best to be careful." He finished undressing and moved to stand by the bed, frowning thoughtfully down at her. "You should get as much sleep as you can."

"Cold feet?" She grinned up at him, reached up a hand to him. "Don't think I could bear nightmares tonight."

He lifted the covers and slipped in beside her. His body was slight but strong, warm and intensely alive. She snuggled against him, letting that warmth flow through her. The healing contact with other flesh began easing the wounds in her spirit. His hands curved around her shoulders. "Been a long time," he murmured.

"Mmmmh?"

"Never mind." He began stroking her brow, caressing the softly quivering eyespot.

"Don't." She tried to pull away.

"Hush. Be still."

She pressed her face against the hard flat muscles of his chest and let the tears come again, gentle healing tears this time, weeping silently until the touch of his hands and her body's response made her forget why she wept.

THE CHILD: 10

For three nights Serroi trudged across the desolation. The stony ground gave way to rolling sand which took an even greater toll on her failing strength. She ate the last of her food early in the morning of the third day, choking down the dried-out meat and rotting fruit. When she tried to sleep, her rest was broken by nightmares so that she woke almost as tired as when her eyes first closed.

Toward the end of the fourth night she stumbled along, her tongue swollen, her mouth leather-dry, her head unsteady on her neck. As the sun climbed clear of the horizon, she found herself at the top of a slope in the middle of emptiness with no shelter anywhere. Eyes blurring, head burning, she started down, fell, rolled to the bottom of the slope and lay there, dazed.

It seemed to her that she sat up and lay curled on the sand simultaneously as if she'd split into two parts. A vinat came tiptoeing over the sand, nosed at her-on-the-sand, then stood over her-who-knelt, large luminous eyes staring out over the dark-bright sands. The sands stirred, opened up. She was kneeling/lying in masses of blue and crimson flowers. Everything was bright and tranquil. A fire began burning in front of her. A crystal pot came from nowhere and settled on the flames and the liquid inside began boiling. A strange woman veiled in grey stepped out of the pot and moved to her-on-the-sand. With a long bright knife, almost a sword, she cut the crouching body into small sections and threw them into the crystal pot that grew larger in order to accommodate the bits of flesh and bone. They boiled and boiled. It seemed to her that days passed, years passed. The bones were boiled clean, churning round and round in the crystal pot until the fire entered into them, burned through into the marrow, glowed red-gold. Then the grey woman fished them out of the water, slipping her slim white hand into the bubbling, steaming liquid as if it were no more than spring water. She lay the bones back into the shape of a girl child. In the skull-holes she

173

placed two pebbles. The skeleton glowed hot, like lines of
fire; the blue flowers nodded their bright heads against the
bones, the crimson flowers brushed their bright heads against
the bones. Flesh grew back over the bones, the stones turned
into eyes. The grey woman bent over the one-who-lay-on-
the-sand, watching the bones grow flesh around themselves;
the head beneath the veil turned. She-who-knelt quivered as
that dark secret gaze passed over her. The grey woman held
out a hand. Her fingers were cool and filled with life; they
closed over the hand of her-who-knelt, lifted her, flew with
her, the spirit-her.

Spirit-Serroi looked down, saw a hole in the earth. "What
is that hole in the earth?" she said.

The grey woman said nothing, but took her down and
down, spiraling into the hole. It grew larger and larger until
they were skimming over a river that divided into two parts,
one flowing south, the other north. The south-flowing river
gleamed bright as gold; the north-flowing river ran dark and
smoky. The grey woman pointed at the dark river and spirit-
Serroi saw bones floating in the murk; the grey woman
pointed at the bright river, then flew with spirit-Serroi over
the shining water. She opened her hand and spirit-Serroi
drifted gently downward, still calm, even tranquil, though she
fell toward the earth. She slid into the water and it flowed
into her; she felt the life-force energizing her; she turned over
and over in the flood. Then the white hand dipped into the
water and drew her up again.

Where the glowing river fell over a cliff into a second hole
there were two trees, a bright tree and a dark tree, round
fruits hanging on each, ripe round fruits bursting with juice.
The grey woman took her down to the trees. This time she
settled spirit-Serroi beside the dark tree. When she took her
hand away, Serroi drifted toward the bright tree. She reached
for a glowing fruit, but the grey woman slapped her hand
away, took her back to the dark tree. The fruits were purple
and fleshy, dripping crimson juice. Spirit-Serroi plucked one
and ate it, then screamed as pain jagged through her, her spirit
body stretched and twisted, near torn apart by the pain. The
grey woman watched, silent and impassive. Though she said
nothing, Serroi perceived the pain as a test. She fought to
control it, to force it into a small dark knot and expel it from
her while she fought also to maintain the integrity of her
spirit body. At the end of a struggle more intense than any
she'd known, more intense even than the struggle with her

Noris, she cast out the pain. The grey woman took another
fruit from the dark tree and extended it to Serroi. She drew
back. The grey woman forced her to take it. Shivering with
fear she bit into the crimson flesh. She felt nothing. Joy
bubbled in her; she swallowed the rest of the fruit then
laughed and danced around the tree.

The grey woman waved a hand at the shining tree. Serroi
darted to the glowing fruit and ate eagerly. Fire burned in
her, seared her, consumed her; again she fought to control
the burning. Again she won the fight. She thrust the fire from
her, handled it, let it burst into the air over her head.

They flew on, the grey woman taking her many places,
showing her many things, testing her again and again, speaking no word, simply guiding her, letting her do and be.

Then they were back with her-who-lay-on-the-sand, the
vinat standing silent guard over the body. The flesh was on
the bones, the eyes plump under closed eyelids. She looked
worn and hungry, the girl curled up on the sand, lips cracking, feet wrapped in bloody rags, a ragged brown robe half
covering a soiled white shift. The veiled woman bent over
her, touched her cheek with cool fingers, then she looked
back, her unseen eyes fixed on the spirit-Serroi as she spoke
for the first time, her voice low and rich. "Cherish all things
that live," she said, then she was gone, fading into the clear
hard air of the desert night.

The body pulled spirit-Serroi. Wriggling about, pushing,
shoving, she fitted herself back into her flesh.

When she woke, the moons were rising. She tried to sit up,
fell back as her arms collapsed under her, tried again and
trembled upright. She rubbed at her eyes, vaguely surprised
to see no vinat, no blue and crimson flowers. *A dream, just a
fever dream.* She pushed up onto her knees, rested a moment,
then got to her feet and stood swaying as she brushed feebly
at the sand crusting her clothing. Abandoning this, she
straightened and turned slowly while she *desired* water. When
the tug came, it came far stronger than before; through her
weariness and pain she knew a flash of hope. From somewhere strength came into her; like a river of fire it flowed
into her. She could feel her bones glowing. With trembling
fingers she tied the cloth around her neck and began walking
in the direction her eye-spot pulled her. The fire slowly died
but while it was there the desert was eerily beautiful for her,
a continually changing pattern of black, grey and silver.

Nijilic Thedom led the long ragged scatter of moons waxing
to half across the starfields, its milky light shimmering
through the air and touching surfaces into brightness.

As the night progressed, her dream-fire left her and she began drifting in and out of consciousness, sometimes coming
to herself with her face in the sand and no idea of how she
got there. Sand under her feet changed and hardened, was
covered with small stones that struck sharply into the soles of
her dragging feet. She stumbled along, half conscious, weaving around larger and larger boulders until she lost all idea of
direction.

Suddenly her eye-spot began throbbing frantically. She
leaned against a boulder, resting and listening, holding her
breath as she waited. She heard a thready tinkle, a faint bubbling. She pushed away from the stone, walked half a dozen
steps and fell to her knees beside a small, shining pool at the
base of a sharp rise. She dipped a trembling hand into the
pool and stared at the water quicksilvering out of her palm.
Dark and secret, the pool caught the starshine and shimmered
the broken light back to her. She dipped her hand again, not
quite believing that she could come back to life.

She stretched out flat and buried her face in the coolness,
drank and drank until she could hold no more. The water
was joy, in her and on her. Then, as in the dream, her stomach cramped. She gasped and rose to her knees, clutching at
her middle, groaning and throwing herself about as the pain
pulsed through her. After a few moments, though, the
teaching of the dream reached into her and she brought her
body under control. She stretched out, gasping, on the sand
until the sun threw up fans of light on the eastern horizon,
warning her that she needed to find shelter. She dragged herself onto her feet and looked around. A pile of large boulders
leaned against a cliff about twice her height, forming a shallow hollow that looked big enough to hold her. She stripped
off her outer rope, dipped it in the water, then settled herself
in the hollow, the dripping robe spread over her.

She slept the morning through, slept better than she had in
days, dreamed a little without the vivid awareness of the pre-
vious day. She woke at a scurrying sound, a tickling over her
leg. A small grey-green lizard was running up the side of the
boulder by her knee. She watched as it ran in and out of
shadow and finally scurried toward her head. Choking down
her reluctance, she snatched the lizard from the rock and
killed it.

Using a sharp-edged flake of stone, she skinned the lizard, ate the meat raw off the small bones, then braved the sun to wash hands and face at the pool. She took only a few mouthfuls of water, having learned a hard lesson, wet her robe again, and went back to try sleeping the rest of the day away.

She stayed at the tiny spring the next night, continuing to rest and rebuild her strength. She ate more lizards and some of the bitter herbs growing in cracks of the rock. When the sun went down again, she drank as much as she could hold, soaked all her clothing in the water of the pool, then wrapped it around her. As soon as she had her direction, she scrambled up the boulders, dragged herself over the steep rise, and set out for the next water.

The hard earth was littered with small sharp bits of rock that could cut to the bone if her foot came down wrong on one of them. This slowed her, put a strain on her strength; she felt her bones beginning to glow again as if they sucked heat and energy from the stones that threatened her. The fire upheld her for a long time, draining slowly away as she made detours around cracks in the earth too wide to leap over and too steep—sometimes even undercut—to climb.

The sun came up before she found the second water. She wound the spare cloth around her head and walked on until she found a crack with negotiable walls. She spent the day there, dozing and enduring. It was both easier and harder to endure, now that she knew there'd be an end to thirst and pain, now that she was wholly sure she'd get out of this desert alive. She was more impatient than ever to cross the last miles of stone and sand. The day went on and on, seemed never to end.

That night the walking was hard. The land was again rising and there were far more rocks, larger rocks, strewn over the unforgiving surface. The night was bright enough with Nijilic Thedom and his companions hanging overhead, but moonlight was treacherous, fooling her with pools of sharp-edged shadow that was just enough different from sun-shadow to throw off her depth-perception.

When the sun rose, she had not yet reached the spring. The pull on her eye-spot was so strong that she kept on. Before the stone grew hot enough to burn her, she saw dusty green and a few birds soaring on leather wings.

The spring welled up from the rock and ran off to the southeast in a small, noisy stream. There was a patch of stunted brush, birds' nests in holes in the rock and in the bushes, some small rodents.

She drank, sparingly this time, then looked around. A rodent poked a quivering nose out from under a stone, was joined by a second, then a third, all staring at her from bright beady eyes. Again she nerved herself and moved cautiously about, gathering small stones. She closed her eyes, opened them again. The rodents were still there. "The Maiden forgive me, small brothers," she whispered, then threw the stones one after another. Two rodents fell dead and the other vanished.

She rubbed at her eyes, then sighed, sat down and skinned the beasts with a bit of knife-edged stone. The flesh was redder and sweeter than the lizard meat. When she finished them, she explored the nests, took three of the eggs and sucked out their contents, throwing the shells away. She drank again, spat out the first mouthful, drank heavily, then rested a moment, her face immersed in the water.

She stayed at this water for two nights and three days, dreaming and struggling to understand her dreams, growing more and more unwilling to accept what they seemed to be telling her. For the first time she felt desperately lonely, not daring to make friends with the animals she would use for food. She would not, could not, play with them, talk to them, then kill and eat them.

When night fell at the end of the third day, she drank from the pool then began following the stream. The moons were already far into their travels when the sky darkened enough for them to be seen. The little stream picked up their light, sang and shimmered in the milk-white glow. Walking slowly beside the small strong stream, she felt a kinship with the dancing water and a greater peace than she could remember. She felt strength grown hard in her; the trek from the desert had fined her, tested her, and she had won through.

She walked steadily beside the stream, humming to herself. The flight dream and the odd things that happened afterward faded from her mind. She felt physically strong and bubbling with health, ready to dance with the moon shadows. Four moons set, two rode high, the two became four then five. It was a vast and stately dance. The moon shadows of the scattered shrubs danced about in multiples like dark silent laughter. Her own feet danced in flickering shadow. She threw out her arms, swung round and round, shouting her joy into the wandering breeze, splashed into the stream and kicked sprays of glimmering silver bubbles into the air. After a while, she settled to a steady walk, quiet and contented.

When there were only three moons left and these were low on the western horizon, the stream tumbled into a slit in the rock. Serroi dropped to her knees, quivering at this echo of her dream. She stretched up, still on her knees, tilted her head back, flung out her arms. The starfield was blooming and the Dancers rocking like cradles along the horizon. Then she bent forward and listened to the water booming in the hole, felt the boom echoing hollowly inside her. She blinked back tears. "I won't cry, I won't give in." She bent to the water, splashed the coolness onto her face, drunk deeply, drank again. With a great show of energy, she jumped to her feet and walked on. When she was several strides away, she *desired* water, then turned west to follow the tug.

The night wore on. The Dancers set and took the moon shadows with them. Serroi faced her loneliness, her pain, her weariness, and slowly accepted them into her; in this remnant of night she found a measure of calm as she narrowed the focus of her strength to simple survival. Without knowing how she knew, she felt that her ordeal was almost over. She was changed, she could take life into her own hands now and shape it as she wished.

An hour after the Dancers set, the eastern sky flushed vermilion. As the sun rose higher, her shadow walked ahead of her like a flat black giant, jerking comically as her feet moved. She climbed a small rise and began looking about for shelter.

The parched land stretched out on all sides, dipping gradually down toward the western horizon, hard earth, dull brown earth, crossed and recrossed by deep fissures, stones of all sizes scattered like tiles across it. One of the larger boulders rocked back and forth, then staggered up onto four skinny legs.

THE WOMAN: XI

Coperic set the tray on the table, pulled the chair across to the bed and sat down in it, smiling at Serroi. She blinked drowsily, stretched, patted a yawn, then smiled up at him, deeply content. Working a hand out from under the tumbled bedclothes, she stretched it out to him. The food cooled as they sat that way, sharing a long moment's relaxation from a longer tension, sharing affection rather than passion, an affection both needed badly.

Coperic was driven by his needs to hide this side of his nature. Only rarely could he share without subterfuge. He was a complex man, a strange man Serroi could marvel at but not fully understand. She lay warm, comfortable, relaxed, contemplating the dreamy calm on his face so different from that sour greedy mask he wore downstairs. His plots and schemes, most of them of a kind to bring him under the headsman's axe were they discovered, these were as necessary to him as the air he breathed. He was smuggler and spy, master of thieves and vagabonds, cynic and idealist, fanatically loyal to his friends, a bitter enemy to those who injured him.

A minute more, then both broke the hold. Serroi threw the covers back and stood. After putting on the crumpled boy's clothing for one more day, she brushed off her feet and stamped into her boots. Crossing to the table, stepping over Coperic's feet and answering his friendly grin, she picked up the tray and carried it to the bed. "You have many people downstairs?"

"Not open, not for another couple of hours." He rubbed at his long nose. "Lot of my customers are allergic to morning light."

Serroi took a few minutes to eat, then she looked up. "Take care, Pero. Has Morescad got anything against you?"

Coperic shook his head. "I'm too little to catch his eye; besides I mean to keep my head low for the next few passages. No chances for greedy old Coperic."

"Wish I could believe that." She drained the cup. "Take care of the girl for me." She lifted the tray from her knees

180

and set it on the bed beside her. "She's going to kick up a fuss when she finds me gone, but she's a good child and far from stupid. If I don't make it back. . . . She scowled, touched her forehead. "Is the coloring still even on my face?"

Coperic leaned forward and drew his fingertips along the side of her face. "Yes, little meie; you'll have to chip it off with a chisel when you want to be yourself again."

She laughed, then sobered, caught hold of his hand, held it against her face for a moment. "I've got a cold feeling about today."

Coperic freed himself gently, leaned back in the chair, frowning at her. "You have to try it?"

She nodded. "For a lot of reasons. I suppose mostly because I have to live with myself after this." She flicked her fingers at the weaponbelt coiled on the table. "I'm leaving that and the pack with you."

He scratched at an eyebrow. "You're not thinking clearly about this, Serroi. It wouldn't be too hard to slip a message to the Domnor warning him of this plot and do it without blowing my cover or yours."

Serroi shook her head. "You're right, it'd be easy enough. How much would you believe if you got a note like that?"

"Can you be sure he'll believe you?"

One corner of her mouth twisted up, then she shook her head. "No, Pero, but I think the chances are better that I can convince him." She leaned forward. "The Nearga-nor seem to be holding a meeting here; I saw more than a dozen of them on the Highroad coming here. Why? How many of them are actually here? Hern's no fool, he's got to be asking himself what the hell's going on. It's not the Gather; the Norim don't have anything to do with the Maiden if they can help it." She stood. "If I don't come back, tell Yael-mri to remember my Noris, that I smell him in this." She slipped the cap on, tucked in stray wisps of hair. "Can I just walk out?"

He moved to the door and pulled it open. "Just go. No problem."

The side streets were empty and quiet in the clear calm dawn. The east burned with layers of red and gold that were reflected in the scummy pools. Serroi skirted the puddles and made her way to the main street where street vendors had mooncakes already frying in pots of fat. The street was filling with the crisp hot smells of oil and batter. Jugglers and beggars, fortune tellers and gamblers, thieves and acrobats, even a few petty Norids mixed with pilgrims up early on this Moongather Eve, all of them gathering around the cake vendor's stalls or setting up for the influx of pilgrims later on.

The harvest of coins. Serroi strolled along, smiling. For the street people these weren't holy days. What they took in by trick of hand or mind would keep them through the lean days of the Scatter. Jugglers and acrobats crunched down the mooncakes, wiped greasy hands on trousers, began practicing their arts. The beggars settled on their corners, sores flaming fresh. They too were practicing their whines, exhibiting their infirmities to each other. Dancers were warming up, stretching, turning, working their bodies. Street musicians were setting up their stands, blowing experimental trills on flutes, tuning other instruments, the singers humming snatches of popular lays or hymns to the Maiden. Gamblers were trying the sleight of hand on each other. The few early-rising pilgrims were mostly serious; even the laughing, joking visitors kept moving toward the Temple.

Serroi passed one or two of the gamblers who had snared victims, wrinkling her nose as the rustics hunched over shells or cards or scattered tiles, intent on their own impoverishment. She strolled through the noisy, colorful life that filled the main street, her spirits rising until a Sleykyn stepped into the street and began walking down its center. His serpent mask glittered, his scabbard clashed softly against the skirt of metal-inlaid velater strips that protected his groin. His velater-hide whip hung coiled in a leather pouch on his left side, only the handle showing; he could draw and strike with that whip in less than a second as Serroi knew only too well. She touched the shoulder where the cut still itched. He wore heavy leather gloves with metal inlays and thigh-high boots striped with the velater hide that could rip a man's skin off with a single glancing blow, the skin from the great dark predator of the sea depths whose scales had razor edges. He walked with a heavy arrogance that no one cared to challenge. For several minutes after he passed the street was empty, then it filled again with people talking and laughing a little too loudly.

Serroi moved unnoticed toward the Temple, a small dusty boy like countless other children—quiet and exuberant, awed and indifferent—brought to Oras to celebrate the Gather. Lost in this stream of pilgrims she rounded the curve of the Plaz-walls and saw the Temple ahead, crossing the end of the broad avenue. Around her she heard sudden intakes of

breath, angry curses, the faltering of pacing feet; she faltered
herself as she stared at the gathering beside the Temple gate.
Black-clad Followers of the Flame swaying and chanting
around a Son who stood high above them on a makeshift
stage, chanting in counterpoint as he shouted a diatribe
against the Maiden, naming her Hag and Whore, Demoness
and Deceiver. The pilgrims muttered uncomfortably, an-
grily—with no one daring to confront this affront to custom
and piety; under the anger there was a current of fear and
uncertainty that told Serroi with a terrible eloquence how
powerful the Sons of the Flame and their Followers had become.

She moved closer to a small family, mother and father and
three children, trying to seem a part of it as she moved past
the glaring eyes of Plaz guards wearing black armbands with
the circled flame embroidered conspicuously on them, moved
through the gate and down the tree-shaded walkway to the
Temple itself, letting the peace inside the walls lighten her
despair and soothe away the disturbance stirred up by the
demonstration outside.

Old but still unfinished, the Temple was a forest of pillars,
each with its unique carving of the Maiden. Every year or so
a new column was added, the figure a gift of another sculptor
and patron or group of patrons—wood and stone, ceramic
and mosaic, every medium but cold metal. Everywhere she
looked, Serroi could see images of the Maiden, stern or tender, laughing and light of limb, or formally gracious. Each
artist had carved or shaped his or her own vision of the great
Her. Somewhere within the forest of columns—a thousand at
the last count—a pilgrim could find that image of Her that
matched his or her inner vision. Serroi had come here half a
hundred times during her ward; even now in her preoccupa-
tion she reacted to the beauty and mystery of the place. Since
the columns were not roofed in but supported a delicate lat-
tice of stone, the morning sun painted lacy shadows on the
muted tessera of the mosaic floor. The noises of the street
were closed out by the massive walls; once she moved into
the columns they ceased to exist for her.

There were already many pilgrims here, telling their prayer
beads or sitting in quiet contemplation of the Maiden. A few
were wandering among the columns searching through the
hundreds of images for the one that spoke to them. The street
crowd had ignored the small boy; here, in the shadows and
the silence, the pilgrims took even less notice of her. She

moved quietly toward the central court, disturbed by the evil
she carried with her, the jarring she felt between her inner
turmoil and the holiness of this place.

She stepped out of the shadow onto the court's mosaic
floor. The fountain in the center of the court sang soft music
to her. At the far end of the large open space were the Door
and the Dais where the Daughter would enact the rite of the
Moongather, her chant echoed by the thousands of pilgrims
filling the court and all the space within the forest of
columns. She hesitated a moment by the coping of the fountain; she had only to cross, turn to her right at the far side
and follow the sanctuary's wall until she came to a small
plain door—until she was there, until she pulled the bell cord,
she was safe in her disguise. The small lump of the tajicho
was warm against her skin inside her boot, reassuring her as
it warned her of hostile search. She looked up, touched the
hand of one of the maiden figures in the fountain; it seemed
to her that the fingers warmed to hers a moment. Then she
shook her head, ruefully acknowledging her desperate need
for reassurance.

She walked quickly across the court. The silence was thick
and tense. She moved down the side of the simple rectangular
building that housed the Daughter and her acolytes. At the
small door, she raised her hand, touched the bell-pull. It was
carved from a large piece of amber into the shape of a slender, graceful hand. To sound the bell she had to take the
hand in hers and tug. The amber fingers felt warm and welcoming in hers. Her heart thudding, her breathing ragged, she
tugged and heard the muted sound of a bell ringing inside.

The door slammed open. She shrank away as she stared up
into the face of a Plaz guard, a big scarred man in carefully
smoothed tabard and clean leathers. He scowled down at her.
"What you want, boy?"

Serroi swallowed, her mouth suddenly dry. She cleared her
throat and croaked, "Message." Her tongue flicked along dry
lips. "Message for the Daughter," she said.

"Give. I see she gets it." He held out his left hand. Some
brawl in the past had taken the little finger and the top joint
off the fourth.

Fighting down a fear that was making her sick to her
stomach, Serroi shook her head. "Mouth message," she said
huskily. "Say to the Daughter this: She who milks the wind
and sows the dragon's teeth has words for the Daughter."

The guard grunted and leaned forward to peer skeptically

at her with slightly nearsighted eyes. "Stay here." He slammed the door in her face. She sank onto the pavement and tried to stop the shaking of her knees. With a trembling hand she wiped sweat from her face.

It's Moongather, she thought. *Except for the trouble Tayyan and I brought on our order, that guard would be a meie; though with the fuss the Sons are stirring up about us, maybe not, maybe it's not all my fault. Still, probably nothing to worry about. The Daughter has to be guarded. At least he wasn't wearing an armband. There must be some guards who aren't involved in this plot.* She rubbed at her nose. *Doesn't matter. I'm a boy, a Mouth, not the meie they're all looking for.*

The door jerked open. The guard beckoned. "Come on, boy," he growled.

She followed him inside. There was a small dark foyer that smelled strongly of wax and polish, than a hallway lit by oil lamps, scented oil, a sweet fragrance that reminded her of spring on a mountainside. The guard stumped ahead of her. His attitude began to bother her. He didn't seem to give a damn where he was, seemed deaf to the tranquility he shattered with each heavy step.

"In here, boy." He pulled back a curtain and motioned her through an archway, then clumped off as she stepped into the bare room where peace touched her fear like a benediction.

The room was a little longer than it was wide. Tapestries on the walls were dark blue with scattered white dots and line figures. After a moment she saw that these represented star groupings; the dots were stars, the white figures the legend images. At the far end of the room two chairs were pulled up facing each other. As she hesitated the tapestry by the chairs split and a veiled figure stepped inside the room. The slender graceful figure wore a long grey robe and over it a translucent grey veil so fine it seemed to float on the still air. The woman sat, beckoned to Serroi.

Heart pounding again, she crossed the room and stopped beside the empty chair. A graceful hand came under the veil; with a fluid gesture it invited her to sit and speak.

Serroi edged around the chair and sat, her toes dangling a handspan from the floor, feeling uneasy and becoming a bit angry at this treatment. The woman in the veil folded her hands in her lap and waited. Serroi bit her lip, then lifted her head to stare a challenge at the veil. "You are the Daughter?"

The hidden head inclined in a graceful assent.

Serroi waited, saying nothing.

"The Maiden's eyes are like mountain tarns, green and brown at once and filled with a wisdom beyond man's comprehension." The veiled woman's voice was warm, almost as deep as a man's.

Serroi relaxed; she knew that voice. She pulled off her gloves, held out her hands.

"The little meie!" The Daughter's veiled head turned from hands to face. "You said you have a message?"

Relief like euphoria swept through Serroi; she could lay her burden in this woman's hands, rid herself of the awful responsibility she carried; she leaned forward, spoke eagerly. "I beg you, doman Anas. Believe what I tell you now."

"Speak, meie. I will hear you." The coolness in the deep voice warned Serroi she'd better be convincing. The words tumbling from her lips, she recounted the events preceding her flight from Oras, finishing, "Please, doman Anas. Believe me and get me to the Domnor so I can warn him."

The Daughter lifted her hands, clapped twice. "Oh I do believe you, little meie." A low rippling laugh. "I do indeed." She stood.

Serroi heard a rattle behind her. She whipped up and around.

A Sleykyn came through the arch at the far end of the audience chamber.

She wheeled.

A second Sleykyn stood just behind the veiled figure.

"Why, Daughter?" There was anguish in Serroi's voice. "Why?"

"Don't fight, little meie." The Daughter's voice had taken on a hard edge. "The Sleykyn will have the meat off your bones. And you don't have much to lose, do you."

The tapestry parted again and a Norit walked through. Serroi's eyes widened as she recognized the Minarka she'd seen on the Highroad. His russet hair was pulled back from his face and tied behind his head with a narrow black ribbon whose ends he'd pulled forward to hang fluttering on his chest. His eyes were copper mirrors, cool and measuring, giving nothing away. He let his hand drop on the woman's shoulder and stood staring intently at Serroi. After a moment of this, he frowned. "Something is protecting her."

The Daughter lifted a slim white hand and rested it on his; her casually possessive air sickened Serroi. "She hasn't been searched. You heard what she said?"

"Of course. One wonders how many have heard her little tale." His eyes ran over Serroi again. "Still, she makes little difference. The thing is almost done. When this business is finished, I'd like to explore her anomalies. Tuck her away in the Plaz dungeons and forget her till then." His hand closed on her shoulder with bruising force. She leaned her veiled head back against him, breathing hard enough so that the puffs of air from her lips blew the grey veil about. "You can play with her then, my sicamar." His words held a hint of amusement, but his face was without expression. He squeezed the woman's shoulder again, then stepped back behind the tapestries.

Serroi swallowed, swallowed again, finding what she'd just seen almost impossible to believe. The Daughter—she who should be closest to the Maiden, strongest, wisest, sanest. "Why?"

"Why not?" The Daughter's voice was filled with contempt. She would neither justify her actions nor bother to debate one who had no power to threaten her. Serroi began to shiver. *A Nor's toy. Again. Maiden bless, again.* The Daughter watched in a hot silence, her breathing fast and hard, as the Sleykyn took Serroi's arm and led her away.

Not again. Not again. Not again. No more betraying. Not another Tayyan. No more animals done to death with my help. Hold out. Say nothing. Don't betray Dinafar or Coperic. Say nothing. Not a sound. If I can. Make them kill me. Say nothing. Over and over the words pounded through her head in time to the sound of her feet as the Sleykynin marched her through the arch and along the back way from the Temple to the Plaz, one on each side of her, holding her arms delicately in their gloved hands, hands that could rip the skin from her if they closed hard. A few ragged urchins saw them, faded away before them. She hoped Coperic would learn she'd been taken and be warned. *Be ready to leave at the slightest hint of trouble. Hear and be warned, my friend. I've sworn to say nothing, but such swearings have been betrayed before.*

They took her in through the small door in the Plaz wall that had admitted the Norid and his escort that other night. One Sleykyn opened the secret door, the other shoved her inside and followed close behind. He took her arm again, delicately again, and took her along the dark musty corridor whose blackness rapidly became complete as they left the entrance behind. Then light flared behind them. She risked a glance over her shoulder and saw that the second Sleykyn followed with a small torch.

They marched past the meeting room, then began winding downward through the rat-hole in the walls, emerging finally into a vast sub-basement, torch-lit and well furnished with the tools of torment, rack and screw, whipping posts and burning irons and all the other aids to reaming what truth the torturer wanted to hear from the reluctant bodies of his victims.

THE CHILD: 11

The creature staggered around, head swaying at the end of a long skinny neck, honking unhappily. It stumbled toward her, wincing, as cracked pads came down on bits of rock. Giggling, dizzy with relief, Serroi raced down the slope and stopped in front of the beast, gazing up into its mild silly face. "Jamat," she said. It ducked its head and nudged at her shoulder. She scratched between small round ears and slipped her fingers under the worn patched halter it was wearing. Fluttering from the tether ring under its chin, a bit of frayed rope slapped at her stomach.

She caught the rope and turned the beast. Walking along beside it she thought, *it must have been scared by something, broke away, then ran off in a panic and got itself lost.* She put her hand on its side, feeling the trembling, the labored breathing. *Poor thing, it's weak with hunger and thirst.* She glanced at the sun, then started leading the jamat forward. *No choice now, got to find water.*

Half the morning passed before she reached the spring. She had to use the animal control she'd learned in the Tower to keep the jamat moving. Again and again it tried to kneel and let itself die; again and again, she prodded it back on its feet, got it moving, though it honked mournfully and blew slime bubbles in her face. She was shaking with exhaustion when the jamat lifted its head, twitched the rope out of her hand and broke into a shambling trot. *It smells water.* She sighed and pushed the damp hair off her face, then began trudging after it—and found it blissfully sucking up water from a bubbling pool in a deep hollow. There was plenty of brush, dried grass, even some late flowers. She sat on the damp earth beside the pool, grateful for the rest and the touch of coolness. After a moment she stretched out and drank. Then she drove the jamat back so it wouldn't founder. As it browsed contentedly at the thorny brush around the pool, she killed and skinned two of the rodents that poked their noses up to see what was happening. She ate hungrily then buried the skin, entrails and bones.

The sun burned down. She moved to the spring and rolled into the water. Dripping and picking up grit on her knees, she crawled into a clump of bushes. The earth was covered with a layer of short dry grass and half-rotted leaves, a softer bed than she'd had for days.

She woke late in the afternoon and found the jamat kneeling close to her, its long neck drawn back, its head tucked behind the upthrust of its hipbone. Chuckling, she crawled out of her hollow, stood and stretched. Without disturbing the snoring beast, she raided nests for eggs and killed a fat lizard. After eating, she drank deeply, then stripped off her robe and let herself slip into the pool. With handfuls of sand she scrubbed herself clean, body and hair, until she tingled all over, then she began on her tattered robes. When she was finished, she pulled the robes around her and crawled back into the shade.

She woke again after the sun was down and toed the jamat awake. It rocked alertly to its feet and turned its head in a half-circle, a look of mild astonishment on its silly face. It stretched out its long neck and sniffed at her hair, her face. She pulled the bony head down against her chest and scratched behind round yellow ears until she was bored with that and shoved the head away. She moved along the barrel body, looking carefully at legs and ribs. Not a tremble left. Food, water, rest, these had restored it.

She chuckled, grabbed a handful of the thick curly hair that covered its body and drew herself up onto its back, kicking and wriggling about until she was up and astride. The jamat honked its disapproval and immediately went down on its knees, front end first, nearly precipitating her over its head, then dropping its hind end, jerking her backward. She blinked, resettled herself, then snorted her disgust. Using her animal control skills, she goosed it back on its feet, clutching desperately at the corkscrew fleeces to keep herself from being rocked off. She kicked her heels into its sides and hung on as it moved off at a slow jog that sent her insides rolling.

For the first hour, riding was a struggle. After that she settled into the proper rhythm and relaxed enough to consider her direction. *You're Pehiiri raised, if I'm right about where I am. Probably ran away from a mouscar—one not too far away, a day or two at most.* She rubbed at her nose, suddenly nervous at the thought of meeting people after so many years alone with the Noris. *Seven years. Ah well. . . .* She closed her eyes and *desired* humankind, then turned the jamat's head in the direction of the developing tug.

Her spirits began to bubble up; the feel of warm life under her eased her loneliness. For the moment she was happy. As the jamat rocked along, she watched the earth flowing past and reveled in the speed of its passage, giggling occasionally as she pictured her own short legs scissoring like mad to cover the same ground. She leaned forward until her cheek was turned against the jamat's shoulder. Overhead the moons danced their slow pavanne while she drowsed, warm and comfortable, the jamat humping and swaying under her, the multiple moon shadows dancing over the barren earth. A while longer and she wound her fingers in the fleeces, let herself drift off to sleep.

Shortly before dawn the jamat honked loudly and repeatedly. Serroi started awake, nearly falling off. Righting herself, she rubbed at her eyes and looked around.

She was out of the desolation into an area of scattered brush and patches of thick dry grass. The jamat's pace quickened. She bounced up and down, struggling to settle herself; after biting her tongue, she clenched her teeth together and simply hung on. The jamat topped a low rise then ran full tilt down the slope toward a cluster of long, low tents. Before she could do more than take in the scattered sights, the jamat was rubbing noses with others of his kind clustered in a rope corral. She straightened; tense and a little afraid, she tried to evaluate the situation.

Pehiiri came out of the tents and stood a little way off, staring at her. Five grim-faced pehiiri separated from the others and came toward her, one of the men yelling and shaking his fist at her. She cringed as the man grabbed at her leg and growled a command. Pehiirit wasn't one of the languages she'd studied; she shook her head, spread out her hands to show him she didn't understand what he was saying.

Those actions sent the blood into his face; roaring with fury, he started to jerk her off the jamat's back. The beast roared, twisted his skinny neck around and snapped long yellow teeth close to the man's arm. He leaped back. As Serroi watched helplessly, a second man raised a crossbow and aimed it at her; she sucked in a deep breath, looked frantically about for a place to jump as his finger tightened on the trigger.

THE WOMAN: XII

Dinafar woke with the sun in her face. It shone through broken shutters, painting odd shapes over the bed and floor. She stretched, yawned, got out of bed and dressed in her spare clothing, wrinkled but cleaner than those she'd worn on the walk to Oras. She unbarred the door and stepped into the hall.

Coperic came through the other door as if he'd stood behind it waiting for her. "Your brother's gone out already," he said sourly. He nodded at the tray in his hands. "Want something to eat?"

"Gone!" She started for the stairs.

Two quick steps and he was in front of her, the tray catching her just below her small breasts. "Don't be a fool." Before she could protest, he took her arm, his fingers tight enough to hurt, and pushed her back into her room. He shouldered the door shut, swung her around, shifted his hand to the middle of her back and shoved her gently onto the bed. He set the tray down on the table and stood watching as she wriggled off her face and bounced up. "Don't try it," he said quietly.

"You can't keep me here." She pushed her hair back from her face and glared at him.

"No?" He jerked his head at the door. "If I have to, I'll put you behind the wall and keep you there long as you keep acting stupid."

"Stupid!"

"You heard me."

She stared defiance at him, rubbing at her arm. "You hurt me."

"What do you expect when you go to putting the meie in danger?"

"I wouldn't." She swallowed, pushed her hands back over her hair. "I wouldn't."

"You were about to chase out after her yelling your head off."

192

"No." She slapped her hands down on her thighs. "I wasn't going to do that."

"Might as well. If she wanted you with her, you'd be with her now. Going to calm down?"

Dinafar looked around at the ugly little room. "I'm not going to spend the day here."

"Meie thinks you can keep your mouth shut when you have to." He eyed her coldly. "I wonder."

She started to protest, saw the look in his eyes, caught back her words and nodded.

His mouth curved in a sour tight smile. "Good enough. You want something to eat?"

She tried smiling. "I am hungry."

He gazed at her a moment longer, then picked up the tray and left. She moved to the door and listened to the stairs creak as he went down. When she heard the downstairs door slam, she stepped quickly into the hall and crossed to the meie's room.

The meie's pack and weaponbelt were on the table. The bed was unmade, the covers tossed about as if the meie had spent a restless night. Dinafar plumped the pillows and tugged at the sheets until they were tight. She smoothed the quilts up until the bed looked right to her. She started to take the weaponbelt, stood with her hand on it, feeling abandoned and useless; this was all she could do for the meie now, this and keeping her mouth shut, keeping away from the guards. Slowly, unhappily, she left the room as Coperic came up the stairs. He saw her, raised an eyebrow, then followed her into her bedroom.

"I fixed her bed."

"I didn't ask." He set the tray down on the table, fished in an apron pocket, pulled out a handful of copper coins. "When you're wandering about, you might like to buy yourself something." He dropped the coins with short musical clinks beside the cha mug.

"Thanks."

He turned to go, then stopped and leaned against the door, his deepset eyes moving over her a last time, a fugitive twinkle in them, a twitch to the ends of his mouth. She sat up straight, smiled tentatively, waited.

"Want to do some work for me?"

She shook the hair out of her eyes, her smile widening to a grin. "Sure."

"Keep your eyes open while you're rambling about. Count

the Norim and Sleykynin you see. Listen to what the Sons of the Flame are saying, what the pilgrims are saying. Don't ask questions. Don't stick around too long any one place, don't be obvious about listening. Don't press. Just pick up what comes your way. Got that?"

She frowned thoughtfully. "Anything special you want?"

He grunted. "You heard me. Meie says you're intelligent. Anything that catches your attention. How's your memory?"

"Good enough."

He scratched at an eyebrow. "Got some prayer beads?"

"Huh? No. Why?"

"Local color." He pulled out of his pocket a string of worn wooden beads. She took them and held them, as his mouth went grim. "If anyone seems to be taking too much notice of you, head right for the Temple and spend the rest of the day there. Don't let yourself be followed back here if you can help it, but don't let it bother you too much if you are. Just let me know and I'll take care of anyone who sticks his nose in unasked." He scowled at her. "You be careful, you hear. Meie'll have my skin in small pieces if you get hurt." He started to leave, glanced over his shoulder. "Don't you talk to anyone, you hear?" Dinafar nodded, hiding a grin behind her hand. He snorted and walked out.

Dinafar drifted through the crowds on the main street, bought a mooncake, strolled on, crunching on the crisp sweet pastry, watching with wide eyes the colorful and varied life swarming around her. She wriggled through circling clumps of pilgrims to watch jugglers and street singers, her ears open to what people around her were saying. She looked into shops, fascinated by the marvelous array of things she could buy. The coins burned through her skirt, even through the handkerchief she'd tied around them. She itched to spend them but there was so much that she couldn't make up her mind what to buy. Everything she saw seemed more desirable than the thing before, and there was always something more. She was enjoying herself so much she felt occasional small bites of guilt. *With the meie maybe in danger, how can I feel like this?* Then she gasped as a snake charmer wound a long serpent about her painted body while her partner played an eerie tune on a flute.

As the morning passed, she began to lose some of her earlier euphoria. There was an undercurrent of uneasiness about the pilgrims that they covered by talking and laughing too loudly. She never heard this formless anxiety mentioned in any of the fragments of conversation she overheard, was not even sure that the pilgrims themselves were aware of it, but it was most evident among the chanting, ranting groups of black-clad men and women sporting a circled silver flame. She knew little about these Followers of the Flame—they had no place at all in the fisher village where she'd grown up— but she knew how scornful the meie was when she spoke of them and she saw the way the pilgrims edged around them and began to feel a cold knot in her stomach.

The Norim were thick in Oras. Already she'd counted half a dozen of the ominous black figures. The street was silent and twitchy a good five minutes each time one of them passed. When she counted her sixteenth Sleykyn, she rubbed at her stomach, feeling the coldness spreading.

She was buying a meat pie and a shaved ice drink when she saw Tesc and his family ambling toward her. She paid the vendor then ducked hastily down a side street. Coperic had said not to talk to anyone and anyway she didn't feel like answering questions. The twins could cram more questions into a single breath than anyone could answer in fifty. She sighed and began circling back to the main street.

Sucking at the ice, chewing on the hot juicy pie, she wandered on until she came to the Plaza. She strolled around the great pile of stone, staring up at the towers. When she came to the small alley of the meie's story, she looked down it, curiosity itching at her.

Three Sleykynin were leaning against the corral fence, watching her. Another lounged against a building near the entrance. Forcing herself to move slowly and calmly, she went back toward the main street.

She glanced back once, saw nothing, walked on, weaving herself into the crowds strolling the main streets. When she stopped to watch a troupe of acrobats performing, she felt the silence grow behind her, looked around, saw a Sleykyn watching the troupe. He was not looking at her, very carefully not looking at her.

Dinafar moved on, sweat beading on her forehead, her heart in her throat. Remembering how the meie had stayed calm and waited for an opening, she walked slowly toward the Temple, winding about pilgrims, trying to keep several of them between her and the Sleykyn. Though he paid no attention to her, he was always there, always about the same distance behind her; she didn't know what had provoked his interest, perhaps it was simply the fact that she'd bothered to look down that particular small alley, but she couldn't waste attention on that puzzle; she had a greater worry. When she saw the gate of the Temple, she had to stop herself from running in panic toward it, but the clot of Followers there was enough to cool the heat in her blood. Imitating the meie without being aware of it, she attached herself to a large pilgrim family and slipped inside.

Standing behind one of the pillars, her prayer beads dangling from shaking fingers, she watched the Sleykyn stroll past the great gate. He couldn't come in without leaving his weapons behind, so he wouldn't come in. She sighed with relief, blessed Coperic, wiped the trickling sweat from her face and arms. The peace of the Temple beginning to calm her racing heart, she began wandering about, marveling at the ever-changing Maiden figures.

As the afternoon wore on, more and more pilgrims moved into the Temple. By the time the sun went down, Dinafar was wedged in between several large families, mothers hissing children to silence and respect, fathers clouting those who refused to listen. One family brought out their prayer beads and began to chant the Praises. Another family took up the chant; the murmur spread quickly through the forest of columns. For the first time Dinafar felt a deep sense of the Maiden's presence; her fear and her anxiety forgotten, she quivered with an awe that grew into an exaltation of the spirit that lifted her momentarily out of herself.

The chant died to a murmur as the Daughter and her maidens came through the Door and mounted the Dais, a veiled grey figure flanked by silver maids, waiting in silence as the families around the columns rose and placed lit candles in holders high up on the columns. Thousands of candles. The Temple glowed with flickering golden lights as the clouds gathered overhead in the final Moongather Storm. The shadows danced as hands rose and fell. The Daughter began the Moongather chant, wheeling slowly, lifting high the silver Sword of the Maiden, the slender blade catching and throwing back the candle glow.

For Dinafar the evening dissolved in a glory that lifted her high again, made her one with the great chanting crowd until it seemed to her the Maiden stooped from the shimmer of the moons as the clouds broke apart to reveal the Gather itself swimming over them, that the Maiden Herself stooped from the Gather and brushed her cheek as the meie had done, touched her cheek in a tender blessing and a welcome.

When Dinafar came out of her daze, the families were gathering their belongings and moving off. Lightning was beginning to flicker and gusts of wind were blowing out the candles. The Moongather was complete, the moon's going now into Scatter. She was suddenly cold. It was very late and Coperic was probably worried about her, the meie too—if the meie had come back. She got stiffly to her feet then touched the hand of the nearest Maiden figure. "Keep her safe," she murmured.

A few pilgrims were settling for an all-night vigil, but the rest were pouring out of the Temple, anxious to avoid as much of the storm as they could. Dinafar hesitated. She could stay here too. She stretched and twisted, her body sore, her stomach empty. Stay until she starved. She sighed, then began working her way into the middle of the stream of departing pilgrims. She passed through the gate, hidden from the watching Sleykynin—two of them now, though the Sons and the Followers were gone—by a large fat woman herding a batch of giggling girls. With rain splashing down around them, they bustled off, Dinafar with them until she was sure the Sleykynin had missed her; she turned into a side street when she was far enough from the Temple and began working her way back to the tavern.

The alleys she traversed were dark and silent—and empty. The rain was coming down in sheets. She splashed through puddles, her sodden skirt slapping against her legs, as far as she could tell the only living thing stupid enough to be out in this.

The lantern beside the tavern's door was dark. She pushed against the panel, holding her breath, wondering if she was locked out. The door resisted her, then swung open with a shattering creak. She shied back, then slipped inside. Coperic stepped from the taproom, a lamp in one hand, a sword in the other. She saw the lamp quiver infinitesimally though his face kept its sour scowl. "You took your good time getting back, girl."

"I went to the Temple."

"I see." He glanced past her at the door. "Bring company?"

"Don't think so. I tried not to."

"Wait here." He handed her the lamp as he went past her, then vanished through the door. The warmth of the flame was welcome. She stood dripping in the foyer, suddenly very tired, her whole body aching, her head throbbing. *She can't be back, something must have happened, she'd be here if she was back, the Sleykynin spotted me, they must have caught her, they must have caught her.* . . .

Coperic came back in, wiping rain from his face. "You're clean. No one sniffing along your trail." He took the lamp from her. "You're soaked, go on up and get out of those clothes. I'll be up in a minute to hear what happened."

"The meie. . . ."

"Not here," he hissed. He caught her by the shoulder and pushed her toward the taproom. "Scoot, girl."

He knocked on her door a few moments later. Dinafar let him in and went to sit on the bed, wrapping her shivering body in the cleanest of the quilts. "What. . . ."

"Patience, girl." He poured a cup of hot cha and brought it to her—and she saw him like the Intii's mother fussing over a favorite grandchild, something she'd never experienced herself, only observed. Feeling odd, she took the cup and sipped at the hot liquid, trying to discipline her impatience.

He pulled the chair around and sat watching her, his forearms crossed over the back. "Early this morning some boys saw the meie taken to the Plaz by two Sleykynin."

She dropped the cup, spilling cha over her legs. "What are. . . ?"

He interrupted her. "Be quiet. There's nothing you can do. There's nothing I can do but wait. And get the news back to the Biserica for her so her death won't be useless."

Dinafar pressed her hands over her mouth.

Coperic rubbed at his eyes, then smiled wearily. "I don't think we should count her dead yet, child. The little meie might just surprise them and bring herself out of the trap."

Dinafar pulled her hands down and began rubbing absently at the cha-damp quilt, rubbing and rubbing, remembering the other times, remembering the meie saying she was taught to use her wits to make up for her smallness. She lifted her head and smiled. "You're right." Feeling around in the folds of the quilt she found the cup and held it out. "I'm warmer than I was but some more cha would feel good."

He filled the cup and returned to his chair. "Now, my girl, tell my why you spent so much time at the Temple."

"A Sleykyn started to follow me. . . ."

A bell rang, interrupting her. Coperic was up and out of

the room before she could ask what was happening. The quilt still around her, she padded out of the room and stood at the head of the stairs listening to voices, muffled and unrecognizable, drifting up from below.

THE CHILD: 12

A big woman with arms like trees came storming up to the men; she slapped at the crossbow, knocking it to the ground. Discharged by the shock, the quarrel went skittering into the brush. Ignoring the growls around her, she waddled over to Serroi and stood examining her, hands on her broad hips, elbows defiantly out. The five men shuffled about, silent and glowering, then turned and went back to the tents.

The morning light was cruel to the big old woman, lighting up every pock and blemish with pitiless clarity. Her face was webbed with thousands of small wrinkles. Deeper wrinkles rayed out from big dark eyes, made larger and darker by uneven lines of kohl painted around them. Two loose folds of skin hung from the edges of her narrow, hooked nose, around her generous mouth, meeting in a roll of fat hanging loose under her chin. Her hair was thick and yellow-white, twisted into braids disappearing under a head cloth pinned tight to her head by a loop of coins. Long clanking earrings dangled from the elongated lobes, all that was visible of her ears, earrings of elaborately filigreed silver set with polished lumps of opal. Heavy silver rings, none too clean, sank into the solid flesh of her fingers. Around each thick wrist clanked half a dozen bangles with more coins wired to them. Coins hung around her massive neck, several chains of them, tilting out over her bosom, shifting noisily with each breath.

Shrewd eyes—shifting between brown and green in the morning light—moved from Serroi to the jamat, back to Serroi. Beaming up at the girl, those luminous eyes twinkling, her face open and welcoming, the woman said, "Mek-yi, meto."

Much of Serroi's apprehension melted under the impact of the old woman's friendliness, though she held back a little, not quite trusting what she saw, wondering why the woman would be so different from the man in her reaction to Serroi's arrival; her experience with the Noris had burned her too deeply.

"Tarim'sk ashag, meto." Grunting with the effort, the old woman bent and waved her hand at the ground, then straightened, her face red. She took a long step closer and reached up to Serroi.

When their fingers touched, force jolted between them, knocking the old woman back, sizzling up Serroi's arm, almost shocking her off the jamat. She tottered, grabbed a handful of the fleece on the jamat's shoulders. Shuddering, she stared at the woman. "What happened? What was that?" She hugged her arms tight across her narrow chest, feeling the bones hard under her skin. *I don't know what to do*, she thought, *I want to trust her, but.* . . . She looked past the woman at the people moving about the camp, stopping to watch her. Nothing welcoming about them.

The old woman was frowning. "Damkil sta?"

"I don't know Pehiirit," Serroi said slowly, clearly. She frowned and searched her memory for the other languages she'd studied, though reading them and speaking them were two different things. "Gavarut vist-blec?" she asked, her tongue stumbling over the syllables. The old woman shook her head. Serroi licked her lips. "Um . . . mosmuswei-wend?"

"N'alalam iy." Again the shake of the head, the dull jangle of the earrings, the soft flop of the braids.

"Mmm. Spaeken mijloc?"

"Ah. Mijloc." The old woman nodded vigorously, her earrings bouncing wildly.

That's a help, Serroi thought. She wriggled around and slid off the jamat, then patted the big animal and pointed to the desert. "I did not steal him," she said very slowly, again struggling for words. "I found him out there." Words began coming more smoothly as she spoke. Relaxing a little, she grabbed at and caught the frayed chin rope. "See?" She nodded as the old woman took the rope end from her and rubbed her broad thumb across the frays.

The old woman dropped the rope with a casual shrug. She obviously wasn't much interested in the jamat, only in Serroi. "Desert. You?" Her accent was thick and Serroi had to puzzle a moment over the words, then she nodded, smiling. The woman smiled back. "Testing?"

"Testing?" Serroi blinked at her, not understanding what she meant, then she thought of the Noris and shivered. "I don't know. I don't know what you mean by testing." She moved restlessly, eyes scanning the tents and the unfriendly people moving about them. "What do I do?"

The old woman dropped a broad strong hand on her shoulder; the force leaped between them again, but she hung on until only a rather pleasant tingle was left. "You have pass the dark gate and come back. You not know this?"

"There was a dream." She shook her head. "It was only a dream."

"You say it to me soon. Your people, they tell you nothing of the dreamtest? Ah! Pay me no mind, meto." She laughed; the chains danced again and those earrings swung some more. She began coughing, beat on her chest, laughed some more. "I forget courtesy when I want to know things. Come. Hungry, little one?" She led Serroi to a tent set off to one side. Behind it, a girl crouched beside a black pot, stirring petulantly at the contents. Hate flared in her black eyes when she saw Serroi following the old woman. "T'mek!" she hissed.

The old woman strode over to her and jerked her to her feet, shook her, snapped, "Davan, fena'kh!" She shoved her back down, pointed at the pot then at a pile of metal bowls sitting by the fire. "Kulek chak m'lao." She looked over her shoulder at Serroi. "Sit, please, little one. Food soon, when this young viper remember how to act."

The girl glared at Serroi then shook the tangle of hair out of her face. "Siy!" she spat. "Gidahi hich yilan-sa!"

The woman's big hand swung in a blow that sent the girl sprawling. Ignoring her wailing, the woman picked up a battered bowl and ladled some of the boiled meat and wild grain into it. She stooped and picked up two flat greyish objects from a low square table beside the fire. With a last glare at the cowering girl, she swept over to Serroi and thrust the food at her. "Eat, meto. Apologies for the bira there. She say she die before she feed you." The old woman shrugged and walked away.

Serroi held the stew bowl in one hand and the two leathery loaves of bread in the other. She stared down at the warm flat loaves. Hungry as she was, she felt a bit dubious about them, then remembered the raw lizards she'd eaten in the desert and chuckled at herself. She set the loaves down and rested the bowl on her knees, looking about for something to eat with. The big woman came back from the fire, smiled at her, then settled herself comfortably, tore off a piece of the bread and used it to shovel some of the thick stew into her mouth. Serroi sniffed at the meat, smiled with pleasure, then imitated her hostess. In spite of her hunger and her delight in the warmth and taste of the stew, she soon could eat no more. She set the bowl on the ground by her knee and watched the girl as she waited for the woman to finish her meal.

On the far side of the fire, the girl crawled back to the pot. Her hand on the spoon, sullenly she looked out of the corners of her eyes at the old woman. "Cayalts, Janja?" Her face was still ugly with resentment and jealousy.

"Caiz." The woman watched the girl ladle stew for herself, a complex of emotions playing over her broad face as she chewed slowly at the bread. After a few moments she snorted with disgust and turned to Serroi. "Idiot bira." She narrowed her eyes at the food remaining in Serroi's bowl. "Is enough?"

"Is more than enough." Serroi patted her stomach. "No room."

The woman grinned at her then slapped a hand on her wide bosom, making the money chains jingle and all her bangles clank fearsomely. "I nomen Raiki-janja."

"I nomen Serroi."

"Ah, Maiden bless." Raiki sucked in a breath, tapped a broad forefinger against the side of her head. "Hunt for words make my head hurt. You learn Pehiirit?"

Serroi hesitated, uncertain whether she wanted to stay with these people long enough to justify the effort. She felt adrift, no direction left for her now that she was out of the desert. Her eyes moved slowly around the encampment, watching the men sitting by their fire, talking, spitting, sipping at small glasses of cha, at the women working over cook fires or spinning jamat fleece into yarn, at the berbec herd moving slowly off to the grazing grounds under the guidance of the mouscar's boys. She sighed. "Janja, I bring trouble." She nodded at the scowling girl crouched over her bowl. "And not just with that one."

"I am Janja." The heavy head came up proudly and the old chatoyant eyes looked about, fierce as a predator's viewing a herd of prey animals. "What I want, I do. You janja too."

"Me?" Serroi stared, then shook her head. "No."

Raiki nodded. "You feel the power. You and me, we sisters. You do me joy if you stay, janja-meto."

Once again Serroi hesitated; she looked into the old woman's smiling face, felt again—almost like a fire bathing her—the warmth radiating out from the janja, caressing Serroi, welcoming her. She trembled, tried to smile, nodded. "I stay. Awhile."

"Ah. Maiden bless." Raiki pointed at the fire. "Atsh. Fire." She uncrossed her legs and pointed at her high-arched battered bare feet. "Ayk. Foot." She slapped a hand against the ground, scraped up and let fall a pinch of dry soil. "Lek't."

The lessons continued as Serroi trailed Raiki about the camp, watching with curiosity as she tranced then healed an ailing baby, worked an amulet for a woman whose last child had been born dead, went out into the desert and collected herbs and several kinds of beetles. After mid-meal the rounds began again, and the pehiirit words kept coming until Serroi was dizzy with weariness.

Raiki finally acknowledged this by clucking in distress and leading Serroi into her tent. The air inside was warm and saturated with the woman's smell. Accustomed to the antiseptic cleanness of the Noris's tower, this casual attitude to dirt and smell repelled Serroi. As Raiki pulled out a sleeping rug and tossed some pillows into a corner of the tent, Serroi struggled to hide her disgust. She settled on the cushions until Raiki left, then she pulled the rag off her head, ran her fingers through her hair, stroked them across her eye-spot, then concentrated on the pillows, evicting the vermin in them and in the sleeping rug, driving them before her to the tent wall and out into the gravel beyond. She heard a chuckle behind her and wheeled, feeling hot in the face. Raiki stood just inside the tent, hands on hips, a twinkle in her liquid eyes. Serroi lifted her hands, dropped them. "I didn't mean to. . . ."

"Insult me?" Raiki threw back her head and roared with laughter. Still chuckling, wiping at her eyes, she shook her head. "Little one, you don't. Those small lifes sneak in through my tightest spells." She cocked her head and examined Serroi with considerable interest, reached out and stroked her face. "The patches are starting to meet. You're a misborn of the windrunners." Her wide mouth spread into a grin. "Do me, by the Maiden." She swung her massive arms out and up. "Chase 'em, child."

Serroi giggled, then both were laughing as the small forms skittered down Raiki's arms and legs and scuttled away.

Raiki sat on the cleaned pillows beside Serroi. Quietly, soberly, she touched Serroi's hand, her thumb moving gently over one of the few remaining rosy patches. "Best keep away from the rest of the mouscar; they don't understand difference, meto." She was becoming more fluent in mijloc as she continued to speak it. "And be careful of Yehail. She'll try to hurt you if she can." Raiki sighed. "I don't know what the Maiden means with her; weren't for the fact she's the only one with sign of talent, I'd run her home before tomorrow dawn." She shook her head, passed a hand over her forehead. "And I'm old." Her voice low and dispirited, she murmured, "Yehail's jealous and simmering with more resentments than these pillows had fleas. Worse, she's greedy and short-sighted, not in the eyes but in the way she looks at things. She hasn't the temperament to be a good janja. I've searched them all, not a touch of the talent, even the unborn." She sucked in a deep breath and let it whoosh out. "You, meto. Let me teach you."

"No!" Seeing the hurt in Raiki's face at her sharp refusal, Serroi went on hastily, "I've seen . . . I've felt. . . . No, I can't touch power, Raiki-mother, I'm not fit." She closed her eyes, the Noris's face dark in her mind. She remembered the sick triumph in her when she shared the Noris's victory over his challengers. Remembered what the quest for power had done to him and everything around him. Shivering and weeping, tired and afraid, she huddled on the pillows until Raiki caught her in her warm arms and rocked her back and forth, cooing to her, comforting her.

The next morning Serroi drifted awake, feeling warm and content, opened her eyes and saw with momentary confusion a slanting tan wall rising close beside her. She freed her hand from the tangled rug and touched it, feeling the coarse yarn and the tough, tight weave. As she blinked and smiled, memory returning, she heard voices outside raised in argument. She pushed the rug back and yawned, ran her fingers through her hair, wondering if she could have a bath, wrinkled her nose because she still smelled strongly of jamat.

The tent flap was jerked aside and Raiki came storming in. When she saw Serroi sitting up, her scowl shifted into a smile. "You slept hard, meto."

Serroi yawned and smiled sleepily at her. "I was tired."

"Got some things for you." She dropped a pair of old sandals beside Serroi, then shook out a long wool robe, a tubular garment woven of undyed berbec wool. Serroi looked dubiously at it, unhappy at the thought of putting on another person's dirt, though it seemed clean enough. Raiki looked thoughtfully from the robe to Serroi and back. "Might be a bit long," she said after a moment. "Try it on, see how much fixing it needs."

As the days of summer drifted slowly past, Serroi was Raiki's shadow. She continued to refuse to learn Raiki's magic, recoiling from it with a fear that was burned deep into her; she wanted nothing to do with magic. What she did with her life she was determined to accomplish through the strength of mind and hand alone, it seemed a cleaner way of living, though she couldn't deny Raiki's goodness and the need her people had for her. She sternly repressed all mention of her initiation dream in the desert, refused to dream again.

The Pehiiri mouscar counted five families, the most that their barren territory could support. This territory wasn't so much a slice of land as a migration route and series of wells that the mouscar had dug and now maintained. They moved in a year-long loop, south in the winter along the inner line and north in the summer along the outer arc of the loop. When Serroi joined them they were close to the northernmost well.

They camped at the present well for another passage, then packed the tents and moved on. Serroi helped Raiki fold up the tent and lash her belongings on the jamat's back, then walked beside her as the mouscar began its leisurely progress to the final well.

The days were hot and dusty and slow. They were forced to move no faster than the grazing berbeci. Serroi walked silent beside Raiki, a small dark shadow, listening while the janja schooled her apprentice. Yehail never forgot that Serroi followed. Her eyes continually swiveled around to her, glinting with triumph when she thought she was monopolizing Raiki-janja's attention, glaring with hate when her inattention to the lesson brought her a scolding.

Nights were hot and breathless. There was no water for bathing; hardly enough water for the ritual glasses of cha the men took around their fire at night. Food was scanty; there was no time for searching out the wild grains, roots and herbs to supplement the greasy stews. The families slept in their clothes, huddled in a mass of rugs, women on the inside, their men in a ring of hot snoring flesh around them. Raiki and Serroi slept apart, but the night sounds of the uneasy sleepers surrounded them, then groans and snores, the wails of hungry babies, sharp staccato slaps at wandering sand fleas. In the rope corral, jamati shifted about, pawed at the sand, honked mournfully, resenting their daily burdens, restless under the moons. A bit farther out, the berbeci whined and cried out, rose and wandered aimlessly about, sometimes dodging and twisting to get away from the night-herds. When one succeeded, the boy who was nearest would curse, call to his companion, then trot out into the shadowy plain to chase down the escapee through the shifting moon-shadows that made such intrusions a continual stumbling and falling.

The mouscar reached the Northwell at the end of the ninth day. The tents went up as the women and girls worked quickly to spread the tent cloth and set the poles and drive in the pegs. The men had scattered to look over the grazing lands, checking grass and browse to see how well they'd renewed themselves in the passages of rest. Serroi helped Raiki set up her tent, arrange the rugs and pillows inside and quietly drive out the vermin that had crept back from the jamat and the sand they'd slept on during the trek. Yehail had returned to her family for the night, leaving the two janjai in comfortable silence, stalking away, seething with anger and jealousy.

Serroi frowned over her cha, watching the girl until she merged with the dark cluster of figures around her family fire. "Raiki, she's going to make trouble for you. Because of me. She doesn't even try to understand."

Raiki sighed. "Even half a chance, I'd send her home for good. I've tried with her, meto. I can't make myself like her. Can't." She sipped at her cha. "She'll be my death, damn her. Saw it when I went through the gates." Her eyes, more brown than green now with brooding, moved over the camp. "Them too, meto. She's going to kill a lot of them. There's a dark hand reaching for her, the dark hand that loosed you to me, you know what I'm talking of. But she's the only one with the talent, the only damned one."

Serroi stirred restlessly, feeling the pressure of the janja's desire. She looked up, stared, as five figures left their fires and came over to them.

Four of the men stood back, willing to support, unwilling to speak. Yod vo Rehsan stepped forward, scowling at the janja, ignoring Serroi. "There is an outsider, janja."

Raiki sat without moving for a long moment, then she rose with slow massive force and stared back at him, her lined face expressionless. "I see no outsider, Yod. There is a guest. My guest."

Yod glanced swiftly at Serroi who sat beside the fire, her arms wrapped around her legs. His dark sunken eyes were shiny with dislike. He was a man of quick and violent temper but he had a cunning tongue and was the mouscar's leader, if that loosely organized collection of families could be said to have a leader. The group lived too close to the edge of subsistence for wide differences in the status of its adult males. Co-operation was essential to their continuance as a group. Yod had an abrasive persistence that wore down opposition. The other men were here now because he'd kept at them until it was easier to go along with him than to keep arguing. While mildly disturbed by Serroi's presence, they'd come to accept her as the janja's pet, but Yod was Yehail's father. When Raiki's eyes swept over them, they plucked at sleeve fringes and kicked at the sand.

"Guests stink after three days. We got no place for strangers." Serroi could see his face darkening even in the dim light from the clouded stars. "I speak for the mouscar, we don't want her here."

Raiki chuckled dryly. "You speak for yourself, Yod. And that daughter of yours." She moved her stern gaze from one face to the other, leaving each man distinctly more uneasy than before. "You going to let an adder-tongued girl tell you what to do?" She snorted. "Yod, you keep pushing this, you push your janja out too. Understand me, man. I won't let you stick your nose into my household. So you might's well trot yourself back to your fire, teach your girl to mind her manners and her business."

One of the other men laid a hand on Yod's arm. "Let it go," he muttered.

Raiki sank down on her heels and poured another cupful of cha, her shoulder turned on the men. She smiled at Serroi, tilted the pot, offering her a refill.

Serroi held out her cup, watching out of the corner of her eye as the men walked back to their fires. She bent her head over the rising twist of steam. "I said there'd be trouble."

Raiki snorted. "Pay them no mind, meto. They need me too much to make trouble."

"Would you really leave because of me?"

"Yah, meto." Raiki chuckled, then drained her cup. "Wouldn't stay away, couldn't, you know. But I'd shake them up a bit. Won't happen." She sighed. "I wish you'd let me teach you, but you're right, even if it is for the wrong reasons. I doubt if they'd ever accept you, not with Yehail backbiting."

The mouscar stayed at the Northwell for three passages then began to trek south, the long leisurely trek from well to well as the grass grew greener and the days warmer—and Yehail grew more jealous, more dangerous. She spied on Serroi continually, and when she wasn't spying, prodded at her, trying to force her into a hair-pulling fight. Serroi managed to swallow her anger, unwilling to hurt Raiki or further damage her standing with her people. By a combination of luck and close observation, the janja often caught Yehail before she went too far, sending her rolling with one of her backhand swats or cowing the girl into temporary submission with a vigorous tongue-lashing.

For Serroi this was a time of drifting. She clung close to Raiki as the only certainty left to her. Even her body began changing. She grew several inches taller, her breasts budded and she woke one morning with blood on her thighs. The herdboys took to coming by the janja's tent, laughing and shoving, until one of them found the nerve to call out to her, then they'd all mill about laughing and joking for a few minutes before they ran off to join their family groups. As the mouscar moved slowly from well to well, working its way south, she grew restless, gradually becoming aware that she didn't want to continue living the meager life of the Pehiiri. She hungered for the small luxuries she'd had in the Noris's tower, though she couldn't endure thinking of him. Clean clothing, daily baths, good well-cooked food, books, beautiful things around her. Above all, quiet and privacy. Raiki was mother and sister and friend; the warmth that had sprung between them from the beginning had grown quietly. Each time she thought of leaving, the nightmares came back. She'd dream of the Noris, wake up sweating, crying in Raiki's arms.

When the winter mooncycles had passed and the year was turning to Spring, the Mouscar reached Southwell, the most elaborate of the wells, small fields enclosed within stone walls and covered water pipes leading from the well to the carefully mulched land. As soon as the tents were up, Raiki was intensely busy with fertility rites for the land and planting ceremonies. Serroi was left to herself. She wandered out away from the well, sat looking down the long slope to the lusher valley far below.

Raiki found her still sitting there late that night, watching the sprinkle of lights in the valley, yellow-gold fires in clusters like a paler starfield on the darkness.

"You didn't come to supper." Raiki settled beside her with a series of grunts as she made her unwieldy body as comfortable as she could on the coarse earth.

"I wasn't hungry."

"Ah." Raiki sat silent a long time, then she raised a large arm, bangles clanking like lonely bells, and pointed at the nearest group of lights. "Sel-ma-Carth." She sighed, the chains around her neck clashing softly. "The Shessel fair will begin in a few days. The men will be going down." Her hand dropped into her lap.

Serroi glanced from the moon cluster to the lights of the city. "It's time."

"Yehail?"

"In truth, Raiki my friend, she's only one of many reasons." Serroi leaned against the old woman, slid her hand between arm and body, hugged Raiki's arm against her.

"What're you going to do?"

"I don't know. Work my way across to the Biserica probably. I'm old enough finally."

"Watch out for them, those lowlanders." In the silence that followed her words, the rising wind picked up grains of sand and sent them skipping around between patches of brush. Over the plain below clouds were gathering. The lights began going out. "They're not to be trusted, meto. Cheat you, kill you, rape you." A big hand patted Serroi's thigh. Serroi could feel her trembling. With an agitated clinking of chains and coins, the old woman moved away. Serroi heard heavy breathing, more rattling of coins. She turned to see Raiki working three of her coin-chains over her head. The old woman thrust them at her. "Take these," she urged. "You'll need money down there."

Serroi jumped to her feet, pushed the chains away. "I can't take that. Raiki, your dowry!"

"Dowry!" Raiki's mouth stretched into a broad smile. "More like burying money. Got plenty for that, meto. Who'd I leave the rest to? Yehail?" She snorted. "Not likely. It's mine, got honest, mine to give where I choose." She fell silent. The moons floated quiet and silver overhead, dipping one by one into the cloud layer over the valley. "I give where my heart goes, meto."

Serroi threw her arms around her friend, pressing herself anxiously against the warm soft body. "I want. . . ." She started crying.

"I know, meto-mi, I know." Raiki patted her on the back awhile, then pushed her away, stood her straight. "I know. Well, that's enough. Come with me, meto. Something I want to show you."

In her tent Raiki opened a chest and pulled out trousers, vest and a loose smock like the men and boys wore. She tossed them on the rug by Serroi's feet. "You're a bit of a thing and still flat enough to pass for a boy half your age. Be safer that way with Lowlanders. Don't trust them, meto. They'll steal the skin off your face and sell it back to you." She grunted as she settled her bulk onto a pile of cushions. "Come and see me if you can. You know how we go." She looked down at her hands. "You'll stay until the men have left?"

Two days later, Serroi slipped away from the Well and followed the track the men had taken down the long slope to Sel-ma-Carth and the Shessel fair. After hours of brooding, her goal was set—the Golden Valley, the place where the Noris couldn't go, the place that had welcomed her.

THE WOMAN: XIII

Serroi's chains clashed softly as she shifted position on the plank bench bolted into the cell wall. Some distance away down the dark stinking corridor she could hear the rise and fall of male voices but couldn't make out the words. She stirred and the chains clanked again, drawing her eyes down to the iron cuffs tight about her wrists, to the rusty chains looped over her thighs. She shivered then reached down and touched the lump in her boot. The tajicho was cool again. The Norit couldn't care less about her. She leaned her head back against the damp stone and listened to the voices, to the silence. The dungeons were empty as far as she could feel. *Hern*, she thought. *Wait till Lybor has her way. No. Not Lybor. The Nearga-nor. Ser Noris, Ser Noris, what's the point of all this?* She felt the stone cool and damp through the double layer of vest and tunic. *That Norit didn't know about me. Why? Are you using them too, Ser Noris? Pushing them about without their knowing it? That so, then I'm a rat in the walls going to steal their prize.* She caught her lip between her teeth. *Half a chance, blessed Maiden, give me half a chance.*

She stood, shuffled to the door. Pressing her body against the hardwood planks, closing her hands tight about the bars, she tried seeing down the corridor; because it slanted a little away from the cell where she was imprisoned she could see dark forms pacing past the end of the corridor. Words floated back to her, cut off as each figure passed out of sight. ". . . that crazy mare . . . set up . . . race . . . got the legs . . . dlebach . . . beat . . . decset . . . three decsets for . . . the meie . . . play with her . . . damn Nor . . . leave us the bones . . . no meat on her. . . ." Finally the two men sat at a table just beyond the end of the corridor and their voices came more distinctly. "Stickin' around here after they finish with fat boy?" The speaker jerked his thumb at the ceiling.

"They promised us gold. Who's gonna stop us takin' what we want."

"Sons, that's who; too many of them got their noses in this.

No drinkin'. Don't mess with the women, run the hoors outta town with they heads shaved, ever tried a bald-headed woman? I say gimme the gold and I cut out for the Southcoast where they somethin' to spend it on."

"Hunh, better not let ol' yellow-face hear you talkin' like that."

"Know what I want right now?" The speaker leaned forward and for the first time Serroi saw that he wore the Sleykyn mask. He tilted the bottle over his mug, watching the last drops trickle out.

"Yeh, and you ain't gonna get it. Can't touch the women in these walls, not even that." The second Sleykyn waved vaguely toward Serroi.

The first drained the mug and stood, not swaying but holding himself with careful dignity.

"Nor said to stay here." The seated one leaned back and brought his hand down heavily on the tabletop.

"Stingy shit only left us two bottles. Maiden's tits, I go get some more, he going to be busy, you keep you mouth shut, he won't know nothin'.." He stalked off, moving out of Serroi's limited range of vision, his heels stomping harder than usual on the stone.

The second Sleykyn sat slumped in his chair staring gloomily at the mug in his hand. Serroi watched a moment longer then went back to the bench.

She reached into her boot and twitched out the lock-picks. Leaning back against the stone, she began working on the cuffs of her manacles. The crude locks were no problem; she caught the manacles as they cracked open and set them on the bench beside her, then dealt with the chains on her ankles. Pick in hand she moved silently to the door.

The Sleykyn was still alone, head fallen on folded arms, the mug on its side with a small spill of wine by its mouth. His shoulders moved and she heard a sputtering snore. Hastily she began work on the door's lock; with one Sleykyn gone off somewhere and the other far gone in wine and asleep she had her best chance. No time to waste, no time at all. The door lock was worse because it was bigger and more complex, but she forced it as silently as she could, her breath caught behind her teeth, her heart juddering at each squeal.

After checking the Sleykyn a last time, she eased the heavy door open just enough to let her slip into the corridor. There was a torch set in a holder by her cell, but that was the only one, confirming her sense that the other cells were empty. She ran on her toes beyond its light, then sank into a crouch, supporting herself on her toes with fingertips touching the filthy floor as the Sleykyn muttered heavily, lifted his head for a bleary look around, then dropped it back on his arms. As soon as he started snoring again, she stood very slowly, making no sudden moves. She drifted like a shadow down the three steps to the cellar floor, then circled around behind the Sleykyn.

She was halfway across the place of torment when the uncertain light from the low-burning torches and the clutter on the filthy floor betrayed her. Focused too intently on the Sleykyn, she stumbled over a hardwood rod lying beside several enigmatic instruments of torture. It bounced off these with a clangor like the ringing of the war-bells and bounded away across the stone, clattering loud enough to wake the dead.

The Sleykyn bounced up, swung around, the whip snicking out of its pouch, the tip slashing her arm before she had time to move. She dived behind a rack, scrambled along it, narrowly avoiding a second slash. At the end of the platform, she looked back along the crank and nearly lost an eye to the flickering whip. It coiled around the crank until the Sleykyn jerked it loose, giving her time to scurry away. He was still hazed with sleep and half drunk, his timing just a fraction off. She crossed to the other side of the rack, looked rapidly about, then dashed for a pair of heavy whipping posts. The lash tip caressed her ankle. She pulled free, then straightened, using the thick posts as protection.

The Sleykyn came rapidly down the side of the rack, stumbling and bleary-eyed. She shifted to keep the posts between her and him, searched frantically about for some kind of weapon, saw cutting tools in a frame on the wall. Ducking and weaving, gasping with pain as the whip found her twice, she darted across the open space and slid behind another article of torment. Flaying knives, high over her head. She dived at the wall. The knife was in her hand as the whip coiled about her hips, cutting through the thick material of her trousers, searing her skin, drawing more blood. Whimpering with pain, the knife held away from her, she crashed to the floor, her weight freeing her from the whip. Before the Sleykyn snapped the whip back, she was up again and running, ignoring the pain, bent low, weaving and elusive in the smoky torchlight.

The Sleykyn's boots were loud behind her as she dived

once more behind the rack. He drove her from this shelter, chased her a second time around the room, getting closer and closer to trapping her as the drink wore off. While she fled, twisting, weaving, running full out from point to point, she tested the balance of the knife. At the point of exhaustion, bleeding from dozens of cuts, there was no way she could get close enough to use the knife on him. She had to throw it. If she missed, she'd have to try fighting him with bare hands, something she didn't like thinking about.

She circled the rack a third time and dived for the twin posts; the Sleykyn was so close she could almost feel his breath hot on her neck. Praying that she read the knife right, she circled the posts, seeking the intangible feel of the whole, forcing herself steady, slowing her breathing. She saw his whip hand go back, saw the triumphant glare in his bloodshot eyes, saw the thick column of his neck rising from his unbuttoned shirt. With a breathed prayer to the Maiden, she threw the knife, saw it turning in a silvery wheel through the air, saw it thud home in his throat.

Filling the cellar with an absurd soft bubbling sound, he crumpled onto his face, blood running from his mouth, his eyes glazing over. Serroi clutched the post, knees shaking, sick to her stomach, gasping for breath. Slowly the room steadied for her. She pulled herself up, feeling pleased with herself for being alive. She kicked out one leg, then the other, testing her knees. They seemed capable of holding her, so she pushed away from the post and tried standing. She took one step then another, then laughed aloud with the sheer joy of surviving.

She crossed to the Sleykyn. He was dead. The blood was no longer flowing from his neck. She rubbed her hand across her face, wiping away beads of new sweat, then knelt beside him. Grunting with the effort, she turned him over onto his back and started working on the buckles to his knife belt. She had to have a weapon. With grim distaste she pulled the belt from around him and rebuckled it; it was too big for her but she could wear it like a baldric. Succumbing to a sudden intense curiosity, she drew the blade from its sheath and turned it over slowly, very carefully. A Sleykyn poison knife. The blade was bone rather than metal, the tip discolored for about an inch above the point. She was very careful not to touch the stain. "Enough," she murmured. The knife back in its sheath and the belt draped across her narrow torso, she leaned over and gently closed the Sleykyn's eyes. "Maiden give you good rest." She stood, stretched. "I think I'm very tired of this killing." Again she rubbed wearily at aching eyes. "I'm a fool; let me get back to the Biserica and I'll do what they've always told me I should, start studying to be a healer."

As she neared the exit she heard a rumbling drunken singing echoing down the corridor. Sliding the knife from its sheath, she ran on her toes to the wall, then flattened herself beside the opening. When the second of her guards came unsuspecting through it, cradling a wineskin in his arms like an overplump baby, she slashed a deep cut in the back of his hand, then darted away.

She watched him die with foam on his lips and twisted horror on his face. The hand that still held the bone knife shook; she looked down at the death-white blade with revulsion, wanted to hurl it away from her; instead, she replaced it carefully in its sheath and crossed to the dead man. After closing his staring eyes and sending him to rest with the blessing for the dead, she picked up the wineskin and walked into the corridor. As the fever from her own poisoned wounds began to work in her, she searched out the panel that would let her back into the maze of passages within the walls.

In stifling darkness, somewhere deep within the maze of hidden passages, she worked the stopper loose from the wineskin and drank, then drank again. She could feel the heat from her wounds whenever she held her arm close to her face. *The lash tip was infected some way,* she thought. *I hurt, but the wounds aren't that bad. I shouldn't be so sick, not so soon.* She drank more wine, then settled herself onto the floor and leaned against the cool stone, wondering what she should do. *I can't stay here. Domnor Hern . . . at least I'm inside the Plaz.* She giggled. *I told Coperic the Daughter would get me inside the Plaz. Not quite like this though. Dinafar. I wonder what she's thinking. Maiden keep her safe—and don't let Coperic get tricky with her.* She pressed the back of her hand against her forehead. *Fever. I wonder what the hell they put on those tips. Domnor; better find him.* She got heavily to her feet, drank again from the wineskin, then wandered off along the passage, turning and twisting, stumbling up and down crazy flights of stairs until she had no idea where she was or what level of the Plaz she happened to be on.

When she was too exhausted to keep moving, she sank

down, sat with her back against the wall, her legs stretched out across the width of the passage, the wineskin like a child cuddled in her lap. In a few moments she was deep asleep.

She woke with small feet pricking over her legs, small wet noses pushing into her. It was too dark to see; she was dizzy, her brain on fire, forgetting where she was, forgetting what she had to do. She reached down and felt about with shaking hands. She touched a quivering snout, slid her fingers past large delicate ears, then down a knobby spine to a hairless tail. "Rat," she muttered, then giggled, then caught her breath. Rats came pattering along the passage, crawling over her until her legs were covered by writhing furry bodies. They kept coming. She could feel their small wet noses nudging into her, the pinpoint claws scrabbling at her. Given what she knew about rats she should have been terrified; she wasn't. It seemed to her that in her sleep she'd called them to her—or something had called them.

Behind her aching head the stone vibrated with tension, the air around her was thick. The rats huddled close to her, half-maddened by it, licking at the blood dried on her cuts, pressing against her, more and more of them as the minutes passed until the passage was full of them. She pulled the wineskin free, heard the rats she knocked loose chittering with fear and irritation. She drank, drank again. Her head throbbed. She reached up, screamed when she touched her eye-spot, it bulged out from her brow, hotter than the fever that coursed in her blood. Something held her; something held it, called the rats to her, was burning her, burning the fever out of her. She blinked, she could see again, her night sight, could see in tones of green and grey and black. Could see the lumpy shifting carpet of small bodies crawling over each other, crouching, trembling, her body was covered by them, covered to the waist, they were behind her, on her shoulders. Warm pulsing vermin. Around and over her. She should have been terrified, she knew that distantly as from a part of her standing far off looking down on herself. She was hot with fever, hot with the thing in her fighting the fever. She couldn't remember, there was something she needed to remember, she couldn't remember, it was important . . . she slept again.

When she woke, she was cramped and stiff but her body was cooler; whatever had been on the lash tip had done its worst and was passing off. She blinked. Her eye-spot throbbed and her night-sight came back. The carpet of rats

quivered and shifted about, chittering nervously. A roach
whirred out of haze and settled beside her head, clinging to
the stone of the wall behind her. More came, crawled over
the stone, over her, roaches came and came and came, flights
of them whirring about her, crawling on her head and arms.
She chuckled, roaches coming to avenge their ancestor,
stopped chuckling when the sound grew too shrill. "Army,"
she muttered. It was hard to move her mouth properly to
speak. The whip had touched her face, opening a cut at the
corner of her mouth. Her cheek was swollen and her whole
face felt stiff.

The dark in the passage was timeless. Only the throbs of
her heart clicked off the minutes for her. She was thirsty,
drank again from the wineskin. She felt cooler all over
though the wine was heating her gullet. There was a small intense hot-spot on her leg where the tajicho burned hotter and
hotter as time passed. She began to remember what had happened and why she was here in this stifling darkness. She sat
up, dislodging roaches and rats, staggered to her feet, peeling
them off her like a lumpy blanket. She swayed, slapped
her hand onto the wall to keep herself from falling. It had to
be time for the Norid's rite. Close to it, anyway. The Norid
was busy, the tajicho's fire told her that. She closed her fingers and slammed her fist into the wall, angry that fear, fever
and the Sleykyn's whip-poison had held her impotent for so
long until now, until the Norid's Moongather spell gained
momentum.

She let her nightsight dim and spent her strength searching
out Domnor Hern. She turned her head slowly as the eye-
spot throbbed and the immaterial search-fingers spread out
and out, wavered, finally tugged upward and to the right.
With roaches whirling about her head, clinging to her tattered
clothing, with rats swarming like dingy foam about her boots,
she began the climb through the walls to the Domnor's bedroom.

Up and around, up narrow stairs where the flood of rats
lengthened before and behind her, up and up, then around in
a squared spiral up the central tower. Up and around, wading
against a wind that tried to push her back, that grew stronger
and stronger until she was leaning into it as one leans into a
gale, fighting for every step.

Until she stopped before an exit like the many she'd passed
before. She stopped, knowing without doubt that the Domnor
was there. The rats piled up around her. She could feel the

whole mass trembling until she feared the building would topple; they crouched around her without a sound, ominously, unnaturally silent. The roaches whirred about her head, then settled around the exit, clinging to the stone, so close they touched, like brown scale mail covering the wall. She leaned her head against the planks of the door. It was hard to think; she had to fight against the steady pressure of the force flowing out of the bedchamber.

Lifting heavy, clumsy arms, she fumbled at the catch, locking the spyhole shut. As she turned them back, she felt her eye-spot go still. She blinked slowly, startled, then leaned to the hole, hardly daring to breathe.

The Domnor sat in a straight-backed chair, his back turned to her, his short pudgy body stripped naked, his arms and legs bound to the chair. His thick mop of straight hair—black liberally streaked with grey—was tousled, one lock standing like a lizard's crest above the rest. His body was still but his strong blunt fingers were working patiently at the ropes, shifting them slightly, working a knot closer and closer. The ropes were cutting painfully into his flesh; every movement had to be a minor agony, but he showed no sign of that. With iron patience he kept working, all the while seeming to concentrate his attention on the Norid. Serroi caught her breath, astonished. She'd seen little of the man during her ward. In spite of her contempt for Lybor, she'd let herself be influenced by that viper's contempt for her husband. Still, there was what Tayyan said. She closed her eyes, the pain back. Tayyan said he was a terror with a sword, said you wouldn't believe how fast he could move when he wanted to, said he could ride a macai better than most Stenda even. She blinked again, able to believe this as she watched him coolly and stubbornly working at the ropes while the Norid stalked about the room making preparations with an arrogance that held the other two in Serroi's field of vision reluctantly silent even when he bent double and began tracing a pentacle around them, muttering a complex chant under his breath as he drew the circled star, dragging the thick greasy crayon over the inlaid floor. The rugs had been kicked aside to lie in tangled mounds against the wall. When he finished the pentacle around Lybor and Morescad, he turned to the Domnor and drew a second pentacle around him. When that was closed he set a thick black candle at each of the points, then stepped back, frowned, black eyes searching restlessly about the room, bothered by something.

Serroi moved her foot, feeling the heat in the tajicho against her leg. His eyes had a wild look to them; his stiff black hair was tied back from his face with braided gold wire that crackled with the energies flowing around the room. Watching as he placed white candles at the points of the pentacle around Morescad and Lybor, Serroi thought, *He's Norid, not Norit at all. I was right. One of the little Nor, reaching over himself out of greed and ambition, backed, I suppose, by the Nearga-nor or he wouldn't dare.* She shivered, sick to her stomach at the sight of him. *Power enough to light a match on a hot day and he terrifies me.* All the time she'd watched him moving about she was trembling, sweat thick and slippery over her body. Her hair clung to her head in ragged oily strings; her eyes blurred and cleared, the thudding of her heart seemed loud enough to wake the whole Plaz. It took a strong effort of will for her to hold her eyes at the spyhole when she wanted to run and run, to get away from the Nor. . . .

And all the time she knew that the Norid in the bedroom was a nothing, a fool, as much a fool as Lybor and Morescad.

The Norid stepped in front of Morescad and Lybor. "The demon will materialize within the pentacle drawn about the Domnor's chair." He thrust his hand into a pouch dangling at his belt and drew forth a knobby stone, dull black streaked with red. "I shut the demon's soul in this sjeme. Who holds it will control the Domnor once the demon swallows his soul and animates his flesh."

"Give it to me." Lybor started to step out of the pentacle.

"Don't break the line, Doamna," the Norid cried hastily. He thrust a hand out, pushing at the air in front of her. "Or I can't answer for your safety." Sweat beading his forehead, he tossed the sjeme carefully into her cupped hands.

She caught it eagerly and cuddled it against her breasts, her eyes glittering, her face drawn in harsh lines of greed. Morescad narrowed his eyes, then smiled indulgently and slid his arm around her shoulders. Lybor shuddered, smiled stiffly at first then with her practiced charm. "When do you begin, Ser Nor?"

"Soon." He glanced at a large hourglass placed on the seat of a chair. There was about a fingerswidth of sand left in the top bubble. "Soon."

Serroi moved her head away from the spyhole, then braced herself against the wood, her eyes closed, her body trembling.

The tajicho was a fire eating into her flesh but she didn't dare pull it out; it was shielding her. Shaking and sick from too many memories, she pulled in a deep breath and put her eyes back to the spyhole.

Lybor and Morescad were talking in low tones that held a touch of acrimony. One of Morescad's big hands was resting over Lybor's, the tips of his fingers touching the sjeme.

Serroi forced herself to watch the Norid and found her fear diminishing as she in a sense confronted him and it. The rats pressed closer against her. Several roaches half-fell, half-flew from the wall, landing on her head and shoulders. The touch roused her, set her wondering, but she shook off her questions and brought her attention back to the room.

The last grains of sand were trickling past the waist of the glass. The Norid circled Morescad and Lybor, flicking a finger at the white candles. One by one they flared up, then began to burn steadily, giving off a thick greasy smoke and an appalling odor. Ignoring Lybor's exclamation of disgust, he commanded fire from the black candles around the Domnor. Their flames burned an acid green, releasing a mist that smelled of rot and death. Lybor stirred, protested. "Must you?"

"Silence, woman." The Norid's voice was unemphatic, but Lybor closed her mouth and snuggled closer to Morescad.

The Norid faced the Domnor. The air shivered around him as his hands moved through a complex sign and he began a guttural unpleasant chant. Inside the pentacle the air thickened and a bilious green smoke slowly changed from a mist to a billowing shape, many-armed with a great gaping mouth.

Serroi's skin started to itch; her eye-spot throbbed with pain and power. She dropped a hand to the Sleykyn's sheath and closed her fingers tight around the hilt of his poison knife.

The Norid groaned and swayed, sweat popping out on his face. Within the pentacle that shape was solidifying, a huge warty thing curving over the Domnor.

Serroi shivered, remembering too much, eyes blurring, mouth dry. *Maiden help me, I can't go in there. I can't. Tayyan, help me. Ayyy, I can't.*

THE CHILD: 13

For a year Serroi worked her way south over the plain, gaining fluency in the language, begging at times, other times working in stables and for farmers, staying in one place for a day, a week, sometimes even a month until she found enough money or other means to move farther south, following her eye-spot's tug, hunting the Golden Valley. She kept away from people, trusting no one, making no friends, fending off questions about the green color of her skin. At times she was desperately lonely with no one to talk to; even the animals weren't enough. She needed an outlet for her strong affections and there was no one; sometimes she felt like she was going to burst in a thousand pieces, sometimes she almost turned back to find Raiki-janja, but she never quite lost the urge to find the Valley. She slept in stables on straw, bathed out of buckets, found no way to wash her clothing, discarded it when it was soiled beyond bearing, buying new things when she could. She kept nothing she couldn't carry easily, went across the Cimpia Plain as a small grubby boy whose wizard's touch with animals won him a job whenever he wanted it. At times the steady attrition of small irritations wore her down until once again she considered giving up. There were no great dangers to be faced, nothing but dirt and hard work and loneliness, but they wore her down until she thought seriously of turning back. The stubborn core that made her fight the Noris, that kept her alive in the desert, kept her moving toward her goal.

Toward the end of her thirteenth year she was working in the stable of a busy tavern in a small trade city on the edge of the Plain when she felt something like a blow in the stomach, though no one was near, no one touched her. She closed her eyes, felt warmth suffusing through her. The hostler led in two lanky high-bred macain and cuffed her for dreaming on the job. "Clean 'em good, boy." He snorted. "They belong to a couple of high-nosed meien. Old Poash is in there kissing their feet." With a sneer he muscled the animals into two stalls. "Lick 'em clean, brat." He wandered off, leaving her alone to do the work.

Two meien. Excited and fizzing with a new hope, she stared after him. *Going or coming?* If the meien were going home, perhaps they'd take her with them. She sighed and began washing the macain, cleaning their neck fringes, scrubbing their backs, working the tiny stones and other irritants from between their toes and out of the cracks in their pads. She pushed out the claws and polished them until the white-grey horn gleamed dully. The macain whined and burbled, nosed at her until she scratched behind their ears and under their chins. Finally she fed them an extra helping of fat yellow liga seeds and left them crunching happily.

She walked through the quiet stable, checking on the other animals, stopped by the door and looked around. A lamp lit by the door, the stables swept clean. Gear hanging neatly on pegs, wiped clean. She nodded to herself, stretched, yawned. All work done. She was supposed to stay around and tend the needs of any late customers when the hostler took himself off to the battered hedge tavern outside the walls where he drank up his wages after grudgingly giving her the few coins he allowed her for doing the work. She was pleased enough by this. The hostler hadn't the wit to see her as anything but the boy she pretended to be—and he wasn't put off by the color of her skin, a color all too evident in the day though she tried to tone it down with smears of greasy dirt. He was too glad to have a silent, willing worker to ask her any questions.

She wandered a last time along the line of stalls then stood in the stable's doorway looking at the busy bright tavern. She hesitated, but the temptation to see the meien was too strong. Slipping into the tavern behind a group of laughing townsmen, she squatted in a shadowed corner where few were apt to notice her.

The meien were sitting together at a table across the room, their backs to the wall, their shoulders almost touching. They were relaxed, talking quietly together, the current of affection between them waking a powerful need in Serroi, a need that twisted her stomach and blurred her eyes. She blinked, folded her arms tight across herself, and tried to focus on less disturbing aspects of the weapon-women. From their chosen table they could see most of the room, the stairs up to the sleeping rooms on the second floor and the two doors leading into the taproom. One was a broad-shouldered, broad-hipped woman with a round face and a dusting of freckles over a

snub nose. She wore her hair short, a shining nut-brown hel-
met following the lines of her skull. She was far from pretty
but had a smile that shimmered with charm and dancing dark
eyes that accepted and loved everything she saw. The second
meie was slim and golden. Golden skin, golden eyes, hair a
slightly darker gold; she wore it long, braided and wrapped
about her head. Both women wore leather tunics, divided
skirts made of the same leather, knee-high boots, a weaponbelt with a slender sword on the right and a grace blade on
the left. Everything about them was plain, without any orna-
ment but the pride that kept them clean and polished.

She gazed hungrily at the two women, wondering if she
could ever have their quiet assurance, the bone-deep serenity
that she could feel even through the noise and confusion in
the taproom. Serroi stirred in her corner, knowing she should
be getting back to the stables. The meien helped her resolu-
tion by finishing their meal and mounting quietly to the second floor. A drunken townsman called an obscenity after
them but was forcibly silenced by his two companions. The
meien ignored the incident and turned down the hallway
toward their room.

Serroi slipped out and returned to the stable. She had just
time to take a last look at the animals before the hostler
came stumbling in, drunk and feeling mean. He snarled at
her, picked up a whip. She backed away, avoiding easily his
clumsy rush. He forgot what he was holding the whip for,
staggered to an empty stall and fell asleep on the clean straw
inside. Serroi waited until he was snoring then blew out the
lantern and climbed to her own blankets spread out on
sweet-smelling straw in the loft.

The meien came for their mounts at Dawn. Serroi was up
and dressed, but the hostler was still snoring off his drunk in
the stall. She saddled the macain for the women and led the
animals out, ran back inside and fetched her blanket roll,
then stood leaning against the stable wall, looking cautiously
around before she dared approach them. She could see the
serving girls from the tavern hauling in water but there was
no one within earshot. As the women swung into the saddle,
she ran forward. "Meien," she called, her voice hoarse with
tension.

The meie with the freckled face rode over to her, smiled
down at her. "What is it, boy?" Her voice was a musical contralto, her eyes still pleased with the world.

"If you're going to the Biserica, take me with you." She clutched at her blanket roll, waited anxiously for their answer.

The freckled meie shook her head. "I'm sorry, boy. We only take girls there, and even they have to be twelve or older. If you want arms training, well, the army might take you when you're a bit bigger." She turned the macai's head and started away.

Serroi caught at her ankle. "I'm not a boy and I'm a lot older than I look, near fourteen. Please, meie."

The golden meie gave an exclamation and rode back to them. After swinging her macai's head around, she bent down and looked intently at Serroi. "It might be," she said slowly. "You're a windrunner, aren't you?"

"A misborn," Serroi said bitterly, scrubbing at her face to let the green show through the dirt. "You guessed right, meie. I'm tundra born."

"I see." The freckled meie smiled down at her, her face lit by amusement. "Well, little one, get you up behind me. I want to hear your story. I suspect it's wild enough to keep the two of us entertained for days." She chuckled, the sound warm with acceptance and interest, reached down toward Serroi.

The hostler staggered out of the stable, stood gazing blearily at the small group. "The boy botherin' you, meien?" he growled. He stumbled forward a few steps. "I'll have the skin off his back for that." His eyes were bloodshot and glazed with the pain in his head; he was unshaven and his clothing bore last night's wine stains and a dusting of chaff from the straw.

The two meien's eyes met; the freckled one raised an eyebrow; the golden one nodded. Together they kneed their macain between Serroi and the hostler. The golden meie spoke sharply, "Go back to your stable, man. This is none of your business." While she spoke, the freckled meie caught Serroi's reaching hand and lifted her up behind. With a shared laugh both meien sent their mounts trotting out of the stable yard.

Serroi looked back at the gaping hostler, then forgot him. She thrust her arm through the strap of her blanket roll and settled it comfortably across her back, jerked off the boy's cap and enjoyed the free play of the breeze through her curls. She held tight to the high back of the saddle and let a bubbling joy expand through her body. In a few days—days!—no longer passages to wait through and work through—in a few days she'd be in her Golden Valley, free at last from fear, free of the Norid. She laughed her excitement, her delight, heard the meie's answering chuckle float back to her, then settled down to ride, a little tired but deeply content.

THE WOMAN: XIV

The rats pressed against Serroi. The roaches left the wall in brief flights, whirring in a rusty cloud about her head. In the bedchamber the silence was tense, the air stiff as glass, as the Norid's laboring voice rose and fell, forcing the demon to take shape within the pentacle. The solidifying figure writhed and moaned, fighting the call. The Norid sweated, his face twisted, his voice flat and hoarse.

Serroi pulled her head back and looked down at the writhing mass of rats pressing harder and harder against her legs and against the exit's planks. She sucked in a deep breath, felt a flicker of amusement through the shreds of her terror. *My army,* she thought. Reaching out with her animal touch, she meshed with the life swarming around her and pulled the Sleykyn poison knife from its sheath. *Whoever called you to me thought I'd know how to use you. I hope I'm right, Maiden bless, I'm right.* Knife in her left hand, she slid back the bolts with the right until the exit from the passage was free of restraint. Again she hesitated, swallowing and swallowing, trying to overcome the fear that still plagued her. She straightened her back, seeing Tayyan's eyes again, staring at her, accusing her. She slammed her palm against the panel and leaped into the room as the exit exploded open.

Stirred to a frenzy by her prodding, the vermin army swept past her, the rats and the roaches pattering and whirring across the room, swarming over the two in the pentacle, knocking over the smoking white candles. They attacked Lybor and Morescad, the rats biting and clawing, the roaches diving at their eyes. Lybor shrieked and tried to scrape roaches from hair and face, frantic with horror and disgust, kicked out at rats who sunk curved yellow teeth into her flesh. She dropped the sjeme, writhed out of the pentacle's useless protection, kicking, screaming, a mass of hairy flesh, brown whirring wings. Cursing and beating at the roaches and the rats who found his boots and leather trousers more of a barrier, who nonetheless found vulnerable spots and sank

227

their teeth into his flesh, Morescad stumbled about, his sword cutting futilely at the air as often as it bit into rodent flesh.

While this happened behind her, Serroi slowed and circled cautiously around behind the black figure of the Norid. He was so lost in his laboring conjuration that he noticed none of the uproar around him. She caught the Domnor's attention. His cool grey eyes flickered then went flat and expressionless again as he began rocking his chair back and forth, working it toward the edge of the pentacle. Crouching painfully over him, the demon was nearly solid and beginning to turn its head about, the crimson eyes aware and angry. The thickening arms moved a few inches either way, testing solidifying muscle.

Shaking so badly she could hardly keep her fingers closed around the hilt, Serroi lifted the poison knife and stared at the narrow black back, its straining muscles clearly visible beneath the cloth. With a gasp and a breaking cry of rage and pain, she plunged the knife into the Norid's back, slamming it under his ribs. Leaving it there with blood bubbling and boiling around the hilt, she reached across the pentacle lines, broke into sweat, moaning softly as her skin burned, dragged the Domnor out, tumbling him and his chair onto the floor. She knelt and began tugging frantically at the knots of the rope that bound his hands.

Screaming with pain, the poison working in him, wrenched disastrously from his spell casting, the Norid stumbled forward. Every muscle jerking, he took one step after another toward the pentacle. Hands flung out, eyes staring, mouth foaming, uttering gobbling, incoherent sounds, he began crumpling; dead on his feet, he fell across the pentacle's line, slamming into the demon.

The crimson eyes swiveled down, the great fanged mouth opened, roared a hollow booming challenge that shook the room. It wrapped its arms about the Norid. There was a sudden intensifying of the stench, a confused mingling of Norid and thinning demon. A last scream. A gobbling mutter. With a loud pop, demon and Norid vanished.

With the disappearance of the Norid, the intensity of the vermin's attack began to diminish. They started scuttling off, melting away into the passage. Lybor crouched and whined, bleeding from hundreds of ragged cuts, then went down again as the rats swarmed over her. Morescad kicked across the heap of rat bodies and ran at Serroi, his sword drawn back for the deadly lunge, his eyes streaming, his face contorted with rage.

Serroi twisted away from the Domnor, tumbling into a controlled roll, then exploded up again, kicking at the General's wrist, connecting painfully before he could swing the sword down on her. In his anger and his contempt for a woman's ability to fight, he'd been careless. His fingers snapped open helplessly as her foot slammed home, his sword clattering onto the floor beside the Domnor. Serroi fell back, coiled again, slammed her heel out into the General's knee. He stumbled backward, arms flailing. As he fought for balance, she was on her feet, snatching up the sword, slashing at the Domnor's bonds.

Morescad scowled at her as he began circling toward the end of the bed, limping a little, his breathing hoarse as he fought to control the fury that weakened and distracted him.

"Hurry it, meie," the Domnor said softly. "He's going for my sword." His arms strained against the rope, muscles bulging under the layer of fat. When the General came bounding back into view, he gave a last great burst of effort and snapped the weakened rope. He rolled up onto his feet, light and alert, snapped out a demanding hand, closing his fingers around the hilt of Morescad's sword. He kicked at the ropes still clinging weakly to his legs.

Serroi looked around, saw the sjeme rocking in the middle of the floor. She scooped it up and hurled it at Morescad as he rushed at the Domnor who was still bothered by the clinging rope. The General dodged; the sjeme flew past his head to crash on the floor behind him, releasing a stinking black fluid which flashed into a roiling cloud that rapidly thinned to nothing.

As soon as the sjeme left her hand, Serroi seized a dead rat and hurled it at Morescad's face. Hurled another and another. Screaming with rage, he forgot the Domnor and charged her a second time. Serroi fled, throwing herself to one side to avoid the sword. She rolled and came up on her feet, flung herself aside again, escaping by a hair as Morescad began to master his temper and attacked more coolly.

"Morescad." The Domnor's voice was frozen steel.

The General twisted hastily around, leaped to one side so he could keep both the meie and the Domnor in sight.

The Domnor was a pudgy short man; he had a broad chest whose strength was masked by excess flesh that rounded into a soft belly like a pillow. Morescad was long and lean with clean articulated muscle; he looked regal and dangerous with his haughty face and fine body—far more a ruler than the Domnor with his round guileless face, wide smiling mouth, lazy rather beautiful eyes. Standing naked, sword held lightly by his side, Hern looked even less impressive than usual. As Serroi turned away from them, the two men began prowling around each other, swords moving gracefully, each man searching for an opening in the other's defense.

Serroi crossed to Lybor, glancing repeatedly at the two men. The woman was curled up, knees against her breasts. There was a drying pool of blood under her head, staining her draggled golden hair. Serroi knelt beside her, lifted her head, let it fall back, nauseated by the red, raw hole gnawed into the slim throat. *The rats. That last wave that washed over her.* Serroi shuddered and jumped lightly to her feet. Looking about for a weapon, she found the Domnor's ceremonial dagger and shoved it into the Sleykyn's sheath, reminding herself to be careful about the poison in the point. She settled herself on the curtained bed, watching the testing going on between Morescad and the Domnor.

They were moving rapidly about the room, each exchange brief and tentative. Her respect for the Domnor, which had been growing since her first glimpse of him fighting for release while the Norid went about his preparations, rose to a new high. He was cool and still not breathing hard; each movement was graceful and economical; he was smiling slightly, his green-grey eyes gleaming with confidence. Morescad was sweating and much stiffer in his movements with a wildness in his eyes that betrayed his fear. He outreached the pudgy little man facing him by several inches, he was fast and skilled and superbly fit—but he was afraid. The steel kissed, slithered, kissed and the General leaped back. Hern was on him, shurri-quick on small, high-arched feet. Touch. Slither. A sudden lunge.

Morescad stared down at the sword transfixing his body, then he toppled forward. The sword hilt struck the floor, turning him to one side so that he fell on his back to lie with mouth open in a silent scream of outrage.

Hern moved briskly to him, knelt, pried his own sword loose from the General's death clutch. He stood, grinned his triumph at her, suddenly remembered his nakedness and flushed a dark purple. Hastily he sidled to the bed and snatched up a fleecy robe. He thrust his arms into the sleeves and slapped the ties around his waist. Settling the robe about his shoulders, he turned to face her, looking more comfortable. He jerked a thumb at Lybor. "What happened to her?"

"Rats."

"Too bad. Waste of a damn beautiful woman." He grinned slyly at Serroi. "Wilder'n a sicamar in heat."

Serroi, too tired to respond to his teasing, wondered what he was getting at.

He climbed onto the bed beside her. "Relax, little meie. A viper may be beautiful but one lives more comfortably in its absence." He swept the room with cool measuring eyes. "Quite a mess." He grinned at her. "You know how you looked throwing those damn rats at Morescad?"

Serroi giggled. He hugged her, laughed with her until tears ran down his face. Finally sobering, they fell back on the bed to lie side by side, gulping in air until they were breathing steadily again.

The Domnor turned his head and frowned at Serroi. "What the hell's going on?" He sat up, bouncing a little as the bed jiggled in response to his vigorous movement. "Not that." He flicked a finger at the bodies on the floor. "That's obvious."

Serroi grimaced, took hold of the embroidered cover and pushed up. "Nearga-nor. They've got together somehow and are moving on the mijloc, using them. . . ." She pointed at Lybor then Morescad—"the Sons of the Light, Maiden knows what else. They already hold Sankoy."

"What's the Biserica doing about this?"

"I don't know. How should I know? You better start thinking what you're going to do. The guards out there are in on the plot, have to be or they'd have been in here long ago to investigate the noise."

Hern grinned. "Rather thought they might be, little meie. Morescad came tramping in at a decidedly awkward moment." He looked embarrassed, turned away, slid off the bed and padded around the end. His voice came back to her. "While I'm getting dressed, how bad is it?"

Serroi scrubbed a hand across her face, wincing as she touched the whip cut. The long strain when she drove herself back to face the Norid and her own terror, the fever-ridden hours in the darkness, the last intense battle—all these had drained her until she was dizzy. The Domnor's question blurred in her tired mind. She clasped her hands together in her lap to quiet their shaking. "I don't know much. The Daughter is corrupted. That I found out. There was a N-n-

norit. . . ." She swallowed hastily. "A Norit in the Temple
with her. She turned me over t-t-to him. Sleykynin brought
me into the Plaz, put me in a cell in the dungeon. I g-g-got
out and k-k-killed both . . . both Sleykyn. I think . . . most
of the guards must be in the plot. Three-four days ago, a Tercel and his men picked me up." A questioning sound came
from behind the bed. "Oh yes, they're dead too." She closed
her eyes, swayed back and forth, her head swimming with fatigue. The words tumbling out unconsidered, she told again
the convoluted tale of her flight and her struggle back to
Oras. With a driven incoherence she returned again and
again to Tayyan's death and her own panic-flight, her betrayal of love and duty. She kept enough control to avoid
mentioning Coperic except as Dinafar's uncle. When she
came to the end of her story, she sat numbed and silent, then
gradually became aware of warmth creeping into her icy
hands. She opened her eyes to see Hern bending over her, his
hands closed around hers.

"You're worn to the bone and no wonder." He freed her
hands and took hold of her shoulders. "Rest awhile." With a
nod at the windows beyond the end of the bed, he pushed her
down, stroked a hand gently down her cheek. "It's storming
out there. We won't be interrupted here awhile yet. Guards
will see to that, even if for the wrong reasons." He smoothed
short strong fingers gently over her eye-spot, smiling down at
her, his green-grey eyes shining with amusement.

The bed was soft; her body went limp, her last strength
draining out of her. The Domnor slid off the bed. She could
hear him padding about the room, still hadn't put his boots
on, then a short moment of silence, then the sound of boot
heels as he stamped his feet down in the boots. "No," she
whispered. "No time." She pushed against the bed, tried to sit
up, could not. Her head was heavy; she had no force left in
her muscles. "No." She called on her stubbornness, that tough
inner core of her being that refused to give in, shoved again
and managed to sit up. Hern came around the end of the
bed, stood scowling at her. "You don't take orders well, do
you."

In her boot the tajicho was beginning to burn; on her brow
the eye-spot began to throb. Ignoring Hern, she looked anxiously around the large battered room; the door into the passage hung open, the opening itself was a rectangle of black
against the pale gold of the wood paneling. "Maiden bless,
more. . . ." With some difficulty she drew her leg up and

rested her calf on her other knee. Thrusting her fingers into the boot's top, she pulled out the small crystal and stared down at the fire glowing in its heart. "He's coming here," she muttered.

"Who's coming?" Hern buckled on his swordbelt then disappeared around the bed without waiting for an answer. He came back. "Here." He tossed her a soft cap and a heavy cape. She stared at the cape then up at him. He was dressed in dark simple clothing, a tunic and close-fitting trousers tucked into mid-calf boots. He snapped a finger at the cape. "You're a bit of a thing, but I'm not that tall myself. Who's coming?"

"Some Nor. Can't tell who or what rank." She stuffed the tajicho back in her boot. "Another one. Let's get out of here."

"Wait." He dropped his cloak on the bed and began working his way purposefully around the room, opening small cavities in the wall, pulling out trinkets and gold coins, stuffing them into a large pouch he slung over his shoulder. Serroi moved shakily to the end of the bed, stood holding onto a bedpost, breathing deeply, feeling her head begin to clear as nearing danger stimulated her, helped her throw off the lethargy induced by the letdown after intense activity. She watched him a moment longer, said, "You don't have to come with me."

He grinned over his shoulder. "I've got a feeling, little meie, me, I've got a feeling that the Plaz ain't too healthy for me right now." He came back to her and took her arm. "I need a hole to dive into if I want to be alive come morning." With a soft clucking of his tongue, he snagged the soft hat from the bed and pulled it down over her head. "You got any preference for where we go to earth?" Snapping the cloak out, he swung it around her shoulders. "You need a keeper, child. It's pouring out there." He took her arm and started for the opening in the wall.

Serroi patted a yawn. "Not a keeper, a bed. And sleep, a whole passage-worth of sleep. The fisher girl's uncle has a tavern by the wall. If you pushed me, I'd say he dabbled in a lot of small illegalities, smuggling, buying stolen goods—you know." She shrugged. "It's a place to stay." She felt a sudden flare of fire against her leg, something like a blow against her head. Swinging around, she stared at the door.

Floarin swept in, the Daughter and the Minarka Norit behind her. "Well, Hern," she said.

The Domnor's eyes moved over the three of them. He smiled tightly. "Greetings, Floarin."

"You're a fool, Hern. Always have been."

"Suppose so. I should have known Lybor and Morescad didn't have a brain between them. What now?"

"The Plaz belongs to me, Hern. No place for you to run. I wouldn't bother keeping you alive, except that the Guard has this prejudice against a woman giving them orders. Relax, love. You'll have a lovely comfortable life, just like mine used to be. Don't keep fighting, this Nor's no fool, not like that one." She stepped aside, smiled up at the Minarka.

The Domnor unlaced his cloak and dropped it to the floor. Serroi caught his arm as his hand closed around the swordhilt. "No, Hern, not now. Let me." She stepped in front of him, dipped down, slipped the tajicho from her boot.

The tall golden man was centered in a shimmer of power. Chanting in a sing-song polysyllabic tongue, he manipulated a loop of string through a series of increasingly complex patterns. Serroi felt the air thickening about her wrists and ankles. She caught her breath, brought her hands to heart level, opened her fingers. The tajicho burned like a miniature sun. Long thick strands of golden light issuing from the Norit's hands looped out and around, then were sucked into the crystal. The strands stretched and stretched—spreading out in great spectral arcs springing from the Norit's hands, curving to touch the walls, drawn in again into the tajicho. The air thrummed with the power precariously locked into the golden arcs.

With a sudden brazen twang the golden lines broke, snapped back, coiling round and round the Norit until he was helpless in a cocoon of light.

Serroi shoved the tajicho into her boot, slapped at the Domnor's arm then dived into the passage, Floarin's raging yells following her. As soon as Hern was through the opening, she tugged the panel shut and slapped the bolts in place. "Keep close," she hissed and started off into the darkness. Behind her she could hear hoarse shrieks and thuds as someone began pounding at the exit. Hern laughed. She spared a moment to wonder what he was thinking and to be grateful for his quick unquestioning compliance with her commands.

They plunged down and around until Serroi's legs ached. Down and around, then through the maze of passages on the ground level. The darkness greyed. The still air stirred, blew into her face. Flickering candles lit the last section of this rat hole. She pulled up suddenly as her eye-spot began to throb. Hern slammed into her, knocking her off her feet. "What. . . ." He caught her shoulder and pulled her up.

"Man ahead," she whispered. "Sleykyn, I think."

"One?" His mouth was close to her ear; she could feel the warmth of his breath against her flesh; she was, abruptly, very aware of him.

"Yes." She was trembling in a way that had little to do with the danger ahead and he knew it. He laughed, a soundless amusement she felt in quick puffs of air caressing her cheek. He caught her chin, turned her face to him, kissed her slowly, sensuously, until she sagged against him. Then her sturdy practicality reasserted itself. She wrenched her head away. "Fool," she breathed. "Of all the times to. . . ."

He laughed again, still soundlessly, his chest moving against her breasts. "My turn, little meie. Wait here while I take care of the thing plugging our exit." He swung his cloak from his shoulders, dropped it over her and was gone before she freed herself.

She leaned against the wall, her nipples tight and sore. *I can't believe this,* she thought. *Maiden bless, what an idiotic thing to happen.* She rubbed at her breasts but found no relief. *And I called him a fool.*

"Meie." She started, stared at the figure silhouetted against a faint glimmering coming around the corner, relaxing as she recognized the short broad outline. "Come," he said, his voice sounding too loud to her.

"Already?"

"Careless, half-asleep. No problem. Sleykynin are damned bad guards. Been one of my men, I'd have him flogged." He touched her cheek. "About over. That bed's waiting. Ready?" When she nodded, he lifted a hand and moved his fingertips across her eye-spot with a gentleness that startled her. "Any more ahead of us?"

She caught his hand and pulled it down. "You distract me."

"Mmmmh."

"Hah! That's no compliment."

"Point of view, little one."

"My name's Serroi." She freed her hand, pulled away from him and started toward the exit. The Sleykyn was around the corner, sprawled on the stone under a guttering candle. She stepped over his legs and trotted on, anxious to get out of the passage.

The rain was coming down in sheets. Serroi stopped in the wall opening, catching the heavy cloak close to her body. "The Gather is complete," she said quietly.

Hern's hand dropped on her shoulder. "Now the Scatter."

Serroi rested her cheek a moment on his hand then stepped out, lifted her face to the rain, letting the cold water bite away some of her fatigue. "Keep close," she said. "I'm taking a long way to the tavern. Don't want to bring Floarin down on Dina's uncle." *Don't want you to know too much either.* She moved quickly across the garden, firmly shutting out memories of the last time she'd been here with Tayyan, helped in that by the rain that blanked out everything but the cold wet roar of its fall.

Outside the wall the rain slanted more, the wind driving it into them as they stumbled through puddles, sloshing the scummy water over boot tops. Serroi moved through a maze of side streets and alleys, deliberately choosing a complicated route to the tavern, nearly losing herself before she found the dark decaying structure.

The tavern was almost afloat, water a foot deep lapping at the walls. She splashed across the street, mounted the stairs and tugged at the bell pull. The Domnor was close behind her. She could smell the damp wool of his cloak, could feel his solid body, though he wasn't touching her. The wind was howling, the rain hissing down. Biting at her lip, her hand flat on the door, she hesitated, then she twisted around, slid a hand behind his neck, pulled his head down until his ear was close to her lips. "He thinks I'm a boy," she said. "Let me do the talking."

"Right." She sensed rather than heard his chuckle. He turned his head farther, kissed her lightly.

She pulled back. "Idiot!"

The door swung open. Hern put his hands on her shoulders, turned her around and pushed her inside, following close behind her, hand on the hilt of his sword.

Coperic was waiting in the dim red glow of the single lantern. He looked sourly at them, cradling a crossbow in his arms. "Where you been, boy?" He scowled at the dark figure beside her. "Who's that?"

"A man who needs a room and can pay for it."

"Pay? How much?" Coperic leaned forward, peering at the Domnor, trying to make out his features. "Ain't no inn, this."

"He don't want an inn, uncle. Three decsets the night?"

"Can't he talk for himself?" Coperic shrugged. "No matter, it's enough."

"I'm wet to the skin and freezing, uncle. Let us up."

Coperic stepped back, waved them past and followed them up the creaking stairs. Serroi pushed open the door to her room. A single candle burned on the table, only an inch high now, the flame flickering and uncertain. She smiled affectionately at it. *Dina. Still trying to take care of me.*

The Domnor looked around. "Hole is right."

"Don't like it, then git," Coperic snarled.

Shrugging, the Domnor crossed the room, swung the chair around, sat. He let his cloak fall, slipped the pouch strap off his shoulder, dipped into the pouch and pulled out the three decsets. He tossed them one by one onto the bed.

Coperic ignored him. "Talk with you, boy. Outside."

Serroi nodded. Outside in the hall she led the way to Coperic's filthy hole. He followed her in, dusted off a chair, watched as she shut the door. "Why bring him here? What happened?"

"You know who he is?" She dropped into the chair, crossed her legs, smiled up at him.

"Damn right I do. What the hell were you thinking about bringing him here?"

"Far as he knows, you're Dina's uncle, a disreputable tavern keeper." She pushed at her hair, plucked at her sodden clothing. "Maiden bless, I'm tired. Pero, things sort of blew up in my face. Floarin has the Plaz, the whole city, for all I know. The Nearga-nor owns the Daughter."

Coperic tossed the crossbow onto the tumbled bed. "I see. You're loose now. What are you going to do?"

"Get out of Oras. Nothing more I can do here." Her mouth twitched into a brief weary smile. "Take care of yourself, Pero. Don't hang around here out of stubbornness or because you happen to like taking crazy chances. They're going to be bad, these next few years." She laughed at the wry twist of his face, then said with a forced vigor, "Get me a boat and supplies. I want Dina and me out of the city before sunup."

"Ready and waiting." His thin mouth curved into a smile as he waved at the wall. "You can go out through there, down a rope ladder. Boat don't look like much, but she's a goer." He jerked his head toward the hall. "What about him?"

"Don't worry, Pero, I won't leave him on your hands. If

he'll come, I'll take him south with me. South to the Biserica. Maiden bless, that sounds good—going home. I'm so damned tired of scrambling." She started toward the door. "The sooner we get away the better. Floarin was having twenty fits last time I saw her." She paused in the doorway, tugged at her ragged, sodden trousers. "I was going to change. No point in that, I suppose, just get soaked again." She raised an eyebrow. "Any chance of some hot cha?"

Coperic chuckled. "Get your party on its feet; I'll see to a warm meal. And collect a damned good fee from our distinguished guest."

Laughing together, they started back down the hall.

THE CHILD: 14

Serroi stroked her palm over the leathery shell, feeling a quiet joy as the foal moved under her hand. Across the stall, the mare craned her neck around, uneasy because her egg was near to hatching. She'd been fighting the sling for days; Serroi was there to keep her from hurting herself in her agitation. The mare kicked at the partition with her uninjured foreleg, waggled the splinted one, began swaying in dangerous arcs that came close to pulling her off her hind feet and that made the supporting beam groan as her shifting weight put new pressures on it. Serroi jumped to her feet and ran to her, soothing her with voice and eye-spot. Whispering soft nonsense, she scratched at the loose skin under the mare's chin until she calmed a little, patted and scratched her a little longer, then returned to the egg.

When she touched the leathery sac, it leaped under her hand. Behind her the mare began kicking and groaning, wanting to get to her egg. Hastily Serroi dug it out of the nest of blankets and straw and staggered with it across the stall. She set it down on the straw under the mare's nose, knelt beside it, holding it steady as a small yellow tooth drove through the tough skin. The egg ripped apart and the tiny foal tumbled out, kicking clumsily with all four feet, the curved egg-tooth like a tiny horn in the middle of its soft nose. A moment later it was staggering onto wobbly legs, falling, staggering up again. It whimpered, a high hooting whinny, its head moving blindly about, searching for the mother just in front of it.

The mare was hooting desperately, stretching her neck trying to reach down to the hatchling. Serroi wrapped her arms about the foal's velvety trembling body and lifted it until mother and son could nuzzle each other. When her back got tired, she set the foal on its feet and urged it along the mare's body until it found the teat and began suckling eagerly. She brushed herself off and sat back on the straw, deeply content as she watched mare and foal.

As the afternoon waned, she began to wonder if her

teacher would remember to send her something to eat; she was getting very hungry. The foal was curled up beside her, its head on her thigh. She moved her fingers along its neck over skin softer than new spring grass, chuckling at the silly grin on the new face. "You're glad enough to be out of that egg. Right, funny face?"

She heard soft steps coming toward the stall and looked up to see a tall skinny blonde stopping outside. She had scraped knees, a tear in the sleeve of her tunic, a bit of tape on her nose—and a basket over one arm. She grinned, hung the lantern she carried on its hook, and strolled into the stall. Bending with an awkward grace, she set the basket beside Serroi, straightened. "You're the new one?"

Serroi nodded.

Her hard blue eyes softening, the girl knelt beside the foal, holding out a long narrow hand for it to smell. Very slowly she edged the hand close enough to touch the quivering nose, finally stroked it until the little macai honked its pleasure in a series of treble squeaks. Blue eyes dancing, the girl settled crosslegged in the straw facing Serroi. "My name's Tayyan. Haven't been here long either. Where you from?"